FALLING FOR FAIRY TALES

LAVENDER FALLS SERIES

ISABEL BARREIRO

Published by Isabel Barreiro

Paperback ISBN: 979-8-218-28210-3

Falling For Fairy Tales

Genre: Small town paranormal romance

Edited by: Jennette Perdomo

Cover Design: Jennette Perdomo

❀ Created with Vellum

AUTHOR'S NOTE

Our main characters are Portuguese American, much like myself and therefore reflect on how I grew up.

TRIGGER WARNING: There is an anxiety attack during **chapter 29.** As someone who deals with anxiety Lilianna was a way for me to express what I sometimes struggle to convey to my friends and family.

This is a slow burn **open door romance** and the spicy scenes are in **chapters 24, 25, first half of chapter 30 and the epilogue.** So to my mom, her friends and my brother you can totally skip those.

Open door romance: my characters have sexy time

Celestino's POV ^

Lilianna's POV ^

To me, you'll get there
To the chronic over-thinkers and deep feelers
Para minha avó, porque você não consegue me ver crescer, mas eu sei que você está olhando de cima

PLAYLISTS

<u>Lilianna:</u>
1. Slow- Shy Martin
2. Eterno- Anjos
3. Slow Burn- J. Maya
4. POV- Ariana Grande

<u>Celestino:</u>
1. I Like Me Better- Anthony Del La Torre
2. I Hear a symphony- Cody Fry
3. Life's A Mess- Spence Hood
4. Amor Perfeito- Mariza

Full playlists for Lilianna and Celestino are on Spotify!

CHAPTER 1
HE'S BACK

Fuck Cinderella. Politely of course. She made it look so easy in the movies. Side note, the third movie was top tier. Anyway, she would sing a little tune and the animals would be at her beck and call, helping her with her chores. I, on the other hand, ended up getting chased by a duck. And not just any duck. A *mother* duck. She had gone full Hulk on me, chasing me around the front of my office building, snapping at my ankles. I felt like I was getting chased by an orc. And not the kind in my romance novels.

With a flash of a vicious white feathered monster nipping at my ankles, my eyes glazed past the river in front of me. River was definitely an exaggeration. As I curved to side step the creature my foot slid into a puddle (not a river) and I fell on my ass.

Today was proving to be exceptionally disastrous. Did I wake up on the wrong side of the bed? Yes, but only because I had stayed up late coming up with marketing concepts in order to attract more tourists to our town's Full Moon Fall Festival. Try saying that five times fast.

Did I make it on time to work despite stopping at Coffin's Coffeeshop for a cup of their steaming caffeinated nectar? Yes. Did I happen to stop right in front of the office to help baby ducks cross the sidewalk towards the edge of the woods of my office building? Yes, I'm not heartless and they looked defenseless. Was my kind heart the reason the mother duck decided to go full Hulk on me thus causing me to slip into a puddle and spill the steaming cup of coffee all over my blouse? Yes. This is not what I needed when I was running on only three hours of sleep.

At least I had some form of sense and managed to lean sideways in order to avoid falling into the puddle. That's somewhat of a win, right? The sky was hazy and I groaned out loud before glancing down at the brown stain seeping into my white blouse. Of course today is the day I decided to wear white. My bra was already peeking through.

Maybe if I just sat soaked in coffee on the pavement I'd melt into the ground like most witches do in the mundane version of fairy tales. That seemed like a painless way to go. But if I melted would I feel all of my bones and organs liquify? Or would the pain be so intense that I'd black out?

A familiar bronzed hand obscured my vision, breaking my tangent thoughts on the pain probability of melting witches. My eyes followed the hand to a thick arm and slowly up a very well sculpted bicep that was basically molded beneath a navy button shirt. My eyes continued their perusal until I crashed into the eyes I thought I wouldn't see for at least a few more years.

These eyes haunted me my whole life. A shade of green that changes every day. They reminded me of a Takahe bird; pear green feathers that melted into glorious golden brown and then a startling brilliant blue. I used to look at those eyes every day and imagine different ways to describe the ever changing color. Thick dark eyebrows furrowed. His bow shaped lips that used to play in my fantasies pulled into a smile.

"Posey," his voice was gravely and my body tightened in a familiar way. Nearly 10 years later and he still had a magical effect on me.

"Celestino," I said, my voice sounding small in my ears. I took his hand and tried not to enjoy how much I loved the feel of his calloused hand under my soft skin. I wondered why they were rough. More importantly, I wondered what he was doing here. It wasn't a major holiday. If it was, he usually didn't come back.

Did something happen to his mom? His sister? Did his apartment catch on fire and he lost everything and had to move back?

"Still the same Posey," he said with a slight smirk. I brushed off the dirt from my knees and snorted.

"I was just trying to help the baby ducks cross the road," I said, pulling my bag tighter against my shoulder as if to shield my pulsing heart. Celestino looked up at me slightly, eyes narrowing. A part of me relished at him having to look up. It always gave me some form of control and confidence around him.

"Like I said, still the same Posey," he said. I rolled my eyes.

"It's been over 10 years since that incident, when are you going to drop that nickname?" I questioned. He let out a chuckle and I mentally cursed as I felt a flush creep on my face.

I've known Celestino Santos since we were practically in diapers and that's when my crush on him started. Somewhere between sippy cups and learning to read. Being around him felt like bathing in sunlight and I was too scared to risk getting sunburnt by asking for more. The one time I was going to confess to him got ruined by the soccer team. I took it as a sign to give up and that we were better off as best friends. Instead I just carried a silent torch that only our mutual best friend Eleanor knew about and Lola.

We both went to separate colleges after graduation and therefore parted ways. It was hard to stay connected between classes, studying and activities. After college I moved back with Eleanor to work for our town and he stayed away in the city.

I glanced at his body briefly. I was taller than him by two inches. We used to argue about who was taller and then one day I kept growing and he didn't. I stared at him now. He looked different yet still the same boyish superstar athlete.

He left Lavender Falls as a lanky pretty boy and came back a burly man with a rough edge. His dark hair was longer than I've ever seen it, the ends curled into waves at the nape of his neck. I wonder if it was as soft as it looked. His eyes briefly glanced at my coffee soaked blouse and I inwardly cursed. Of course the day he decided to pay a visit I would be a mess. His eyes met mine and he glanced away quickly. Nope. I was not going to overanalyze that.

"You know I like calling you Posey." His stubbled smile stretched across his face again.

My stomach twisted. Crap. Those feelings were definitely still there. I decided to ignore the childhood nickname and move onto a more pressing topic.

"What are you doing here?" I asked tentatively. He glanced at the building hesitantly.

"I've decided to move back. I actually got a job as Ben Chaves's assistant," he said casually. My eyes widened. *Oh.*

"You're going to be working here?" My voice squeaked.

But he didn't seem to notice because he just let out another chuckle, his shoulders shaking slightly. My stomach flipped as I continued to make him laugh. I remember I used to do anything to get him to react. Whether it was a laugh, a smile or even a snarky come-back. Because when he did react, it was with his whole body.

"Yeah. I just felt like I needed to come back home, you know," he said, sounding lost.

I nodded silently. He's home. And he's definitely not leaving. The hamster in my brain that was running was now being chased by a fire. This meant we would occasionally be working together. Me in market-ing, him in event planning. Us. Together. In close proximity.

I shook my head mentally. He was back. Which was not a big deal because we were just friends and I was happy to have him back. It'll be like old times and maybe I could finally squash my school girl crush once and for all.

"I was going to message you but it was kind of hectic moving back," he said, his hand reaching to scratch the back of his head.

Was he nervous? My phone beeped reminding me of the meeting I was-*we* were supposed to be getting too. I glanced back at my shirt. Yep, my bra was definitely making an appearance. *Fuck.* Mental note: white blouse equals nude bra, not blue. But I was too high on no sleep to even bother with proper fashion etiquette.

I was just trying to be nice. I didn't want the baby ducks to get run over. Why couldn't the mother duck see that? Why didn't I just cast a spell to float them to her? I groaned inwardly. A spell would have sufficed but I never think of using magic first.

"Well I gotta take care of this. I guess I'll see you inside," I said, inching towards the front door of *our* office building.

Celestino cleared his throat and rushed to hold the door open. I tried my best to not look like I was sprinting to the bathroom as he called out, "see you at the meeting!"

Definitely still have butterflies. Or more like sprites.

ELEANOR WALKED into the bathroom huffing. "There you are," she said with an exasperated tone. "I've been looking everywhere for you!"

Her bright auburn hair was pulled into a slick ponytail and whisked back and forth excitedly as she busied herself attempting to help me. Her eyes were wide with worry. Today her right eye was more brown then the left, which was green. She must be in a good mood. I wonder why.

"I woke up late because of work. Showed up on time. Tried to be a decent witch and save some baby ducks only to have the mother go feather fucking ogre on me," I took a breath as Eleanor stared at me. "Anyway I ended up falling and well as you can see..." I said, face flushed as I pointed to my clothes.

Eleanor bursted out laughing. She couldn't help it. Poor me, Lilianna Maria Rosario, born with the worst luck. Always had. Constantly get into the most impossible situations that would have you believing I was lead in a comedy movie. An ancestor must have been cursed and I was the unlucky generation that got its repercussions. Or maybe I was the Fates pet? They did love making things go askew.

Who gets pooped on by a bird not once but three times in one day? Who gets a flat tire on the day of their last final exam of university from trying to avoid running over a squirrel? Who finally works up the courage at the awkward age of 13 to confess their life long crush to their best friend AKA captain of the soccer team only to get a bucket of ice accidentally poured on them which then causes her white dress to show her floral underwear? Me. Lilianna Maria Rosario is who.

Stars, I'm surprised I wasn't wearing a floral bra under this blouse. So Eleanor's reaction was perfectly normal because things like this were normal for me. I even laughed at the ridiculousness.

"You know I always have a spare blouse with me in case right?" Eleanor raised an elegant eyebrow and handed me a pink silk blouse.

"Guess who's back in town," I said through gritted teeth.

Eleanor bit back a smile. "Someone is back," she questioned innocently.

"Oh," I recognized that tone. It's her *I swear I'm completely innocent* voice. So that's why she's in a good mood.

"You and I both know *you* know who I'm talking about because *you* would have seen his resume." She let out a giggle as she helped me button the sleeves.

"I was going to tell you but I knew you would have spent days freaking out over seeing him again," she said.

"Well instead of having days to mentally prepare myself, I'm freaking out now," I hissed.

"So you still have a crush on him?"

My cheeks turned the same color as the blouse I was now wearing.

"No," I said tensely.

All she did was hum in response as we walked out. I didn't need this right now. What I needed was to get through this meeting, plan a few social media posts, pray my idea gets approved and sleep. And coffee. Definitely in need of coffee.

Then I felt it. An itch began to prickle the at back of my skull. I was late. I hated being late. Being one minute late made my stomach tighten and the world tilt on its axis. It was fine. I was fine.

Walking in, I tried to keep my breathing even despite the fact I felt like I ran a mile. Mayor Kiana Humphrey sat at the head of the table. She was my chemistry teacher in high school but decided she was tired of the curriculum the school was dealing with and became mayor to make serious changes.

Also in attendance were a few council people; Leo who was the department head for Communications (my boss). Chelsea was in charge of Finance and a few other departments like Planning, Zoning and Code Compliance sat around the table. And then sitting across an empty chair was Celestino—cool, confident, collected and devastatingly handsome.

I tried not to grumble while heading to my seat. I could feel everyone's eyes on me. My brain began prickling with the new attention I was being given. We were all here to discuss the plans for the Full Moon Fall Festival.

It was a citywide effort to put the festivals on. This festival in particular was my favorite, a weekend fall festival that let the town dive deep into its mystical magical history and it was near Halloween. Made sense given the fact that our town, Lavender Falls, was mainly made up of witches, warlocks, vampires and just about anything spooky.

For example, Leo is a werewolf and therefore is always excited for the fall festival. Something about the shiny rock hanging in space really does it for him. And Eleanor, my soul sister, is a pixie and not like Tinker Bell although she does have an affinity for tinkering. I, on the other hand, am a witch. But not just any witch, one who comes from one of the founding families. Which always held a certain level of pressure.

Thankfully I never had any path to follow that was set by my mom or my last name. She was always the "finish college then follow your dreams" kind of person. But also whatever I did needed to be financially stable. And I was doing that. I loved my job.

Even though there were plenty of times I lost sleep, I enjoyed creating content and coming up with ideas to bring the community together. It felt natural to me like magic…well for the most part.

"I'm so sorry for- " I began before Mayor Kiana cut me off.

"Don't worry Lily, we haven't started yet." I frowned. Mayor

Kiana was always a stickler for time. It was odd they hadn't started the meeting by now.

The Mayor cleared her throat and smiled at each of us. "Now that we're all here it's time we begin."

Swallowing hard, I kept my head down. I wasn't ready to face anyone's eyes yet. I needed to calm my nerves even if I was technically on time.

"I would like to introduce everyone to Celestino Santos. Most of you know him seeing how we've either watched him grow up or grew up alongside him," she said, glancing around the room.

"He'll be Ben's assistant and will be a great asset in taking our events to the next level as we continue to expand Lavender Falls into a growing community."

Everyone clapped and I glanced at him. His eyes met mine and he shot me a smile. I wanted to melt on the spot. I looked over to Eleanor who was busy trying to hide her smirk. I was *not* going to hear the end of this from her. Leo cleared his throat.

"If I may?" Leo smiled at me. Oh creatures of the deep. "Lilianna sent over a draft of new ideas for our social media front that will gather the eyes of the tourists along with a fresh festival idea."

Heat slowly crawled back into my face. I didn't think he would start with me. I didn't even think he would read my email. I sent it at three in the morning, high on exhaustion. All eyes turned to me, waiting. I took a deep breath, desperately trying to spell together my thoughts despite being decaffeinated.

"We already have the carnival, the maze and the haunted house which Alex will be sending over the theme soon and other events we normally do but I thought how fun would it be to have a pub crawl. We can create a fun map, maybe make it like a scavenger hunt?" I took a deep breath. "It can send people to the different pubs around town, mix in some of our local lore."

Everyone's eyes lit up, naturally at the mention of something spooky and alcohol.

"Brilliant!" Mayor Kiana clapped her hands excitedly. "And you'll spearhead it," she continued, her tone definite.

Her eyes were more serious than a troll protecting their bridge. She, for whatever reason, expected me to take the lead. I glanced at my boss who was beaming. There was no way he was going to let me be in charge. Would he?

I was just his assistant. Sure I gave amazing, out of the box ideas occasionally and made sure certain things ran smoothly but I was never in absolute control. I wasn't the lead person. I always needed his approval and honestly even if I didn't I would still ask for it. Would I even be able to handle it? It would be so much responsibility.

"Of course she will. She can do it but..." Leo trailed off.

My heart began pounding. Was I hallucinating? Was being sleep deprived making me hear things? Also why did he say *but*. But what? Did he not think I could do it? I barely registered that Leo was looking at his twin brother Ben, who was in charge of Cultural Affairs and Special Events. A slow smile slid across Ben's face which was covered in a thick red beard.

"She can't do it alone. Not on top of her other work. So my assistant Tino will help," Ben suggested. I bit the inside of my cheek. It took every ounce of self control to keep my reaction neutral. Celestino and I were going to be working together. Platonically working together. Well obviously platonically because this isn't a workplace romance book. He's my best friend. Wait, would that make us a friends to lovers romance book? I knew I shouldn't have listened to that audiobook last night. Now my head was swimming in book tropes.

Oh stars, they're still talking to me. *Get a grip,* I told myself.

"Yes," Leo said, still smiling.

Celestino cleared his throat, attempting to recover from the shock.

"Us," he sputtered out. Everyone nodded in agreement.

"You guys will do great. You've done amazing things," Ben started. He turned to face Celestino. "I think this is a great way for you to reconnect...with the town. This is also an event and you have more experience in putting them on," he pointed out. That was true. I've never been in charge of an event. I just showed up with ideas to promote it. Leo smiled wide.

"And who knows, maybe it'll be a good stepping block from assistant to something with a legit name plate," my boss said.

His words were all I needed to be convinced to work with Celestino. I could finally be on the same playing field and of course the money would be great.

I took a deep breath. Celestino and I worked together all the time growing up and we were great…when we weren't bickering. But something in the back of my head was saying this was going to be different. I took a deep breath, mentally preparing for what was going to be a long two months.

I could work with Celestino, get rid of my crush, put on an amazing event and get a promotion. Although I wasn't a werewolf, I could practically howl at the sight of my name on a shiny gold nameplate.

This was my chance.

CHAPTER 2
I'M BACK

It felt weird to be back in Lavender Falls. Back in the town that I grew up in. The town I stayed away from for almost 10 years. I didn't do it on purpose. I love my town. I just wanted to experience something different. I thought maybe I was made for a bustling concrete jungle and not a small town. I was wrong. I knew the second I graduated college I was wrong.

Then I thought maybe getting my master's would lead to a better paying job and erase this feeling of being lost. While I was happy with my masters I was wrong again.

I went from following my parents expectations growing up to not knowing where I belonged anymore. But one thing I was sure of was that I was tired of the city. Tired of the noise and coldness of the people. I needed to escape the pollution of it all. I felt myself suffocating under the mask of fake smiles, snake eyes (not the shifter kind) and half hearted promises.

I missed waking up to a quiet town. I missed the familiar faces and warm hellos. I missed the feeling of being connected to a place and its people.

A part of me also missed *her*.

I knew moving back into town I would see her again. My best

friend. And I was counting on it. I wondered if we would slip back into our friendship. College was hard. We both had busy schedules and distance didn't help. Would we fall back into place like two puzzle pieces? Or had our pieces become too jagged from life during our time apart?

I thought my repressed feelings faded away but they bubbled back to the surface during my interview with Eleanor. Having my infamous party pixie best friend Eleanor conduct my interview for the job I was overqualified for made me laugh. Who knew the queen of parties would be the second in command to our beloved mayor.

We all have been friends since diapers since our moms grew up in neighboring villages in Portugal. We were a trio. I was the jock, Eleanor the drama queen cheerleader and Lilianna, our artistic book-worm. She was always the nice, quiet girl however I knew better. She held a fiery passion inside of her. If pushed too close to the edge or if someone crossed her inner circle she was like a dragon, ready to attack.

As we grew older I began noticing things I probably shouldn't have about my best friend. I noticed the way she would bite the inside of her cheek when she was keeping herself in check. She would tug her earlobe when she was nervous. The way her magic smelled like the ocean and would burst out when her emotions began surfacing.

Or how my hands always itched to tuck a loose wave behind her ear. I slowly began realizing how much of a temptress my shy witch was. Okay she wasn't mine…yet…if she wanted.

I noticed things about her that I shouldn't have and Eleanor knew. She always gave suggestive eyebrows and secret smiles when she caught me staring at Lilianna. I wasn't blind to Eleanor's smirk when she oh so casually mentioned that Lilianna also worked at the office.

"WELL YOU DO KNOW that by working for Ben, you're working for the town which obviously comes with some perks like insurance, benefits

and that Lily works in the same building."

I was nodding along until her name popped up. I felt my cheeks flush. Eleanor stared at me, her contrasting eyes filled with amusement.

"Eleanor." I gave her a pointed look. She held her clipboard up innocently.

"What? I'm just saying. You're going to see a lot of familiar faces now that your back and Lily happens to be one of them. She also happens to work in the same building." She gave her infamous Cheshire smile.

"It will be nice to see familiar faces." I did my best to keep my voice even. Eleanor tapped her polished nail against her chin.

"Yes it will. Anyway, welcome home Tino."

ELEANOR WAS WELL ACQUAINTED with my unrequited crush on Lilianna Maria Rosario. We all grew up together and I've held a torch for her ever since we were about 12 years old.

Lilianna was fidgeting in her seat during our meeting. It was different seeing her in person rather than on social media. I watched her slowly become someone else, someone breathtaking via a small screen. My heart would flicker whenever I would see her post. But in person? It was pounding.

During our meeting I couldn't help but try and catch her eyes again.

When our eyes connected outside the office I felt something snap within me, locking me into place. She was always beautiful but now she was almost painful to look at. Like a celestial being. If I stared too long I would go blind. But for her I would, knowing she would be the last thing I saw.

Her eyes flickered back to me after the announcement of our joint partnership for the pub crawl. My stomach sank at her reaction. This was not how I pictured our reunion going. I knew she would be shocked since I haven't been around.

But I figured I would get one of her smiles. She has a smile where her eyes brighten like honey in sunlight. I imagine that in our reunion she would throw her arms around me as I crushed her to my chest. Okay the hugging may have been more of a hopeful fantasy.

A quick tap got my attention. I looked over at Mayor Kiana who raised an eyebrow. Ben, my boss was giving a speech and I was daydreaming about my best friend.

I gripped my hands, remembering our conversation outside the meeting room.

"MAYOR KIANA, A SECOND," I called out. The mayor was one of the town's brightest witches and also my old chemistry teacher. Gotta love small towns.

"Good morning Celestino." Her red lips stretched into a smile that was warm and inviting.

Today she wore a bright orange tailored suit. Her deep ebony skin shined against the vibrant color. I felt my stomach twist and in two seconds I was back to being 16 and in her class.

"Um...well I was wondering if..." my brain was short circuiting. I hadn't actually thought of what I was going to say.

"Yes?" She raised an elegant eyebrow.

From the corner of my eye I saw Eleanor, slip out a pink blouse. I knew who it was for. She would look nice in it.

Focus. My eyes caught Eleanor's briefly and she gave a slight nod.

"The haunted house! I was wondering if maybe I could help out," I blurted. Eleanor winked at me and was gone.

"I appreciate your enthusiasm for wanting to get back into the community after being away for so many years but don't you think

that's a question you should be asking Ben? He is your boss." She crossed her arms and I felt sweat at the back of my neck.

She knew I was asking this for something else. I did my best to keep her gaze but the more she looked at me the more I felt myself unravel.

"He is! You're right. But...the thing is he might not let me help with everything we're doing and I really want to get more into building. You know how much I've always loved carpentry. I'd figure you'd back me up since I built your son his play kitchen last Christmas when I came," I rushed out. She let out a hearty laugh.

"That's right! Listen anytime we start cooking dinner we let Ethan cook a mini plate in his kitchen. It's been so amazing. He's quite the little chef. Thank you again for that." Mayor Kiana turned to continue walking towards the meeting room. I followed closely behind.

"You know what Tino? I will. I'll let Ben know it's a great idea. Plus the more help the merrier." A smile stretched across my face.

I let a whisper of my magic float out, hoping to gain a sense of Lilianna. We stopped in front of the meeting room. Before opening the door Mayor Kiana looked at me over her shoulder, a hand on the door handle.

"Oh and don't worry. Lilianna just walked out the bathroom so congrats on helping her not be late. I guess some things never change." With a wink she opened the door and walked in.

OF COURSE she knew what I was up to. She always knew everything. Almost every other day in high school I stalled Mayor Kiana before class to give Lilianna a chance to make it on time because her math class was across campus. It was like I was 16 again. I guess she was right, some things never change.

With a deep breath I focused on our meeting and prayed I didn't promise to do any more idiotic things for the woman who silently bewitched my heart.

CHAPTER 3
STUPID SEXY SMILE

"This is fucking great!" Eleanor cackled into her caipirinha.

After work we had gone to our favorite pub, The Drunken Fairy Tale Tavern because it had been the longest day in my life. Well one of the longest days. There was that day where the local grocery store, Griffin Groceries, ran out of coffee.

Poor Griffin forgot to order coffee and it took about three days for it to come in. Could we have casted a spell for fast delivery? Of course! But Griffin uses special coffee beans from a undisclosed dimension and if you ever tasted it you would wait three days for it too. That was a dark day for all in Lavender Falls.

Eleanor couldn't stop laughing since our morning meeting ended. She kept chucking notes over my desk like we were back in the fourth grade about Celestino and I sitting in a tree.

"It's not funny," I said into my cider. Eleanor wiped a tear from her eye. Naturally my best friend was over the moon over my distress.

"Think of the bright side you guys might be able to get rid of that weird tension you've had for years," she teased. I scoffed.

"There is no tension," I said.

"Listen, they *loved* your idea which was a given and there's a chance of a promotion which you *will* get," my pixie friend continued, ignoring my very truthful denial.

I sighed, leaning into the hardwood back of our booth. It was the most secluded one and the perfect spot for me to be around people but not feel obligated to socialize.

"I know but now I have to work with *him*," I said before taking a swig of my drink.

"Who is this guy and do we hate him?" a voice asked, sliding in next to me.

I turned to Sailor with a smile. His blue eyes were the same color as the mediterranean sea. His golden hair was pushed back, his sun kissed skin practically glowed in any lighting. At the right angle if you looked closely at his cheeks you could almost make out iridescent scales.

Sailor was a siren who moved into our town about a year ago. We all became fast friends and he was the best bartender The Siren's Saloon had ever seen.

"So Celestino Santos is our best friend. We've all been together since practically diapers. He recently moved back into town and our witchy sister here has had a crush on him since forever. Those feelings are clearly still there." Eleanor sat back triumphantly. Sailor nodded, soaking it all in.

"So we like him right?" he asked. That got us to laugh.

"Yes Sailor, we like him. Although some more than others." Eleanor snickered. I bit the inside of my cheek.

"That was a silly childhood crush okay? I'm over it," I said somewhat confidently. Sailor tucked his chin into his hand, his eyes held a knowing glint.

"Really? Because that's not the vibe I'm getting," Sailor said with a cheeky grin. I squinted at him.

"Are you using your magic on me?" I questioned.

"Why use my magic when your face makes it obvious?" He smiled.

Eleanor nearly choked on her drink. And then I felt a zap up my spine. He was here. I could feel him. My magic was trembling beneath my skin.

"Hey guys." A deep velvet voice pierced through the smoky haze of the tavern music and wrapped around me like tentacles. I needed to calm down with the kraken romance books. Celestino stood in front of us.

"Tino," Eleanor exclaimed. Celestino glanced at me before zeroing on Sailor's arm which was hanging around my shoulder.

"This is Sailor," I said, hoping to keep my voice even. He turned a strained smile to Sailor.

"Hey, man. Nice to meet you." He offered a hand and Sailor smirked.

"I've heard so much about you," Sailor said. Celestino held onto his hand a second too long, his eyes narrowing.

"Good things I hope." Both men glanced at me quickly.

"Very good things," Sailor teased.

"Why don't you get a drink and join us," Eleanor offered as I sipped my cider, avoiding Celestino's eyes. He nodded and pointed to the bar silently.

"I'll join you Celestino. Another round ladies?" Sailor asked. We nodded and watched the boys walk away. The second they were out of ear shot Eleanor leaned in.

I was walking towards the bar with this unknown friend of Lilianna's and somehow it was getting under my skin.

Eleanor had never mentioned a guy. I felt my hands twitch and bile in my throat. Whoever he was, I didn't like him.

I glanced back at Lilianna. Pinched eyebrows, tensed eyes,

hunched shoulders. I felt that urge to wipe that look off of her face. I wanted to smooth the wrinkles between her eyebrows and relax her muscles beneath my hands. She was probably feeling overwhelmed from the meeting and from me being back in town.

Eleanor had texted me to grab a beer. She was one of the few people who knew about my feelings for Lilianna. And it was by complete accident.

Okay, maybe not an accident. It was graduation night and we were at some party getting drunk. Everyone was there except for Lilianna.

"WHERE OH WHERE COULD SHE BE?" I sang, my words slurring. Eleanor raised an eyebrow.

"And who do you mean by she?" She smiled. I rolled my eyes. We both knew who I meant.

"Lilianna," I grumbled, throwing back some green colored shot, wincing as the burn slid down my throat.

"Lilianna? Don't you mean Posey?" She leaned against the makeshift bar and placed her head in her hand, staring intently. I felt my face heat up. It was probably the alcohol. But before I could respond Eleanor continued.

"She's very selective with her crowds as you know but also she said she had some work to get done, some last minute scholarship essay. Honestly she always has something." Eleanor sipped her drink.

I sighed deeply. My Lilianna was always working. I shook my head. Eleanor's eyes traveled to the dance floor where Sally was dressed in a tight red dress and looking our way.

"But it's graduation," I whined. Eleanor rolled her eyes.

"I know," she said, throwing back a shot.

"She's pretty," Eleanor said, motioning to Sally. I glanced briefly at her cheerleading co-captain who has practically been on my ass this

whole year. Sure she was what most people would call beautiful but she wasn't Lilianna.

"She is," I muttered flatly, fidgeting with the cup that had the disgusting shot.

"But?" Eleanor edged on.

"Lilianna looks better in red. But if Lilianna were here she would probably have to pull her hair in a bun thingy because it gets poofy in a crowd like this. She has pretty hair," I rambled. Eleanor let out a laugh.

"Celestino, are you finally admitting your feelings for Lilianna?" she asked.

"There isn't a word that describes my feelings for her. She's beautiful and s-smart. Like wicked smart and so fucking hard working. Like fuck I wish she's would just take a break and come out with me-us. You know? She deserves to relax." My eyes wandered to the crowd. I felt my brain switching onto autopilot.

Now that I started spilling my guts I couldn't keep my mouth shut.

"And her lips? Her legs. I don't even care that she's taller. Her laugh? I could get drunk on her laugh. Oh my fucking stars what am I saying right now? Why can't I stop? What is wrong with me?" I looked at Eleanor whose eyes were wide in disbelief. She had her phone out.

"Why is your phone out? Fuck don't send this to her! She can't know!" I began reaching for Eleanor but she moved away from me.

"Oh don't worry I won't send this to her. This is for me to keep…in case."

I GOT drunk once during high school and spilled my guts to Eleanor. I wondered if she still had the video from that night and what the fuck she's done with it.

"You and Posey seem close," I said. Sailor smiled.

"I wondered how long it would take for you to say that," he said. I cocked an eyebrow. He just kept smiling. "*Posey* and I are very close," he said, leaning against the bar. He looked like a spoiled prince with his tousled blonde hair. I didn't like my nickname for her on his smug lips.

"I call her Posey," I forced out. The fucker smiled widely.

"You like her," he said plainly. I choked. Who just blurts that out after meeting for five seconds?

"No I don't," I said. Sailor let out a laugh.

"He does like her," a deep voice grumbled. I turned to the voice coming from behind the bar.

"And who the fuc-Caleb?!" I stared at the voice in shock. The elf smirked and offered his hand. "Dude what are you doing here," I said, taking it.

"I moved here after I graduated. Took over the bar. I'm actually Greg's younger brother," Caleb said, opening a bottle of Guinness.

"How did I not know that?" I asked.

"Divorce. I stayed with my dad and my siblings stayed here with my mom. In the summer they would come over. But I decided to move here after we graduated. And well, you know I never talked about my family much," Caleb explained.

I nodded along. Caleb and I were roommates in college. He never talked about his family. He always kept to himself. Whenever I would bring up Lavender Falls he would shut down which now made sense. I guess his parent's divorce must have really affected him. But looking at him now something was different.

"Small world," Sailor said, smiling.

"The usual?" Caleb asked him. The usual? A stab of green envy snaked its way inside. Back in the city I never had a usual. Most people were too busy to stop, talk and get to know their drink orders.

"Wait, what do you mean I like her?" I asked, circling back. Caleb rolled his eyes.

"You were always going off about your best friends. Once I moved here I put it together. It was pretty obvious you liked *Posey*." He smirked. I took a sip of my beer. Did I really talk about her that much back then? I glanced at Sailor who was smiling.

"You mean like. Present tense," Sailor interjected. I rolled my eyes.

"What are you smiling for," I said, slightly irritated by him.

"It's okay if you like her," he said.

"Why?" I asked, looking away. I bit the inside of my cheek.

"Because it is." The tension in my shoulders eased. I'm an idiot. I was being jealous. And he knew. Caleb knew too I bet.

"You don't have to hide your feelings," Sailor said. I looked at his eerie blue eyes and opened my mouth to say something. "I'm a siren Celestino. I can see straight through you so don't even deny it," he interjected. My eyes widened. He smiled at my reaction.

Fuck.

"Now come on best friend. Let's get back to our ladies," Sailor continued, grabbing their drinks and heading back. Caleb grunted and turned away. "Oh by the way I am the person you'll be working side by side with for the haunted house," Sailor said, patting my shoulder. Great. He took a step towards Lilianna's direction and I sidestepped him to take the seat next to her. I don't care if they were just friends. She was *my* best friend.

"He's jealous." She gave a mischievous smile. I cocked an eyebrow at her.

"Jealous?" I questioned. I glanced over at the bar.

"He was practically sending laser beams at Sailor's hand being on your shoulder," she squealed. I sighed.

"Eleanor please. The man probably thinks we replaced him with Sailor," I said pointedly. She scoffed.

"Oh no. He was definitely jealous. Let's see who ends up sitting next to you." She leaned back into her seat.

"Sits next to me? What are we in middle school?" I downed the last bit of my drink.

Even though it felt childish a tiny part of me couldn't shake the feeling of hoping she was right. That Celestino *was* jealous. Maybe he did feel something for me. I bit the inside of my cheek. I was being ridiculous. Celestino and I were friends. Always have been and I was perfectly fine with that.

"They're coming back," she hissed.

I looked over to see the two men walk towards us, drinks in hand. My eyes connected with Celestino and I watched as he side stepped Sailor to slide into the booth next to me.

My heart skipped. I didn't dare meet Eleanor's eyes. I was not going to read into this.

"So the ladies told me that you guys will be working together for the pub crawl? I'm a bartender at The Siren's Saloon," Sailor said nonchalantly.

"I gotta stop by sometime. Is Carrie still the owner?" Celestino asked, twisting his beer bottle around. He was nervous. It was his tell-tale sign. He always fidgeted with his hands when he was nervous.

"Yep. Actually I gotta head over for my shift. Ladies until we meet again." He drained the last bit of his beer. "And I'll see you later in the week boss man," he said, clapping Celestino's shoulder. I raised an eyebrow as Sailor walked away.

"Boss man?" I asked. Celestino smiled and I tried to focus on *not* staring at his lips.

"Yeah, we're working together for the haunted house," he said. I nodded silently.

"Ooh, tell me when. I love watching men perform manual labor," Eleanor said a little too loudly.

My eyes flew to the elf bartender who just so happened to flick his ears in our direction. I bit back a smile. I looked at Eleanor who was smirking. Celestino glanced between us.

"Am I missing something?" he asked, clearly out of the loop.

"I'll explain it to you later. I'm going to leave you two to talk about work. Now children," she said, getting up. "I expect you to work together and put on the most amazing pub crawl ever. And remember, don't turn anyone into toads." She winked and glided away.

"That was one time," I called out.

I swear by the stars she'll never let that go. We were cramming for our chemistry exam. I was a bundle of nerves and barely slept two hours. One second we were arguing over chemical formulas and their correlation to potion making and the next second I accidentally turned her dog into a toad. It was a slip. My emotions were all over the place. I was tired and it was an accident. An accident I fixed swiftly might I add.

Celestino slipped out to take her seat and his warmth was replaced by cold air. I already missed his presence.

"So what's the game plan Posey?" he asked. I fought the urge to roll my eyes at the nickname.

"How do you know I already have a plan?" I asked. He gave me a dumb look.

"Listen. I may have been gone for a few years but I know you. You have a plan. You always do." I felt my cheeks heat. I hated that he still knew me. A part of me wanted to prove to him that I wasn't the same shy bookworm he grew up with.

Celestino gave me a cocky grin, one that made my heart skip.

"Stop that," I said. That only made him smile wider.

"Stop what?" he asked innocently.

"That smile. I know that smile."

He sipped his beer. "And what smile is that?"

Was he really doing this?

"That smile you smile when you think you can get whatever you want. It's aggravating." I huffed. It was a smile that twisted my insides and made me weak in the knees.

"Aggravatingly charming," he suggested. I bit my cheek. No. This wasn't happening. This couldn't be him flirting. Not with me, his best friend. Or was I thinking too much?

"Possibly. Anyhow we are getting off topic right now. I do have a plan." He straightened himself and set his beer to the side.

I reached in my bag to pull out my planner. We needed to come up with a schedule and then I could go home and get my heart and brain in order.

"Does that book say, *The Lady and The Kraken?*" he asked.

I froze as I stared at what I placed on the table. My paranormal romance book. How the fuck did I mess that up?

"Yes. I still read. I like books. Even paranormal romance ones. They're...nice," I said, while internally screaming, *Celestino Santos has discovered you read dirty smut.*

I grabbed the book hoping my face didn't give anything away. Why did I pull that out? Why didn't I look inside my bag first? The most important question was, why was my planner the same size?

I took a breath. It wasn't a big deal. It was just a book and I've always been a bookworm. I sat up straighter. This was me freaking out for no reason. I noticed a weird look in his eyes as he did his best to keep his face neutral.

That was interesting. I've never seen him struggle with his expressions, not like me anyway.

"That's an interesting cover." His voice was low.

His eyes melted into me and every nerve end in my body clamped up. I felt my magic pushing against me.

"By interesting do you mean suggestive? If so, then it makes sense given the context of the book," I said matter of factly. My mouth was on autopilot now.

His tongue peaked out to wet his bottom lip. "And what exactly does it suggest, Posey?" he asked. I felt my mouth go dry.

"Well..you know...sex." I said quietly as my hands trembled against my planner.

"Are you uncomfortable with us discussing sex?" He raised his eyebrows.

How the stars did we get to this conversation? We haven't even asked the normal questions yet like, how was college, how was the city, did you know I've had a crush on you since diapers?

His eyes were dark, teasing. I bit the inside of my cheek. I wasn't going to let him tease me. We were both adults now.

"O-of course not. We're both adults. Sex is a natural thing that happens and there's nothing wrong with the fact that I like reading about krakens using their tentacles to fuck-"

"Alright Lilianna I didn't mean to tease you so much." He cut me off. He hardly used my name. Ever. I wanted to hear him say it again. I cleared my throat.

Well this was awkward. His usual cool green eyes looked tormented. His cheeks flushed. Something was bothering him.

"Well, let's lay out some ground rules. First and foremost no mentioning of my fondness for paranormal romances or romance books in general," I started. "Two, we have to agree on everything. Teamwork involves compromise and I want to make sure we agree on the work we're doing."

Celestino stretched in his seat, shoulders finally relaxing.

"Three, we split the work 50/50. We still have our other jobs to do and we need to pull our weight evenly," he added. I nodded at his rule. Taking another sip of cider I racked my brain for another rule. I needed something. I couldn't leave it at three. Something popped into my head.

This should put him in his place.

"Four, we put the town ahead of your ego," I said with a satisfied smile. He snorted.

"I think you mean *our*," he said.

Downing the last bit of my cider, I slid to get up out of the booth. I felt my magic hum beneath my skin for the fourth time today as I stood beside him. I met his eyes confidently.

"Oh no, I mean yours. We *all* remember how you have a big ego." And to show him I wasn't the same timid girl he grew up with I boldly glanced at his lap, a smirk spreading across my face. "You know what they say about big egos." I gave him a wink. I heard him bark out a laugh as I walked away.

"Care to find out?" I heard him call out from behind. I threw up a middle finger without glancing back. This was going to be a long two months and for the first time in a while I was truly excited.

CHAPTER 4
SHE'S A GODDESS

I watched Lilianna walk out and sat in the booth in disbelief. One, I hadn't expected her to be so matter of fact over the fact she likes to read books with fucking. She said it so casually not realizing she was setting me on fire. And that book?

Now I have to fucking look up at the book to see what she likes and figure out a way to show her I can give that to her. Krakens was it? Maybe there was a spell I could find.

I shook my head. She used to get nervous about all of that stuff. Stars forbid if Eleanor ever brought up one of her midnight rendezvous with her boyfriends.

But now? Now she was casual about it in public and I was the nervous wreck. That look she gave me? I've never seen her look at me that way. There were sparks of desire behind her warm brown eyes. It was a look that begged me to drag her into the back office and-

I groaned, my head hitting the back of the booth. She even looked at my cock. Thank the stars for the lighting being low or she would have fucking seen what I've been trying to hide.

And rules. She gave us fucking rules. A part of me wanted to break her rules. Break them, bend her over-

"Tino, Tino, Tino," Eleanor sang, breaking my thoughts. I groaned again.

"Ellie," I said flatly. She had the biggest smile on her face.

"This is going to be so much fun." She slid back into Lilianna's seat, chin in her hands.

"What?" I asked.

"You folded so fast," she pointed out.

"She surprised me. For a second I felt like I had to be on my toes. I wasn't sure what was going to come out of her mouth," I confessed. Eleanor nodded.

"On your toes. Your back. Sitting down." She twirled the ends of her hair. My face flushed.

"Well someone is still the same," I said. She let out a laugh and from the corner of my eye I saw Caleb glancing this way. She turned to face him.

"See Caleb. That is how you make a woman laugh."

I looked over at him. For the first time I saw the man's cheeks darken. He turned away quickly. I wonder if this was why he seemed different. I looked back at Eleanor and I pointed between them.

"Are you two…?"

Eleanor sighed. She shrugged her shoulders. Oh Loch Ness Monster, if anyone can crack into that elf's armor it might be her.

"We've all grown up a bit, Tino. You have a lot to relearn. But just be patient with her. You know she was always slow when it came to her feelings," she said.

Her feelings? I raised an eyebrow at Eleanor and she zipped her lips. I messed with the label of my beer bottle, my thoughts and feelings rolling around in my head.

Lilianna had a delicious fire she only let out every once in a while. And stars, did I love bringing it out. I may have come back to town because I missed home but I missed her as well and I haven't even had her the way I've always wanted to.

By the end of the Full Moon Fall Festival I was going to capture that cozy witch's heart in whatever way she'd allow me. My eye caught Eleanor's who was looking at Caleb. Our best friend was clearly okay with this and that was all I needed.

"Good luck," Eleanor said, smiling with a gleam in her eyes.

I would definitely be needing it.

CHAPTER 5

RULE NUMBER 6

I woke up with the sun cutting through my curtain and the sound of ridiculously happy birds singing outside of my window. I wanted to set them on fire. I stayed up late. Again.

This time it was to mentally prepare for spending practically a whole day with Celestino. I methodically wrote out our rules on a document with a nice header and font that matched the style I was going for. I created a loose sketch of the map for the scavenger hunt and a list of all the pubs that would participate. I was massively over prepared but I couldn't sleep last night and decided to get a jumpstart.

I couldn't stop myself when my worker bee brain was buzzing. If I didn't I would have stayed up late staring at the ceiling or succumbed to the storm of doom scrolling on social media. Why do that for a few hours when I can get work done?

Stretching out of bed, I began to get ready. I needed to look my best to feel confident in order to handle what Celestino made me feel. Feelings that I shouldn't be feeling. Feelings that made me distracted. I twisted my wavy hair into a messy bun, a few strands spiraling out around my face.

I reached for my favorite distressed graphic tee paired with my beat up sneakers that my mom wanted to burn. I would be meeting

Celestino in half an hour at Coffin's Coffee Shop and definitely needed caffeine before I could put up with his irritatingly sexy smirk.

I still couldn't believe he was back in Lavender Falls. I was happy to have him back, truly. The town felt more like home with him in it. Yesterday the part of my brain that kept my filter under control was off and today I needed it up and running to keep everything in check.

Stopping to glance at myself in the hallway mirror, I took a deep breath.

This was going to be fine, I told myself.

But my brain, on its own accord, went back to what I said last night before leaving him. My magic began prickling. It was there on the surface of my skin as I thought about him. It was begging to be near him. My brain recalled the way his eyes melted whenever he looked my way during the meeting. That made me nervous. It twisted my stomach and made me think of things I shouldn't be thinking. I couldn't deny I had a crush on him since we were kids.

Despite the teasing he always held a softness around him. I became familiar with the way his eyes were always calculated, waiting to step in when need be. He was always so open with himself and his feelings while I've always been guarded.

Celestino, Eleanor and Lola were always there to protect me, to help me get out of my shell. But now we were adults. I didn't need to be protected or looked after. Sure, I still had a shell. But I knew when to step out and when to retreat…typically.

My teeth dug into my bottom lip as I remembered the way he watched me as I sipped my cider. It was permanently etched in my brain and going to be on replay in my fantasies. I could feel there was a shift in the air. I shook my head. I couldn't deal with this. Not now at least. I had way too much swimming in my brain that was trying to stay afloat.

I grew up seeing the downside of love. I saw how it could break a person into a million pieces. And with how much Celestino means to me, I couldn't take that chance…not yet. The possible outcome might be too big for me to give in. It was too unpredictable and I didn't have time to figure out the risks. I needed to focus on my job.

STEPPING into Coffin's Coffee Shop was like bathing in warm ectoplasm. Okay, that kind of sounded gross. It was more like a bubbling cauldron. With mood lighting and a slight medieval flair, the coffee shop felt like the home of a royal witch. It immediately relaxed my nerves. And it wasn't because I constantly got free snacks since I spent the majority of my time working here.

"Lily," Madame Coraline called out.

The old crone witch had salt and pepper hair that was pulled back by her wand and fell to her waist. She had pale gray eyes that were sharper than a blade. Wrinkles barely etched her face.

"The usual?" she asked. Madame Coraline smiled warmly and it felt like a grandmother's hug. I nodded and made my way to the back of the shop, praying to up above that no one took my table. I had a specific table in the corner that allowed me to see anyone coming into the shop and was situated by the window so the sun would come in to keep me warm.

I froze. Someone was at *my* table.

Well, it wasn't my table exactly. It's not like my name was carved into it, although that was seeming to be a good idea. I glanced around quickly trying to assess a backup. I usually always had a backup seat at every location I frequented. But before I could find it the man at my table spoke up.

"I made sure to get your table."

My eyes widened seeing Celestino. His eyes were more green today due to his olive shirt beneath his black plaid flannel. He stood up gesturing to me to sit. Always a gentleman. He wore fitting black jeans and his family pendant hung around his neck. He looked good. Really good.

Stop it.

I needed to focus. His dark wavy hair was swept into a low pony-tail. I wondered how it would feel to slip my fingers between the strands. I bit the inside of my cheek. I needed to keep these thoughts to myself. Did I find him attractive? Okay, maybe yes. I've been here less than five minutes and my brain was turning into mush.

We didn't stay in touch throughout college. Eleanor and I were roommates. Our friendship withstood late night study sessions, pixie dust covered shenanigans and puking in frat party bathrooms. However, with Celestino being further away it was hard to stay connected. We grew up and grew apart. He also didn't update his social media very often which I did occasionally keep track of.

I looked at Celestino again. I had an inkling that spending time with him meant that these *'few times a year'* late night thoughts would be constantly flooding in. My eyebrow twitched realizing he was here way earlier than expected.

"Oh," I said quietly.

He offered the chair he was sitting in; the one I always sat in because it gave me a view of the whole shop. I liked to keep a loose eye on who walked in and out. You never know when a creature from Fauny's Farms might escape. I squeezed past him as a waitress walked by, my shoulder nearly hitting his chin. A zing went up my spine from the brush of contact. My magic woke up.

"What do you mean by my table?" I asked, pulling out my laptop. He cocked his head with an amusing grin.

"This is the table you always sat at. Or do you prefer a different table now? It was probably stupid of me to assume. It's been eight years." He was babbling. That's new and cute.

"It's still my go-to table. Thanks," I said.

A grin slowly broke out across his face and I wanted to burn it into my memory. It was like the sunrise, slowly peeking out from the clouds, warming every inch of me. At that moment Madame Coraline stopped by with her signature mocha latte and warm buttered croissant.

"The usual," she snickered. She clearly overheard our conversation. My coffee preference and seating have apparently not changed in all these years. I smiled at Madame Coraline who sauntered away with mysterious pep in her step.

"Okay so there are a *few* things that haven't changed. But I like it here. Sometimes I'm here for the ambiance and to catch up on read-ing." I leaned in close. "Sometimes…I even switch my seat," I whis-pered. Celestino chuckled. I took a sip of latte letting the flavors glide over my body like a hug on a brisk fall day.

"You mean sometimes you come here for the ambiance while you hunch your shoulders, wrinkle your eyebrows and tap on your laptop like some zombie while occasionally reading your romance novels," he said, arching an eyebrow. I scoffed at him.

"I like to think I have better skin than a zombie. And you know some are nice. Greg, who works at the cemetery, is a sweetheart," I said. "Also don't forget rule number one," I continued. Celestino grinned.

"Greg is nice but I mean you're just always working according to Eleanor. You're successful now. You can relax every once in a while." He glanced away towards the window. People were strolling by, enjoying the breezy weather that was signaling the approaching autumn.

"I wouldn't say successful. I'm still just an assistant," I stated.

"And you're successful. Look at everything you've accomplished. Look at how much the tourism in town has gone up. That's because of you, Posey," he said firmly. My eyes widened at his conviction. I guess he was keeping tabs on me. Or the town. He smiled at me tenderly and my magic sang.

"Regardless of your job position that doesn't mean you don't deserve a break every once in a while."

I bit back a retort because he was right. "I do let loose," I coun-tered, turning on my laptop, eyes focused on the screen.

"Not according to Eleanor," he fired back. He wasn't going to let this go.

"Eleanor needs to stop talking to you about me." I mentally cursed. That was a dumb response and he knew it. They were best friends, of course they spoke. It's not like I'm opposed to going out either. It's just that my social battery can be like a broken phone. It has a tendency to drain quickly.

He shrugged his shoulders and pulled out his laptop and notebook.

His laptop was covered in stickers; food puns, skeletons, bands and cities. It seems like he's been to a lot of places, so many adventures I wasn't aware about.

"I like karaoke," I said in a low voice. He looked up in surprise.

"Karaoke? You know that involves standing in front of people and singing."

"I know the definition of karaoke and the people I'm singing in front of are drunk majority of the time." I narrowed my eyes on him.

He bit back a smile and I forced myself to not glance at his lips.

"Little Posey likes to serenade. Sure you're not a siren?" he joked as if it was the most confounding thing he discovered.

"Only on girl's night because the drinks are usually half off and I can get a basket of fries for the same price," I continued.

He cocked his head letting a full smile, dimples and all, spread across his face. I felt my heart thump against my chest. My magic hummed, wanting more.

"I never would have guessed," he said softly.

"You have about eight years worth of things to catch up on," I pointed out jokingly. When I looked back at him his face softened. His eyes crinkled at the corners.

"Well I would like to catch up," he said gently.

His words hung in the air like clouds and I wanted to pluck them and keep them close to my heart. Because it wasn't just what the words were but how they were said; with longing. Those seven words stirred something inside of me that I never truly felt before. He leaned towards me.

"I forgot how pink your cheeks are. Like a cherry blossom," he said. My eyebrow twitched.

"A cherry blossom?"

He nodded, settling back into his seat.

"I had a floral competition event I had to put together once and I learned a lot about different species of flowers."

I sat back in my seat. A floral competition?

"That might come in handy for the spring festival." I made a mental note to tell Eleanor. "I don't think I would say my face is like a cherry blossom. More like a rose. Always red," I said. He shook his head.

"There's a difference between you blushing and your rosacea," he smiled. I scoffed.

"And you can tell the difference?" I asked.

Suddenly a soft glow of light appeared by my hand. A small sprite appeared with a package.

"Hi from Pricilla's Potions and Lotions. You have a delivery! Here is your calming cream. Just sign here please!" The sprite's voice was soft and bright.

"Impeccable timing," I said under my breath. After signing for my package and slipping into my bag I looked at Celestino again.

"I can always tell when you're blushing. I just don't know if it's for the reasons I think." He broke eye contact and tapped away on his laptop.

I tugged at my earlobe as my heart pounded. I didn't expect him to say that. What were his reasons? Were they the same as mine? *Focus.* I shook my head forcing my thoughts to be over the conversation.

"I worked on a few things last night," I said. I was fully in work mode now. Celestino straightened his shoulders, his full attention on me, waiting. I liked that.

"I have our rules on a document. I just shared it with you. I also sketched out some designs for the scavenger hunt and a list of all the pubs that should participate. We can work on the map for the order together and come up with riddles." A light bulb flickered in my head. "Oh but the riddles should be based on the pubs participating so you should probably contact them first."

We needed to make sure all the pubs were willing to participate. He looked pensive. I felt a flicker of nerves rise.

"What?" I asked, nervously. He crossed his arms over his chest and I glanced back at my screen to avoid looking at the way his flannel tightened around his biceps.

"That's way more than 50% and we've barely even started. We agreed to split the work evenly," he said. I chewed my bottom lip.

"I mean if we were to get technical on it we don't have a baseline for what we consider to be 50% due to the fact that we haven't made a list of everything that has to get done to divide it up evenly," I said. He scoffed.

"Really Posey? You want to get *that* technical?" he asked, arching an eyebrow. I straightened in my seat.

"Well I'm right," I said confidently. And I was. We hadn't drawn up any plans to form a proper conclusion on what we each considered to be 50/50. Why was he taking this so personally? It wasn't a big deal.

"By you going ahead and working before we laid down the groundwork on what *we* would consider to be 50/50 is past 50/50. You took over instead of giving us the opportunity to draw a line."

I blinked at him, clenching my jaw. He smirked, realizing he caught me. My nostrils flared and my magic came alive again. I hated being wrong. In this case by a small technicality he was right. I could tell by his stupid smirk he was happy he caught me. I felt like a kid again, arguing over magical monopoly. He would steal all my apothecaries and I would buy up his hotels.

"So now what?" I asked.

"Well before we discuss the whole 50/50 thing there's something else we need to talk about."

Oh no. I didn't like his tone. It was the tone he used when he wanted something.

"And that is?" I asked.

It happened slowly. His green eyes darkened. His body leaned across the table, hand closing my laptop to get my full attention. He tilted his head down so whatever that was going to pour from his lips would only be heard between us. My stomach was in knots. The people in the shop faded into the background and a bubble formed around us. It felt like it was only Celestino and I.

"Punishment for when one of us breaks the rules."

My heart stopped for a second and my lungs needed more oxygen. Celestino Nuno Santos just used his flirty tone on me.

On me.

I've heard him use it on countless girls growing up. I used to dream of him using it on me. But those were dreams, fantasies, hopeful wishes that I never thought would turn into a reality.

It was the way his voice slightly dipped on the word us. *Us*. There was a pull in his tone that drew me in. Like a moth to a flame. His pupils slightly dilated with excitement and his cheeks were flushed.

"P-punishment," I stuttered. He nodded, eyes still holding me in place.

"Like what?" My question came out breathless.

"Truth or dare."

It took a second before his words registered, breaking me out of his spell. A giggle escaped.

"Truth or dare? What are we twelve?" I asked, pulling my hand back. But he wouldn't budge. Instead he applied more pressure to keep my hand down. His strength flooded my body with heat.

"Truth. Or. Dare." He emphasized each word but my only focus was his hand pressing down on mine, his magic running up my arm, seeking mine. I felt it tug me. I took a deep breath trying to push it back. He raised an eyebrow, waiting.

"Fine. Truth or dare it is," I bit out. He finally let go of my hand and a soft sigh escaped me. I felt like I could breathe again. His smile was smug.

"Well then Posey, which will it be?" he asked.

What did I want? What if I pick dare? Would it be something innocent or dirty? If I pick truth, what would he ask me to reveal?

"Truth," I decided, hoping it would be simple. He cocked his head to the side, mulling over whatever choices his brain was concocting.

"Did you miss me?" he asked. I stared at him in shock.

My heart gave a tiny crack. I wasn't expecting that. I wanted to ask why he felt like I didn't. Of course I did. I missed my best friend. I missed the way we bickered. The way we laughed together. The way he made me feel safe. The easy answer was yes even though it didn't feel that way. It didn't feel like enough to just say *I missed you*. Staring at him I noticed he looked...lonely.

"Yes Celestino. I missed you a lot," I answered sincerely. His shoulders relaxed and he nodded.

"Cool. Let's make up this list and maybe you can avoid breaking rules," he said, rolling his shoulders. But I wasn't done. He didn't notice he also broke a rule.

"Truth or dare?" I asked him. His head popped up, confused. "You mentioned my romance books in the beginning of our conversation. That means you broke a rule." I crossed my arms over my chest. He let out a chuckle. *Just like old times.*

"You're absolutely right," he smirked. "This time," he said with a wink. I bit my lip to keep myself from laughing. He scratched the back of his head in contemplation.

"Truth," he said. I smiled, pleased at his choice. There was something I needed to know.

"Well did you miss me?" My heart squeezed as I forced each word to come out. Did he think about me in college? Did he wonder what I was up to? He never came around much for the holidays, always busy working and frankly so was I. It was like throughout these eight years we kept circling each other, like magnets trying to pull closer.

His green eyes looked dejected, lonely, and fuck I wanted to erase it. I didn't like that look on him. He was always carefree. Looking at him now I wonder what broke him and if I could be the one to put his smile back together again.

"Yes," he whispered, turning away. My heart swelled briefly. It was confusing. A part of me was happy he missed me but the other half of me felt hurt. I felt somewhat responsible for our disconnect. Maybe I should have reached out. Maybe if we kept our friendship throughout college we both wouldn't feel so…lost around each other. Either way he was back and I wasn't going to let him go again.

WITH THINGS CLEARED up it was time to get back to work.

"First things first is that you should call the pubs before we move on to anything. We have to know who's participating in order to handle the rest," I said.

"Yeah that would make sense. You want me to call?" he asked to clarify.

"Well if you want *me* to do it, it's going to be by email. I don't like phone calls and getting an email back might take longer than we want," I said, clicking my pen. He smiled.

"Right. That's fine with me. Have you thought of a name for the crawl?" he asked. I blinked and he stared at me.

"I hadn't thought of that," I said. My brain was too busy thinking of all the other little things that had to be done. I let that detail slip between the cracks. The Haunted Pub Crawl wasn't bad but I wanted something else.

I took a bite of my croissant, savoring the buttery goodness. A small moan escaped my lips and Celestino looked away quickly, shifting in his seat.

"Well that's why it's a team effort," he said, jaw tight. His laptop pinged with all the documents I shared. "Wow you really went all out," he remarked. His voice was slightly breathless with admiration. He cracked his knuckles dramatically and I shook my head, smiling.

"This is the rule list?" His eyes roamed across his screen. "I'm going to color code the rules. Don't give me that face," Celestino chuckled. "I want to track who ends up making the most rules. My bet is on you. And let's agree on a name before I contact the pubs. We should also give them a deadline so we can try the drinks. We don't want tourists accidentally turning into rats or the drinks tasting like swamp water," he finished.

I couldn't stop myself from grinning. My brain was beginning to relax. It felt nice to share the workload with someone else. Especially someone who was willing to point out the things I missed in a non-condescending way.

"Once we have a title I can come up with graphics for the socials and flyers to be handed out to the shops," I added. He nodded in agreement. It felt good telling him what to do without him having a snarky comeback. It was refreshing and hot.

"So names…" he began.

"Spooky, cursed, maybe ghostly," I began trailing off synonyms of haunted in order for an idea to spark.

"There's tavern, bar, potion, elixir, or tonic," he added. We leaned into our laptops searching synonyms, shoulders hunched, brows furrowed. Maybe I was like a zombie.

"Cursed Bar Hopping," he offered.

I wrinkled my nose.

"Hopping makes me think of Easter. Paranormal Drink Fest?" I asked.

"But we have the Full Moon Fall Festival," he pointed out. I bit my lip.

"The Cursed Bar Crawl," I suggested. It was simple, to the point, no mistaking what it was. Plenty of spooky creatures crawl anyway. Celestino thought about it for a minute.

"I'm good with that. Come up with the graphics and I'll start calling the pubs. You want them come up with a signature cocktail for the event?" he asked. I nodded. He read my mind perfectly and a part of me was a bit flustered by it.

The eight year gap in our friendship was slowly closing. It was much easier bouncing ideas off of someone, especially someone who kept up with my brain.

I started to work on the graphic designs only half paying attention to Celestino's phone calls.

My eyes flickered up at some point as I confirmed the colors I would be using. He leaned back against his seat, stretching his arms as he talked to the manager of Boogeyman's Bar. His muscles made the flannel stretch again and I lost focus for a second. His neck strained as he arched his back and I wondered how his pulse would react if I kissed the spot right below his ear. His five o'clock shadow accentuated his cheekbones.

My eyes traveled to his hands. His fingers looked rough. He always had a knack for building. He took carpentry in high school and would make the most amazing things. I used to walk by during his afternoon workshop classes just to catch him.

He chewed his bottom lip, which arguably shouldn't be as plump as it was or the perfect shade of dusty rose. The smell of the ocean tickled my nose. When I glanced up my stomach tightened. He wasn't chewing his lip out of habit. No, he was chewing his lip to keep from laughing.

Fuck!

He caught me. He caught me staring at him like he was the last red velvet cupcake at Godmother's Patisserie. My face erupted into flames. My heart was catapulted into overdrive. I needed to calm down or my magic would explode.

Celestino didn't say anything as he continued to call The Siren's Saloon, The Plastered Pixie and Highwaymen Haunt. No, instead he bided his time. He knew I was expecting a response from him and I knew he was enjoying having me twitch in my seat.

My knee bobbed up and down manically, waiting for him to say something, anything. My stomach was in knots over it. My magic kept rolling my pen away from me as I tried to relax. I took a deep breath. I didn't need to be worrying over something as small as a look. He wasn't making it a big deal so why should I?

"So all the pubs have agreed. They're very excited. They're going to send their logos so we can attach them to the graphics and I gave them two weeks to finalize their menu so we can try them," he said.

All I could do was nod. I was grateful that he was one that dealt with the conversational part but I couldn't bear to meet his gaze. I took a sip of my latte, letting whatever warmth it still had calm my body down.

"Did you know most elephants weigh less than the tongue of a blue whale?" My voice was strained. What the fury fuck did I just say? Did I really talk about whale tongues? I could feel his eyes on me.

"Posey," he said. The softness of his voice *almost* tempted me to look up.

"Rule number five: we won't speak about you catching me checking you out," I rushed out, my heart hammering faster than a bat's wings. He laughed softly and I couldn't stop my eyes from seeking him anymore. He was shaking his head, causing some strands to fall forward. Stars, I wanted to brush it back with my hand. *No. Stop it!*

I looked away as he started packing his things. I assumed he still needed to head to the haunted house. I still kept my eyes glued to my laptop even when his scent of sandalwood curled its way through my senses, suffocating me in the most bewitching way.

"I gotta go help with the builds but that wasn't simply checking me out," his breath tickled my ear. My eyes fluttered, relishing in his nearness. "Rule number six: you can eye fuck me anytime."

My pen flew across the room and nearly smacked a kid as Celestino walked away. The second he walked out the door I went over to convince a family I didn't purposely try to hit their kid with my pen.

Fuck me and I don't mean in that way…I think.

CHAPTER 6

A Nudge

I couldn't stop my smile as I walked over to Atticus's Antiques. I hadn't been back to enjoy the festival in years. It was always my favorite time of year. That and the Winter Wonderland festival. Every year Atticus's Antiques would transform into a haunted house. Mainly due to the fact it was the only building on the block with a finished basement that wasn't used for storage and had plenty of rooms that connected.

The day had been going great. It felt natural to be working side by side with Lilianna again. It felt good. We had a name for the crawl. Pubs were contacted and confirmed. Next was social media which Lilianna was great at according to everyone. And honestly I knew she was. I always kept tabs on Lavender Falls socials ever since Eleanor sent me a funny promotional video Lilianna did. She got dressed up as a giant pumpkin, skipping down city hall throwing candy. She looked adorable.

But the real reason I was in such a good mood was because I caught her checking me out. I watched her eyes devour me. She hadn't noticed I was watching her. I could barely focus on the phone call with the owner of Boogeyman's Bar, Mr. Salazar.

She felt something. There was no way I was imagining it. Not with the way she reacted when she realized I caught her. This had to be why Eleanor was okay with me making a move.

"Looks like someone is in a good mood," Sailor chimed as I stepped inside Atticus's. Damn the stars. I forgot I would be working with him. Seriously, who the fuck names a siren Sailor? Like how much more cliche could it get? What was he, the prince of the sea? I chuckled.

"What are you laughing at?" he asked as I made my way towards Atticus's office.

"Nothing" I said flatly. I slipped my bag inside the room, locking it in the closet.

"I don't know boss, you're in a much better mood compared to last time. Did you see Lilianna?" His eyes were too bright. I strangely felt compelled to tell him yes. He better not be using his magic on me.

"No," I lied, heading to the bathroom to switch clothes. The fish man followed me.

"Are you sure? Because I think you did."

I slammed the door in his face. "Space Sailor. I don't need help changing," I grunted. He laughed and it sounded like a fucking song.

"Who knows? You might put your pants on wrong, thinking too hard about Lilianna."

This was going to be the longest two months of my life. When I got out Sailor was leaning against the wall humming what was probably a sea shanty.

"Do I need to remind you I'm a siren," he said, raising an eyebrow. I sighed.

"Okay. Yes, I saw her today. We had a work meeting and it was nice," I confessed. I dropped my clothes in the office before heading to the back of the store.

"Nice as in, it was so nice to reconnect with an old friend and work together," he started. I was going to agree but he rambled on, "Or was it more like it was so nice to reconnect with an old friend that I've secretly had a crush on for years?"

I waved my hand up and his mouth instantly closed.

"Sailor there are people around here working," I hissed. He

widened his eyes, nodding profusely and I let my magic release him. We walked out the back door into the outside where we would be spending our time cutting wood and building set pieces. I was grateful that Sailor finally got the hint to keep his big mouth shut. I handed him the paperwork with the sketches of what we would be working on today. He nodded and went to pull up the wood.

"So it was definitely the second one," he called from over his shoulder.

I groaned. I wonder if I could staple his mouth shut.

"Are you sure you can handle working on the festival, help Lilianna with the bar crawl *and* transform Atticus's Antiques into a haunted house," Ben, my boss, asked me during our meeting the next day. After working on a few decor pieces for the haunted house, I had a meeting with Ben. We were working through a long list for the festival and needed to make sure we had everything.

A lot of stores would be closing their doors to open booths and a few at home small businesses would be setting up shop. We needed to put together a map for where they would be stationed. The football field would be clear to host the carnival rides then we had to figure out if Patty's Pumpkin Patch would be having the infamous haunted hayride and corn maze. There was also the matter of finding and confirming the food truck vendors.

"This is a cake walk compared to the b-list celebrity charity events I would help put on," I responded. Which it was. A small town festival was a breeze compared to the jobs I had done in the city.

My mind was pulled back into a memory of putting on a fancy charity ball at The Plaza. It was a total schmooze fest with sleazy men getting drunk and some women hoping to get lucky. I got bitched out by the lady in charge because the champagne glasses were organized wrong on the waiter's trays.

That didn't even come close to the time when I was told I was incompetent because the sun didn't rise at exactly 7:01 but at 7:03 for an outdoor ceremony for a mafia wedding. At least I swear they had to be the mafia.

It was just little thing after little thing. And stars forbid they found out I was from a small town. *No wonder,* they would say, as if that explained the reason I couldn't control the gravitational pull of the Earth so the sun would rise at the time they required.

Ben gave me a look, one I didn't want. He pushed away his keyboard.

"What made you want to move back?" he asked.

I was dreading this question. I knew it would come up and I was prepared for it but it didn't make me like it any more. Everyone wanted to know why someone successful in the city of New York would move back to his hometown. I sighed, sinking further into my chair.

"I was tired of it, Ben. People were fake. Not everyone of course but it just never felt right. I felt like I was constantly putting on a show. Like I couldn't be myself." I sighed. "They looked at me like I was a speck of dust, littering their prestige chandeliers. I was sick of it, even though the pay was great. I…I was lonely," I confessed.

He stayed quiet for a few minutes. "Well it's good to have you back," he said. I nodded, pulling up our list.

I knew I would like working for Ben. He was straight laced. You knew what you were getting with him. You didn't need to use flowery language or over explain to him. He didn't question you constantly, making you feel inadequate. It was a breath of fresh air.

"How does it feel to be working with Lilianna?" he asked nonchalantly. My heart did a weird thing. I glanced up at the smirking werewolf.

"What do you mean by that?" I arched an eyebrow. He placed his hands behind his head.

"What do *you* mean by that?" he asked innocently.

"Your tone," I said flatly. He shrugged his shoulders.

"I'm just saying. It's been a few years since you've talked, hung out, seen your *best friend.*"

I felt heat creep up my neck. Fuck, did everyone know I had a crush on her? Was I that obvious back in the day? I mean I was very good at covering myself. But then again this was a small town. I went out with other girls knowing Lilianna would never go out with me. I tried to shove the feelings aside. But at some point it just felt wrong to try to be with someone else when the person I wanted was within arm's reach.

It's why I gave up relationships during my senior year. I just wanted to focus on enjoying my last year with my friends before leaving. And during college? I had a few flings here and there but it never lasted long. Nothing ever felt right.

"I'm going to ignore your tone and just say it feels nice to reconnect with old *friends*," I said, emphasizing the plural of friends. Because now that I was back I was happy to be with Eleanor, Lola and Caleb too. I still couldn't believe I grew up with his siblings and never pieced it together. Ben let out a laugh.

"The real question is why did you stick me with Sailor? He's irritating," I grunted.

"Sailor can be intense but he is one hell of a carpenter. Don't worry he'll grow on you," he said. I shook my head.

"Like a mole," I muttered.

"Work together…like a clownfish and an anemone," he said. I couldn't help but chuckle.

"Really? An ocean simile?" I asked.

"He is a siren," he shrugged.

Ben and I laughed. It was definitely good to be back.

THE WEEK WAS FINALLY OVER. At least with one job. My eyes wandered back to my computer. I was waiting on some permits to process. I made sure Lilianna had all the logos she would need because she didn't just need the pubs logos but now she had to make sure she was promoting vendors that would be a part of the festival. I squeezed the back of my neck. I couldn't stop the bubble of worry that was brewing. It felt like she had a lot on her plate. But stars so did I. I was going to be spending the weekend with fucking Sailor sawing and putting together wood frames and carving styrofoam to look like Greek statues.

Tomorrow morning I would be meeting Lilianna at The Drunken Fairy Tale Tavern to go over the riddles we needed for the crawl. My fingers tapped against my desk. I couldn't help it. I had always missed her but now, being back in town and having only a few meetings with her, I felt like our friendship was falling into place.

My phone buzzed against my desk. It was Eleanor.

ELLIE

You+Me+Karaoke= hungover and sleeping in

Love, your amazing, beautiful pixie best friend

Karaoke? Did that mean Lilianna would be there? She mentioned she liked karaoke. Without any questions I texted her back yes.

I felt my stomach tighten. Would I see her tonight? I stared at the time on my clock. Two minutes until I could leave the building, might as well start packing now. I slipped my notebook into my bag and turned off my computer for the weekend. I waved goodbye to Ben before making my way to the elevators. My phone buzzed again.

FISH FACE

1pm tomorrow right boss man?

I sighed deeply seeing Sailor's message pop up. I stepped into the elevator ignoring his text.

FISH FACE

I know you saw my text boss man

I slipped my phone in my pocket. A second later it buzzed again.

FISH FACE

You left me on read boss man

Sailor blew up my phone with emojis and gifs and I was ready to chuck the device against the wall. The elevator doors opened and I felt a shiver run up my spine. My eyes connected to a familiar pair of brown eyes.

"Posey," I said as I stepped in.

"Hey there," she said casually. The doors dinged closed. I felt a hitch in my breathing once we stepped inside. We were alone in an enclosed metal box. My brain began running rampant with wild ideas that involved me pressing the emergency stop button and propping her up on the railing. My eyes flickered slightly up at her.

"How was your day?" I asked, trying to keep it cool. She gave a small smile and it sent my magic humming.

"It was okay. Got some graphics ready for vendors," she said. I nodded. I wonder if Eleanor texted her.

"Eleanor and I are going for happy hour. Want to join? Get the group back together?" I hope I didn't sound needy. But I was. I needed more of her presence. Getting the gang back together was a good way of being around her. A way that didn't involve work.

She started chewing her bottom lip. "I can't. I'm trying to get a certain number of things done before the weekend but next time."

She finally looked at me. Her brown eyes locked on mine and it was as if everything faded away. My eyes took in the state of her wavy hair pulled back in a ponytail and the dark smudges under her eyes. Her cheeks were slightly flushed and she was gripping her bag tightly.

"An hour?" I asked. She needed to relax. I could tell she wanted to say yes but she was holding back. I took a step closer and her pupils dilated slightly. I raise my hand slowly, my finger grazing her cheek to tuck a stray strand of hair. I hope she didn't notice my hand trembling.

"One hour," I said. I just wanted one hour with her. 60 minutes of no work, just us...and friends. I looked at her, pleading. Her chest rose and fell.

"You're giving me that look," she said. I bit back a smile at her remark.

"And what do you mean by that?" I asked. Her eyes widened slightly. She didn't mean to say that out loud. I arched an eyebrow and she straightened herself.

"You're giving me your 'green doe eye' look. You used to do it all the time when you wanted something," she said as the beep of the elevator droned on. She knew me so well. I let out a chuckle and took a step closer. She was either going to make me regret getting in her space or not.

I look down at her lips quickly. They were slightly open and her eyes dipped down my face. I was so close to her. I could almost feel the brush of her blouse against my chest. I clenched my fist to keep my magic from pulling her in.

"Please Posey," I said in a low voice. Her hand fidgeted with the strap of her bag again. A look crossed her face.

"The thing is Celestino," she leaned her face slightly down towards mine and I swear I stopped breathing. She was so close. So fucking close. The breeze of her magic wrapped around me and I felt its pull.

"That look never worked on me before and it certainly won't now," she said as the elevator dinged open. "Bye," she tossed over her shoulder. I step outside, my eyes glued to her retreating figure. I wish she would turn around and see how much of a mess she left me.

I STRETCHED my back and glanced around. The tavern was slowly becoming packed as people finished off their work day. I waited for Eleanor to arrive. Caleb handed me a Guinness.

"How does it feel so far being back?" he asked.

"Honestly? It feels like nothing has changed yet it has. Like I know everyone here but it's been eight years since I've really been around.

Everyone has their place and I'm trying to find mine again." I took a sip of my dark beer.

"You have a place here, always have and will," he said firmly. I rolled my eyes at his serious tone.

"I know, I know. I guess I spent so long away that now I'm confused about where I fit in." I fidgeted with the glass.

"I get that. I'm from here but I grew up away from everyone for the majority of my life." Caleb glanced around the pub. " It took me a while to feel like a part of the town I've always had roots in," he said.

I held up my beer in salute.

"To finding our place," I said. He chuckled and grabbed a cup of water.

"Sláinte."

At that moment Eleanor twirled into the seat next to me and Lola appeared on my other side. Eleanor had her hair pulled back by a headband and was still in her work clothes.

"Hey boys," Lola said smiling. Her green and purple braids sat on top of her head and she was dressed in overalls.

"Gardening?" I asked Lola. Her smile widened.

"Yep! A certain someone had to help me set up my portion of the community garden," she said smirking. Eleanor tapped the bar with her fingers.

"Give me the dirty details later. Anyway hey bestie," Eleanor said brightly. She snuck her arm around my torso giving me a gentle squeeze. Her face dropped as she looked up at Caleb.

"Caleb," she said his name nonchalantly.

"Eleanor," he said in a low voice. They stared at each other for a few seconds before Caleb turned to walk down the bar. I tried to cover my laugh while Lola rolled her eyes.

"So are you going to catch me up with how you, my best friend and my old college friend seem to be having something?" I asked. Lola snorted.

"Please catch him up," Lola teased. Eleanor rolled her eyes.

"It's hard to have anything with that brute. He hardly says anything and when he does it makes me want to slap him with pixie dust and not the fun kind," she scowled. I shook my head.

"You're having problems getting someone?" I stared at Eleanor in disbelief. Eleanor always had the magical ability to have anyone and anything wrapped around her tiny finger. The fact that Caleb seemed immune to Eleanor's charms must be a challenge.

He came back with a drink and dropped it next to Eleanor's hand. Eleanor didn't even spare a glance. Caleb crossed his arms, waiting for her to say something.

Lola leaned into my ear. "Watch carefully," she whispered.

Caleb cleared his throat. With a bored expression she finally looked at him.

"An appropriate response would be thank you," his deep voice rumbled. Her eyes flickered to the drink.

"An appropriate manner for a bartender would be to ask me what I wanted to drink," she threw back. Caleb leaned in.

"You get the same drink every time Starburst."

Eleanor's face flushed. "Well maybe I want to switch it up," she said, crossing her arms. Caleb scoffed.

"And what would that be?" he asked. Her eyes slid down the bar to a man drinking what looked like scotch.

Eleanor smiled sweetly and with a loud voice she said, "I'll have what he's having."

The man looked up. Eleanor waved and sent a wink. The man smiled and began walking towards us. Caleb turned to glare at him.

"No." His voice was borderline murderous. The man spun on his heels immediately and went back to his seat.

"You realize you can't stop me from going over there right," she said. My eyes bounced between the two. I needed fucking popcorn. This was incredible to watch. This was the most animated I had ever seen Caleb.

Caleb spread his hands on the bar and leaned in. Damn, I wish Lilianna was here to see this. Although she's probably aware of this thing between them. Caleb kept leaning closer while Eleanor held a bored look on her face. I have to applaud her for the commitment.

"And what's stopping me from kicking you out of my bar?"

Oh, shit.

"You wouldn't dare," she bit out. Caleb smirked.

"Is that a challenge?" he asked.

"Kick me out and I'll end up at another pub with a man making me a decent drink," Eleanor said with a mischievous smile. Lola was desperately trying not to laugh as I looked around. Apparently I wasn't the only one watching. Everyone in the bar was staring, waiting.

"No one else in town makes your drink the way you like it. Not like I do and we both know it," he grumbled. Eleanor lifted her drink and took a sip from the tiny straw. I swear his cheeks turned pink.

"Remind me who was the one that taught you to make it how I like it." She raised an eyebrow. My heart was pounding. I felt like the third wheel. This was some cheesy romcom shit. They stared at each other for another minute before Caleb backed off.

"Drink your damn drink," he muttered, walking to the other side of the bar. Eleanor sat back triumphantly as Lola clapped.

"I can't believe I've been missing this. How long has this been going on?" I asked, setting my beer down. Lola and Eleanor glanced at each other.

"He's been in town for four years. So since then," Eleanor said.

My jaw dropped.

"And nothing has happened?" I asked. She sighed disappointedly.

"He just backs away every time we start to get close," she said. I bumped her shoulder.

"He's always been kind of reclusive if that's any help. I guarantee you I've never seen him that vocal in all the years I've known him and I've lived with him in college," I said. Her eyes lit up.

"Can you tell me stories from your college days?" Her eyes widened in excitement and I laughed.

"Don't leave out a single detail!' Lola's eyes shimmered.

"Of course. One time we were at a party and we didn't realize the jello shots were infused with a dance potion. Caleb ended up having a few, stripped down to his boxers and-"

I felt a smack at the back of my head. I turned around to see Caleb with his hand raised.

"How the heck did you get here so fast?"

"We don't talk about those days." And with that he turned and went towards his office. I glared at his retreading figure. I looked over at Eleanor and Lola and sent them a wink. They nodded in silent agreement.

"How was work this week?" Eleanor asked, shifting the conversation. I looked around the room.

"It was fine. Workload is about the same but I can breathe now," I said. Eleanor smiled at me from behind her glass.

"And how's working with your bestie?" Lola asked. At the mention of Lilianna I felt my beer threatening to come back up.

"It's been…nice. Kind of like the old days," I responded calmly. Eleanor hummed next to me.

"Just like old times? So feelings and everything?" Eleanor asked. I glanced at her. She had the dumbest grin.

"Ladies," I warned. They gave me an innocent look.

"What? I distinctly remember you mentioning at that party eight years ago: *there isn't a word that describes my feelings for her. She's beautiful and-* actually I still have the video." She reached into her purse.

"You still have it?" Lola leaned past me, towards Eleanor.

"No, no. Not here," I said, grabbing Eleanor's hand. "Pause, you know about the video?"

Lola giggled and patted my cheek. "My sweet Celestino we were all at the party," she said.

My face flushed. So everyone in town definitely knew about my crush. *Fucking fury.*

"Do you still have feelings?" Eleanor asked, raising an eyebrow. I tapped my fingers against my beer, a blush creeping on my face. Eleanor smiled. "So what are you going to do?" She cocked an eyebrow at me and Lola snorted. I scowled at her question.

"What do you mean?" I took another long sip.

"Eight years ago you drunkenly confessed that you had a crush on her. You admitted to us now, sober, that you still like her. So what are you going to do?" Eleanor rolled her eyes.

"When in this conversation did I admit such a thing?" I asked. Lola glared at me.

"Celestino Nuno Santos," Eleanor said firmly. I forgot how persistent Eleanor was. I bet Caleb was well acquainted with that part of her personality. Annoyed with how long I was taking to answer, Eleanor placed her drink on the bar and gripped my shoulder.

"What do you expect me to do," I pleaded. Lilianna didn't see me anymore as a friend and sure there were signs that she obviously felt attracted to me, but something was holding her back and I didn't want to push her. I *wasn't* going to push her. She tightened her grip on my shoulder, brows furrowing. I try not to flinch. I forgot how strong she was for a pixie.

"You need to man up. You're not a teenager anymore. Make a damn move. This is us officially giving you permission as her best friends,"she said. I stared wide-eyed at them.

"This is your chance. It's now or never," Lola said, grinning.

My heart rattled against my chest.

Maybe I'll give her a nudge.

CHAPTER 7

RIDDLES ARE SEXY

It was the end of the week and I was feeling like a zombie. I probably looked like one too. Maybe I could stop at the cemetery to visit Greg and we could hang out. He was the nicest zombie in town. Actually he was the only one.

It was going to be a peaceful night with a superhero movie on in the background as I sipped a glass of wine and did some work. But something absolutely horrible happened. I was happily walking to my couch when I tripped and spilled said glass of wine onto my coffee table. The table where my laptop innocently laid wide open.

I stared wide eyed at the crime scene. My innocent laptop was splattered in red liquid. I could practically hear it crying. I stood in shock for about five seconds before a string of curse words flew out of my mouth. Of course this would happen. A part of me wished I had said yes to Celestino. I could be with them at The Drunken Fairy Tale Tavern right now having fun. This probably wouldn't have happened if I had gone.

"Fury fuck," I kept mumbling over and over again. I ran to the kitchen to grab some towels but they kept flying from my hand. My magic was buzzing around, opening and closing kitchen cabinets.

Everything was out of whack. I needed to get my magic under control. I needed to breathe.

"Okay magic. Listen to me. We need the towels to clean the mess so stop making them fly away," I said with a deep breath. I closed my eyes briefly letting my magic flourish within. A surge of warmth pulsed through me. I concentrated on what the towels would feel like in my hand and nudged the energy around to follow my directions. I flicked my fingers and the towels landed in my hand.

With a deep breath and tears in my eyes I wiped my laptop. It could still work. It could definitely still work. But from the state of the wine seeping between the keys of my keyboard I knew it would take a miracle.

Fuck, how did I even trip? I frantically looked around. The floor was clean. Typical. I tripped over my own damn feet. I pressed the power button, praying to the stars it turned on.

"Please," I whispered. Nothing. It wasn't working. Not even a flicker of light to showcase my precious laptop was hanging onto some form of life. Now I was going to need a new laptop. Which meant I had to spend money. I sighed against the couch.

Maybe I really was the Fates favorite.

MY PHONE BLARED against my nightstand. I groaned, covering my head with my blanket. I felt tired. Depleted. I could feel the sun shining through my window, warming my back. Wait…sun? I sat up immediately.

"Fuck," I croaked out. I reached for my phone and noticed the missed calls and unanswered texts from Celestino. I was supposed to meet him two hours ago. I was *supposed* to wake up before the sunrise to cleanse my apartment as the first sunbeams of the day hit my windows and wash my hair. All before meeting Celestino at the tavern to go over the riddles for the Cursed Bar Crawl.

"Fuck, fuck, fuck," I repeated over and over again. I threw a flannel on top of my pajama tank and stuffed my legs into joggers before slipping on some sneakers and reaching to grab my bag. Except I couldn't grab my bag.

As I reached for the bag my magic frizzed out and shot it two feet away from me. This couldn't be happening. Taking a deep breath I reached out to my bag with my magic, and this time it came towards me. Throwing it over my shoulder I ran out.

People were bustling around. I called Celestino while running to the tavern. He wasn't picking up. Why would he? I was two hours late. He was probably furious. I would be. I hated being late. Being on time made me anxious. If you were on time, you were late. If you were late…I shuddered at the thought.

I could already feel my stomach clenching, intestines twisting, cold chills grating over the goosebumps on my skin. I should have gone to bed after I transferred everything to my new laptop. But no, I had to get the work I had planned on doing done. I continued my cursed chanting even when I threw open the tavern's door.

I sensed him sitting in the same booth we all sat in last time. Celestino looked annoyed. I was ready to throw up. My brain was wracking a way to either cast a spell that could turn back time or fancy words that would make the lines in his face go away. I stood before him, hands clasped together to keep the trembles at bay.

"Hi…I'm..sorry…" I said, trying to catch my breath. He just looked at me. His eyes were more of a muddy green today. His shoulders were tense. A feeling began gnawing at my inside. *Disappointment.*

I hated that it was my fault. If I hadn't stayed up late. If I had just gone to bed or set ten more alarms. Something familiar was slowly clawing its way to the surface. A feeling I needed to keep locked up.

"You're late," he said.

I took a deep breath. "I've been swamped with work and my laptop broke when I accidentally spilled wine on it because I tripped over myself and so I got a new laptop and had to relearn how to use it and instead of going to bed like a normal witch I was tweaking the graphics and so I stayed up ridiculously late and I overslept and I'm never late okay never ever which you must remember since I was the one always making sure Eleanor was on time. Except for chemistry class, although the only reason I was almost late to that class was because it was across campus. Anyway, I'm so sorry." I gasped for air, throwing everything at him in one breath.

His mouth twitched. His face was fighting back an emotion I couldn't decipher. I felt my magic pushing beneath the surface. It had me on edge the past few days and that *feeling* was there again.

Celestino stood up silently, grabbed my bag from my shoulder and sat it in the booth next to him and walked towards the bar. I sat down reluctantly, casting a glance at him. I began chewing my lip and squeezing my hands to keep from reaching for my ear. This was uncomfortable. I wondered what he was thinking. He went to talk to Caleb.

A few minutes later he came back and sat across from me. My seat faced the doors. I wondered if he did that on purpose. I opened up my laptop and notebook to prepare to tackle our to-do list.

"I am sorry," I said, breaking the choking silence. He nodded. Was he mad? "Aren't you going to say something," I begged. He tilted his head to the side watching me. It was bothering me that he wasn't answering. I needed to know how he felt. I needed to fix this. But before he could say anything, Caleb approached our table with two cups of coffee.

"Your food will be out momentarily," Caleb said in a gruff voice. I turned to Celestino confused.

"Food?" I asked.

"I doubt you ate anything by the state of your attire. I see you still like cats," he said, smirking. I glanced at my tank top that was covered in baby black cats wearing witch hats....and no bra. My eyes widened.

"Fuck me," I hissed, buttoning my flannel.

"I would like to go on a date first," he said with an eyebrow raised. I shook my head.

"I'm not mentally awake to deal with you yet," I murmured into my cup. The taste of mocha slid down my throat. *He remembered.* I used to always get mocha lattes our senior year. It's where the addiction started.

"So, new laptop?" he asked. I grimaced.

"Couldn't you have casted a clean up spell on your old laptop or taken it to Reece's Reparar Restore," he suggested, rolling up his henley.

I froze. *Why the fuck didn't I think of that?*

He chuckled at my face. "That didn't cross your mind?" he asked. I covered my face with my hands.

"Fury fuck me," I mumbled into my hands. Why did things like that slip my mind?

"Like I said, take me on a date first," he said, shrugging his shoulders. I balled up a napkin and threw it at him. That got him to chuckle.

"I was two hours late," I said grimly.

"It's okay Lilianna. I know I have a lot of catching up to do. I know you're not the same person I grew up with. But I remember how much you value time."

My heart skipped. He had called me by my actual name. Not Posey. Not Lily. My name.

"I'm not sure whether I like you saying my name," I mumbled. His lips twitched.

"I can tell by your face you liked it," he said. He didn't say my name often and I kind of liked it when he did. I wanted to hear it again. To hear the different ways he could make my name sound.

He took a sip of coffee, his eyes looking away. I bit back a smile. I noticed his cheeks were a little flushed. That made him somehow less intimidating. I guess it made him shy.

Celestino? Shy? I wanted to laugh at the thought.

"Anyway, what's on the to-do list?" he asked. With the subject on track I looked at my list.

"Alright. Scavenger hunt and riddles. Although we need to figure out the order of the bar crawl first," I said.

"Drunken Fairy Tale Tavern should be last," he stated.

"Agree. Maybe start with The Boogeyman's Bar? Isn't their signature drink tagline you'll be bumping all night? Sounds like a good one to start with." I took another gulp of coffee. Exhaustion was deep in my bones.

He nodded. "Let's do Siren Saloon's after. Their signature and Boogeyman's involves tequila," he suggested and I smiled. I had a soft spot for tequila. Unlike some of my friends, I didn't spend my college days drowning in tequila shots and so I still enjoyed the taste.

"Did you smile at the word tequila?" He cocked an eyebrow.

"No…maybe…okay yes. It may or may not be my weakness." I watched him scribble something in his notebook. "Did you just write down that I like tequila?" I stared at him, a laugh on the verge of escaping, I reached for the notebook. He pulled it to his chest, shaking his head.

"1. Karaoke. 2. Tequila. I gotta remember these things," he said with a grin. I bit my lip to keep the sleepy giggles at bay.

"And let me guess. You're a…whiskey guy," I stated confidently.

"You guessed right," he answered. "Dare I ask how'd you got it right?"

I rolled my eyes.

"We grew up together. It would be hard not to notice the things you like," I said. He leaned forward.

"Do you know what else I like?" he asked. His voice had dipped and it compelled me to come closer. The air around us stalled and my heart pounded in my ears. A part of me was screaming to look away but the other half wanted to see where this conversation would go.

But before I could answer Caleb showed up with plates of food breaking the spell. Scrambled eggs, eggs sunny side up, french toast, sausage and bacon. I pushed my laptop to the side.

"Is all of this for us?" I asked in shock.

"I hope so," Caleb grumbled before stomping away.

"I didn't know if your taste in breakfast had changed so I got a few things." He gestured to the plates.

"I still like scrambled eggs," I said while taking the plate. He nodded and began taking a piece of french toast and dripping it into the yolk of his eggs. I stared at my soft scrambled eggs. I quickly glanced to make sure Celestino was focused on his plate before taking a bite. I did everything in my power to ignore the feel of the eggs moving around my mouth.

"Are you okay?" Celestino asked. I met his eyes.

"All good. Thanks for ordering the food." I continued eating, this time hurrying. I really didn't want him to notice. I pushed my plate away, half of the eggs gone. Celestino reached over to finish them.

"You could have said something," he said. I glanced at him.

"What do you mean?" I asked.

"Your eggs. You could have said something and I would have asked Caleb to have them be cooked more." I felt my face flame.

"I...I was late and you ordered all this food. I didn't want to be anymore of a bother," I confessed. He sighed, shaking his head and added another sausage to my plate.

"You are not a bother Lilianna. I don't know who made you feel like you could be but you're not. Is it the texture?" he asked. I bit the inside of my cheek. *You are not a bother.* My heart skipped at the statement.

"Yeah. Certain textures just...feel wrong," I confessed. He nodded with a soft smile.

"That's okay but you need to eat more," he said, pointing to my plate. I rolled my eyes.

"You sound like my mom," I stated.

"*Você é tão magrinha. Precisa comer mais,*" he said, mimicking the popular phrase we all grew up hearing. I rolled my eyes.

"*Sim senhor Celestino,*" I said teasingly. His eyes darkened.

"Posey," he warned, wiggling another sausage at me. I raised an eyebrow at the sausage bobbing up and down. I slapped a hand over my mouth and my laughter came out as a snort.

"Just eat it so we can work," he said with flushed cheeks.

"Fine," I said, giving in. My smile stretched across my face. I missed this.

"That doesn't rhyme," I said.

After eating breakfast and figuring out the scavenger hunt we began working on the riddles. At each bar their signature cocktail would come with a cute little saying and a riddle. They would tell the tour guide the answer and be led to the next pub. But right now we were both arguing about writing the riddles. The few patrons that were around glanced in our direction.

"It doesn't have to rhyme," Celestino said.

"It's a riddle," I said with annoyance. I forgot how much we would bicker. Whether it was which condiment worked best on french fries or what to watch on movie nights, we had different opinions half of the time.

"And therefore because it's a riddle it has to rhyme?" he asked.

"I know it doesn't have to rhyme but *you* know it'll be more entertaining if it does," I said. He groaned.

"You just want to be right," he said, rolling his eyes. I smiled.

"I am right," I replied. There was a sparkle in his eyes. I bit my cheek and squirmed in my seat under his gaze. He sighed.

"I've always liked this side of you," he said.

"And what side is that?" I asked. His eyes traced over my face, briefly flickering to my lips and I felt my stomach bottom out.

"The part of you that likes to put me in my place." His voice pulled me in once again.

"I do." My mouth betrayed my brain. Did I just fucking say that? Out loud? He raised an eyebrow.

"And how do you want me now," he whispered. My heart was rattling against my chest like bat wings. How did I want him? There were a few ways flashing through my mind. All of which involved being alone in my apartment. Was this his way of telling me something? Was he daring me to cross that line?

"The unicorn is the national animal of Scotland," I blurted out. Celestino covered his face, chuckling. He slid out of his seat and came to place a kiss on the side of my temple.

"I'll get you more coffee, my unicorn," he said. I froze. He kissed me. I felt the heat spread from my face down to the pit of my stomach.

My lips stretched into a smile. I rubbed the stupid smile that was spreading across my face. My plan was to stay focused and get what we needed done. Which was happening…until we got to the riddles. Who knew stringing sentences with double meanings and rhyming words would get under his skin.

My mind wandered to what he mentioned before. Did I like putting him in his place? Yes, I did. Something about having him under my finger thrilled me.

My leg was bobbing up and down manically as my brain continued to float around with images of Celestino and I. The smell of coffee soon brought me back to my senses. I turned to see Celestino walking over to me with a small smile. He handed me my coffee and I mouthed thank you.

I worked in complete silence as I wracked my brain to put the riddles together.

BOOGEYMAN'S BAR -> Siren Saloon
> *What captures your heart in just three words*
> *With a flick of their tail they'll be gone in a blur*
> *To a place where drinks are served*

"WHAT RHYMES WITH STRIFE?" I asked after 15 minutes of uninterrupted silence. He looked up from his laptop. He was busy designing the festival map so that vendors knew where to go.

"Um…knife, life, wife-" he began.

"Thanks," I said, cutting him off.

SIREN'S SALOON -> Highwaymen Haunt
> *A change of song is in the air*
> *From sea to land you must beware*
> *To take a carriage is to ask for strife*
> *At your next stop you risk your life*

. . .

HIGHWAYMEN HAUNT -> Plastered Pixie
> *We're short, not tall with tiny wings*
> *We crack jokes, we don't sing.*
> *At home you'll find us near a tree trunk,*
> *But where do we go if we want to get drunk?*

PLASTERED PIXIE -> Drunken Fairy Tale Tavern
> *Once upon a time we set off on a quest*
> *To find where cocktails are made best*
> *Everyone is always welcome here*
> *You never know what fairy tales may appear*

I FOUND MYSELF SMILING. I missed this. Writing like this. This was a different type of creativity that helped me loosen. I found it relaxing to pluck words from thin air, find a common thread between them and intertwine them together until the melody of their sounds were pleasing to the ears. It was a breath of fresh air from the limitation of 140 characters for witty captions. I giggled to myself.

A tingle ran up my spine. "I guess we're even," I said.

"Even?" he asked.

"I just caught you staring at me," I said. He shrugged his shoulders.

"You can be very distracting," he said. I scoffed instinctively.

"You can be," he said. I crossed my arms, starting to feel uncomfortable with this kind of attention.

"Well you can be as well," I said. He smirked and leaned in.

"Really? Care to tell me how?" he questioned. I rolled my eyes.

"You know you're attractive," I said plainly. His fingers drummed against the table.

"But do *you* find me attractive?"

I swallowed as his green eyes baited me to say yes. "Don't look at me that way," I hissed, my heart skipping. He cocked his head to the side in question. "You're baiting me to answer with flirty eyes," I said. He barked out a laugh.

"Flirty eyes," he teased. I rolled my eyes.

"Yes and you know it."

"If I'm giving you any look it's only because you started it," he pointed out. I flushed.

"No I-we need to work," I said, hoping to cut the conversation short. He smirked.

"Rule number seven: don't start what you can't finish Posey."

CHAPTER 8

MÃES ARE ALWAYS RIGHT

I couldn't help but smile while leaving the pub. She said I was giving her flirty eyes and I was. My heart was beating out of my chest. She caught me and I couldn't help that I liked getting caught. I also couldn't help how my body reacted so quickly to her, longing for more. The way her eyes lit up with a challenge. Her magic called to mine. I felt it deep in my bones.

I sighed, walking down the familiar path towards the office. People waved hi and sent warm smiles. It felt nice to be home. It felt like I could finally breathe easier. In the city I was overworked and undermined all the time. Here? I had trust. People listened to me with respect. A flash of dark hair caught my eye. I turned to the window of Pricilla's Potions and Lotions. The outside was painted in a pale lavender. Flowers decorated around the window. A wooden sign hung from above with golden calligraphy. Pushing open the pale yellow door a bell twinkled and jingled. I was met with the smell of sage and oranges.

I saw Pricilla in the back helping a customer. Her dark hair had streaks of purple and practically floated around her. Her amber eyes met mine with a smile. I offered a polite wave. I made my way towards the woman by the window.

"*Bom dia mãe*," I said above her shoulder. My mom turned around with a gasp. Her dark hair curled around her shoulders much like mine. Her green eyes widened behind her glasses.

"*Meu deus* Celestino," she said, playfully smacking my shoulder. I couldn't help but chuckle. I tossed a hand over her shoulder and squeezed. She wrapped her arms around me, her head on my chest. Then she smacked the back of my head.

"Ow. What was that for?" I asked, rubbing the spot.

"You scared me!"

I couldn't help but laugh. My mom might be one of the most powerful witches in town but she could jump at a fly.

"*Por quê você está aqui?*" she asked, her eyes going back to the rows of candles. My mom wasn't asking me why I was here nonchalantly. No, what she really wanted to know was why I wasn't in the office when she knows very well I don't need to be at an office desk to be working.

"I had a meeting with Posey. We're working together for the festival," I said as evenly as I could.

"Lilianna? You two working together?" she asked. My stomach twisted at her tone.

"Yes. We have to do this bar crawl. People solve riddles, learn some fun facts while walking to the different bars drinking," I said explaining. I don't know why at almost 29 I felt like I needed my mom's approval. She placed a candle down and picked up a new one, nodding along.

"It was her idea. A great one. My boss, Ben, decided it would be best for me to help her since I've put on events before."

My mom simply nodded some more. She didn't say anything, just continued picking and sniffing the candles.

"I know what a crawl is. I'm not that old. But you and Lilianna… together again. Interesting."

I cocked my head, eyeing her more deeply. She was sensitive to the future and usually had feelings on what was going to happen.

"What do you mean by interesting?" I asked. She turned to look at me and I felt a zing run up my spine. There was a small light around her eyes. Her magic was awake. She handed me a candle.

"Trust her," she said.

"What do you mean?" I asked, taking the candle. She gave me a warm smile. And with those two words she left me standing in the middle of the store holding a candle called *Ocean Breeze*.

I was tidying up my apartment waiting for my mom to drop by and visit. She lived on the edge of town and I was anxiously dusting every-thing. I needed to make sure everything was orderly so I wouldn't hear, *"Ah, Lilianna you know a little vinegar and water would clean this up."*

Nitpicking on the state of my apartment was something I mentally couldn't handle today. Instead of knocking on the door like a normal witch I heard her snap her fingers in order to unlock it. I rolled my eyes.

"Oi, *mãe*," I called out. My mom stepped into my living room with two tote bags.

"*Querida,*" she said with a warm tone. I always loved the sound of endearments in my mother tongue. This word was particularly my favorite.

"You know there's a few normies staying here for vacation. What if they saw you," I pointed out. She brushed me off with a wave of her hand.

Her wrists were covered in gold bracelets. A golden pendant, the Heart of Viana swung on her neck. She wore a long skirt with a cream blouse tucked in. Her short dark hair brushed her shoulders. Crow's feet edged around her eyes showing a woman who had experienced life and laughed despite it. I smiled as she made herself comfortable in my kitchen.

I felt a sting in my chest. It was hard noticing how much older my mom was getting. She came to this country before I was born and taught herself english. She raised me on her own. She had to do so many things alone. I felt the weight of guilt settle within me.

She was the reason I was working so hard. One day I want to be able to give back everything she gave me. I bit the inside of my cheek. I felt like I was still waiting for my break even though I graduated nearly ten years ago. A part of me felt like I was behind everyone else. I shook the thoughts away. Not now.

"*Chá, café ou porto?*" I asked my mom. It was typical that when anyone came over a Portuguese household you had to ask if they wanted tea, coffee or a small glass of port wine. And it didn't matter the time of day.

In my mom's village people would come over to my avô's house at nine at night and you still offer. And they had to accept. You don't say no to food or drinks in a Portuguese house.

"*Querida.* You need to eat." Her accent was thick. Despite the years of living here she never lost it. It hadn't even been a full two minutes before she started to pester me. I sighed, and strolled to place a kiss on each cheek. Setting the bags on the kitchen counter she began pulling out containers of food.

"*Café.* Here, food," she continued and I started making her coffee.

"I do eat," I said. She grunted, already reorganizing my fridge.

"*Não.* You always work and with this festival you don't remember." She gave me a look. A look that screamed, *you know I'm right.* And she was. Whenever I got swamped with work I would forget to do simple parts of my routine like eating and drinking water. Problems of a workaholic with a hyperactive brain. I handed her the coffee and she smiled, nodding.

I sat down on the couch, letting her heat up some food to share. The smell of tomatoes, garlic and wine trickled in the air. It smelled like home.

"So tell me. How's work?" she asked. I automatically tensed.

"Good. Tiring. They put me in charge of something I came up with and if I do well I'll get promoted," I said with a hesitant smile. My mom came to the couch, smoothing my frizzy hair.

"Finally!" Her lips pulled into a wide smile. I felt a surge of pride course through my body. I was constantly worried about making her happy and not letting her worry.

"I see some pictures online. They look nice!" She waved her hand for two plates to float out the cabinet. I always marveled at the way magic just came to her. She used magic like it was an extension of herself. It flowed out of her like a stream.

But with me it was different. It's not like I was afraid of it. I loved magic. I loved the rush of warmth it gave me. It was just sometimes when I was too nervous, too on edge, it went erratic. I would lose control. Like when the paper towels and my bag flew away from me instead of towards me.

Honestly sometimes I would forget to use it because my brain would be focused on a logical solution.

My mom handed me a plate of *carne guisada*. The smell immediately brought me comfort.

"What's wrong?" Her words stirred me out of my thoughts.

"Nothing!" My voice was slightly pitched and she offered a reassuring smile.

"Celestino Nuno Santos," she teased. My mom was fully aware of Celestino.

"He's more cute now. A good looking man." She eyed me. I rolled my eyes. My mom was very much like Eleanor in the *'we should be together'* department.

"It's just work," I muttered before taking a bite. She squinted at me.

"Before it was just studying."

I continued to eat my meal in silence. He was back and I felt twisted inside. It felt easy to slip back into our friendship but a part of me wanted more, wanted *him*. And sure he was noticing all the little things I thought I kept hidden, like loud noises and being uncomfortable in social settings.

But at some point he would feel overwhelmed. Once he knew me in a more intimate way it would be too much for him to handle. Wanting more always led to mistakes. Or maybe he- *smack.* My mom lightly tapped the back of my head.

"*Comer,*" she demanded.

"I am!" I said. She hummed in disbelief.

CHAPTER 9

CLOSET OF SECRETS

I was sitting in Coffin's Coffee Shop waiting for Eleanor and Lola to join me. My stomach was in knots. My brain was wracked with things to get done for the bar crawl. There were regular city posts that I needed to keep up with, laundry, text my mom, Celestino, making sure the flyers got hand-*wait*. Did I just add Celestino to my list? I groaned into my latte. I couldn't get his green eyes out of my head. He made my magic buzz which was something I was trying very hard not to notice.

At that moment I caught a whiff of cinnamon and sage. Eleanor strolled in, glitter to accentuate her high cheekbones, purple blush to set off her golden undertones and her hair was slicked back into a high bun. She was decked out in a pale pink cropped sweater with yellow mom jeans and paired with white cowboy boots. A glossy smile graced her face.

Lola walked in with her laughing at something Eleanor said. You could see a hint of fangs. Ever since biology in the ninth grade Lola would join us for weekend brunches. While I loved having Celestino and Sailor in our friend group it felt nice to have some girl time. Lola was around my height and her hair was twisted into box braids with silver cuffs and charms that fell at her waist in a balayage of purples and greens. Her deep, ebony skin shimmered against her white shirt that had the Loch Ness Monster on it. She wore a long tight jean skirt with sneakers and a cardigan.

"Lily," Eleanor said excitedly. I smiled at her. Lola leaned down to kiss my cheek.

"It's been forever," she exclaimed. My worries melted into the background as my favorite girls sat down.

"Ah, why are my friends the prettiest?" I asked. Eleanor rolled her eyes. Lola snorted, shaking her head. "I ordered an iced lavender lemon tea for Eleanor and for you, Lola passion fruit iced tea with raspberry syrup." They each smiled.

"Oh thank the hollow tree! It's been so crazy at work," Eleanor sighed. Lola and I nodded silently. Eleanor took a deep breath before diving deep into the cauldron's pit of what it's like to be the mayor's assistant. She had to be on top of all the Mayor's appearances, speeches, schedules all while making sure the other departments were running on time with the Full Moon Fall Festival preparations.

Apparently there was a missing invoice in the finance department and it magically ended up wedged between the fridge and coffee machine in the break room. Not sure how but it did.

"I am so glad to be back," Lola said, leaning back into her chair. She just finished graduating from vet school and recently moved back into town.

"You have no idea how much I've been missing our girl dates," Eleanor confessed. I giggled.

"Well now that I'm back, so will our regularly scheduled Sip and Spill sessions! And...I've heard someone else is back." Lola's eyes slid over to mine. I groaned.

"Lola, not you too," I said. She smiled.

"You do remember I would sit between you two in science right," she said. I shook my head.

"He's back. You're back. Looks like my favorite people are back home." I smiled, moving past talking about Celestino. Lola nodded her head and flicked her braids over her shoulder before meeting my gaze.

"May I ask which one of us is your favorite. Celestino or me," she smirked.

"Well obviously you Lola. You're prettier," I said. We laughed.

"But seriously Lily, how is it having him back? How's working together?" Lola asked, drumming her fingers. Eleanor nodded along.

"So far it's been okay," I said honestly. "Graphics and flyers will start circulating this week. This Saturday Celestino and I will be trying the signature cocktails while figuring out where the riddles will be placed in each bar," I said. I chewed my lip. "We have to find someone to lead the bar crawl and make sure they have a basic outline of what to say. I'm hoping Hallie can do it since she helps out with the community theater. We also have to intertwine the pubs' history," I said.

"I knew I wouldn't have to worry about you guys." Eleanor sat back with a happy sigh. Just then a short girl with jet black hair cropped close to her jawline appeared with Eleanor and Lola's tea. She shot Lola a toothy smile revealing a fang.

"Thank you," Lola said brightly.

"Of course Ms. Luna," the vampire girl said. Lola smiled, "just Lola is fine." The waitress nodded and left us.

"Oh by the way! Alex set the theme for the haunted house. We'll be able to start advertising that soon. I just have to finish the graphics to reveal it," I mentioned. The haunted house was everyone's favorite in town and a great hit with the tourists.

Every year was a different theme. They would transform Atticus's Antiques into a haunted house since it was one of the few places with multiple finished rooms and floors. One year it was a *Magical Menagerie* where it started out with a beautifully whimsical world of different creatures and the further into the house you went the more twisted it became. Another year it was *Haunted Portraits*, famous portraits from history coming alive to seek revenge.

"What's the theme? I know they started working on props and staging since Ben sent over the invoice for supplies," Eleanor paused to take a sip of her tea. "I have to call the high school for volunteer actors," she said. Her eyes darted to the window.

"The theme is simple: Addams Family. They were thinking of

mythical mysteries but…we all grew up with some scary myths we would rather not touch," I said. "Also isn't that Ben's or Celestino's job?"

"I figured I would help. You know me. Anyway, I love Addams family! You're totally dressing like Morticia. And good call on axing the mythical theme. Who knows what could have happened," Eleanor shuddered. "We might have accidentally summoned something like that one year," Eleanor said.

"Don't remind me." Lola shook her head. The first year I moved back, Lola was visiting and someone accidentally summoned a mummy. The theme was, *The Riches, The Rags, The Fallen*. It was not pretty and required a lot of toilet paper. The mummy didn't want to return back to the dead unless they were wrapped in the softest toilet paper we could find which is understandable. You want to be comfy in the afterlife.

At that moment Eleanor's eyes became razor sharp. Her look went from lovable to cunning. I braced myself.

"So Celestino," she said slowly bringing him back into the conversation. I felt my cheeks heat up.

"Yes. Give us all the dirty details," Lola said with a smile.

"One, there are no dirty details. Two, it has been nice to work with him. He has helped my stress levels go from level 100 to 95. That is all," I said, biting the inside of my cheek to calm my body down.

"A mere 5%? For you? That says a lot. I wonder what other areas he could help you with," Eleanor said as her lips pulled into a smirk. Lola took a sip of her tea to keep from laughing.

The door to the coffee shop dinged and I felt a pull. The charming warlock strolled into the coffee shop. He wore a loose yellow tank top, the sides revealing tan muscles and a tattoo. *That was interesting.* I didn't know he had a tattoo. He wore olive green running shorts that revealed sculpted legs. I knew Celestino was more than likely to be fit given his love for carpentry and sports growing up but I never imagined this. Well I did…technically. His hair was in a high bun this time, strands sticking to his face. His beard was cut short.

His chest was puffing out as he tried to slow his breathing. His cheeks were pink from the excursion and I wondered if his face looked like that when-

"Earth to Lily," Lola called out, breaking my train of thought. My eyes widened.

"Mangalicas are the only pig breed to have a wool coat," I blurted. Lola and Eleanor glanced towards the cash register and began laughing.

"I know! They're so cute," Lola said.

"You knew and didn't tell me?" I asked. Lola rolled her eyes.

"From now on I promise to give you random animal facts. 'Tis my duty as a vet," Lola said, crossing her heart.

When I looked back at Celestino he wore a giant grin. *Fuck.* I was caught again. Celestino grabbed his water from the vampire girl who was looking at him with heart eyes. My fingers twitched against my cup. His green eyes connected with mine again and my magic pulsed.

"Rule number six," he called out before walking out the door. Two pairs of eyes stared at me.

"What's rule number six?" Eleanor asked with a serpentine smile. I felt my cheeks blaze.

"Nothing. We just have rules in place to keep us on task," I said, avoiding their eyes. The table wobbled as they shifted in their seats. Lola placed a hand on her chin, eyes wide with delight. Eleanor leaned forward, swinging her tea back and forth.

"Why do you need to be kept on task?" Lola asked. I flicked a napkin at her. She swatted it away.

"The more important question is what happens if you break a rule," Eleanor questioned. I fidgeted with my hands.

"Truth or dare…" I mumbled.

"Oh he's definitely naughty," Lola said, crossing her arms. I rolled my eyes.

"Agree. Who knows maybe you guys will get to rule 69," Eleanor said. My magic snapped and the ball of napkin caught on fire.

Eleanor and Lola jumped back. Eleanor swiped her hand over the tiny flame, sending pixie dust down to douse it. Lola gathered the ashes into a pile on top of another napkin.

"Eleanor," I hissed. This is what happens. If my emotions flare, so did my magic. It had sparked out of control for a second. Last time, I whacked a kid with a pen and this time I set an innocent napkin on fire. What was next? Giving snails wings? Making flowers talk?

"Well clearly by your magic's reaction you're not opposed to 6-" Lola began. I reached over to cover her mouth. She shoved my hand away.

"It's cute how he makes you blush," Eleanor said. I rolled my eyes.

"My face is always red," I said.

"There's a difference," they stated. I bit my cheek remembering how Celestino said the same thing. I picked at my crematorium cupcake.

"Honestly I don't know why you just don't give in to him. You clearly find him attractive and for a while I might add." Eleanor gave me a pointed look while Lola nodded along.

They have been wanting us to get together since high school. And sure I had always harbored a secret attraction to him but I was too much for everyone in the past.

People had a tendency to be messy with my emotions. I was either too emotional or not enough. Being single was easier. It was easier than having to constantly worry about making sure the other person was happy enough with me so they wouldn't leave. I sighed.

Celestino and I have been friends our whole lives. Naturally he knew me but honestly? How I am now is nowhere near how I was. My early 20s taught me a lot about myself. I spent my life with someone else being in charge of my routine and structure.

So when I went to college it felt like a LEGO set. But the instructions I had didn't make sense. I couldn't figure out how to put the pieces together when everyone else could.

It took a long time to figure out what worked for me. Even now there were times where I would mess up. It took a lot of pain to get to where I am.

Now with Celestino and I falling back into place in each other's lives, I felt afraid of destroying what we were rebuilding by wanting more.

I needed to change the subject before my brain continued on its downward spiral.

"What about you and Caleb?" I asked. I noticed the way Eleanor constantly tried to weave her way through Caleb's armor. She had a crush on the poor elf. But Caleb was like an iron statue. Eleanor huffed.

"Oh yeah! How's that going?" Lola asked, excitedly.

"I think I have pixie dust in my ear. What about you Lola?" she asked, deflecting. I shook my head giggling.

"Me? Ellie I just got back. I need to settle in and see if I can get a job at the vet clinic before dealing with any romantic feelings," Lola said. Eleanor smirked.

"Doesn't have to be romantic to get some action," she teased.

"Isn't that why we have toys," Lola fired back. We all laughed together and I glanced at Eleanor again.

"You think after four years of you guys circling each other something would happen?" I asked Eleanor. She rolled her eyes.

"You're one to talk," she snickered before dropping her gaze. "I think I'm just going to give up honestly."

That was surprising. Eleanor never liked to give up. I looked at her. The shadows under her eyes were peeking through her makeup.

"Everything okay Ellie?" Lola asked softly. She picked at the burnt napkins.

"I'm just tired, you know? The holidays are coming up and it's not my favorite time of year," she said. I nodded. Eleanor had a strained relationship with her family and holidays were usually tough for her. Her eyes were bright with unshed tears. Lola wrapped an arm around her.

"Make *you* happy, Eleanor." I offered a reassuring smile. She dabbed her eyes.

"Do me a favor Lily and take your own advice." Eleanor smiled.

"Get to rule 69," Lola said grinning. We laughed into our drinks. It felt great to have my girls again.

I WAS SITTING on my couch, staring at the ceiling after getting off the phone with my mom. She had called to tell me to give Lola good news. Apparently she heard from the gossip train of Lavender Falls that Ms. Heinstien was looking to hire another veterinarian. Before I could put my phone down it rang again. This time it was my boss, Leo.

"Hey Mr. Chaves," I said, sweetly.

"Good afternoon Lilianna. Just wanted to see if everything is going well?" he asked. I reassured him that everything was happening on schedule.

"I knew I could count on you. Are you two working well by the way?" There was a hint of something at the end of his sentence, something suspicious. I took a deep breath.

"Well I haven't turned him into a frog yet have I," I said.

"If you did, you know true love's kiss would break the curse," he said with a laugh.

"Sir," I said in disbelief. Why did I feel like the whole town had eyes on Celestino and I?

"Oh Lily, can you do me a favor?" he asked. I bit back a sigh. I didn't have a good feeling about this. And I was right.

Thirty minutes later I stood in front of Atticus's Antiques with a wheelbarrow of wood. I sighed for what felt like the twentieth time today. I had no idea why Leo couldn't have just dropped off the wood but here I was. I distinctly remember this *not* being on the list of duties when I was hired.

"Excuse me," I called out from the front door. Different workers poked their heads in the entryway. I smiled as I saw the rooms being decorated. Magic was buzzing in the air. I could feel it vibrate against my skin. Taking a deep breath I let my senses open up. With new eyes I could see the faint hint of shimmer in the air and hear soft bells. Magic was flowing in abundance and I couldn't stop smiling. It was marvelous.

"Lilianna," Ben called out. Although Leo and Ben were twins they were very much opposites. Leo excelled in the Communications Department. He was warm and loud. You always knew when he was in the room. Ben ran Cultural Affairs and Special Events. Sure he was just as loud as Leo but it depended on the situation. He preferred his brother to take the spotlight.

"Oh thank the moon you brought the wood. Can you take it around to the back of the shop please?" Ben's beard was filled with wood chips. I stifled a laugh and nodded. Picking up the wheelbarrow, I made my way to the back of the shop.

I could hear the sounds of a saw table. Sailor was working on cutting some wood. I stood off to the side not wanting to get too close to him while he was operating machinery that could decapitate me. After a few minutes he stopped and glanced up.

"Hey there," Sailor said with a bright smile. His energy felt like a warm summer day. I felt a strange pull to him, like a leprechaun to gold.

"Your wood." I managed to get out. Did I just say his wood? Like his-w*hat was wrong with me?*

"My wood? Oh the wheelbarrow! Thank you so much." His voice was like an ocean wave pulling me under. He began walking towards me and I noticed a dusting of freckles. His lips were pulled into a wide smile as I took a step forward.

"Sailor!" A deep voice called out. In that instant, it was like a bubble popped. I turned my gaze to meet the eyes of Celestino. He was shirtless, sweaty and in soccer shorts. The pull to Sailor was no longer there. I kept my eyes up, not wanting to stare at Celestino's naked chest or the fact that his tattoo swirled up the side of his hip and up his chest. My fingers itched to trace the lines.

"Stop using your magic on her," he grunted. I looked at Sailor.

"When I'm working and get tired sometimes I sorta lose grip on my power." He scratched the back of his head. "Sorry about that," he said sheepishly.

"Oh! No it's okay. You know I get it," I said. He gave me a smile and lightly nudged my shoulder.

"How's it going Lily?" he asked, wiping his hands on a towel he kept in his back pocket.

"Not bad. Going to start promoting the haunted house soon," I said. He waggled his eyebrows and flexed his bicep.

"Awesome. Let me know if you need anything for the Saloon."

"Don't worry. I'll definitely be there for content," I said. Celestino coughed, getting my attention.

"Posey, we need to talk about something." Celestino's voice sounded annoyed.

"Okay. I'll text you, Sailor," I said before making my way through the back of the shop, following Celestino.

"Can't wait," he called out. Celestino snorted up ahead.

"What's up?" I asked. Celestino seemed tense and not just because of his voice but his whole body looked tight. Both in a sexy way and a stressed way. My gaze wandered down his back. His shoulders were wide. I noticed a sprinkle of beauty marks across his skin. Every summer when we all went to Boogeyman's Swamp, I would play connect the dots with them. All in my head, of course. Because friends don't touch each other's half naked bodies.

"Rule six," he said, breaking my trance.

"The only reason I'm staring is because you're literally walking in front of me." I pointed out. He chuckled.

"I know. I'm reminding you of when you were at Coffin's with the girls."

I ignored the flop in my stomach. He turned left into a room. It was covered in vines and broken Greek statues. It reminded me of Morticia's garden. There was a door in the back that Celestino was heading towards. A tiny closet painted to blend into the background of the room. If you looked closely, the painted vines looked like they were moving...or were they?

He stepped inside. I leaned against the doorway. The dimmed closet was extremely small and made me feel a bit antsy. From the looks of it it was meant to be a coat closet. I doubted no more than two people could fit inside...maybe.

"Are you going to ask?" I asked. I felt my stomach twist. I wanted to be home and not in this room alone with him. Especially one that felt this small. Celestino grunted while trying to attach some vines to the top of the ceiling, his body stretching.

Eyes up.

"Truth or dare," he grunted. I picked truth last time. It would only be right if I went with dare. I kept my eyes on his face.

"Dare."

He nearly dropped the screwdriver. He stared at me with wide eyes.

"Did you say dare?" he asked in shock.

"Yes. I pick dare," I said, slightly agitated. I began shifting my weight as my nerves began rattling inside of me.

"Oh no. You need to give me some time. I need this to be good," he said. I rolled my eyes. Celestino continued working, ignoring my presence.

"So am I just supposed to stand here and watch you do whatever it is you're doing until you've decided?" I asked, breaking the insufferable silence. Celestino finally looked at me, arms still up. A wicked thought skated across my mind and my skin prickled.

"Yes. Would you prefer to be watching Sailor," he grunted out. My heart skipped. Was he jealous? Sailor and I were just friends which he knew. But a part of me enjoyed that Celestino could be jealous.

"He's my friend just like how you're my friend," I said, reminding myself of our relationship. He snorted. "Are you jealous?" I asked. His eyes clashed with mine.

"Excuse me?"

"Are you jealous?" I asked again. He huffed before dropping his arms. His hands twirled the screwdriver.

"Yes," he admitted.

I stared at him in shock. I didn't think he would admit to that. I guess I could see why. With Sailor he's probably reminded of what used to be and now that he's back he feels left out. Yeah, that's probably why. I swallowed, fingers twitching against my jeans.

"You don't have to be," I said softly. He met my eyes again with an emotion I was scared to read into. He stretched up trying to screw some sort of mechanism to the lighting. My eyes drifted back to his tattoo, a combination of ocean waves and lavender. My leg started bobbing up and down. I needed to get out of here. Celestino still hadn't given me my dare and the longer he took the more anxious it made me.

The screwdriver kept slipping and his eyes squinted with the dim lighting.

"Just turn on the light," I said. Feeling frustrated I stepped forward to pull the cord from the light above.

"No," he called out. But it was too late. I fell forward as the door swung closed. Pulling the cord caused the mechanism he was working on to kick start, shutting the door behind us. *Not* turning on the light. My hands automatically flew to his sweaty and very naked chest to steady myself.

"W-what was that," I stuttered. His chuckle echoed in the room and his chest rumbled against my hands.

"Someone is going to be hiding in here to scare people. It'll be jarring to have the door snap open and closed then use magic to make it flow." His breath felt hot in my ear.

"Someone," I squeaked.

"Yes, *someone*. It's a little tight with two people don't you think," he said, near my ear. His warmth began to seep into my bones. His chest rose and fell against my hands. I felt the urge to slip my hands around his neck, pull him close and feel his lips against mine. Or I could move my hands down to feel his abs move under my fingers.

"Well we could just pull the cord again and it'll open." I said, reaching to pull it. Celestino grabbed my wrist. His grip was soft yet firm. A shiver traveled down my spine. I wanted him to grab both my wrists and press me against the wall.

"I haven't finished fixing it yet. It won't open." His voice was low.

Of course I would be trapped in a closet with him. This felt like something out of a romance novel. However if this were a romance novel, this would be the moment where we stare into each other's eyes causing the tension to be so thick the only way to snap it would be with a kiss filled with longing and passion.

Eleanor would be screaming if she was here. Actually her and Lola would have been the one to trap us inside. My heart picked up as the fantasy unfolded in my head.

"You're still impatient," he chuckled.

"You were taking too long with the dare," I said, a bit breathless. We stood in silence, our breathing becoming one at some point.

"I didn't like how his magic was influencing you," he confessed.

"He didn't do it on purpose," I whispered. I turned around to wiggle the door knob, hoping to break out of this weird tension and closet. Celestino grunted as I brushed against him.

"This is a tight space," he said. My hips grazed his as I turned back around. Celestino pressed himself as close to the back wall as possible.

"Dammit Posey, stop moving around," he said through gritted teeth. I saw his face through the cracks of light shining around the door. His eyes were clenched closed and he was breathing heavily through his nose. He placed a hand on my hip, pushing me away which wasn't by much seeing how tight the closet was. Goosebumps traveled up my body. I wanted his hand to keep moving up.

"You're breathing fast," I said.

"Posey. I'm in a tight space with a beautiful woman. What do you think is happening?" My heart was beating erratically against my chest.

This was bad.

This was very bad in a sexy dangerous way.

Celestino was confessing something that I desperately wanted to explore. The air around us felt charged. My magic was trying to push me closer.

"I'm sorry," my voice squeaked.

"It's okay. I should have given you the dare." He finally opened his eyes. A tender spark glowed.

"I shouldn't have messed with what you were working on without asking what you were doing,' I said, laughing nervously. "I still need to work on my patience."

We were quiet for a few moments staring at each other. Comfort began washing over me. That's what I always felt with Celestino. Comfort. Safe. But now new words are being added. Hot. Desire.

"Lilianna," he whispered. Would I ever get used to him saying my name? Would it always send a tiny thrill throughout my body? "I have the dare now," he said gently. I pushed the lump in my throat down.

"I dare you to see if we can learn to be closer." He said it so softly I swore I heard wrong. Did this mean what I thought? His hand cupped my cheek. It felt deliciously rough against my skin.

"Only if you want and at whatever speed you want," he said quickly. My throat closed. His voice was sincere, kind and patient. Everything he's always been and what my heart wanted, *needed*.

But I felt it. The tendril of fear was snaking its way around my heart. Celestino had always been a friend I could trust. I just didn't know if I could trust him with my heart in that way. Or if I could trust myself to give it to him. He leaned forward, closing the thin space between us.

"Posey?" he asked softly. His thumb traced a line across my cheek, coaxing me into submission. It felt good. I could feel my body relaxing into his touch. He was soothing away every raging doubt. My magic began seeking him out, wanting to be closer. I watched his eyes roam over my face. "Is the dare okay with you? I can change it?" he asked gingerly.

"I-"

"There you two are," a mischievous voice called out as the door swung open. I jumped back falling on my ass and looked up to meet the cheeky eyes of Ben.

"Did you know The Addams Family started out as a comic that was released in the 1930s," I blurted out, praying he didn't notice how red my face was.

"That's so interesting. Using it for a social post?" he asked with a grin. I smiled weakly. "I just wanted to thank you for the wood and make sure you gave these papers to Eleanor," he said, helping me up.

"Yeah no problem!" My voice was pinched. I grabbed the papers from him, my hands trembling. "Well thank you and I'll let you get back to it," I said, making it hastily out of the room. I needed to get as far away as possible. I could hear footsteps trailing behind me as I exited out the haunted house. A warm hand wrapped around my wrist.

"Posey." Celestino yanked me back and my heart sped up as my body remembered how close we were.

"Yes?" I asked, not willing to meet his gaze.

"The dare. I can change-" but before he could finish I cut him off.

"I don't know."

His gaze hardened but his grip on my wrist remained light. Celestino had always been more straightforward than me. Unlike him I needed time to think, to process the variables and weigh the scales of my choices and their effects.

"Is it because you're confused or afraid?" he asked. My body tensed. I wanted to deny the truth of his question. I didn't like where this conversation was heading. My stomach cramped. *Fuck.*

"I just need to think about it," I said, yanking my hand away.

CHAPTER 10
LIKE OLD TIMES

My magic was pushing me to run after her. My hands were shaking as I walked back to the Atticus's. I shook my head. That was a dumb move. I should have just opened the damn closet door. But she was so close to me. Her magic had begun to wrap around me. I felt drunk on it.

I needed to cool down. I needed to not think about how soft her skin was under my hand or the way her cheeks flushed and how relaxed she was.

I *dared* her to cross the line of friendship. Why did I dare that? I could have said, *'I dare you to come to karaoke next time.'* Which would have resulted in us hanging out in a non-work environment and then I could have nicely suggested a conversation about the state of our friendship. But no, I fucking *dared* her. I covered my face, groaning. I was going to nudge her, not push her. She clearly was conflicted about what I asked and I just kept pushing for an answer. Stars, we just reunited after almost eight years! I needed to-

"Trapped in a closet eh?" Sailor's voice snapped me away from my thoughts. I met his eyes.

"It got stuck," I said, my voice tightening.

"Really?" he asked. There was an edge to his voice I didn't like.

"Yes," I gritted out. My brain automatically pulled up the memory of seeing Sailor and Lilianna together. The way her cheeks were flushed in his presence. The way she smiled so carefree with him. Sailor smiled wider.

"Couldn't you have casted some spell to get out?" he asked teasingly. My eyes widened. I could have. But I didn't want to. Something flashed in my mind. She didn't use magic either. My heart skipped with hope. Or maybe she didn't remember she could.

"You both seemed to have enjoyed it," he said with a shit eating grin.

"Clearly not. You saw the way she ran out of there," I said, tightening the elastic in my hair. Sailor shook his head.

"All I saw were two very flushed people who were upset they got interrupted."

I looked away from him. I always forgot how in tune he was with emotions. Then again he was a siren. They could figure out anyone's emotions and if needed to…manipulate them.

"Nothing happened," I said disappointedly. Sailor tossed scraps into a bin.

"Are you sure?" he asked, a bit gentler this time.

"We're just friends and she's probably mad at me now." I sat on the step, clenching my fists. Sailor nodded silently. We stayed like that. Sailor sawing wood, me staring out.

I needed to make it up to her. I needed her to know that she could decline. She didn't need to feel pressure to do anymore or *be* anything more. I was her friend. Her best friend and if she wanted us to stay that way I would be okay with that.

After finally coming home and being back in her life I realized I would rather have her as a friend in my life than as nothing at all.

"Do something that makes her happy," Sailor's voice sang out, pulling me out from my spiral. I looked at him feeling hazy. The smell of the ocean filled my senses and I was reminded of Lilianna again. Sailor shook the saw dust off of his gloves.

"Do something that makes her happy," he said. I racked my brain through our memories. I could make her happy. I know what makes her happy, at least I knew what did.

AFTER WORK I stopped by to pick up a cherry coke and hot fries. This was always my go to for her whenever she needed to be cheered up because she failed a test or was feeling down.

My heart was in my throat as the elevator of her apartment building kept bringing me closer to her. Eleanor gave me her apartment address and asked to hear all about the dirty details which I assured her was not going to happen. Details? Yes. Dirty? No.

I bit the inside of my cheek. Guilt racked me. She pulled away from me and that hurt. We were just getting back into the flow of things. I should be taking my damn time. Taking a deep breath I knocked on her door. There was a groan from the other side.

"Um. Posey, it's me," I said. There was a grunt. "Posey, are you okay?" I could easily open her door with my magic but that would be an invasion of privacy and I didn't need her to have another reason to be upset with me. I heard muffled curses as the door cracked open. Her brown eyes glared at me.

"Yes?" Her voice was soft despite the look. I held up the snacks and offered a smile.

"I wanted to apologize and make sure you were okay," I said. She eyed me skeptically. My heart was rattling.

"Apologize?" she questioned. I cleared my throat. Well this felt fucking awkward.

"For the closet. That shouldn't have happened and I'm sorry. It was wrong of me to dare you something like that. We haven't spoken in years." I glanced away from her. "It wasn't right to dare for something more when we still need to settle back into being friends. Also we were trapped in a closet. I took advantage of the situation," I confessed. She looked hesitant, chewing her bottom lip.

"But you're willing to change the dare if I'm too uncomfortable with it right?" she asked. I nodded. "I just need some time to sort my feelings," she said. Hope flickered.

"I'm okay with that," I said. And I meant it. However she wanted us to be, however long it took I would accept it. "Anyway, here," I said, handing her the coke and chips. She reached out a hand, still hiding behind the door. But then her eyes widened and she yelped, gripping the door.

"Posey?!" My heart dropped at her pain. "Posey, what's wrong?" I asked. She moved back. Her face was scrunched up in pain. I dropped the snacks on the ground and lightly placed a hand on her shoulder. She seemed to relax to my touch, leaning slightly towards me. She took a shaky breath.

"Just cramps," she said.

A light bulb went off in my head. I stepped in and slipped my arms around her, lifting her up. She let out a startled gasp.

"Celestino!" She tried to move in my arms and I held on tightly.

"To the couch," I said. I whispered softly and closed her door with my magic.

"What are you doing?" she asked. She stared at me with wide eyes.

"I'm placing you on the couch, wrapping you in a blanket and turning on a movie. Do you have a heating pad?" I asked.

"Celestino. I can take care of myself. I've been getting my period since I was 10," she said. She wiggled in my arms.

"Yes and I'm going to help like I did all those other times," I said. She rolled her eyes but let me tuck her in with a blanket.

"It wasn't all the time," she muttered. I looked at her face. It was pinched in pain and the bags under her eyes were darker. I grabbed her chin and watched her pupils dilate slightly. *Fury fuck.* Her eyes could get me to do whatever they wanted. They shimmered with flecks of honey and green.

"What do you need?" I asked. She turned her gaze away.

"I'm fine," she said again, clenching her stomach in pain.

"Tell me Lilianna," I demanded. She sighed, too tired to put up a fight any longer.

"Bring me the coke and chips. I don't have a heating pad because mine broke. I want *folar* but I'm too lazy to make it." Her eyebrows scrunched in concentration and I chuckled. "Oh and I need Pricilla's special raspberry leaf tea. It's in the pantry," she finished. I couldn't help but smile. She hated being waited on but I loved waiting on her.

"I'm going to bring you the coke and chips. I'll make you the tea. Then I'm going to step out and buy the ingredients to make *folar*," I said, heading towards her kitchen.

"Be careful. I could get used to you serving me," she said. I smiled.

"I'd do anything you tell me to M'lady," I said in a fake British accent. Her soft laughter filled the apartment and eased the tension in my shoulders. Her eyes widened quickly.

"Wait, you know how to bake?" she asked in shock. I chuckled and handed her the snacks. She unfolded herself from the blanket and that's when I noticed the large familiar hoodie she was wearing. I looked away quickly. Nope. Not right now. I didn't need those thoughts running through my brain and down my body.

"Is it my turn to remind you that some of us have changed?" I threw her words back at her and went to the kitchen to make her tea. I snuck a glance at her and watched her fight back a smile.

We stayed in comfortable silence as the smell of raspberry, ginger and honey filled the air. I needed to ignore how right this all felt. I moved to her fridge and found lemon juice.

"Celestino could you add some-"

"Lemon juice? I remember," I said, mixing some in. She smiled. Taking a deep breath I walked back over to her with her tea. She sighed into the cup. I brushed her hair back from her face. She always had horrible pain the first few days. And when her and Eleanor and Lola synced up? It was painful to watch.

"No working while I'm out," I commanded. She snorted and I stared at her hard. "No. Work," I emphasized. Instead of responding she turned to the tv, tucking herself further into her blanket. I shook my head.

"I'll be back, Posey," I called out, heading towards the door. Once outside her building I pulled out my phone and called my mom.

"*Ei mãe*, question. How do you make *folar*?"

CHAPTER 11
BAKING DISASTER

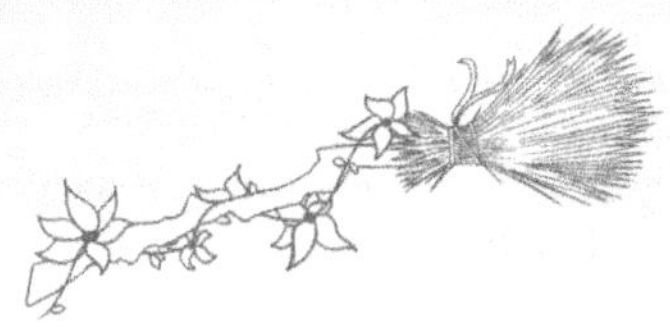

This could not be happening. Celestino was in my apartment. He was in my kitchen. Baking! The man couldn't even handle making butter in the fifth grade. I snuck a picture of him pouring flour and immediately sent it to the girls.

ELLIE
That man does not bake

Well he's clearly baking!

LOLA
He loafs you

Lola that's cheesy even for you

ELLIE
All you knead is loaf

LOLA
Specifically his loaf

These puns are getting stale…

ELLIE
LOL anyway why is he baking you bread?

95

My period has made her grand entrance

ELLIE

Bitch

I have hot fries

LOLA

Damn. Imagine when it's going to be all three
of us again

Anyway I'm currently planting some new
seeds in the garden but if you guys need
anything let me know!

I left my phone on the table and I waddled over to Celestino. He must have stopped by his place before getting the ingredients. He was wearing a gray hoodie, sleeves rolled up and dark sweatpants. His hands dug into the dough and I couldn't help but admire them.

The way he was kneading it I could only imagine how his hands would feel on me. I felt myself blush. I focused on the dough and not his hands. The color was yellow enough which meant he probably used the right amount of eggs.

However, watching the dough stretch beneath his hand, something was off. I looked at his face and his eyebrows were scrunched in concentration.

"Are you sure you've done this before?" I asked, tentatively.

"Of course. I used to help my mom when I was younger." He grunted, using his other hand to add more flour. That was a slight improvement although he needed to add more.

"I can add the flour for you," I said as I made my way to the sink to wash my hands. I gasped as something wrapped around my waist. The blanket fell away from my body. An invisible force gently pushed me backwards until I was back to back with Celestino.

"What is this," tumbled out of my mouth. The magical force made me arch my head back onto Celestino's shoulder. My stomach twisted but it wasn't because of cramps. This was him, his magic. It felt hot and filled my blood with temptation. It smelled like sandalwood and a bit of citrus I think. It was hypnotic.

I sucked in a breath, letting my eyes adjust to see his magic. A fog of light purple was floating around us. From the corner of my eye I saw him turn his face to the side. I bit my lip not wanting to make the indecent sound that threatened to pour out.

"Now didn't I tell you I was going to be taking care of you?" His lips were near my ear. The timber of his voice created an inch on my skin. His magic was still lightly pressing down on me. I wondered how else he could use his magic. "Posey?" he asked, breaking my thoughts.

"But I can help," I said.

"But I want you on the couch," he said. How? Laying down? Sitting? Oh stars, I needed to stop.

"But-" I began to say.

The grip of his magic tightened around me. A tiny gasp escaped. Our eyes stayed connected in a silent battle. Me wanting to help while all he wanted was to take care of me.

"On the couch, curled up," he said.

Yes, sir.

His dimples popped as if he read my mind. I was doomed because of his damn dimples. I gripped the end of my hoodie.

"Fine. But one condition," I said quietly. He raised an eyebrow in question. With a gentle tug of my own magic I pushed off of him, turned and pressed my chest against his back. I wrapped my arms around him. I leaned my head on his shoulder, enjoying the mix of our magic in the air.

"Add more flour," I said gently in his ear. He chuckled, a faint blush on his cheeks.

"Yes ma'am," he said. Ma'am? I kinda liked that.

I picked up my blanket and made my way back to the couch and settled into the corner. Celestino's magic slowly drifted away and I wished it lingered more. Priscilla's tea had a magical effect to dull the ache of cramps for about four hours. I would be needing another cup later.

My front door slammed open. Celestino jumped, nearly sending the bowl of dough onto the floor. Quickly as he jumped I felt his magic crack through the air.

"It's me! Relax," a familiar bright voice shouted. I heard her kick off her shoes before strolling in with grocery bags and dressed in purple sweats.

"What's up wenches?" Eleanor's voice was extra shrill. Celestino glanced at the bags.

"Don't tell me…," he trailed off. She placed the bags filled with most likely snacks on the coffee table in front of me.

"Oh yeah," she said, crawling into my burrito blanket. "We're still period sisters," she grumbled into my chest. I couldn't help but laugh as I wrapped my arms around her in a hug.

"Menstruating misses," I replied.

"Mother nature's bitches," she said, stretching.

"Dragon's piss. It really is like old times now," Celestino mumbled.

We've have always been in sync more or less. In high school when Lola joined, we would spend the first day of our periods together and Celestino would insist on eating junk food and watching rom coms with us if he didn't have soccer practice. She peaked over the couch to eye him.

"Hey Tino," Eleanor's voice was laced with sugar. He placed a dish towel over the bowl to keep it covered as it rose.

"If the *folar* doesn't come out right I'm kicking you out." Her tone dropped, eyes narrowing in on the warlock. After drying his hands he made his way over to the couch and sat at the edge.

"Only Posey can do that," he said, crossing his arms. Eleanor turned to me and I looked at Celestino.

"If it doesn't come out right, I'm kicking you out." I grinned.

AN HOUR later we were all still on my couch, stuffing our faces, binging the How To Train Your Dragon movies.

"I'm going to check on the dough," Celestino said, getting up. Eleanor wrapped an arm around my shoulder.

"He's baking you bread," she whispered into my ear.

"And?" I asked, giggling. She took a sip of Pricilla's tea.

"You know what that means, right?"

I rolled my eyes. Here we go again. Just like me, Eleanor was Portuguese and grew up on many superstitions. Being pooped on by a bird meant good luck, owls were a bad sign, and whistling at night meant you were calling bad spirits.

"What does a man baking bread mean, oh Great Eleanor of Pixies?" I asked in a mysterious voice. She glanced at Celestino who was prepping to roll out the dough.

"His baguette rises for you," she whispered. We bursted into a fit of giggles. My face flushed.

"You do remember Celestino has always done whatever we wanted when we had our period right?" I eyed her. I took a sip of my mug letting the flavors and Pricilla's secret ingredients attempt to keep my pain at bay.

"Especially you," she teased. I rolled my eyes before glancing at Celestino. When I looked back Eleanor was staring at me. Oh no. I fidgeted with my blanket.

"Lilianna," she said with a parental tone. She eyed me. "You're not telling me something," she continued, leaning closer. I snuck a look at Celestino who was concentrating on slicing the *chouriço*.

"He may have dared me to do something," I whispered. Eleanor's eyes widened and she slapped my shoulder.

"Bitch," she hissed at me. I shushed her and casted another quick glance at Celestino. I definitely didn't need him to overhear this conversation. Although I'm pretty sure he knew that I would tell the girls about our conversation. I grabbed my phone and gave her and Lola a quick rundown.

ELLIE

YOU FUCKING WITCH

LOLA

Lily I need you to say yes so I can live
through you. Help me out.

You want me to accept just so you can live
vicariously through me?

LOLA

Of course not! What kind of vampire do you
think I am? I want you to do it FOR YOU

Living through you is just a bonus

ELLIE

I'm going to suffocate you with pillow

@Lola don't you think a certain someone is
available so you don't have to live through me

@Eleanor if you suffocate me I'll never
answer his dare

LOLA

HA! The man spends too much time
complaining about my gardening techniques

ELLIE

@Lily Does this mean you're going to answer
his dare

@Lola we know you want to secretly get into
his plants

He can water your garden

LOLA

BYE I'M LEAVING TO WATER MY OWN
GARDEN

And I do mean my own garden. My sage
plant is doing so well! Look!

Lola's sage plant really did look good. She's always had a green thumb and a passion for growing her own veggies and fruits. She got a spot in the community garden and has spent most of her time being back getting it all set up.

Eleanor bumped my shoulder and I glanced at Celestino. He had begun rolling the dough to place in the oven.

"I said I needed time," I whispered. She rolled her eyes.

"You and I both know you do not need time," she said. "Take the dare. Just give it a try. Trying is just an attempt. It doesn't mean anything has to come of it," she said.

"I'll talk to him later," I promised. I knew nothing was going to go anywhere if I didn't address my feelings and confusion towards Celestino. Especially if I just kept him in the dark about it. But confrontation had never been my strong suit. Celestino placed the bread in the oven and we all continued our movie marathon.

IT WASN'T BAD. The bread was fluffy enough and the *chouriço* and bacon seeped into the dough creating a symphony of flavors. Garlic, salt, butter, smokiness and spice. It was exactly what I needed. Although Celestino could have spent a few more minutes kneading the dough. We stuffed our stomachs and Eleanor was currently passed out on my lap while we were watching the third How To Train Your Dragon movie.

"Hey," Celestino whispered. I turned to look at him and my chest tightened. The moonlight filtered through the window casting a glow around him. His eyes looked dark in this light. He was breathtaking. It almost hurt to look at him.

"Do you want me to put her in your room?" he asked, pointing to Eleanor who had her mouth slightly open, lightly snoring. I stifled a laugh as she twitched in her sleep.

"Yes please," I said. He carefully picked her up and I led him to my room. It wasn't until we were tucking her in that I realized he was in my room. My private space. The air felt warm. His eyes bounced around, trying to take everything in. There wasn't much. An old dresser with candles, jewelry, an old bookcase that was falling apart and a small vanity. He followed me back out to the couch and I felt like I could breathe again.

"Thank you for the bread and taking care of us," I said, picking up our dishes. Celestino intercepted, taking them from me.

"I can do that," he said. I began to protest. "Go make yourself another cup of tea. I can do this." I rolled my eyes at his bossy tone.

"You don't have to thank me. I care about you guys. Plus it kind of felt like old times," he confessed. I smiled as a memory resurfaced. I moved closer to Celestino.

"Remember that one time we made chocolate chip cookies because Eleanor was craving it," I said, meeting his eyes. He grinned.

"You mean the day she somehow set the oven on fire?" He chuckled. Thankfully Celestino mastered a water spell and was able to extinguish the fire. "The cookies were rock solid," he said, placing the dishes in the sink.

"Tasted like ashes," I replied.

This felt nice. Standing in the kitchen with him, cleaning up and doing mundane tasks.

"I've been meaning to ask you but how was the city?" I asked once we were back on the couch. I still remember when he asked if I missed him and how lonely he looked. Celestino's demeanor shifted. His shoulders tensed and he fidgeted with the strings of his hoodie.

"I did like it. I met a lot of people, made money and made connections," he said. I tucked my legs underneath me and shifted slightly closer as Celestino turned towards me, giving me his full attention.

"I just felt like I didn't fit in, you know? I spent my whole life doing everything my parents wanted which I'm grateful for. I loved being involved in sports and doing all of that." He tugged at his sweats. "But once I was in college I just felt lost. I wasn't sure if anything I enjoyed was because *I* enjoyed them, you know? I loved sports and I loved bringing trophies to our town but that was for our town. My grades? Graduating? My degree? That was for my parents. What was for me?"

I had no idea growing up he felt that way. He never let on about those emotions. I guess we all had our own secrets. I understood though. I followed along with what my mom said I needed to do. Once I got to college I had no idea what I wanted and felt out of place.

"It just wasn't for me and that's okay. I think everyone has a time in their life where they have to figure out who they are and where they fit in. It's also one of the reasons I came back. I just wanted to be in a place where I knew I could be myself," he said. His eyes held a faraway look. Guilt began to settle in my stomach. Staring at him I could see the pain he probably suffered out there.

"And right now I like what I'm doing. I like working with Ben and I love building," he said, glancing at me. I placed my hand on his shoulder and squeezed.

"I'm sorry we lost touch," I said tenderly. My eyes stung with tears. Fuck. Was I going to cry? He huffed out a laugh before turning his face to place a quick kiss on my hand. My heart skipped. With gentle fingers he wiped my eyes and it felt like he was taking my heart into his hands.

"Lilianna we were young. It happens a lot. You make friends and sometimes you go your separate ways. You grow and fall. We were all busy trying to find ourselves and get through college. What matters is that we're here now." His words washed over me. He knew how to pluck the strings of my heart like a harp.

"I know. I just can't help but feel-"

"Don't put someone else's emotions on top of yours. Don't put blame only on yourself when they also had a hand in it," he said, cutting me off. This is why I fell for Celestino all those years ago. He was warm, understanding and kind. The pain in his eyes faded, replaced by something different. I swallowed the guilt. He leaned over to the table to grab my cup of tea.

"Okay *querida*?"

Querida.

I nodded. My face flamed and a cramp worked back into my lower abdomen. Celestino tipped the cup towards my lips and I took a sip.

"Now that you're back, you're stuck with us again," I mumbled.

"I wouldn't have it any other way," he said with a tender smile. I took the cup from him and couldn't stop myself from leaning my body against his, my head on his shoulder.

"Alright. Should we do *Eureka* or *Schitt's Creek*?" he asked.

CHAPTER 12

FREAKING FEELINGS

Apart of me felt lighter after hanging out with Eleanor and Posey. It felt like old times. I didn't realize how much I missed it until we were all stuffing our faces on the couch and watching movies. It was what I needed. I found myself smiling as I made my way towards the office.

I had a meeting with Sailor and Ben to go over what builds were left to make. I knew they wanted to update some of the directional signs like where the haunted house, hay maze and pumpkin patch were located.

I just need to think about it.

That's what she said. I felt a pang in my chest. I could do time. Whether she wanted to try something more or not I would wait as long as she needed. Warmth spread through my chest. I felt my magic zip up and down my arm from where I held her. I don't think she even realized how she kept naturally leaning towards me. But fuck did it feel right.

"What ya' smiling about boss?" Sailor's voice broke through my thoughts. I straightened my back, my smile dropping. I continued on my walk, ignoring him. "Boss," he called out. He fell in step with me.

"How are you?" he asked. I ignored him. "It's a great day isn't it? I had the best sleep," he continued. I ignored him again.

"I wonder if the meeting will end fast. I have a shift at the pub tonight," he persisted. I bit the inside of my cheek as he kept rambling about mixing sea pearl dust with drinks.

"Did you and Posey make up?"

His question caught me off guard and I ended up tripping over myself.

"Now he listens!" He laughed out loud, catching the eyes of some people. He patted my shoulder and I shrugged his hand off.

"You don't call her Posey," I said glaring at him. The fucker only smiled bigger.

"So did you guys kiss and make up?" He waggled his eyebrows. I felt my cheeks heat up.

"Sailor," I growled.

"What? I'm just saying," he smirked. I rolled my eyes. "Did you take my advice? What happened?" he asked. For some reason my mouth betrayed me and I found myself telling him everything as we made our way to the meeting. Ben was right when he said Sailor would grow on me.

BEN WAS SITTING across from us reviewing our list. We needed to construct the maze, most likely with the help of some Earth fairies, update signs and finish the haunted house. We also needed to double check with the businesses that would be vendors the day of and make sure all of the food trucks were confirmed.

"The haunted house is slowly coming along," Sailor said confidently. I nodded in agreement.

"It's nice to have an extra hand," I admitted. Sailor's smile widened.

"Aw, thanks boss man. I love you too," he teased. I rolled my eyes. Ben let out a chuckle.

"The maze is handled. I'll make sure to confirm the businesses and food trucks. Just focus on the signs, the haunted house and the bar crawl. If I need anything else I'll let you know," Ben said. I nodded and stood up.

"How's the bar crawl coming along by the way?" he asked with a twinkle in his eyes. Sailor settled into his seat, hands folded in his lap with a smirk.

"It's coming along. Promotions have begun. Riddles and the map have been squared away. And this weekend we're going to be testing some of the beverages because...well remember what happened that one time." I arched an eyebrow at Ben who was trying to hold back a laugh.

"What happened?" Sailor asked. If I remember correctly Sailor has only been living in Lavender Falls for a year.

"You know how sometimes humans come and stay in our town for vacation? Well one day a group of college kids were taking shots at Boogeyman's Bar, having a great time. The only problem was one of the humans accidentally grabbed the wrong shot. You know how Red Bull gives you wings? Well that's what happened. Luckily they were really drunk and Lilianna's mom wiped their memory. So now we're all extra cautious," Ben said. Sailor's mouth dropped.

"So that's why you guys have to try the drinks? Why not make them normal? Like magic mocktails," Sailor suggested.

"We do that now. We have a system in place to tell the difference between humans and nonhumans as they walk in. An alarm system of sorts. But we still have to make sure the magical drinks are safe for us supernaturals," Ben said and I nodded in agreement. In each establishment a sign glows above the patrons heads when they walk in letting us know the difference.

"Mhmm. That's really smart. Other towns should implement that," Sailor said, getting up.

"Good work guys," Ben said as we left.

Sailor smiled at my mischievously as we walked out. "I can't wait for you guys to try my drink," he said.

"It better be good," I replied as as we made our way towards my desk. Everyone swears he's one of the best bartenders in town. Even Caleb agreed which was saying a lot.

"Well I know Lilianna is going to like it. I'm making it with her favorites," he said smiling. I felt my heart pinch.

When I left Lavender Falls I was 18. The parties I went to, Lilianna didn't show up half of the time. I didn't know what she liked. But Sailor did. Sailor knew the current version of Lilianna while I only knew the past. I tried to shake the snake of jealousy off but it was slowly taking permanent residency inside me.

The day was finally here. Today was the day Celestino and I would do a test run of the bar crawl. A part of me was excited. Was I excited for the bar crawl? Or spending time with Celestino? Maybe all of the above.

I had a bundle of sprites dancing around my stomach. Our friendship was finally settling in place even though the temptation for something more was growing. His dare had been lingering in and out of my head more often lately. And I wanted to give him an answer. I needed to so it would stop taking up room in my thoughts.

"Lily," my best friend banged on my door instead of barreling in. Which meant some humans were out and about on the floor. Eleanor had decided to come on over and help pick out a look for my *non-date*.

Opening the door Eleanor was once again dressed to impress. Most likely for a certain elf bartender. She wore tight white ripped pants with a lime sequined green halter top and purple leather jacket. She had on sparkly heels and her auburn hair was pulled back by butterfly clips.

"Goddam," I stared at her in amazement.

"I know and now it's your turn!"

She began to drag me to my bedroom but before she went any further I pulled her towards the kitchen counter. Two shots of tequila were lined up for each of us. She smiled wickedly.

"Time to party," she said as we licked salt off the back of our hands and threw back the burning liquid. Biting into the lime we giggled.

"Now I can raid your closet," she said with a wicked grin.

"I won't comment on the amount of black because you know I love you so let me work my magic," she said, flickering through the clothes.

"Hey you know I perfected that hair dye spell," I said as she picked out my favorite skinny jeans. She threw an outfit on the bed. My trusty dark jeans, a black silk lace cami and my favorite leather jacket.

"All black, just how you like it," she said. I smiled at her.

"Alright fine but let me do the spell first."

We headed towards my bathroom. I woke up feeling centered with my magic. My anxiety wasn't twitching beneath the surface which meant I needed to take full advantage. Sitting on my sink Eleanor wore a giant grin.

"Surprise me bestie!" She sparkled. I raised an eyebrow. "Listen I know you have an eye for color so do your best." Eleanor was practically glowing.

"Okay. Let me think."

Eleanor nodded and closed her eyes. Freckles danced around her face and down her shoulders. Her eyelids shimmered with pink. I smiled.

"Twist and twirl. Wave and curl. Hair needs a rethink so how about some pink," I said. A puff of sparkly pink smoke enveloped Eleanor and her wavy auburn hair slowly turned pink. The new hair color made her skin glow.

"Bitch," Eleanor screamed, staring at herself in the mirror. Everything about her seemed brighter. She turned around, a smile stretched across her face.

"Alright it's your turn."

Glitter began sparking out of her fingers. A flick of a brush, a wave of powder and I found myself smiling just as big. I missed getting dolled up. I knew I needed to push myself more to hang out with friends. I was the one keeping myself busy.

"Are you excited for tonight?" Eleanor asked.

"We're just going to test out the bar crawl," I said. She rolled her eyes.

"You and I both know that's a lie." She tapped my nose with highlighter. I snorted. "Especially after that dare that you technically haven't answered," she continued. I glared at Eleanor. "You know you didn't and we both know what you want to say." She set the brush down.

"I don't know," I said, shifting on top of my sink.

"Lilianna. You like him, always have. It's okay to say yes."

We stayed quiet for a few minutes as she continued her work.

"Why are you scared?" Eleanor asked in a quiet voice. I hesitated.

"We've been best friends forever. A million things could go wrong. Sure he likes me as his friend. But dating me? That's a whole other thing. What if I'm too much?"

Eleanor placed her hand on my shoulders. Her mouth was set.

"You are *not* too much. Everyone else is simply not enough," she said with sincerity. I felt tears in my eyes.

Well there goes my anxiety. Something was bubbling beneath the surface again. We were having a good time and I've been centered with my magic today. We were laughing. I didn't need it to ruin the night before it even started.

"I know that. I do. I get that but it's like something else stops me from just going for it," I admitted.

"That's fear," she said, offering me a sheepish smile. I looked away. How do I let fear go?

"Just promise me you'll have fun. Yes, this is to make sure the bar crawl is a hit but something *might* happen with Celestino. Which is okay, especially if you want to make it to rule 69." Eleanor waggled her eyebrows. I broke out in a smile. "Have fun," she said, pointing to the mirror. I took a deep breath.

"I deserve fun," I said firmly.

"Also, Lola texted me before I came over and agreed for you to make it to rule 69," she said, smirking. In that moment my phone beeped.

LOLA

Rule 69

I looked at Eleanor who was still smirking. This was going to be an interesting night.

CHAPTER 13

LET'S GET TIPSY, WITCHES

I was a bundle of nerves. I tugged on one of my hoops multiple times as I waited outside of Boogeyman's Bar for Celestino. A zing snapped through me. He was here. Goosebumps prickled across my skin.

I turned around and my breathing faltered. He wore tapered navy pants that stopped right above his ankles paired with white sneakers. His pants were practically molded over his calves. I liked his calves. Years of playing soccer made his body lean and hard.

He wore a loose white, button shirt that was tucked in paired with a jean jacket. A few buttons revealed his smooth chest and his family pendant. The white of his shirt made his skin glow. I could tell he's been spending all of his time working outside. My throat tightened. He looked like dinner, dessert, and a snack.

His eyes slowly made their way up and down my body. I was nervous from the heat of his gaze. I wasn't used to being looked at that way, especially from him. My leather jacket was beginning to make me feel like I was trapped in a sauna. I tried my hardest not to fidget.

"Good evening Mister Wicked Warlock of The East," I said jokingly to break the tension. He let out a chuckle.

"Hello there Lilianna. You look beautiful," he said, taking a step forward. The corner of my lips tugged. He wasn't going to make this easy. His eyes blazed and he leaned in to graze my cheek with his lips and my heart skipped. His lips left a trail of heat that crawled towards my heart.

"Well let's boogie with the monsters," I said, smiling. He slid his hand around my waist, pulling me forward. Just friends being friendly, I reminded myself.

WE WALKED into the cool air of Boogeyman's Bar. It sat right at the edge of town. Behind the bar was a community garden that was surrounded by a swamp. The garden helped provide a lot of vegetables, fruits and herbs for the town. It grew the majority of the flowers used for the spring festival. Caleb's younger brother Flynn was in charge of the garden on top of being a part time bartender and whiskey maker.

The inside of the bar was decked out as a Boogeyman's wet dream. Dark wood covered every inch. Moss hung in the corners and were tangled with string lights to give the illusion of a night under a swamp sky. The bar was in full swing with blues music filling the atmosphere.

"Hello there!" The sharp green eyes of a slender man behind the bar called our attention.

"Mr. Salazar," I said warmly. I watched Mr. Salazar move with grace across the bar, thin hands working their magic making drinks. His eyes are what always caught my attention. They were an eerie green and seemed to follow every movement. There was a thin yellow circle around his irises if you looked close enough.

I had no idea what kind of creature he was except that he cared about the swamp and honestly I never thought to ask. The one thing I did know was that he wasn't a fan of Sailor, or most sirens in general.

"Hey Sal. We're here to try Boogeyman's Booze. Gotta clear it for the Cursed Bar Crawl," Celestino said in a friendly tone. It was as if he never left. Everyone had welcomed him back with open arms.

I found myself smiling watching them talk. I hope he knew how happy everyone was now that he was back. I hope he knew how happy *I* was having him back. His eyes cut to me and he winked. I giggled, shaking my head.

Sal mixed some green liquid into our drinks. After adding a shot of tequila to each glass he pulled out a tiny glass bottle and added three drops, causing a fog to float out of the drinks. A swell of strange excitement began brewing inside my chest.

"Excited Posey?" Celestino asked. I turned to face him. He had a sheepish smile. I nodded silently. Sal placed the lime green drinks in front of us.

"It'll have you doing the boogie all night," he said, giving us a disco dance move before moving down the bar. We laughed in unison. Celestino tapped his glass with mine and went to take a sip.

"Wait no," I exclaimed. Worry snapped in his eyes.

"What's wrong?" He looked confused.

"You have to make eye contact after we clink our glasses and take our first sip," I said. He snorted. "Come on, it's bad luck if we don't," I said. He shook his head, giving in.

"Fine. Okay."

Our eyes connected and I felt the world slowly slip away. After clicking our glasses I brought the drink to my lips and paused. The smell of acetone, laced with green apple and agave hit my nose. I held Celestino's gaze. Enjoying the way his eyes seemed lighter, brighter. Not like when we were on my couch and clouded in pain.

I stopped tilting the glass once it touched my mouth, waiting for his reaction. His eyes bulged and the vein in his neck jumped out. For a split second his skin flashed swamp water green. I found myself coughing to hold back a laugh meanwhile Celestino choked on his words.

"You..you didn't…" He coughed into his hand.

"I wanted you to try it first," I said with a cheeky smile.

"You little witch," he said, shaking his head. I tossed my hair over my shoulder and raised my glass, stress rolling off my shoulders.

"Well I *am* a witch," I said. He gave me a full smile, one of my favorites. It was big and unapologetically carefree. It made crinkles appear on the sides of his eyes and his dimples were out. I felt a swell of pride at being the one to create and receive this smile.

"It's your turn, Posey." His voice dropped to something huskier. It sent a shiver down my spine. He kept my gaze and stepped forward. I stepped back, needing space. Taking a deep breath I took a sip. It tasted like a burnt apple covered in gasoline. My throat immediately closed and I choked.

"Am I turning into Shrek?" I asked wide eyed as my skin flashed green. Celestino couldn't stop laughing. He waved Sal over.

"Yes? What did you think?" His *s's* hissed out.

"Sal. I love ya man, I do. But let's tone it down a bit and try not to make the customers look like ogres," Celestino said. Sal's tongue flicked out for a millisecond.

"How about one drop from your sparkly bottle and more green apples," I suggested with a smile. Sal dropped his shoulders slightly.

"Yes Ms. Rosario." He nodded with a smile and slithered off.

"I'm happy we're doing this," I confessed. I turned to Celestino who was watching me.

"Me too. Shall we go to the next bar, M'lady?" Celestino leaned away from the bar and offered his arm which I gladly took. This was going to be an interesting night.

She looked devastatingly beautiful and it was a sucker punch to my gut. My hands itched to grab her. I shoved that feeling down. I needed to focus on the task which was trying not to die from the drinks. I definitely will not be eating apples any time soon. Lilianna relaxed while she held onto my arm. I glanced up at her slightly. I don't think she realized just how close she was. Lately I've noticed she's been finding ways to be near me.

Siren's Saloon was only a few blocks away. The outside sign was a piece of painted driftwood. The front porch offered seating for those who wanted to smoke outside. We stepped through the double doors to find ourselves transported to the inside of a pirate ship. Comfy booths scattered around. Nets hung from the ceiling and a giant fish tank separated the front room and the pool tables. The bar itself looked like it came from a cowboy movie.

We made our way towards the bar and a familiar figure was pouring shots for a group of elves. Lilianna's eyes widened in excitement as she let go of my arm to walk over to Sailor. The snake that was buried inside me woke up. Sailor's smile widened. He leaned over the bar to kiss her cheek. He looked over at me and winked.

The fucker. I slid into a stool next to her.

"Hey guys! How was the drink at Boogeyman's Bar?" Sailor asked.

"It was…interesting," I said. Lilianna's smile was open as she recounted what happened to him.

"Are you ready to try my concoction?" His question dipped at the end and his eyes held an alluring appeal. Lilianna smirked and my hand tightened on my thigh. Was he blatantly flirting with her in front of me? No way in a hellhound's lair.

"Yes please," she said leaning in.

"Two," I said, breaking their spell. I scooted closer to Lilianna. I could have sworn I heard her take a quick breath. I snuck a glance at her. There was a faint flush on her cheeks. Was that for me or for Sailor?

"Two Siren's Songs, Sailor," she confirmed. I must have given him a look because he just kept smiling. Her gaze followed Sailor as he turned around to pour drinks. I spun her stool to face me. Her eyes widened at the sudden movement.

"You're here with me," I said, trying to not let my annoyance slip in. She bit her bottom lip, the lips I've been dying to taste. Her eyes twinkled.

"Are you jealous," she teased.

"Yes," I answered with zero hesitation again. I was never the possessive type. But I wanted all of her. My mind slipped back to the closet at the haunted house. After having a taste of it behind closed doors I wanted to be her sole focus. She tugged at her earlobe nervously. She looked away from me and into the crowd. My heart leaped at her next words.

"You don't have to be jealous of him. He's a friend only. Nothing more. Trust me," She said softly. My mom's words rattled through me. *Trust her.*

Without thinking I grasped her chin in my hand and pulled her closer. I needed her to look in my eyes and tell me.

"Don't worry about him, okay? N-not him or anyone else," she said, quietly. I leaned in slightly, being drawn to her. Before I could say anything Sailor placed our drinks in front of us.

"Staying away from water is recommended. Hope you enjoy Lily." I felt my eyebrow twitch. He was seriously trying my patience. We clinked our glasses together and sipped. I tasted sprite, peaches, tequila and something else.

"Fuck," she immediately said. My body twitched in response.

"You like?" I asked, needing to know what her tastes were.

"Fuck yes," she said taking another sip. She needed to stop saying that word. She slowly relaxed in her seat. The sound of sea shanties were being played in the background. I tried to ignore the punching feeling when her eyes slid to Sailor.

"How is it?" he asked.

"It's okay," I said with a shrug knowing damn well it was a lie. This was going to be a hit with tourists.

"It's amazing," Lilianna said gleefully. And it was. She continued drinking. Sailor smiled.

"Great. Can't wait to tell the Captain," he said leaning onto the counter. I shifted in my seat.

"You have to make this a staple," she said.

"For you? Of course." He grinned. The whole exchange twisted my gut. At that moment a guy from down the bar called out to Sailor.

"Glad you came and liked the drinks." He winked and left us. Once again her eyes followed him.

"Rule eight," I said in a rough voice. I leaned towards her, my mouth tickling her ear. I inhaled her scent. Lavender and ocean water.

"No eye fucking anyone else." My voice was cold. I knew it was. I couldn't take it anymore. She raised an eyebrow.

"I wasn't eye *fucking* him," she said with a bit of a bite that sent my blood racing. She was right. But before I could apologize something about the aquarium caught my eye. There was something about the sea blue water that entranced me. There was an assortment of colorful fish and lobsters that were swimming around. Lilianna followed my gaze.

"It's so pretty," Lilianna whispered. I nodded.

"Right? Want to see it up close?" I turned to see her downing the rest of her drink. My eyes widened in shock. She gripped my hand and began dragging me over to the aquarium. I tried to ignore the feel of my hand in hers. Her warm fingers slid between mine. I liked the way this felt. Something deep within was screaming finally.

We pressed our faces into the glass, watching the fishes flick their tails back and forth. It was like a sea of rainbows.

"Wow! They're *soooo* pretty," she said with wonderment.

"I feel like jumping in and swimming with them. I mean look how much fun they're having," I said. My eyes were glued to the fishes doing flips. It was like they were putting on a performance for us.

"But you know what would be better? If they were free to swim in the open ocean!" Her eyes sparkled against the glow of the water.

"Save the fishes," I yelled.

At that moment everything felt like a movie. Sailor jumped over the bar as I tried to lift Lilianna into the tank.

"Stop!" Sailor called out, throwing his power into it.

Everyone in the bar froze. Some people were in mid drink, being unable to stop their beers from pouring down their faces. While my body was yearning to have a pet Flounder I noticed that Sailor was strong enough to have the whole bar under his spell. I guess he was pretty *and* powerful.

"We're saving the fishies. They should be in the ocean," Lilianna whined. I tried nodding aggressively in support of my woman but I was frozen in position. Sailor let out a chuckle.

"The nearest body of water is the one by Boogey's. The ocean is a two hour drive," he said. I wanted to punch his face. How dare he stop my witch's mission to save the fishes?

"She wants the fishies in the ocean. Where there is a well there is water," I said.

"I don't think that's how it goes," Sailor snorted, shaking his head. My hands were still wrapped around Lilianna's waist who was gripping the top of the aquarium.

"Um…can we move now?" she asked, her voice soft. When I glanced up at her, her face was red. Very cute.

"I may have added too much rainbow fish scale." Sailor sighed into his hand. "The fishies are fine. Why don't you go relax at the bar while I fix you up something," he commanded.

I dropped Lilianna gently onto the floor. She squeezed my arm, looking away. We headed to the bar without hesitation. Our bodies were covered in a warm haze that smelled like sea salt. We couldn't deny Sailor no matter how much we wanted to. Sailor cracked open a small bottle in the shape of a clam.

"Just have this and you'll be a little less…shipfaced," he said, offering us a shot of a blue liquid.

"It looks like the water of the aquarium," I said. Lilianna gasped. She turned to me.

"We should save the fishes," she exclaimed.

"Drink," Sailor ordered before we could get out of our seats. The cold liquid tasted like seaweed and we gagged.

"Are we going to be gagging all night?" Lilianna coughed out. She froze for a moment before dissolving into a fit of giggles. I felt a flush crawl up my face.

"I *guess* less fish scale," Sailor said, chuckling. She offered a weak smile.

"Yes please but it did taste great," she said, trying to recover. She did that at Boogeyman's Bar as well. She wanted to comfort him despite the critique. And the drink really was delicious besides the siren call to the water and all sea creatures.

"Well I'm glad you liked it." Sailor was doing that thing where he rested his chin in his hand and batted his ocean blue eyes. I knew he was doing this on purpose. He was trying to get in my head.

I didn't know much about him. The only thing Eleanor told me was that he was from Coralia Coast. But then his eyes slid to mine and there was a mischievous glint. I faintly heard Lilianna sigh as she reached to squeeze my hand. She looked at me, eyes filled with warmth. It wasn't the same way as when she looked at Sailor. This felt intimate. She smiled and the snake slithered back into its den.

"Yes. Less scales. Alright Posey, let's go." I clutched her hand in mine and dragged her out.

"Have fun Celestino," Sailor called out laughing.

CHAPTER 14
LET'S GET TIPSY PRT. 2

Next up was Highwaymen Haunt. The local biker bar was exactly what you would picture. Everything was dark, including the building. It was the only black building on Lantern's Street. Inside, the walls were covered in graffiti and posters of rock bands and there were a few pool tables and darts in the back.

The bar was packed with big burly men. This was the shifter's and vampires favorite place to hang out. Rock music blasted through the haze of smoke. There was a good chance that we could see our bosses here. We headed towards the bar and squeezed our way to sit down, my hand still wrapped around Lilianna's.

Lola was behind the bar, clutching someone's shirt. Poor guy. Nothing escaped Lola's vision and not just because she was a vampire.

"Sorry Lola. I wasn't going to walk out without paying you, you know." His voice became higher the further he spoke. She grinned, revealing her fangs and he dropped the cash before bolting to the back of the bar. Her braids sat at the top of her head and her dark skin glimmered around the dim fluorescent lighting. Her eyes lit up when they met Lilianna's.

"Lily," she exclaimed. It was shocking to see Lola go from badass vampire to a bubble of joy. But that's how she's always been. Her personality was brighter than the sun. Honestly it could rival Sailor's. "Hey there Celestino," she said leaning over the bar to kiss my cheek. Her eyes briefly glanced at our joined hands and Lilianna pulled away.

"By the way, I'm totally stoked about the bar crawl. That's an awesome idea!" She continued as she poured beers for customers.

"How come you're behind the bar?" I asked. Lola sighed.

"I was having dinner with my parents here and felt bad that Colin was the only one behind the bar. Plus I did work here one summer, so why not," she said, shrugging her shoulders.

"That's nice-" I began to say.

"Plus I wanted to be here to witness you guys trying the drinks," she smirked. And that was the Lola I knew.

"Well I hope it's good because the last two places..." I trailed off and shivered. Lola let out a deep laugh.

"Yikes. Let's hope it ends well shall we? I'll get started on them in a minute." She turned to hand the beers to the customers.

Lilianna and I were now alone. In the past two bars the drinks had come fairly quickly and there wasn't space for small talk. But now the seconds stretched into minutes.

I opened my mouth to say something but my words were caught off by a tall man with deep brown skin. He had brown eyes and a warm smile.

"Alex," Lilianna said, smiling. Alex worked at the mayor's office as the finance assistant to Chelsea. And when he wasn't crunching numbers he was helping his wife, Thalia, at her gallery in town that featured local artists. His younger brother Felix was also in charge of the haunted house since his Uncle Atticus decided he was too old to handle it.

Lilianna stood up to throw her arms around him. I smiled. I always liked Alex. We were on the same soccer team growing up. He was a whiz with numbers, cool under pressure and had a killer hat trick.

"Hey Celestino, just wanted to say we're happy you're back. We gotta' do friendly matches on the weekends like we used to," Alex said, tossing an arm over my shoulder.

"Oh, absolutely. We could get Caleb and Sailor," I said. Alex smiled.

"How's Thalia?" Lilianna asked. Alex married his high school sweetheart and they were expecting their first child soon.

"Still pregnant." Alex pointed behind him to where Thalia was dancing. "You guys here to try out the signatures right?" he asked us. Lilianna nodded.

"Once the drinks check out I can-" Alex waved his hand.

"Stop talking about work. It's the weekend," he said, cutting her off. I chuckled.

"Right? Never taking a break," I teased. I glanced at her with a twinkle in my eyes. She scrunched her nose, sending me a death glare. It was cute.

"Fine, fine. This is me relaxing," she huffed out. She crossed her arms over her chest. I couldn't help but steal a glance at the way the skimpy material formed over her breasts.

"Have you seen her dance?" Alex asked with a grin breaking my thoughts.

"Her? Dance? Do we not remember prom?" I snorted. Eleanor had to drag Lilianna on the dance floor every three songs. She stood up straighter and offered Alex her hand.

"Let's show him what this ass does," she said and dragged Alex towards the makeshift dance floor. I watched her leaned down to kiss Thalia's cheek. They exchanged a few words. There were a few couples scattered around swaying to the drum beat. She wrapped her arms around Alex's neck and began swaying her hips. Alex leaned into her ear.

My heart was raging against my chest. My eyes were glued to her body as she swayed against Alex, spun to Thalia and back to Alex. My hands tingled to get themselves on her. She threw her head back, laughing. The things I would pay, that I would do, to be the person that got that sound out of her.

I giggled, feeling happy. I felt lighter on the dance floor. My brain wasn't focusing on my to-do list. I felt like I could breathe on my own.

"So you and Celestino huh?" Alex asked.

"No, we're just working together," I said. Alex spun me towards Thalia. She leaned towards my ear.

"Are you sure about that? Because he's looking at you like he's going to eat you," Thalia teased, wiggling her eyebrows. Alex turned us around so I could see Celestino over his shoulder.

His eyes glowed in the light. I could see a faint humming around him. My eyes widened. *His magic.* It was pulsing off of him. He was looking at me like he wanted to drag me away to a dark secluded corner. But I wouldn't have to be dragged. I would be walking right alongside him.

I stayed quiet and was grateful that Alex and Thalia didn't push the conversation further. I felt myself slipping to the beat, the smoke and the lights. I let the stress of my life fade into the background. A faint whistle called my attention and I noticed Lola lifting our drinks. I nodded. Alex spun me again and I saw Celestino laughing at Lola. I smiled. He looked so happy to be back. I patted Alex's shoulder and kissed his cheek. Thalia came to give me a hug.

"Karaoke later?" she asked, smiling wide. I winked.

"Of course it wouldn't be *Lily's Night Out* if there wasn't karaoke," I said. I blew a kiss to her belly. Thalia took a deep breath, rubbing her stomach. Alex slipped his arm around Thalia. His eyes softened as he glanced at his wife's belly. I smiled at their love, something I've wanted but been afraid to have.

I began walking towards Celestino and my heart picked up. He looked so handsome. His eyes made their way back to me, where I wanted them to stay. His hair was coming loose. He had unbuttoned another button and his tattoo peaked out from beneath. He licked his lips and I clenched my fists. I needed to get a grip.

"You seem to be enjoying yourself," he noted once I stood in front of him. I nodded, reaching for the drink and taking a sip. He raised an eyebrow, probably surprised I didn't wait for him. But I needed to cool myself down for more than one reason.

"I do enjoy dancing occasionally," I said. It was his turn to drink.

"I've taken notes," he said, smirking. The back corner of the bar caught his eye.

"Is that a pool table?" he asked. I looked at him.

"Yeah," I said grinning, an idea forming.

"Want to play," he suggested. The night was still young. It was only 10. Something mischievous swept through me.

"I'm down," I said. As we made our way through the crowd, Celestino offered his hand to steer me through. I nodded and tucked my hand into his. A slow warmth spread throughout me just like it did at Siren's Saloon. I felt my senses relax and even my magic buzzed excitedly. We chose a pool table in the back corner. As we reached for the pool sticks, Celestino suggested a bet. I cocked an eyebrow.

"A bet?" I asked as I reached for my drink.

"Yeah. We could bet who has to do the script for the bar crawl guide," he said. I tilted my head back and forth, thinking. I had planned on doing it but this could be one more thing off my plate. Plus everyone always complained I worked too much. I smiled. This was going to be good. I was going to have one less worry.

"That doesn't sound bad but I'm gonna have to confess, I'm not good at playing pool," I said. His eyes met mine. He grinned. It was cute how he thought he was going to win.

"I could show you a thing or two," he said. I bet he could just not at playing pool. I nodded, ignoring the way my magic zapped to the surface again as we brushed by. He racked the balls into a triangle.

"Just avoid getting the white ball in and the eight ball should be last. I'll shoot first. Whichever one of us scores first that's the pattern we go for," he explained. I nodded, biting back a giggle. The poor warlock had no idea what he was in for. He smacked the white ball so hard it sent the rest scattering but nothing went in.

"Your turn," he said. I straightened my shoulders and bent over the table to where the white ball was.

He came up from behind me and leaned over. "It might be easier if you placed your fingers like this," he said into my ear, adjusting them. If I turned my head slightly we would be in the perfect position to brush lips. A thrill shot through me.

"Yep," I squeaked. He backed away. Taking a slow breath I hit the ball and one of the stripes curved around the socket at the last second.

"Maybe the next one," he offered a sheepish smile. *We'll see.*

He landed a solid, twice in a row and now it was game on. I bit the inside of my cheek, my eyes narrowing in on my target. I rolled my shoulders back. I held the pool stick in a loose grip, lined up my shot and sunk four stripes in a row.

"You're good at this," he said in disbelief. I shrugged my shoulders.

"I said I wasn't good and I'm not. I'm great." I smiled. Celestino looked at me in awe.

"You little witch," he muttered.

"Are you going to keep saying that all night?" I cocked an eyebrow. He twirled the pool stick in his hand.

"You think you can keep it up all night?" he asked, smirking.

"I don't think I would have a problem keeping you up," I said, grinning. Celestino nearly dropped his pool stick. A pretty blush stained his cheeks.

After missing the next shot, it was his turn.

"How did you get so good?" he asked, making it in. The pool pocket. Not me. Yet. Maybe. *Focus.* He slid behind me to take his next shot. His eyes squinted as he lined it up.

"Well it's no surprise I wasn't a party person in college but Eleanor was- still is. I quickly learned I didn't really need to talk to people when I played pool. My brain only had to focus on one thing and it was an easy way to get free drinks for us," I said. It was also fun beating all the guys. "Some of the guys were douches and couldn't handle being beaten by a woman," I continued. Celestino raised an eyebrow. His grip on the pool stick tightened.

"Did any of them try anything?" he asked, voice low. I shook my head.

"Oh no don't worry. We had a few friends from the soccer team who were always with us to back us up. Plus, if someone did try something, Eleanor and I would have used magic," I said.

Which was true. There was only one time we had to use a spell. We were in the middle of a pool game when one of our opponents girlfriend's showed up declaring Eleanor was sleeping with her boyfriend. She wasn't but it got ugly fast. I had to cast a spell to disguise Eleanor as we slipped out. After that night we decided to do ladies night at a different bar.

Celestino nodded. "Good." His voice was short. I walked up to him and placed a hand on his shoulder. Heat was radiating off of him. He turned his head to the side to face me. I squeezed his shoulder.

"We were fine. Always." I reassured him.

"Well if you can kick my ass in pool I can't imagine what else you have up your sleeve," he said with a grin.

THE GAME ENDED QUICKLY since I stopped holding back. Celestino took a gulp of his drink.

"Darts. Let's play darts," he suggested. I rolled my eyes.

"You technically lost though," I pointed out. He shook his head.

"Two rounds of darts. That'll be the deciding factor," he urged. I laughed. I forgot how competitive he was.

"Bring it on," I said. But this time I was nervous. Darts wasn't my thing. At all. One time I almost stabbed the quarterback in the arm and I wasn't even drinking. Celestino nearly lost it as soon as he realized he would be winning the first round of darts and I found myself becoming more and more agitated. I downed the rest of my drink. Celestino's eyes widened and he decided to do the same.

"Last round," he said with a cheeky grin. A scowl appeared on my face and I threw the dart with a bit too much force.

"You almost hit me," he yelled. I snickered.

"*Almost* being the most important word and why are you even standing that close to the board?" I asked. He rolled his eyes and reached for the darts. It didn't take long for him to win round two.

"That's not fair, you knew you were good at darts," I shouted over the music. A crowd was beginning to gather.

"You want to talk about fair? You played me at pool," he fired back.

"We need another thing to decide," I said looking around.

"I beat you twice," he taunted. We both stared at each other and then the end of the bar.

"Race," we called out at the same time before sprinting down the bar. Everyone around us immediately parted, laughing into their drinks.

But Lola stood at the end, arms opened and ready to tackle us. When we realized what she was going to do it was too late to slow down. Lola wrapped her arms around us and I felt my stomach bounce.

"How about you two sit before destroying the bar with your competitions and I fix you a drink," she suggested. Her tone was laced with magic. Like a siren, vampires had an ability to sway and we eagerly complied.

"Whoever finishes the drink wins the bet," I said, my heart pounding with adrenaline.

"You're on," Celestino agreed, pulling himself away from Lola to get to the bar.

Lola sighed, "I think I added too much venom."

We waited at the bar impatiently, fingers tapping and legs bobbing up and down. Lola began concocting a shot with clear liquid. We eyed each other, anticipation building. She set it in front of us, chuckling.

"On my count…1, 2-" she began.

"Wait! On 3 or after 3?" I asked. Celestino nodded furiously. Lola chuckled.

"After 3 Lils. 1…2…3," she yelled. We both dove for the glass and threw our heads back, like we were back in college. We each slammed our glasses down.

"Tino," Lola called out. The bar erupted into cheers. Both of us began shuddering. I coughed.

"How about we tone that drink down," I suggested. Lola was covering her mouth, trying to keep it together.

"Way ahead of you, sweets," she said with a toothy grin. Celestino was rubbing his eyes.

"Remind me to tell you about the haunted petting zoo tomorrow," he muttered.

"Oh I can't wait! I've already made little costumes they can all wear," she said excitedly. Every year we have a petting zoo for the kids and we dress the animals up as little monsters. Although some animals didn't really need a costume. But the tourists didn't need to know that.

"Remember to send the invoice Lola. You gotta get paid for your work," Celestino said.

Lola rolled her eyes. "Aye, aye captain," she said with a giggle. My eyes widened as a reminder popped into my head.

"Ah, Lola!" I jumped. I completely forgot that my mom had called me with some very important news for Lola.

"Yes?" she asked, raising an elegant eyebrow. I smiled.

"My mom told me that because Ms. Heinstien wants to spend more time with her grandkids, she wants to hire another vet," I said. Lola broke out into a huge smile, fangs and all.

"Holy shit stars! Thank you so much Lily!" She threw herself over the bar to hug me. She was squeezing me so hard I could hardly breathe. But it was worth it to see Lola's reaction. Celestino laughed. "By the way we need to plan a brunch," she said as she pulled away from me.

"Yes! I found a new french toast recipe to try," I said, excitedly.

"That will go perfect with the syrup I made from the *ginjinha* you gave me," she squealed. *Ginjinha* is cherry liqueur with notes of cinnamon, cloves & nutmeg. My cousin had sent me some from Portugal recently and I gave an extra bottle to Lola when she graduated. She's always loved finding new recipes and remedies.

"And me?" Celestino asked, butting in. We both turned to look at him.

"Girl's only," we both said before dissolving into a fit of giggles. He rolled his eyes at us and slipped a hand around my waist.

"Well we still have places to go. We'll see you around," Celestino said, pulling me away. Lola bounced up and down excitedly. I glanced back at her and she sent me a wink.

"*Rule 69*," she mouthed.

ONCE OUTSIDE A LIGHT breeze cut through me. The moon was hanging high in the air.

"That was nice of you," Celestino said softly as we walked to Plastered Pixie. I felt my body loosen up. This was exactly what I needed.

"I was just letting her know. Lola has wanted to be a vet since we were kids, remember? She just graduated and this is going to be amazing for her." I smiled, staring at the stars.

They twinkled so bright. I bet the stars weren't lonely. Why would they be? They had so many to keep each other company.

"What's going on in there?" Celestino asked, softly tapping the side of my head. I glanced at him.

"What do you mean?" I questioned. His eyes crinkled at the sides as he smiled. He looked so…at ease.

"Something is worming around in that brain of yours." He gave me a pointed look. I began fidgeting with my hands. Was I always this easy to read?

I chewed the inside of my cheek as we walked. He didn't ask again, instead he gave me time to decide on whether or not I wanted to tell him. But I felt like I could share my thoughts with him. It was easy with him, like breathing.

"The stars," I blurted out. He cocked his head to the side.

"The stars?" he asked, slightly confused. I took a deep breath and tightened my jacket around me. My brain was always swimming with thoughts. Half of the time I just kept them to myself.

"They all shine in the sky. Sometimes we can see them and sometimes we can't. Do they still shine even if we can't see them? Do they feel sad when no one notices them? Do they feel lonely even though there are a thousand of them around?" I felt my cheeks heat at my confession. Maybe I saw myself in the stars. Always around, always noticeable but never feeling *seen*.

Celestino took a moment to ponder before responding. I felt my heart opening up as he spoke.

"The stars shine even if no one notices because they can't help but shine. And sure not everyone might see them for what they are but there are some people who do," he said, grabbing my elbow gently. "You, yourself, are willing to think about them. That's more than enough. And do they feel lonely? Probably. Sometimes we all do. Just remember you do have people in your corner. Okay," he said.

I felt tears prick my eyes. I did want to be seen. I wanted to be seen by Celestino. I nodded, taking a step closer to him as we walked. He smiled tenderly.

THE PLASTERED PIXIE was in full swing as we came up to it. It was a building, covered in vines. A bright glowing pink neon sign hung above the door. As we opened the door, the smell of sugar and strawberries carried us towards the bar.

Plastered Pixie was a sweet tooth's heaven. The floors were checkered and each wall was a different pastel color. Basically it was like the candy land board game threw up inside. The trunk of an old pine tree sat in the middle of the bar wrapped with lights and surrounded by bean bags. Behind the bar was Pearl.

"You guys," she called in a high pitched voice. She had strawberry blonde curly hair and her eyes were a bright blue. She was decked out in a poodle skirt that was so short the 1950s would faint. I grinned widely.

"Hey Pearl," I said. Celestino offered me to sit first and I saw Pearl's eyes assessing him. A shot of envy popped up while she boldly checked him out.

"Pearl long time no see," Celestino said. His voice sounded a bit too flirty for my tastes. I stuffed the green feeling to the back of my mind. He wasn't flirting with her. We've only been here for two seconds and even if he was he could. We're not together.

Because you didn't answer the dare, my mind chastised me.

"We're here to try the signature cocktail for the bar crawl. Gotta make sure it doesn't have too much of an effect," I said, making sure to keep my tone even.

"You wouldn't believe the trouble they've been causing," he said. Pearl leaned onto the bar. Strangely this reminded me when we were at Siren's Saloon. I noticed there was some tension with him and Sailor.

"Ooh trouble," she said mischievously. I looked away, feeling awkward as Pearl flirted with him. "I'll be right back ya'll," she said, twirling away. It's been so long since I felt like a third wheel. It was a feeling I was used to with Eleanor but it's been years since I felt that way around Celestino.

"Posey, are you okay?" he asked. I plastered a smile.

"Absolutely. Just getting a bit tired. I may have tried a bit too hard at darts," I said. Celestino looked at me skeptically.

"You nearly shot me," he pointed out.

"It was an accident," I exclaimed. He snorted. Pearl twirled back to us.

"Here it is folks! Love Potion #1. Prince Not Included." The pixie waggled her eyebrows at both of us. The drink was a pretty light pink color that was drenched with sparkly dust that made it glow. I could smell the hint of raspberry and lemonade. Oh, I was going to like this one.

"I find that princes turn to frogs more often," I muttered. Celestino raised an eyebrow.

"I'd make a great prince," he said confidently, tapping my glass with his. I let out a laugh.

"You're the 'riding on the white horse in shining armor' type," I teased. Taking a sip of the drink I let the tart flavors wash over me. The drink was the perfect combination of sweet and sour. This was dangerous. I could easily have four more. I squinted in thought. "Wait, you're more like Chris Pine in Princess Diaries 2," I said. "The first half of the movie when he's annoying," I quickly clarified. Celestino chuckled into his drink.

"What's wrong with the second half of the movie?" His eyes glowed with something that had me flushing.

"This is good," I said, trying to change the subject.

"I like the balance of sweet and sour," he said.

"Yes! That's what I was thinking!"

He grinned. The bar was filled with people mainly occupying tables for hangover snacks like mozzarella sticks and chicken wings. I noticed a cute couple in a corner. Upon further staring I realized it was a vampire and a siren. Both of them were very pretty. They were talking closely with each other, sharing words and smiling. I felt a tightness in my chest.

"They're so cute. I wonder how long they've been together," I said absentmindedly. I couldn't stop my mind from wandering into the realms of 'what ifs.' I wonder what it was like to love someone who wholeheartedly cares for you despite your flaws. To love someone who accepts you for you and helps you grow into the best version of yourself; someone who doesn't make you feel small.

But sometimes love felt awkward. It requires you to lay everything out and I rather stay hidden underneath a blanket.

Watching other families, other relationships always felt like a puzzle I couldn't figure out. Like my piece never quite fit. I dated, but I always struggled to show my affection or the right amount of it.

According to my past, every emotion I emoted was either too much or nonexistent. I constantly worried about too many things. I was either too busy or too needy.

Honestly, it was such a headache trying to be everything. Even with Eleanor and Lola there had been moments where I had to force myself to be present, smiling, making eye contact.

Celestino interrupted my thoughts. "I bet they just met tonight," he said. I swirled to look at him.

"No way! Look how cozy they're being," I said. His arm was around her chair, they were both leaning into each other. The siren's cheeks were pink and the vampire's eyes were practically sparkling. They shared words and laughter. Celestino scoffed.

"They could be both looking for a hookup." He took a sip of his drink, smirking.

I bit my cheek. He was probably right. The hopeless romantic side of me was peeking out. I could never have a one night stand. I tried once in college but there were too many issues. The negatives outweigh the positives and so it didn't work out.

Celestino took a sip of his drink. "I bet he had a good pick up line. Especially since she's a siren. It's hard to get their attention."

I raised an eyebrow. "Experience?" I asked. He shrugged his shoulders.

"College was an interesting time," he said. Did Celestino have a hard time? I couldn't imagine that. He was handsome, kind and obviously had a great six pack. And the tattoos? Stars, his tattoos replayed in my head constantly.

"A good pick up line?" I asked, curiously. He nodded. I sat up straighter and turned to face him. "Tell me your best," I stated.

A part of me wanted him to flirt with me again. I liked being the center of his focus. He set his drink down. With his hand back on his chin he gave me a toothy grin, stealing my heart.

He cleared his throat. "Do you like raisins? How do you feel about a date?" he asked. I tried to keep my face neutral but I could feel a laugh bubbling up.

"The Great Celestino Nuno Santos chooses that as his pick up line? Also I don't like raisins, remember," I teased. He mocked a gasp.

"I'll have you know that the line worked on Beatriz in the 6th grade," he said.

"That was weak." I rolled my eyes, taking a sip.

He scoffed. "Well, show me your best, Posey," he challenged. Excitement coursed through me. This was going to be fun. I took a sip of my drink to mentally prepare myself. I met his green gaze.

"If I could rearrange the alphabet, I'd put 'U' and 'I' together." Unlike me Celestino didn't hold back his laughter.

"That was corny," he said.

"Corny is cute," I stated.

"I have another one," he said. Apparently it was going to be the battle of cheesy pick up lines. He smoothed his hand over his shirt and I glanced at the tattoo that was peeking again.

"Feel my shirt. Know what it's made of? Boyfriend material," he said confidently. I set my drink down and leaned over. My knees were cradled by his. I placed my hand on his shirt like he asked, my thumb lightly grazing over his exposed skin. I felt his heartbeat pick up. A bolt of awareness ran through my spine.

His heart raced from my touch.

"I think it's your turn Posey," he said, his voice sounding strained. I glided my eyes from his chest, up his neck, past his lips and to his eyes. At this distance they seemed more hazel. The golden brown was seeping from his pupils to bleed into the green. My hand dropped to his thigh.

"Just call me Nemo….'cause I wanna' touch your butt," I said. He fought back a grin. Keeping my gaze, his hand reached over to grab his drink.

Over his glass he whispered, "Can I call you beauty? 'Cause I'd like to introduce you to my beast." He held my eyes, waiting for my response. I froze. One part of me wanted to giggle, the other wanted to slide my hand over his cock and follow through with his line. My eyes slid down to watch his neck move as he drank. My body began feeling warm and my magic resurfacing sluggishly, seeking him out like usual.

"Is that a lightsaber in your pants or are you excited to see me," I said without thinking. His eyes widened and I swear his pupils dilated.

He placed his hand on top of mine and he tightened his legs to keep mine trapped. His chest was rising and falling faster than before. Celestino leaned closer.

I felt time freeze. All the noise faded into the background. His lips held my attention. A dusty rose and the bottom slightly full. They were begging for a kiss. I *needed* to kiss him, to feel his lips claim me. I needed him to make me forget my worries by dragging me into the nearest corner.

"Rule seven?" he questioned.

Don't start what you can't finish. That was the rule and here we were teasing each other with pick up lines. We were once again tempting fate. We were like the ocean, pulling and pushing away from each other constantly. Maybe I was tired of pulling away. I swallowed and began leaning in.

"My friends!" A familiar voice interrupted us. We snapped away from each other.

"Fun fact grizzly polar bear hybrids exist," I blurted out.

Pearl slapped her hand on her face and Eleanor bursted into a fit of giggles. Why did my best friend choose now of all times to interrupt us? Celestino glared at Eleanor.

"Nice timing, Eleanor," he muttered. I felt my face get hot. Now that we were pulled apart I felt my thoughts becoming clear. There must have been something in the drinks. Maybe it was a good thing we didn't kiss. *Yet.*

"Pearl, I think you added a bit too much pearl dust," Eleanor suggested.

"I don't know what you mean," Pearl said innocently, spinning away to the end of the bar. Eleanor shook her head at her. She wrapped her arm around me.

"So how's it going you guys?" she asked. Chewing my lip I decided to state the facts.

"It's been interesting." Which was the truth. The night had been fun, a little wild and kind of gross. By the look on Eleanor's face I could see she knew there was more to what I was letting on. She smirked.

"Have you done anything I would do absolutely sober?" she asked. I rolled my eyes.

"I don't think we've reached that point yet," Celestino said. Eleanor punched his shoulder. "Actually I've found out that I'm not Prince Charming but Chris Pine from Princess Diaries 2," he said with a smirk.

"The first half," I said quickly. Eleanor smiled wickedly.

"You mean the movie that you watch religiously every year because you absolutely adore him," she snickered. I wanted the floor to open up and swallow me whole or for an ogre to carry me away.

"Oh rea-"

"Karaoke," I shouted before Celestino could finish his sentence. They both laughed as I dragged them out the door.

CHAPTER 15

LET'S GET TIPSY PRT. 3

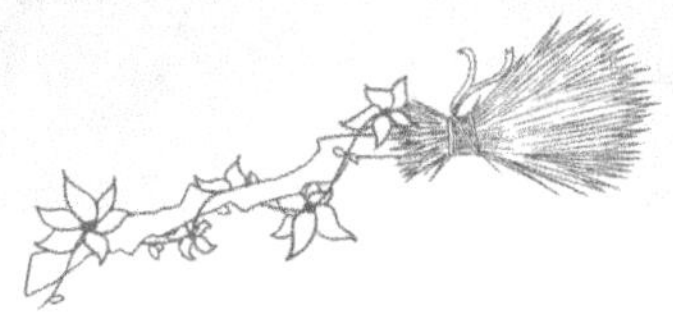

The Drunken Fairy Tale Tavern was in full swing. Everyone was drunkenly singing and dancing. I loved watching people be happy. Their infectious mood easily slipped into my bloodstream. I felt the bundle of nerves and anxiety that had been threatening to resurface slowly fade to the background again. Celestino pushed his way through the bar. Eleanor and I followed behind. I marveled at the way he commanded himself. It was hot.

Squeezing our way to the bar, I noticed that Caleb, Bridget and Flynn were manning the fort. The elf siblings were swinging bottles and sliding drinks. It was always amazing to watch them work. They were constantly in sync. It was a wonder how they never crashed into each other.

Eleanor sat on the bar stool, hand in her chin, looking bored. I smiled. It was always fun to watch her play cat and mouse with Caleb. I noticed Caleb's pale blue eyes glance quickly at Eleanor. I made a mental note on how he did a double take. His gaze slid over her face and down to take in her lime green top. I swore I saw him take a deep breath.

"Your hair is pink," he stated, not meeting her eyes.

"Nice to know your vision works," she said, pretending to sound uninterested. Her eyes glanced around the room. At that moment Caleb peeked at her again. This was always my favorite pastime. Watching them go back and forth.

"Your starter shot," he stated, giving her a shot first. Their gazes met and my heart squeezed. It was so obvious. I wondered why Caleb was being so stubborn.

"Nice to know you remember," she said, taking it. He snorted.

"Not hard when you have a routine."

Eleanor hummed in appreciation and the corner of Caleb's lips perked.

"Well you guys do have the best-" she started, but stopped when a plate of monster-ella sticks appeared in front of her. Eleanor broke out in a wide grin. Caleb turned to Celestino and I.

"Two Crone's Curses please. Gotta' try it for the bar crawl," I said over the music. He nodded silently and got to work. Celestino tapped my shoulder.

"Hey, I'll be right back," he said. I nodded silently and he squeezed my hand. We were standing close again. His eyes were bright with excitement. I watched him disappear into the crowd.

Eleanor waved a cheese stick in front of my face. I giggled, taking it. The cheesy greasiness warmed my body. The Drunken Fairy Tale Tavern really did have the best cheese sticks.

"I might have to start making my own rules," she huffed. I raised an eyebrow.

"Celestino and I have rules to keep us on track with work…mainly. What you want is the opposite." I bumped her shoulder. Eleanor rolled her eyes, throwing back her shot. She furrowed her brows.

"Is what I want really all that different from what you want?" she asked. Caleb placed the crone curses in front of me.

"Rules wouldn't work on you because you would purposely break them," he said before walking away. Eleanor sat with her mouth hanging slightly open.

"I didn't know anyone could shut you up," I said laughing.

"I'll just find someone else to cure my appetite tonight," Eleanor stated, scanning the crowd.

"Who are we thinking?" I asked, immediately slipping into my wingwoman persona. I glanced at Caleb. He tensed, the veins in his hands popping out as he poured the cachaça into a glass for Eleanor.

"I just need someone to make out with for a bit," she said tapping her chin. "Someone with nice lips," she said, her voice rising. I sat back, trying to keep my composure. Like clockwork, Caleb popped up with her drink.

"Drink," he grunted. She smiled sweetly.

"Thanks." Turning her back to Caleb, Eleanor pointed to a werewolf in the back. "I've always had a thing for werewolves. Something about their dominant nature just gets my blood pumping."

I knew she was well aware that Caleb was still behind her. He was staring at the werewolf with murderous intent. Then he did something Eleanor and I were not expecting.

Caleb leaned over the bar, his hand on the back of Eleanor's neck. I heard her take a quick breath, her cheeks immediately reddened. He leaned into her ear. I felt incredibly awkward to be watching all of this.

"Leave with that werewolf and I'm never going to kiss you."

Our eyes widened. I could see Eleanor was itching to break into a smile. She quickly looked at me, eyes lit up with excitement. She tried to turn her head to the side to look at him.

"Were you ever going to?" she asked, her voice soft.

"Stay after we close," he said and turned to walk away.

Holy stars, were they finally happening? Where the fuck was Celestino? Another bolt of electricity shot through me. My eyes found him and I felt a familiar rush go up my spine. Celestino looked at me, a smile hanging off his face. He was so painfully handsome and I wasn't the only one noticing him as a few people casted glances at him.

"What did I miss?" he asked, looking between us confused.

"Just Caleb and Eleanor being Caleb and Eleanor," I said cheekily. He looked over at Caleb who was mixing drinks.

"Rule seven?" he asked. I elbowed him, giggling.

"Rule seven is don't start what you can't finish. And clearly I will be tonight, at least one way or another," Eleanor said pointedly.

"Maybe you'll get to rule 69," I teased. Eleanor shook her head and left to go dancing. Celestino took her bar seat.

"Rule 69? Did I miss when we made the first 68?" he asked, raising an eyebrow.

My face burned like hellfire. I handed him his drink. Hopefully because Caleb was behind making the drink we wouldn't have any strange side effects.

Taking a breath, we both tapped the glasses. This drink was a mixture of lemonade and apple. Delicious. We waited a few minutes, sipping our drinks as we watched the people around us enjoy themselves. Celestino leaned towards my ear.

"Feeling normal," he said. I nodded. Thank the stars for Caleb. The host of karaoke interrupted the music.

"Come on ghosts, ghouls and heathens. Sign up for killer karaoke now!"

I jumped in my stool. "Shots," I called out, waving to Flynn. Flynn was Caleb's younger brother. He had dirty blonde shaggy hair and brown eyes that screamed '90s heartthrob.

"Are you really going to do karaoke?" Celestino asked. Flynn set out three shots. One for Celestino, Eleanor and I. Before I could respond we raised our glasses.

"To the stars above and monsters below!" We cheered together. His face was pinched as he swallowed. I smiled. Guess he wasn't a fan of tequila.

"I always do karaoke when I go out," I said, feeling myself loosen up. A group of vampire girls drunkenly made their way to the DJ. *'Evacuate the Dancefloor'* began bumping throughout the bar. Eleanor magically appeared.

"That's our song," Eleanor said and grabbed my arm to drag us to dance. We both swayed to the beat of the music. Eleanor bumped her hip against mine.

"How are you feeling?" she asked.

"Happy," I shouted. Eleanor smiled. She was just grateful that I was out and not home buried in blankets with my laptop and so was I. I needed a reminder to let go and enjoy life. Eleanor wrapped her arms around my neck as we danced.

My eyes found Celestino who was chatting to Caleb. Caleb actually cracked a smile. Celestino pushed a loose strand of hair behind his ear. My heart thumped as I stared at my best friend. We watched each other grow through the good and the bad. From learning to read spells and braces.

There was so much history between us. What if by giving into our history, it gets torn apart? Could I risk that? His gaze turned to me and immediately softened. I felt my heart squeezed. Why did his eyes do that? Why did he have the uncanny ability to ease my mind, make my magic sing and my body flush? It was scary.

For the first time in a long time, Celestino awoke something in me. It was a feeling I wasn't sure I could trust but might possibly risk for him. I twirled around so my back faced him. I was afraid of what would happen if I kept looking in his eyes. Afraid he might see how much I wanted something deeper with him but was too scared.

"So how's the date been so far?" Eleanor asked in my ear.

"It's not a date. It's a work thing," I hissed back. Eleanor rolled her eyes.

"Okay. Work thing. But how is it? You guys seem to be enjoying yourselves." Eleanor gave me a hopeful look. I glanced at her feet.

"What if it ruins things? What if it makes things awkward? What if it turns out to be a mistake?" Eleanor waited for me to finish my nervous rambling. "Things feel…different between us," I confessed. That was the only word I could think of to encapsulate whatever was going on between us.

"Is it a good different?" Eleanor asked carefully. I met her eyes this time. I nodded, hesitantly. Eleanor squealed so loud a few heads turned to look at them. The feelings I have now felt different from when we were kids. They were slowly becoming bigger, like a hot air balloon rising. But I wasn't sure if I could trust them to not break my heart. A hot air balloon will come down at some point, won't it?

"You know what this means?" My pixie best friend was practically floating.

"What?" I asked, hesitating.

"Duet," she squealed even louder. I threw my arm around her shoulders.

"I'm down. Which song?" I asked. Eleanor's eyes slid over to where the men were chatting.

"Something to grab their attention." She tapped her chin. I glanced back at Celestino who raised his glass in my direction. I waved at him.

"Let's do *Wannabe by Spice Girls*." Eleanor declared and dragged me to the DJ booth. She leaned over to tell DJ Fantasy which song. My eyes wandered back to Celestino who had a big grin while watching. My stomach twisted in knots.

I felt Eleanor tugging me on stage. DJ Fantasy handed us each a mic. I stared at the screen, letting the beat of the music seep into my bones. I turned to the the words on the screen and forced myself to focus on the song and not the hot warlock at the bar.

I couldn't stop staring. How could I? The witch on stage was a completely different person. She wasn't the shy girl I grew up with who kept her nose buried in her laptop and books. Or the woman who always seemed to teetered on the edge. No. On stage, belting *if you wanna get with me, better make it fast,* she was confident and carefree. Then there was her voice.

I forgot how beautiful her voice was. Like a siren's call. Lilianna captured every single person in this bar. Her eyes met mine and I swore her smile got bigger. I felt compelled to walk out to the dance floor and wrap my arms around her. It was then I noticed *everyone's* eyes on the girls. A sea of green coursed through my veins. Caleb leaned over the bar.

"Are you good?" he asked, smirking. My face heated and my magic was buzzing. I glanced over at Caleb who was clearly watching Eleanor.

"Are you ready for the after hours shenanigans," I teased back. Caleb choked on his water. When the girls left to the dance floor he confessed what he said to Eleanor. Apparently he just couldn't stand the thought of her with the werewolf so he said the first thing that came to his head. Though I think it was with his other head.

Everyone clapped in a round of applause and Lilianna had one of the biggest smiles on her face. It was like my whole world tilted and she was the center holding me up. She was my moon, keeping my gravity centered. This was it. She *was* it. I knew at this moment I was going to do whatever it took to get her to smile like that again and always.

The girls came stumbling to the bar, asking for another drink. Lilianna threw her arms around my neck and squeezed. I wrapped my arms around her, savoring the feel of our bodies. My cock twitched in my pants. She pulled back smiling, her eyes darting to my mouth. My hands tightened on her hips and I wanted to rock her against me, desperately.

"Isn't she amazing," Eleanor said, bouncing up and down. Lilianna quickly pulled back and looked away, sliding into the bar stool I had kept open for her. My hands twitched to bring her back into my arms.

"Phenomenal," I said. Lilianna looked at me, fighting to keep her smile at bay.

"Are you sure you're not a siren, little witch?" I asked, staring at her intently. I couldn't stop myself from flirting with her tonight. Lilianna laughed.

"Are we back to doing pick up lines?" Her brown eyes glimmered wickedly. I leaned in slightly.

"Would they even work on you?" I asked. My eyes narrowed at her as if trying to analyze her. Which I was. I was gauging her reaction. I wanted to know how much I could push her. She tilted her head back and forth.

"I like them fictionally, not sure about reality," she said. I cocked my head to the side.

"Your romance books?"

I knew this was going to call for a punishment but by her hand I was more than willing to constantly break the rules. She gasped loudly, hitting me on the shoulder lightly.

"Rule," she exclaimed. "Well, Wicked Warlock of The East, truth or dare?" she asked. I felt nervous all of a sudden. I wasn't sure if it was the amount of alcohol I've consumed or my magic mingling with hers.

"Dare," I said. A part of me hoped she would dare me to kiss her or something. I would gladly do it in front of all these people. But I wasn't expecting what actually came out of her pretty lips.

"I dare you to do karaoke."

Fuck.

Her smile was pure magic and was absolutely going to make me sing in front of a drunk crowd.

"Me?" I asked in shock.

"Yes," she said, pointing to the stage.

"Me? Up there?" My nerves spiked. A smirk curved across her face. She leaned over and the smell of the ocean filled my senses. She batted her eyes innocently.

"Are you afraid?" she asked. I glanced at her lips before looking in her eyes. She was baiting me.

"Afraid of what?" I asked, bringing myself closer.

"Afraid of a challenge?" She cocked her head to the side. She *was* flirting with me. Oh stars, I fucking loved this side of her. The urge to wrap myself around her was nearing the edge. I needed to touch her. I reached out to wrap one of her waves around my finger.

"I think we both know I'm not afraid." My gaze flickered back to her lips. I licked my bottom lip. Her gaze went to my lips. She wanted to kiss me. Needed too. I could see it in her eyes, feel it as she trembled slightly.

Fuck, if I didn't get a grip I was going to-

"If y'all are gonna kiss can we get some shots first. Caleb! Hit me!" Eleanor slurred slightly, breaking our spell. Both of us backed away from each other. This was the second time Eleanor cockblocked me tonight. I was beginning to believe she didn't want us together. I glared at her. Lilianna cleared her throat.

"Don't you mean hit on me Caleb," Lilianna snickered. Eleanor laughed.

"That's what I've been doing," she said, tossing her hair back.

Caleb poured three shots. "Is that what you call it? Hitting on me?" Despite his stoic face there was a warm glow in his eyes.

"There is more I would like to do," she muttered. Eleanor threw the shot back and walked away, straight into the arms of the random were- wolf. A tick worked in Caleb's jaw as he stared at them dancing. I grabbed my shot and glanced at Lilianna.

"What did we just witness?" I asked in disbelief. I couldn't keep up with their banter. Lilianna laughed. I still wasn't used to their constant back and forth. Caleb was quiet in college and never seemed to have any sort of romantic relationship.

"We just saw some high quality sexual tension. Come on, shots, Mr. Wicked Warlock." She tapped my glass again. I rolled my eyes before letting the burning liquid slither down my throat into the pit of my stomach. She smiled at me.

"If I do this, what do I get in return?" I asked. She stared at me in shock.

"One, that's not what we agreed with the rules. Two, I already went up on stage and three, I lost the bet at Highwaymen Haunt. I say you're winning." She was technically right but I couldn't help but be greedy. I needed more. I smiled.

"What if it's something simple?" I asked. She looked skeptical. I was working on something and she could see it.

"Simple?" she asked tentatively. I nodded. She grabbed her earlobe, debating.

"Fine. Now go before I change my mind," she said. I slapped the bar, leaned over and kissed her cheek quickly. Her eyes widened as a faint blush stained her cheeks. Lilianna laughed, shaking her head. I was grinning as I made my way to the stage. Going through the binder of songs I decided to sing, *Put Some Sugar On Me.*

Despite the fact I couldn't sing for shit I was too tipsy to even care. I pointed to her before sliding my hand down my chest to my stomach. Lilianna followed the movement. As I kept singing, my gaze never wavered from hers and she didn't look away despite everyone casting glances at her. The crowd started clapping and hollering.

I was probably going to regret this tomorrow along with the shots. But I was high on the crowd, the atmosphere and her. Lilianna wrapped her arms around herself to keep from falling out of her stool in laughter. When the song ended I practically ran to the bar.

"That…was..wow," I tried getting out. Lilianna wiped her eyes.

"That was amazing," she yelled over the drums of some '80s song.

"I can see why you do it." I smiled at her.

"Nothing like singing songs in front of a slightly intoxicated crowd. They don't care whether you sound good or bad. They're just there for a good time," Lilianna said as she quickly scanned for Eleanor who was still dancing with the werewolf.

"I went up and opened my mouth and next thing you know the song is over and the crowd is cheering." I felt like I was on cloud nine. My heart was pounding. She beamed at me but I noticed something. Her breathing had slowed and her shoulders were relaxed. Her eyes had drooped down a bit. The high of the night was slipping away and being replaced by exhaustion. She waved at Flynn and he handed her a glass of water.

"Drink," she said. I raised an eyebrow. "You're not a fan of tequila I presume. Drink some water," she said. I smiled, taking the glass from her.

"Are you ready to call it a night?" I asked. She looked up at me in surprise.

"Well, are you? I'm fine if you want to stay a bit longer," she said looking over at Eleanor who was making her way back. After taking a drink of water I offered her the cup. She nodded, taking a sip as she waved at Eleanor.

"I'm fine too but it's been a long day and we've gone through a lot of magical beverages," I said. She almost sighed in relief. I enjoyed being able to read her. She was my favorite book and with each chapter I was learning something new about my best friend. She nodded, turning to Caleb who had a new basket of monster-ella sticks.

"Caleb, can I pay?" she asked. Caleb eyed me.

"He took care of it," he said, pointing to me.

"What?" Lilianna turned to face me. "How much was it? I'll cover Eleanor's," she said, reaching for her wallet.

"Cover for me?" Eleanor asked, appearing next to Lilianna.

"It's fine guys," I said.

"You didn't have to do that!" Both Lilianna and Eleanor said. I chuckled.

"I got to spend some quality time with my best friends. My treat."

The girls exchanged glances.

"Come on Posey. Let's get you home," I said, tugging at her waist. She nodded and reached to hug Eleanor.

"You killed it. We have to do karaoke again as a group," Eleanor said excitedly.

"Oh, I'm totally down," I agreed. I leaned over to shake Caleb's hand.

"Don't forget chapstick," I heard her whisper into Eleanor's ear. Eleanor waggled her eyebrows.

"You too," Eleanor said. I bit back a smile. Maybe my little match-maker pixie friend wasn't a cockblocker. Lilianna blushed a deeper shade of pink and my heart skipped. Eleanor sat at the bar and began munching on her cheese sticks. I glanced at Caleb who was watching Eleanor before turning to the woman who stole my heart. She smiled at me and offered her hand.

I took it, happily walking out into the fall air.

CHAPTER 16

ALMOST IS NEVER TOO MUCH

Autumn was in full swing. Lilianna was looking up at the sky. It was getting close to a full moon which meant it was almost time for the festival. She smiled at the stars with a slight shiver.

Tonight was amazing. In the city, I was always racing to catch the last train. I was surrounded by noise and people. It was suffocating. But here everything was open, relaxed. I felt more like me. I walked in step with her, close enough that my body heat warmed her.

"Can I tell you a secret?" I asked. She looked at me. "Caleb covered Eleanor's part," I said. A cheeky grin appeared on Lilianna's face.

"I knew it," she said. "I swear the day they get together…" she trailed off, spinning in the middle of the sidewalk.

"Looks like someone is happy," I said, grinning. She rolled her eyes, walking in front of me backwards so she could keep eye contact.

"You have no idea what I deal with every time those two are in the same room. It's nauseating but also adorable," she said. I felt a swell of warmth. I was glad I came back, surrounded by people I love. I was happy to be around Lilianna again.

"Can I ask something?" I asked. A nervous look flashed across her face. I placed my hands in my pockets to hide the tremor. "You care so much for other people's happiness. You always have. But what about yours?"

Her eyes widened and her shoe got caught on a crack. She began falling backwards. I reached out to grab her. I pulled her into my chest. The smell of sea salt and lavender cocooned me. Her hands tightened on my arms as I stared at her, waiting for an answer.

"Why?" I asked softly. She stared at her hand gripping my arm. She bit her lip.

"If they're happy, I'm happy. I like making people happy," she said carefully. The pad of my thumb tilted her chin lower, forcing our eyes to connect.

"If you're so busy making sure everyone is happy, who is making sure you're happy?" My question slipped out. Lilianna looked conflicted. Her warm brown eyes were filled with so many emotions. Sadness, exhaustion, worry and annoyance.

"I'm plenty happy," she stated.

"Posey, why do you hide?" I asked. She looked at me sharply.

"Hide?" she asked, confused.

"You're hiding," I stated. Her nostrils flared. She didn't like my question. She pushed away from me and I regretted the words. I wanted her back in my arms.

"It's not hiding," she said. I cringed at her sudden change in demeanor. I struck a nerve. She turned to walk down the street and I trailed behind her.

"Yes. You're doing it now. Why are you turning away from me?"

"I'm not running away from you. I'm just selective," she mumbled as she hurried down the street. I quickened my steps to keep up with her.

"What do you mean," I pushed on. She was running away and I needed to know why. She shook her head. "I want to know," I stated. This felt almost messy. Our emotions, words and boundaries were intertwining. She had walls up and I don't remember her ever having walls with me. Lilianna bit her lip. "Please," I said softly. She huffed.

"It's not hiding…exactly. I'm just uncomfortable," she confessed. I grabbed her arm to slow her down.

"Why?" I asked. How do I make this better? How do I make her trust me?

"This conversation," she said. She stopped at a red light.

"Why," I repeat gently, not wanting her to run away again. She sighed. We both knew I wasn't going to give up.

"Because I've had these types of conversations in the past and they never end well. I don't want that to happen to us. I'm worried about saying the wrong thing and it creating a rift between us. I'm afraid if I say something you'll say I'm being dramatic or weird," she said, squeezing her hands.

I felt my throat tighten at her confession. There were tears in her eyes. She couldn't even look at me and it made my heart bleed.

Lilianna had always been more of an introvert in our group but I never saw anything wrong with that and yet someone made her feel like it was something to be ashamed of. They didn't see the beauty in knowing someone who feels deeper than others. To have a woman whose heart was as big as a giant and with emotions like that they needed to be handled with care.

"The only thing you should worry about is saying how you feel. Letting me know what's going on in that head of yours so I can understand you better. That way there won't be a rift," I said. My hands turned into fists.

"Have I ever made you feel that way? Like you were weird or something?" I asked. My stomach twisted as I tried to think about our childhood. She let out a sad chuckle. *Fuck.*

"You and Eleanor never outright made me feel that way," she said. "It was more like I realized I wasn't as outgoing as you both and a part of me felt guilty I couldn't be that way. Sometimes I felt like I couldn't keep up with everyone around me." She paused to take a breath.

"But as I grew up I realized that it's okay. We all have our own way of seeing and living in this world." She looked at the stars and then at me, her honey eyes shining. "I remind you to look at the stars and you remind me to dance under them," she said.

This witch. She owned my soul. She constantly gave so much to everyone.

But not anymore. I was back and I planned to give her everything she needed and more. She deserved it.

"Okay," was all I could say. She looked at me, surprised.

"That's it?" she asked tentatively. I offered a sheepish smile.

"Yes. I just wanted to understand you more." Lilianna was different from the quiet bookworm I left at 18. She had more fire in her, more confidence. But her worries had increased. I wanted to ease them in any way I could. We crossed the street towards her building

"Okay," she said quietly. I walked her up to her building's door. "Thanks for walking me to my place."

"Of course. You're going to go to the library next week?" I asked. She sighed.

"Yeah, probably Thursday. I have the day off," she said absent-mindedly. I took a step towards her and she tensed up. My hand grazed her cheek to tuck a strand of frizzy hair behind her ear. Her hair had poofed up during our bar crawl and it was adorable.

"Can I cash in on the karaoke?" I asked. I kept my voice low. My hand cradled her jaw. She looked into my eyes.

"Yes," she whispered.

"Next time something feels too much or too of anything, tell me."

"Next time?" She hesitated. I smiled.

"Yes," I whispered. She took a deep breath, pulling my hand off of her face. The warmth slowly began to fade and I ached to reach for her again. She held my hand, staring at it as if it was the most fragile thing in the world which it wasn't. With her I felt invincible. Then she wrapped her pinky around mine and looked at me.

"You saying something like that is almost too much," she confessed.

"Almost?" I asked. She nodded. "We'll work on that."

"I pinky promise to tell you next time," she whispered, leaning to kiss her thumb. Keeping her gaze, I did the same. With a tap of our thumbs and a tiny squeeze we let go. I watched her step inside.

As I turned to walk away there was one thought running through my brain. She didn't turn away from me this whole night. She relaxed with every graze of my hands and lips. I glanced at my hand. There was a small ember of hope forming between us and I refused to let it be extinguished.

CHAPTER 17

BEHIND BOOKSHELVES

"Sip and spill," I told Eleanor. We were at Coffin's Coffee Shop. We barely had a chance to talk since Saturday. We both had deadlines to reach with the festival getting closer and Lola was working hard teaching the flying goats to do tricks on the ground. Eleanor sighed as Lola and I eyed each other.

"Nothing," she grumbled.

"What," Lola and I said at the same time. Eleanor waved at us as people casted looks in our direction. I was secretly hoping she was going to say we had the steamiest make out session and he asked me out on a date.

"Tell us everything." Lola demanded, taking a bite of her sandman sugar cookie.

"Well I was helping him clean up because I am a pixie that was raised with manners for the most part. We kept eyeing each other the whole time. The anticipation building. But guess what," Eleanor said. She was tired. I could see it in her eyes.

Eleanor's eyes had a tendency to change colors depending on her mood and right now her left eye, which was typically green, was more hazel.

"We met at the bar after cleaning up. He was like right in front of me. His hand, which was warm and a little rough, slipped to cup my cheek. At this point my heart is pounding. I've been waiting for this moment," she continued.

I was on the edge of my seat. What could have possibly stopped the two from kissing? Did the speaker combust into flames? Did a baby griffin escape from Fauny's Farm again? Lola and I clasped hands and leaned closer in anticipation.

"He leans in. Guys, his lips are so irritatingly close to mine. His mouth brushes my cheek, making my body go all tingly. I swore I was ready to explode into pixie dust. He keeps going up, teasing me. *Edging* me. Then he reaches my ear and whispers, our first kiss won't be in the middle of a bar and not because you demanded it," she said, imitating his gruff voice. Lola snorted and I broke into a wide grin. Of course Caleb would do this. "And then I asked, so we *will* kiss? Because clearly that statement is suggesting that we will. And this insanely aggravating hot elf says to me...," she trailed off, making us lean forward. "We will when the time is right. And then he just walked away!"

We bursted into laughter. Caleb was playing hard to get and despite that, Eleanor's face was bright pink and she had a giant grin.

"And you loved that didn't you?" Lola asked her.

"Of course. The way he just told me what to do? It was so hot. For like five seconds that whole conversation made every single thought I had in my head vanish. I wasn't thinking about work, my family, nothing," Eleanor said, leaning back in a huff. Caleb loved teasing Eleanor the same way Celestino kept teasing me

The thought made me remember our last conversation. He had been so open with me, patient and kind. It was scary. He just accepted me. I took a sip of my latte, shaking my head in disbelief.

"Anyway, did you two kiss? How was the walk?" Eleanor asked, waggling her eyebrows. Lola turned to me, tucking a braid behind her ear.

"Yes! It's your turn to sip and spill. You guys were very cozy when you left Highwaymen Haunt," Lola said with a smirk. I shook my head and gave them a low down of the whole night including the bet.

"Honestly, I'm not surprised," Lola said.

"I agree," Eleanor joined.

"Really?" I asked.

"Well, yeah. Celestino has always been the type to pay attention to everything. Why do you think he's so successful at planning events," Eleanor said, giving me a look.

"He notices me," I said softly.

Lola nodded. "He's noticing your walls. Things are different now that we're all adults," Lola chimed in. I groaned into my hands.

"He wants to break them down," I whined slightly.

"And bend you over," Eleanor said, smiling. I gave them a look but then broke out into a small smile.

"Stop putting thoughts into my head," I said.

"Like those thoughts haven't been in your head," Lola scoffed.

"When are you seeing him again?" Eleanor asked. I glanced at my phone. Celestino hadn't contacted me since Saturday. It was a busy week for everyone.

"Well, I lost the bet so I'll be at the library tomorrow," I stated. Eleanor got a wicked gleam in her eyes and Lola began tapping her chin. I knew those looks.

"Lily, does he know you'll be there?" Lola asked. I thought back to that night. Did I tell him? My eyes widened at her sneaky grin. *I did tell him.*

"No, no, no. Just because he knows does not mean it's going to be a scene from one of our romance novels," I rushed out. My face was hot. Actually my whole body was feeling hot at the mere thought of us alone in a dark corner of the library. My mind wandered into being pressed against the fantasy section.

"Funny how we didn't even mention our books and you went ahead and thought about it," Lola teased. Eleanor shook her head.

"There's nothing wrong with thinking about the fact you might be living out one of your favorite fantasies. I'd say go for it. It's been awhile," Eleanor said, taking a sip of her drink.

"I can also tell you're excited because your magic is buzzing around," Lola said with a cheeky grin. I closed my eyes and took deep breaths. She was right. Our drinks shook slightly on the table. There was a slight vibration running up and down under my skin. I needed to calm my body down. I grabbed my bag as we stood up to start our day. As we were walking out Lola and Eleanor started singing, *My Pony.*

"He's not going to show up tomorrow," I said, trying to convince myself more than them.

THE LIBRARY WASN'T busy today. I had picked the table on the second floor all the way in the back, hidden by bookshelves. I didn't want to feel the constant need to look up every time the doors opened. I also needed peace and quiet. I got zero sleep from thinking about what I needed to do today and fantasizing what could happen if Celestino showed up. And yes, I was in the fantasy section. What better area to have fantasies?

So I came into the library at nine, picked all the books I would need before settling into my little nook. My laptop was open, books laid across the table with a few sticky notes on pages that could possibly help. Today's assignment was creating a script for the bar crawl tour guide. I needed to intertwine some history facts while keeping it entertaining.

I had the introduction done when I felt his presence. It was weird the way I sensed the moment he walked in through the doors. My brain and magic were automatically attuned to him at this point. It felt like a trail of sunshine glided from across the room and settled around my shoulders.

The smell of sandalwood and citrus tickled my nose. I kept trying to type as I felt him wander around the library. *Not looking for me of course,* I told myself.

"There you are." His voice was thick with sleep. It felt like gravel against my ears and awoke my body. Was that how he sounded when he woke up? I looked up to see his wavy dark hair was let loose across his shoulders. Was that how he looked when he just woke up? My gaze took in his black hoodie and sweatpants. He had a book bag slung over one shoulder.

"What's that?" I pointed to the bag. I needed something to focus on that wasn't the way his beard was coming in, making the angles of his face sharp and giving him a mysterious bad boy look. I also didn't need to watch him lick his lips before responding but I did anyway. Stupid libido.

"This is fabric that is sewn together to help one carry stuff around so their arms don't get tired," he snickered. I rolled my eyes.

"What are you doing *here*," I stressed, pointing around the room. He pulled out the chair next to me and plopped down.

He shrugged his shoulders. "Just getting some work done. Figured you needed company." He began opening his bag and pulling out his laptop.

"What work?" I asked. I had a feeling he came to help me.

"Oh, forgot something," he said. Quickly he leaned over to graze his lips across my cheek. "Good morning Posey," he whispered in my ear.

My cheek tingled from his lips. A simple brush sent my heart pounding against my chest. His eyes were more green today. They reminded me of pears.

"I like pears," tumbled out of my mouth.

"I'll bring you some next time," he said, still keeping my gaze. Stars, what was wrong with me?

"What work?" I asked again. Looking at him I felt like we were connected by a string that was pulling me towards him. He was close enough I could smell his cologne and feel the warmth of him. It was intoxicating. Instead of responding he continued to stare at me, his eyes trailing all over my face. My eyebrow twitched. Did my breath stink? Was I forgetting something?

Oh.

"Good morning Celestino." I kissed his cheek, mimicking him. His eyes softened. I cleared my throat. "Now, what work?" I asked. With a satisfied smile he leaned away, his warmth escaping.

"I came to help." He began lifting the books I marked and reading the titles.

"But I lost the bet," I pointed out. He rolled his eyes.

"Even the strongest knight of the realm needs a second in command to carry his armor and ready his steed," he said, bringing back his fake British accent. I snorted.

"So you're a knight now and not a prince?" I asked.

"Most princes are both," he said.

"So are you King Arthur?" I asked.

"Will you be my Lady of The Lake?" he asked.

"Not Guinevere?" I questioned.

He grinned. "You would never betray my heart," he said surely. I blushed. He licked his bottom lip and I met his eyes again. I took a deep breath. I could probably kiss him right now and he'd welcome it. He could probably lean me against the book shelf or even this table. He'd help me live out one of my romance book fantasies.

There was a tiny rumble. One of the books in the corner, behind my laptop, began wobbling. *Fuck.* My magic buzzed with excitement. Celestino didn't seem to notice. I just needed to relax before my magic caused something again.

"Male bees only mate once," I blurted out.

"That's very sweet," he said, turning back to the books on the table.

"You can't help me" I said, reaching behind my laptop to grab the book that was making me anxious. Celestino chuckled.

"I'm helping so deal with it. What do you have so far?" he asked. I chewed the inside of my cheek.

"But a bet is a bet," I stated as he opened his laptop.

"I didn't want to use this but, rule six," he said. My mouth hung open.

"R-rule six? What do you mean?" I asked. He smirked.

"You were checking out my mouth," he said. My cheeks flamed.

"I was just looking at your face!" My voice pinched high at the end. He brought his finger to my lips. I was tempted to bite it but he might like that.

"Shh. We're in a library, Posey. It's okay you checked out my mouth. It's very kissable. Now, truth or dare?"

He was smiling and I couldn't help but smile back. He had something up his sleeve. But what? If I go with dare he would probably dare me to let him help. That's what he wanted. If I chose truth he would ask why I was refusing his help. So my choices were to let him help or open up a piece of myself.

Swallowing, I muttered dare. His grin was like Cupid's arrow, shooting straight through my heart. He crossed his arms.

"I *dare* you to let me help you." He pulled his kissable lips into a smirk.

"Fine," I said, trying to hide a smile. I showed him what I had so far. The introduction was a brief history of the town and at each location the leader would give some fun facts about the bars. Spooky and simple.

Lavender Falls was founded a long long time ago by the seven founding families. A family of witches, warlocks, pixies, fairies, vampires and werewolves. At least that's the story. I suspect they just wore a lot of black, didn't shave and maybe that's why people assumed they were of the supernatural kind.

Anyway, they wanted to have a town where everyone was free to be themselves and live in harmony. To the mundanes who have visited Lavender Falls, they say spooky things happen. Things such as fruits that typically don't survive the winter season thrive. Or how you can hear the sound of a carriage riding down the empty street late at night. Sometimes lights flicker even if the power is off. Honestly those things don't seem spooky but there was that one time with a floating pumpkin head.

Everything was going great. We worked in silence and had two bars left to cover in the script when Celestino's thigh brushed against mine. Throughout the whole three hours I had become acutely aware of his breathing. How every thirty minutes he would stretch his back and bring his arms behind me so they would graze my shoulders.

Or how every time he picked up a book he would begin chewing his bottom lip. I hated it all. I hated how my body and mind kept being consumed by him. He was a beautiful distraction.

"Posey, what do you need," he said, breaking the silence. I looked at him but he kept his eyes on the book.

"Nothing," I said, turning away to stare at the words on my laptop. He grunted.

"Correction. Is there anything that you want?"

There was a lot I wanted. To finish today's work, edit a few posts that were scheduled, have Caleb and Eleanor get together and finish my latest book. I also wanted to have my mom be proud, kiss Celestino along with the success of the bar crawl and the festival. I wanted Lola to be one of the head vets at the local clinic. Also the safe delivery of Alex and Thalia's baby. I furrowed my brows. Too many thoughts were filling my brain from a simple question.

"A break," I said. He nodded and closed his book.

"Why don't I grab us some coffee and we take a bit of a break," he suggested. I sighed. Caffeine is just what I needed.

"A latte, please."

He nodded, leaning in to kiss my temple and walked away. I stared around the table. He was becoming more affectionate with me and I felt myself falling for every whisper of a touch. Slowly over the course of a few weeks with him back in my life I was craving more of him. I was thinking of ways to touch him, to be held by him.

Our laptops were squished together, books opened everywhere. The longer I sat to stew in my own thoughts, the more anxious I became. We were doing everything according to schedule.

In theory, I should be relaxed but I couldn't help but feel nervous. I was worried about the success of the crawl and I was becoming more open to giving Celestino a chance.

Rolling my shoulders back I decided to take out my book and read. I could probably get through some chapters while Celestino was away.

I cracked open my book, *The Mafia's Seamstress*. It was a steamy book between a seamstress and the head of the Italian mafia. They had met when the male lead, Dante needed a suit for a fancy gala. While I thought the romance would be between Dante and Lucia, Dante's cousin Luca was worming his way in.

"So I WOULD BE careful with who you throw that pretty smile to." Luca smiled at me and I clenched my thighs. For a man who could kill with his bare hands he had a pretty face.

"Are you including yourself in that," I said without hesitation.

"I'm number two on the list of men you need to watch out for." His voice was rough and I felt myself being pulled by it.

"And who is number one?" I asked as I watched his eyes trace over my face.

"You've heard about Dante's Inferno right?" he asked. I nodded, afraid to speak. "There's a reason that's my cousin's nickname." He tugged at the tape measure around my neck and wicked thoughts began plaguing my mind. He hummed and his gaze darkened. Then he gripped both ends and tugged hard. I fell into his arms.

"Too bad my cousin isn't here or I'd-

"FUCK," I yelped as Celestino's head appear next to mine. The book went flying onto the table. I was so engrossed in my story, I hadn't heard Celestino walk in and place the drinks on the table.

"I want to know what happens next." He reached for the book. I snatched it before he had a chance.

"Rule one," I squealed. Celestino leaned down to look at me. One hand on the back of my chair, the other on the table.

"You said we can't talk about your love of romance books, not that I can't *see* them." Celestino leaned closer. "But if we must follow the rules…" His voice dropped. I swallowed. The desire in them sent my body on fire.

"Truth or d-dare," I stuttered.

"Dare," he whispered. My breathing became shallow. "Are you

going to dare me to do the things you read about in your books, my wicked witch?" he asked. His scent was entangling me. The need in his eyes reminded me of the male protagonists in my romance books. And my heart pounded to see Celestino looking at me in such a raw and primal way. "Dare me Posey," he urged, leaning towards me. I closed my eyes as Celestino slid his hand into my hair.

"Tell me," he whispered into my ear. He pulled back, looking for an answer. I glanced around. No one was in our area. It was just us in our little bubble. Behind our table was a bookcase. I took a deep breath, mustering every ounce of courage I had and pushed Celestino away. I got up and began walking towards the bookcase when I heard him sit down.

"What are you doing?" I asked. He looked at me with one of the history books in his hand.

"Oh, well…"

This time Celestino's cheeks turned a shade of pink. He thought our game was over. A coy smile played on my lips.

"Instead of telling you my fantasy…let me show you," I said. His eyes widened. He silently followed me. I leaned against the books and he stopped right in front of me, eyes watchful, waiting. I took a deep breath.

"I have a fantasy of having a make out session in a dark corner of a library," I confessed. I looked into his green eyes, bewitched by the swirling color fading as his pupils dilated. He smiled. I was about to slip my arms around his when he grabbed them and laid them at my side. I looked at him confused. His smile widened as he stepped closer. His hands cupped my cheeks and instantly my body relaxed into it.

All of my worries began melting away. If this is how he made me feel just by his touch I couldn't imagine how I would feel kissing him.

"May I be the one to fulfill this fantasy of yours?" he asked with sincerity. He wanted to make sure I was comfortable and my heart wanted to explode. Was this too much? Possibly. But it felt good. I could feel the books press into my spine as if trying to push me towards him.

"That's why we're here," I whispered.

He didn't go for my lips right away. Instead he kissed each cheek, my forehead, my nose and along my jaw. Each soft brushstroke of his lips had me slipping closer and closer to his body. He was teasing me. Despite me being a bit taller we fit naturally. He kissed me from my neck to up my jaw and the anticipation was driving me mad.

He shuddered, pressing his lips gently against mine. We sighed into each other. It was soft for a second and then he pressed his whole body against mine.

I gasped into his mouth as he pulled my bottom lip. I needed to feel every inch of him. I slipped my arms around his waist, gripping the back of his hoodie as our tongues fumbled into a tango. His hands dropped to my waist, tugging my hips against his.

"Lilianna," he whispered as he kissed me. I shivered under his hold. My name on his lips sounded like heaven and I wanted him to worship me. My heart was hammering. I couldn't remember the last time I felt like this. I needed more. I needed *him*. I reached for his face to connect our mouths again when-

"Got coffee," Celestino said enthusiastically, cutting through my fantasy. I jumped, sending my book to the floor. I blinked, staring at him and the two cups of coffee he was holding. "Hey, what's wrong?" Concern crossed his face. He placed the coffees down and reached for my forehead. His hand was cool to the touch. "Your face is red. Are you feeling okay?"

I looked into his eyes, words dead on my lips. Kissing him, holding him, him holding me, the bookcase. It was all in my head.

"Posey?" he asked. His gaze slid to the open book on the floor. What page did it land on? I bent to pick up the book.

"The book was getting good," I stumbled on regaining my composure.

"From your reaction, I bet," he muttered.

"Oh, very much," I said, but I wasn't sure if I meant the book or my daydream. I stopped reading it halfway through the chapter apparently. He chuckled.

"Posey, let's get back to work," he said. I bit the inside of my cheek. The fantasy was fake but was the tension we've been experiencing just a part of my imagination?

I blinked at him in confusion. "I...," I trailed off. What was I going to say? There was no way I could tell him I was daydreaming about making out with him.

"Did you know an ostrich's eye is bigger than its brain," he said. I looked at him confused.

"What?" I asked. My brain quieted for a moment and I felt like I could breathe.

"I read it somewhere," he shrugged.

"You read a random fact?" I questioned. He took a sip of his coffee and nodded. He handed me my cup. "Thanks," I said sheepishly.

"So what do we have and what is left?" he asked. I cleared my throat, my brain switching to work mode.

WELCOME TO BOOGEYMAN'S BAR. Now it didn't get its name because the owner was a big disco fan. Instead it was given the name because the owner had stumbled upon the location on a foggy night and noticed how the swamp gave off boogie-oogie vibes. That...and well the bar oozed a strange green liquid in its pipes for a few weeks. I like to say it was ectoplasm but sources say it was the swamp water. Which is totally safe now. If you look into the water during spring you might find the Loch Ness Monster or a close relative swimming.

THE SIREN'S Saloon isn't named after our favorite red headed mermaid. Although the jury is still out there since I did catch Carrie the owner humming Part of Your World. It was because the original owner was once a pirate, sailing the seven seas before losing a poker game where he won the bar but lost his ship. They say he had the saloon refurbished to replicate his ship so he could always feel like he was back home on the ocean.

· · ·

HIGHWAYMEN HAUNT. As you know back in the day there weren't as many road rules as there are today. They really took the meaning pedal to the metal seriously. Word on the street is that the original owner was driving late one evening after having one too many drinks and a mysterious figure on a horse with a pumpkin head stopped him from colliding with a tree. So the owner bought the bar he got drunk at that night and named it after the mysterious highway figure. Sometimes when the moon is full, you can see a figure or figures watching over the main road.

PLASTERED PIXIE WAS BUILT on the site of an old fae meeting ground where they would hold their festivals. Now the fae would get drunk on both magic and mead after festivals, and the next day you would find multiple fairies and pixies strewn across the clearing. The other story is the owner had a thing for Tinker Bell and alliteration.

AND NOW OUR GRAND FINALE…THE Drunken Fairy Tale Tavern! A pub that welcomes all. Young or old. Big or small. Magic or Mundane. This place all started…

I STARED at the table in front of me, covered in open books and note cards. Words were beginning to blur together and my eyes were straining to focus.

"Have you found anything about The Drunken Fairy Tale?" I asked.

"I've looked through some of the books and I can't find anything," he said. I chewed my lip. How strange that our favorite pub was the only place we struggled to find. We began scouring through every book but nothing came up. Celestino closed the book that was our last hope. "It looks like we're gonna have to talk to Caleb," he said.

I sighed this time, stretching my arms. I was hoping to have everything finished today. Mentally I began pulling a list of all the things I still needed to get done.

"I'll talk to Caleb," Celestino said, squeezing my shoulder and pulling me out of my own head. I looked up at him. I didn't mean to space out. He smiled at me. "A lot going on in that beautiful head, *querida*?" he asked.

"Sorry. Yeah, I was just thinking about everything that has to get done," I said, gathering the books. He moved to help.

"I get it. I still have a few builds to power through."

"I remember one year the haunted house almost caught on fire," I said. It was about four years ago and they did a *Phantom of The Opera* theme. One room was decked out with lit candles. Fun fact: candles and fake spiderwebs do not mix. Since then someone had to triple check that everything was in line to avoid a disaster. Celestino shuddered.

"Don't remind me. My mom sent videos. Thank the stars, the water fairies were there," he chuckled.

My heart was raging as I made my way towards the tavern. Her face was flushed, pupils dilated, lips parted. That face was going to be in my dreams. I don't know why I got so nervous catching her reading her romance book. It's not like it was a big deal. I scratched my chest, feeling my heart beat erratically.

But it was Lilianna. *My* Lilianna. I've never seen her that way and fuck, did I want to again. I shook my head. I needed to think with my brain.

For some reason there was no history on the tavern and we needed that to finish this task. I promised her I would talk to Caleb and that was exactly what I was going to do. I needed to talk to him and then run home for a cold shower.

WALKING into the tavern it wasn't too packed. Caleb was at his usual spot at the bar talking to a man with blonde hair.

"Mr. Boss Man!" The singsong voice was like the cold shower I needed.

"Sailor," I said, nodding to him. He had the biggest grin on his face as I slid into the stool next to him. "Why are you smiling like that?" I asked tentatively.

"Your aura is very interesting," he said with a smirk.

"You can see my aura?" My eyes widened. He kept smiling.

"I can. Some sirens can't. I take it you were with Lilianna?" he asked. I sighed. There was no point in lying when he could tell.

"Yes," I mumbled.

"You guys are so cute. Just as cute as Caleb and Eleanor," Sailor said, glancing at Caleb. Caleb tried swatting him with a towel.

"Shut up," the stoic elf grumbled. Sailor laughed. Glancing between the two it was funny to think they got along. Caleb was like an old dragon and Sailor walked around like sunshine poured out of his ass. And somehow I felt like I had a place between them. Sailor nudged me.

"Everything okay?" he asked.

"Kind of," I said. I turned to Caleb. "I gotta ask you something." Caleb arched an eyebrow at me. An elf of few words as usual. "What's the history with the tavern? Posey and I tried looking for it at the library for the speech the tour guide is going to give during the crawl, but we couldn't find anything." A tick worked in Caleb's jaw. He stopped drying glasses for a second.

"Honestly? Not sure," he said. Both Sailor and I exchanged glances.

"What do you mean?" Sailor asked, somehow now a part of our conversation.

"Well the tavern was randomly left to my family," he continued.

I shook my head in disbelief. "But I thought you guys owned it?" I asked. His family had been running the tavern since before I was born.

He shrugged his shoulders. "According to my dad, someone left my granddad a letter and a key to the place. The rest is history." Caleb turned around to reorganize the bottles behind him. I scratched the back of my head.

"I guess you guys could just say that it was mysteriously left to us or something," he continued. He frowned as he stared at a bottle of gin that was running low.

Lilianna wasn't going to like that. She liked to make sure everything was wrapped up with a neat ribbon and this created a loose thread.

"I have to tell Posey," I said as I felt a pull.

"Tell me what?"

I turned to see the woman currently occupying my thoughts. Lilianna had her hair pulled on to the top of her head, a few strands falling out. She came to stand next to me.

"Caleb has no idea who the owner is or where the tavern came from. It was just left to his granddad one day," I said. Her bottom lip stuck out in a frown and her eyebrows cinched in.

"Fuck," she whispered. Caleb continued shifting through bottles, stacking them on the bar. Sailor reached for one of the empty bottles.

"Is everything alright?" Sailor asked Caleb, holding up one of the bottles. He nodded silently.

"I'll come up with something," she said. It was my turn to frown.

"I'll help you and don't say no." I wrapped my hand lightly around her elbow. She rolled her brown eyes at me.

"Fine. Fine," she said and sat down as Sailor stood up.

"Well, we better leave. The Addams Family house awaits us," Sailor said. And because he loved irritating me he walked over and patted Lilianna's head. She giggled, swatting him away. *Stupid fish face.*

"I'll see you this weekend," I said to her, kissing her cheek again. I couldn't stop touching her all day. I did it in the morning to see how she would react. She smiled and wrapped her arm around my waist to squeeze me, kissing my cheek.

This was definitely good. The second we were out in the open I punched Sailors' shoulder. The siren laughed.

"It's just so easy to rile you up, boss man," he teased.

"Whatever. We got work to do," I said marching down the street.

CHAPTER 18
ANXIETY MONSTER

I stared at the cup of water in my hand as Caleb went through the bottles on display. So, no history. I could make something up. I was creative enough that I could weave a story that tied into the Kiernan family.

But did I want to? I wanted people to learn about what makes our town spectacularly spooky as accurately as I could.

Caleb shot up from the ground causing me to nearly jump out of the bar stool. "Is everything-,"

"Bestie!" A voice called out. I turned to see Eleanor strolling in with a gift bag.

"Hey there," I said, as she kissed my cheek. Her eyes slid to Caleb and she nodded. He nodded back and continued what I assumed was inventory.

"How was the library?" she asked with a suggestive look. I rolled my eyes.

"No fantasies were brought to life so calm down," I said.

"Damn. I was hoping for some juicy details," she said, pouting.

"What's in the bag?" I asked, trying to distract her. Her glossy lips stretched into a serpentine smile. Either this was going to be glorious, hysterical or uncomfortable. Maybe a combination of all three.

"I got you a gift. You've been so stressed lately and I figured you needed something to loosen you up," she said as she handed me the bag.

"That's so sweet of you Ellie," I squeal, opening the bag. My eyes widened as I stared at the object in the bag. "Eleanor!" I hissed.

"What," Eleanor said, shrugging her shoulders. "You've been so wound up with the crawl and you know who that I thought this could help," she said casually.

"So you got me a vibrator?" I asked in shock as I stare at the dark blue contraption.

"I was going to get you the same model I have which has like three different functions but I don't think you're ready for that." She said it so innocently I almost forgot we were talking about vibrators. Caleb coughed. *Shit.* I forgot he was there. His cheeks were slightly flushed. Eleanor raised an eyebrow.

"What? Uncomfortable with vibrators, Caleb? You know they're your friend and not your enemy," she said. I bit my lip to hold back a laugh. He rolled his eyes, holding empty bottles of vodka.

"I know. Toys, ties, tongue." His lips twitched. "I'll use whatever if it benefits my partner," he said, keeping his gaze on Eleanor. His pale blue eyes were sharp. Eleanor flushed.

"Well now I gotta go home," she said, jumping off her seat.

"To use your toy," Caleb teased.

"What else would I be doing," she said over her shoulder as she walked out. And just like that she was gone. I couldn't help but laugh. Whether it was an entrance or an exit, Eleanor Silva always made her mark. Caleb's eyes followed her.

"So Caleb…" I said, trailing off. He cleared his throat.

"I can show you the letter my granddad was given to help with your bar crawl if we never talk about what just happened." His voice sounded tight. I nodded, wordlessly, trying to keep it together. The letter was the start.

Caleb left for his office, returning moments later with an envelope in his hand. I knew the easy way would be to make something up but something inside me wanted to solve this mystery.

"They left this envelope on his doorstep," he said.

"Like a stork dropping a baby?" I asked. He let out a small chuckle.

"You and I both know that's just a fairy tale. Anyway they left a letter entitling my family to take over the tavern." I carefully took the envelope in my hand.

"And they never came back?" I asked. Caleb shook his head.

"My granddad even tried using some magic on the letter to reveal who left it and nothing worked. The person didn't want to be found."

"But wouldn't someone know them?" I asked.

He leaned against the bar. "That's what I thought. But no one remembers anything except that my family inherited it. It was like the person casted a spell to wipe everyone's memory," he said. Well that was interesting. This was probably the most mysterious thing to have ever happened in Lavender Falls and we're a town of supernaturals. I opened the letter. The crumpled paper had yellowed with time and felt fragile beneath my fingers.

Dear Sir Kiernan,

You may not know me but I am the owner of The Drunken Fairy Tale Tavern. I know my identity is a mystery in this town. I've been a nuisance to everyone, an aching thorn in their side and therefore I am leaving. Maybe something waits for me beyond the Gasping Greenwood Forest. Maybe I'll return with a new hope and better understanding. Please take care of it. It means the world to my family.

Thank you, G.G

"G.G. Maybe the town records," I suggested. Caleb shrugged.

"You can try. Maybe you'll spot something my granddad missed," he said, taking the letter back.

I looked around the tavern I basically grew up in. I thought putting on a bar crawl would be easy. But when has anything in Lavender Falls been easy?

CHAPTER 19

IT'S COMING

Today was going to be rough. I could feel it in my bones. I woke up late, the graphic I posted had a typo which I didn't see until this morning (40 people had already liked it) and I had no coffee. So I ran to Coffin's Coffee Shop as fast as I could and then made my way to the office. I ignored the pang in my stomach.

The office building came into view surrounded by gray clouds. It was like I was running straight into a villain's lair. I noticed the duck family was back. No way was I going to help them cross the street again. Nope, I learned my lesson. I eyed the mother duck who magically remembered me and was glaring at me. Who knew a duck glaring could be terrifying? I made it inside, waving to Penelope who was in charge of the front desk.

"Hold the elevator," I called out. A bronzed hand with thick fingers peeked through the doors, keeping it open. They reminded me of-

"Good morning, *querida*." Celestino's morning voice made my stomach twist in a different kind of hunger. I blushed. He smiled at me, his eyes trailing up and down slowly. I began to feel self conscious. What was I even wearing?

Stepping inside I nervously stood next to him. I wore blue skinny slacks with an oversize blouse, a black cardigan and flats. Okay so, casual yet professional. At least everything matched, right? I felt Celestino's gaze on me. I looked at him and he was staring at me intently.

"What's wrong?" I asked. Did I have something on my face? A tick worked in his jaw.

"You were running late?" he asked, his voice gruff. The elevator beeped with every passing floor. I nodded, trying to gauge why he was reacting the way he was. Celestino moved to step in front of me, his back to the elevator door. He reached for my cardigan and tugged me lightly forward. Was he going to kiss me? Did I brush my teeth? I hadn't drunk my coffee yet and therefore the part of my brain that kept my filter in check and stopped me from doing stupid things was still off. I was totally down to do stupid things like make out in our office elevator. I started to close my eyes, bracing for the impact when I realized he had begun buttoning my cardigan.

"What are you doing?" I couldn't stop the irritation in my voice. I didn't mean to sound that way. I was just tired and I stupidly thought he was going to kiss me. Immediately, I apologized for my tone.

"I *know* you're tired. I can tell," he said, buttoning the last button.

"Really?" I asked. When I met his gaze, his green eyes were burning.

"Yes," he whispered. His hands slipped to my waist, pulling me flat against him. My eyes widened. My body was ravaged by heat. He was warm and strong. My eyes closed briefly, savoring the feel of his body against mine.

"You see now?" His lips tipped up to my ear.

"Fuck," I shivered out. I wasn't wearing a bra. I was in such a rush I completely forgot. Now all I felt was Celestino's chest pressed against mine. My nipples automatically tighten and from the look in his eyes he could feel that.

"Maybe Eleanor has one you can borrow, seeing how she keeps spare blouses for you," he teased, pulling away as the door chimed open.

"Doubt it. We're not even the same size." I glanced at him and he rubbed a hand on his face. I handed him my second cup of coffee and he shook his head while taking it.

"It's too early for this. Come on, we have a meeting," he mumbled, taking a sip.

I couldn't stop my leg from bobbing up and down. I planted my hand on my thigh, hoping it would be a reminder to stay calm. I had my notes opened on my laptop. The meeting was going over the Fall Festival. Eleanor was currently speaking. Her hair was pulled back into a low bun with a jeweled headband. She wore a mustard colored blouse, tucked into wide legged, pink gingham slacks.

"So far all the shops have confirmed they'll be vendors, the haunted house is on time in terms of builds and props. The bar crawl is also on track. However I have yet to hear back from the carnival company." Her eyes glanced towards Ben who nodded.

If they hadn't been confirmed, it meant they wouldn't be arriving on time if at all and then I couldn't do the time lapse video I do every year. I bit the inside of my cheek. I needed to come up with a few other ideas. Maybe more videos teasing some of the vendors products and the haunted house. My head began spinning.

"Ticket sales are a bit slow at the moment but surely that will pick up the closer we get to the festival," Eleanor continued and glanced at me. She must have seen something in my eyes because her eyebrow twitched. I nodded and tried to crack a smile.

My fingers began flying across the laptop. I needed to ramp up advertisements. Maybe switch up the graphics, make sure shops got flyers to spread and create engaging videos. I needed to rework some of the captions to be more eye-catching as well.

I felt a familiar twitch in my chest, a heaviness. My breathing was getting shallow. I tugged on my earlobe, needing to distract myself from my thoughts. *Everything is going to be fine.* I repeated the mantra hoping to burn it into my brain, knowing damn well it didn't always work.

My eyes looked across the room to meet Celestino's. Concern was all over his face. My heart pounded against my chest. I didn't need to see that look on his face. It made me want to crumble, to cry. I also didn't need *him* to see me this way. One look from him and my mask was willing to fall. I didn't need that right now.

I shifted my gaze to Eleanor who gave a smile. She could tell that I was trying to keep it together.

After the meeting was over Leo asked me to stay behind. Through the glass I could see Celestino and Eleanor hanging around.

"We have to ramp up promotions," Leo stated. I began typing away on my laptop.

"Already handled. I can come up with a few creative ideas for videos and pictures. I'll promote the pubs and shops that already have a decent following and they can share it as well." I said, pouring confidence into my voice. But I could feel it in the back of my head. A slight crack was trying to break into my demeanor.

"Why don't you let me handle making the graphics and posting them. I want you to focus on the videos. You're great with them. They always do well. You also have the bar crawl. I don't want you over-working yourself," he said. A sigh escaped me before I could stop it. Leo smiled. "You don't have to do everything you know," he said. Leo's eyes crinkled on the side.

I gave a tight lip smile. "I know. I just-"

He waved his hand, cutting me off. "Even though you're my assistant, we split the work Lilianna." His eyes grew serious. I bit my tongue. It was very rare for my lovable goofball of a boss to be serious. Usually it happened around the full moon when his inner wolf was clawing his way out. Which now that I think about it…

"Of course," I said. He smiled and strolled out the door. I let out a breath and sat back in my chair. The exhaustion of the past few weeks was starting to take its toll. Work, friends, family and Celestino. Everything was starting to tread on the trail of overwhelming.

I heard the door open. I didn't need to look to see that it was Celestino. His magic was like a warm cup of apple cider on a cold day and it was calling to me. I stood up, gathering my stuff.

"You okay Posey?" he asked. I took a deep breath and turned to face him with my bag tightly in my grip.

"Yep. Just gotta plan out some work stuff," I said, forcing a smile. I could tell he didn't believe me. He always could and now I could see it. The way he was tracking my every movement. From my eyes, to the way I was breathing slightly faster and how my hands clutched my bag.

"Posey-" he started to say before Eleanor walked in and began grabbing him.

"Leave her," she stated. Eleanor knew that I needed to be alone. Just alone to reorganize my brain. I wasn't having a full blown anxiety attack yet. I was trying to manage it. Irritation flashed across his face as he pulled his arm away from her. He opened his mouth to say something. "Now," Eleanor said fiercely.

Celestino's eyebrows furrowed. It was very rare to see Eleanor stand her ground in an authoritative way. She enjoyed being more carefree but right now she was protecting me.

The truth was Celestino didn't know much about my anxiety. It didn't become an issue until college. I still remember my first anxiety attack freshman year. It was right before my final. I had a group project and one person wasn't pulling their weight. I remember the way my brain short circuited. My throat closed up and it felt like I couldn't get enough air in. My hands started shaking uncontrollably and one word kept playing over and over again. *Failure.* Eleanor attempted to calm me down but I could barely hear her.

Growing up I never really suffered from anxiety attacks but college was different. I was an adult. There was no perfectly structured routine curated by others. Everything was on me. And being alone and responsible began to show how flawed I was.

It was a mix of people pleasing, conforming myself so they wouldn't leave and the masking to fit in. Then making sure things were perfect and I became infatuated with order done my way. I began to hold onto things too tightly whether it was my own emotions or others.

Now at 28 I was more aware of these moments. And deep in my body an anxiety attack was brewing. I could feel it.

"Just text me if you need anything," Celestino said softly. I nodded. I didn't want him to see me this way. I couldn't let him. This part of me was too complicated to sort through.

Once he was out and his presence disappeared from the air, I took a deep breath. My eyes shot to Eleanor.

"It'll be okay. You're good at this," she said sternly. I nodded.

"Leo is going to take control of some things so I can focus on videos and the bar crawl so it'll be fine," I said to Eleanor. She nodded and opened her arms up for a hug. I stepped in. "Everything will be fine," I whispered into her shoulder.

Something was wrong. Something was wrong with her and I didn't know what. She kept picking at her nails when she wasn't typing away at her laptop. Her eyes looked strained. Every few moments she would take a deep breath as if she forgotten to breathe. It was killing me not to go over to her and wrap my arms around her. It hurt when Eleanor pushed me out of the room. Lilianna didn't want me to see this side of her.

I felt helpless. I just wanted to make her happy. I wanted to make things easier for her. She spent so much of her time caring for others, I wanted to care for her. But how?

I was staring at my phone on my kitchen counter. I kept walking by it, fighting on whether or not to call Lilianna. I wanted to make sure she was okay but I wasn't sure if I could or if she even wanted to hear from me. I felt restless, useless. Grabbing my phone I texted the last person I wanted advice from.

I need your help

FISH FACE

You need to redo that sentence

I need your help

...please

FISH FACE

You mean, "I need help from the most glorious, radiant, sexiest siren I know... please"

I knew this was a mistake

FISH FACE

LOL I'm kidding. What's up?

Something is up with Posey and I don't know what to do

FISH FACE

Oh that

You know and I don't know?

FISH FACE

She's very anxious. Just ask her if she needs anything

This is the advice I get?

FISH FACE

I said I was glorious, radiant and sexy not wise

Bye

I sighed into my hands. I felt jittery. I was nervous to text her. *Me.* Nervous to text Lilianna who I've known since I was in diapers. But this situation felt delicate. I didn't want to make things worse.

"Just pick up the phone and text her," I muttered to myself.

> Just wanted to see how you were

I put the phone face down. I didn't want to be staring at the screen, waiting for a text back. My fingers tapped against the counter impatiently. My phone beeped after what felt like forever.

QUERIDA
I'm okay

> Do you need anything?

QUERIDA
No I'm okay

> Posey do you WANT anything?

She didn't respond right away this time and so I used the moment to tidy up. I needed to distract myself. After the meeting today, I called the carnival who did end up confirming which was a giant sigh of relief. They'll be setting up next week. One less thing for me to worry about.

The haunted house was running on time although a few decor and props wouldn't be arriving until next week. I needed to finish building some directional signs. There were at least three food trucks we needed to confirm. My phone dinged and I dropped a cup I was cleaning in the sink and dried my hands faster than fluttering sprite wings.

QUERIDA
Food

Food. She wanted food. I could provide food.

QUERIDA

Give me options

Please

Italian, Chinese, Caribbean or Portuguese

QUERIDA

Caribbean please. Curry chicken. If they have
buss up shot that would be nice. If not any
other roti is fine.

I couldn't stop my face from breaking out into a wide grin. She wanted to see me. Sure it was because I was bringing food but she didn't shut me out despite feeling whatever she was feeling. Now I just needed to get my witch her food.

I was laid across my couch, laptop on the coffee table, mentally kicking myself. None of the trends fit with what I needed in order to gain ticket sales. I chewed my lip. I was blocked. I knew I was. This is what always happened. Being a creative being meant that ideas came in waves. Sometimes they made big splashes and sometimes they were dead calm leaving you with nothing.

I closed my laptop. I needed a break. I needed to take my mind off of work and just relax. The meeting set me very close to a spiral. That night with Celestino, going to different pubs reminded me how badly I needed to take time for myself.

And then he texted me asking if I needed anything. I wasn't sure what I wanted exactly. That's a lie.

I wanted him.

I wanted him to be around me and hold me. His presence had a calming effect. It relaxed my nerves. And so I told him I wanted food, hoping it would mean him coming over and staying with me. Would he stay after dropping the food or would he leave right away?

A million and one things ran through my head. And just like that a small snowball of what if's became an avalanche. My stomach felt like it was getting trampled by orcs.

I groaned into my couch pillow. I peaked at the coffee table and reached for my laptop. Might as well try to use work as a distraction again. Old habits die hard I guess.

I HAD SPENT the last twenty minutes trying to focus on video ideas and flinched when there was a quick knock at the door. I shut my laptop quickly and jumped off the couch. I took a deep breath. This was a normal hang out. We spent many times eating dinner together. Albeit, Eleanor and occasionally Lola were always there.

Opening the door Celestino stood there with a wide grin and two plastic bags. It looked like he ordered the whole menu. He stood in the doorway, wearing sweats. I fidgeted with the end of my hoodie.

"Come in." I did my best to override my nerves in my voice. The smell of curry floated through my apartment. My mouth began watering. He made his way to my kitchen counter and I found myself walking with a bounce in my step. He must have noticed because he began smiling as I stood next to him.

"Excited for food?" he asked. I nodded enthusiastically. He squeezed my hip.

"I have beer in the fridge," I said.

All the food was laid out as he went to the fridge. I couldn't have been more grateful. This was so kind of him and I was the reciprocator of it. But I felt it again. There was a swirl of emotion, deep in my belly that was gnawing to be released. This moment of joy felt slippery. I couldn't trust it because nothing this nice ever lasted. A feeling was scratching beneath my skin.

"You have Guinness?" he asked in surprise. I felt my cheeks heat up.

"You drank it at the tavern so I figured you liked it," I said, messing with the hem of my hoodie again.

"Really?" He turned around holding a bottle of Guinness and Super Bock. I bit the inside of my cheek, shrugging my shoulders.

"I have it for moments like this, for when you come over," I confessed. I bought a six pack after my period and kept it in the fridge in case he came over again, hoping he would. He smiled, nodding along.

"I was thinking maybe we could watch a movie," he said, changing the subject.

I let out a soft exhale. I *needed* this. I liked the way he seemed to fill the space of my apartment with tranquility. He made his way to the living room and began clearing my coffee table. I enjoyed the way he moved around my space as if he'd been here a thousand times. He felt comfortable in my home and I felt comfortable with him in it.

"Sit," he ordered, pointing to the couch. I did as I was told even though I wanted to tell him he couldn't tell me what to do in my own space. But I decided to humor him and by the glint in his eyes he knew.

"Wait," I said, jumping off the couch suddenly. I went to my linen closet to grab a tablecloth to lay on the coffee table.

"Smart witch," he said. My heart skipped. He began laying out all the food in front of me. Everything looked delicious. I grabbed my remote to run through the movies. Celestino slid in next to me and my toes curled at the feel of his body heat.

"That one," he said pointing to the screen. A giggle escaped.

"You really want to watch Princess Diaries 2?" I asked. He tore a piece of roti and dipped it into the curry.

"I have to see how we're like Chris and the princess," he said with a grin. I rolled my eyes.

"The first half of the movie. Also his name is Nicholas here." I said. He shook his head and offered me the bite he prepared. I reached for it and he pulled back. My eyebrows furrowed in confusion.

"Let me?" he asked, his voice dropping. His green eyes seemed to melt. He held the piece of flatbread in front of me and I leaned over to take a bite, my eyes never wavering from his. An explosion of rich warmth, heat and spices washed over me. I closed my eyes, a moan escaping. When I opened them again his face was unreadable. He cleared his throat, coming back to reality.

"I take it you like it?" he asked, eyes casted downward. I nodded, mouth full.

"Good," I mumbled. I ripped another piece and dug into the curry chicken. I held it in front of Celestino, face red. He smiled, dipping his head.

My body tightened as his tongue lightly grazed my fingers when he took a bite. I watched his throat work as he ate. He hummed in delight.

"Good right?" My voice was strained. He licked his lips.

"Very," he said, his voice low. Taking a bite again I couldn't stop myself from doing a happy dance. Celestino chuckled. The taste of ginger, garlic, herbs and peppers were enough to bring me to my knees. My fingers were tinged in yellow and it made me happy. I hadn't had this in so long. I glanced at Celestino and he had a soft smile.

"What?" I asked. He shrugged his shoulders.

"I like feeding you," he said.

"I have no problem if you want to keep bringing me food," I said, giggling. He handed me my beer.

"I'll always bring you whatever you need," he said. And like that, I felt a wall around my heart crumble.

WE WERE HALFWAY through the movie, food gone when Celestino leaned into my ear. "I can see why you think that's us," he said. I let out a giggle.

"I never said that was us." I glanced over at him. His body was angled towards me in the perfect cuddle position.

"They clearly have tension and there was that closet scene," he pointed out. I blushed at the mention of the closet scene. I spent a few nights going over what he said inside the closet in my head.

I dare you to see if we can learn to be closer.

I wondered what would have happened if I responded yes to his dare right then and there. Did I want to answer now? I looked over at him again. But what if things got weird?

I could talk to him about it but I would rather stew in a pot of over-thinking, self-doubt and unanswered questions then face confrontation.

"Can I ask a question?" he asked as I reached to clean up the table.

"Of course," I said.

"Why is this promotion important to you?" he asked, stopping me from cleaning up. A swirl of emotions began brewing. I stared at the empty containers.

"Honestly?" I sighed. "I feel like if I get promoted it'll ease my mom's worries. When I picked my major, she didn't quite understand it. Being in communications, specifically social media, was difficult to explain. And it took awhile before I landed a position. For her, being a lawyer or a doctor equals security." I looked at him and he pulled my hand in his. "I love what I do. I love coming up with creative concepts that bring everyone together and learning how to execute them. It's fun and I know the money will follow eventually but…" I trailed off. He squeezed my hand. This was the part I hated to admit.

"I feel guilty. I feel guilty for liking what I do. For having the kind of job that makes me look forward to the next day. She didn't have a choice on what she could do when she came here, but I did. I get to have that luxury. I just wish she had that or that I could give it to her," I said as tears gathered in my eyes.

Celestino shifted his weight, leaning closer to me. "Our parents did what they had to do when they came here for us. Our parents worked hard so we would have a chance at succeeding. We're just doing it our way. She worked so *you* could have this life. So *we* could have this life," he said, wiping a tear from my cheek.

I stared into his green eyes, my hand and heart in his hands.

"So we should make the most of the life they gave us?" I asked. He nodded, squeezing my hands reassuringly. "Okay," I said, giving him a wobbly smile.

"Let's watch another movie," he said, getting up to finish cleaning up.

CHAPTER 20

UNEXPECTED SLEEPOVER

I liked her like this. This was Lilianna. Dorky and warm with pink cheeks. I wondered how she would feel if I wrapped my arms around her. But despite her being happy right now, I kept replaying her face during the meeting. She was clearly trying to remain calm, but her eyes held the truth of her feelings. She looked like a storm, ready to explode.

The worries on her face seemed to have vanished as we ate in relative silence. Her body was relaxing on the couch as we watched the movie. But I couldn't shake the feeling she was burying whatever she was hiding.

"Can I hold you?" I asked, interrupting the scene where Princess Mia was with Nicholas walking through the garden. Her head snapped towards me at my question. I had no idea what compelled me to say those words, but I knew deep in my gut it's what she needed. She tugged on her earlobe. Her eyebrows pushed together in contemplation. "You can say no," I said gently.

"I've kind of been wanting you too," she said softly. My heart soared like a phoenix rising from the ashes.

She's been wanting me too.

"Oh really," I teased her. She rolled her eyes and made her way over to me. My heart began to beat faster.

"Shut up," she said, crawling into my open arms. I angled myself more so that her back could rest against my chest, my arms coming to crossover her body. I couldn't stop the sigh of relief that escaped me, especially when I felt her muscles relax. This felt right. This felt more than right. The warmth of holding her safe in my arms eased something within my soul. I leaned into her ear and felt her shiver. That reaction sent tingles through my body.

"Rule nine. If you feel like doing something, do it. So if you wanted me to hold you, you just had to ask," I whispered as I tightened my arms around her. "Is this too much?" I asked. She turned to angle her face to me. Her cheeks were flushed against the glow of the tv.

"Almost," she whispered. I placed a quick kiss on her temple and went back to watching the movie.

Almost.

"SHOULD WE START ANOTHER MOVIE?" I asked once the movie ended. She stretched out her long legs, pressing further into me and I grunted. "Do you want to pick?" I asked. She nodded enthusiastically, her bun hitting my face. I chuckled.

Minha bruxinha.

"Why don't you pick while I use the bathroom," I said.

She nodded silently, less aggressively, scooting over. I glanced over at her, feeling a zing go up my body. Her bun was falling apart. She was wearing a hoodie that looked like the one I gave her in high school and had a small smile on her face. She looked perfect. She looked like mine. Just not in the way I wanted yet. Shaking my head I headed to the bathroom.

After using the bathroom I paused at the sink. Where was the soap?

Lilianna's bathroom was impeccably clean but I couldn't find the soap. I bit the inside of my cheek and opened her lower cabinet. There was a brown paper gift bag. I pulled it out to have it out of the way, finding the soap behind it. Putting the bag back, my eyes glanced inside.

I sucked in a breath. Every ounce of blood that was coursing through my body rushed to one area.

"The soap is in the cabinet underneath! J-just behind the bag," Lilianna shouted nervously from the other side of the door.

Fuck. Fuck. Fuck. Breathe Celestino. Get your shit together.

After washing my hands, I took a deep breath, opening the door to see Lilianna leaning against the wall, picking at her nails.

"You know most people keep this in their room," I said holding the bag. Her body visibly tensed. She walked towards me, slowly, my eyes being captured by the gentle sway of her hips. Her hand reached for the bag.

"It was a gift from Eleanor. She said I needed to relax," she said softly. The smell of the ocean seeping through my pores. My magic began humming as it sensed hers. "Besides, it's waterproof," she whispered. I breathed deeply. I needed to relax but the smell of her magic was intoxicating.

"You shouldn't tell me those things." My voice was rough. I stepped into her personal space. Her eyes widened slightly. I gripped her chin, slightly tilting it down towards me. Her tongue peeked out to lick her bottom lip. Her fingers were clutching the bag. "I can still see the hesitation in your eyes." I regrettably let her go and made my way back to the living room. "When you're ready to answer my dare, let me know. And don't worry. I know how to use toys."

Once we were back on the couch I handed her the remote. "You pick, Posey," I said. She nodded silently and crawled back into my arms. I smiled.

Almost.

I WAS SLEEPING PEACEFULLY when the sound of a door closing woke me up. My pillow felt warm and I pulled myself closer. I had never felt more relaxed in my entire life. But something was off. There was a light breeze against my neck. I cracked my eyes open to see Lilianna. I had my arms wrapped around her. Her mouth was slightly open, a slight snore escaping between her lips.

A small part of me wanted to laugh but I refused to ruin this perfect moment. How the stars did this happen? Last thing I remember after the vibrator incident was that we decided to watch the first Transformers movie and then nothing.

My face felt warm. She looked so peaceful. I wanted to close my eyes and continue sleeping. All of a sudden her arms tightened around me and she moved to press against me. I took a deep breath from my nose. She kept wiggling, pushing into my hips. Her eyes were still closed. She pressed her face into the side of my neck, sighing happily. My heart began pounding. Was she awake? That's when I felt it. And I mean *it*.

I bit my lip to keep from moaning as she pressed into my dick. Oh stars, was she rocking? I'm going to explode if she doesn't stop.

"Celestino," she whispered against my neck.

Oh, fury fuck. I went rigid at hearing her sear my own name into my skin. Her voice was low, needy and fuck did it twist my insides in the most delicious way. Was she dreaming about me? But before I could continue my thoughts, she pushed into my morning wood again and a moan escaped my mouth.

Lilianna instantly froze. Her eyes snapped open to see me staring at her. Then her gaze headed south to see her core pressed against my erection. She jumped back and I fell off the couch.

"Stars," I grunted as my back hit the floor.

"Celestino," she called out, peeking over the couch. I covered my face with my hand.

"I'm sorry. I didn't mean for this to happen," I stumbled to say. This has got to be the most embarrassing thing to have ever happened. I sat up, shaking my hair into place. Her face reddened.

"I also didn't mean to fall asleep," I grumbled. I froze as I remembered why I woke up.

"What's wrong?" she asked, tentatively.

"The reason I woke up was because I heard the door close," I whispered. Lilianna's body trembled. "Stay here," I ordered.

I stood up slowly, adjusting my sweatpants. The smell of sandalwood drifted in and when I glanced down my magic had manifested physically. Purple electricity wounded its way around my hand. It crackled through the air. I heard Lilianna stifle a gasp.

I inched my way towards the kitchen. Standing outside the kitchen I saw that the door was locked. So what did I hear? I glanced at Lilianna. She was peeking above the couch. That's when I noticed her magic. With my own active, my eyes could see the magic around us. Hers was a soft gray and sparking everywhere. There was an erratic feeling in the air. A vibration. Her baby hairs were beginning to stand on her head, creating a halo of waves and curls.

A picture frame on the wall began to shake lightly. She glanced at the picture frame. Her eyes widened impossibly more and she ducked. Did her magic scare her? Now that I thought about it, I never saw her use magic much.

The smell of coffee slipped into my nose. My eyes trailed to the kitchen to see two cups of coffee, croissants and a note. I let my magic wave off as I entered the kitchen. I recognized that handwriting.

Dropped in for breakfast but looks like you have a different breakfast in mind. -E

I let out a hearty laugh and held up the note.

"It was Eleanor," I said. Lilianna practically ran over and nearly tripping. She snatched the note, her eyes scanning over it.

"Fuck," she hissed, her hands trembled and the note in her hand lit on fire. She jumped back. The smell of a thunderstorm consumed the kitchen. Lilianna stepped back again as I reached for her.

"I'm sorry. I'm sorry. I'm sorry," she said as she waved around to try and dispel the magic in the air.

"Hey, hey, it's okay," I said, reaching for her. What was happening? I've never seen her freak out like this before. I needed to distract her. I needed to do something to break the waves of whatever thoughts were plaguing her.

"You snore," I blurted. Her eyes snapped to me. *There she is.*

"No I don't…I think," she said, puzzled. More of her hair slipped from her bun.

Fuck, she was cute. I wrapped my arms around her.

"I do?" she asked in a huff. I felt her body relaxing, the magic leaving her body, the air becoming still.

"You do but it's quiet enough it didn't disturb my sleep," I said, kissing her cheek.

"Well thank the stars I didn't disrupt the sleep of the Wicked Warlock of The East," she said, tipping her head down on my shoulder. We both laughed.

Her phone beeped, pulling her mind back to reality. She pushed herself off and went to go find it. I leaned against the kitchen counter, sipping my coffee. I watched her cross the room back to the couch. I liked this too much. I could see this being my future. Her in my baggy clothes with bedhead, walking around our place.

Our place.

The thought felt natural to me. Because she felt that way to me. She felt like home. She was my moon keeping me tethered to this world. My phone beeped and I made my way over to it.

"Wait," she called out but it was too late. There was a message from Eleanor on my phone. She had placed me in a group chat with Lilianna, named *Sexy Supernaturals.*

ELLIE

Good morning love birds! Did you we make it
to rule 69

Attached was a picture of Lilianna draped on top of me. Her hand was clutching my chest, her leg draped over my hip with parted lips. She looked serene. My dick hardened. I had one hand wrapped around her and another on her ass. My hand twitched. Fuck, I wish it was there now, slipping under her sweatpants. I saved the picture immediately.

"I'm sorry," she said.

"Sorry for what? That was the best sleep I've had in awhile." I smiled at her. She turned the prettiest shade of pink.

ELLIE

I'm now in need of a little spoon

We shared a laugh when I got a brilliant idea. Without hesitation I added Caleb into the chat. Oh this was going to be good. After adding Caleb I glanced at Lilianna who was looking at me with a devilish smile.

Want to volunteer?

CALEB

I don't do little spoons

ELLIE

Fine. I'll find someone else

CALEB

Good luck finding someone who can deal
with your attitude

Ellie adds Fish Face

ELLIE

Be my little spoon?

FISH FACE

Name a time and place

QUERIDA

It's too early for this

CALEB

I bet spooning Sailor is like spooning a piece
of driftwood

My witch needs her coffee

QUERIDA

My witch?

Lilianna snorted with a faint blush. She was so adorable in the morning. My phone continued to ring.

Querida adds Lola

ELLIE

By the stars could you guys be anymore
adorable. So rule 69?

@Caleb someone sounds jealous

FISH FACE

I'm not opposed

CALEB

It's too early for this

QUERIDA

Eleanor we slept. As in: a condition of body
and mind that typically recurs for several
hours every night, in which the eyes are
closed, the postural muscles relaxed, the
activity of the brain altered, and
consciousness of the surroundings practically
suspended.

LOLA

LOL did you really look up the definition?

FISH FACE

I'm soooo cuddly

ELLIE

Facts

LOLA

I wanna cuddle

CALEB

My brother is free

LOLA

I rather eat dirt

I held her coffee in my hand. "This coffee is a sweet treat but in need of some heat," I whispered. My palm emitted a soft glow. I came up from behind her and placed the coffee in front of her. She jumped slightly back, pressing into me.

"Coffee," I slightly grunted. She bit her lip. Her body went tense. I knew she could feel my cock, pressing against her ass. I took a step back but Lilianna stepped back with me. She turned around to face me.

The feeling in my chest swelled. A hint of desire filled her brown eyes. It was the same look she's been giving me since I came back. A look of wanting to give in but wanting to keep a boundary and because of that look I refused to cross it. But that didn't mean I couldn't constantly show her I was interested.

"You should step away, Posey," I grumbled. Instead she took a step towards me, pressing herself against me. He tilted his head towards the ceiling, eyes closed. I took a deep breath.

"*Fofinha,*" I whispered. She gave me a hesitant smile. I'm so fucking screwed.

"Celestino," she said. My jaw clenched. I brought a hand to her hip. Her eyes fluttered as I slipped my fingers under the hoodie to play with her skin, drawing goosebumps. Her eyes focused on my lips.

Not yet, a voice in my head said. I couldn't touch her how I wanted yet. I refused to make the first move. So I decided to let go. My hand burned to touch her skin again.

"Why don't I leave you to enjoy your morning," I said, grabbing my wallet and keys.

"What?" she asked in disbelief. As much as I wanted to stay I was painfully aware that she was conflicted. The last thing I wanted was for her to regret this, regret us. "Wait," she called out. I turned around and she handed me two croissants.

"Eat," she whispered. I smiled and took the food.

This was something she needed to settle within herself. I would be here with open arms, as a friend or something more. Whatever she needed from me I would give freely, just like I gave her my heart all those years ago.

CHAPTER 21

MAGIC MALFUNCTION

It was Monday morning and for once I wasn't running late. Instead, I actually made coffee at home and even ate breakfast. Major win. Today was going to be a grueling day. I was going to be visiting different places that would be selling during the festival to gather promo videos.

There was a slight twitch in my eye. I had stayed up way past 2AM to find trending sounds that were longer than nine seconds and missing being wrapped in Celestino's arms.

My first stop was at Pricilla's Potions and Lotions. Pricilla's shop was perfect for all things skincare and candles. It was where I always got my rosacea cream and her ginger lemon balm tea always helped with my anxiety.

It was run by Pricilla, hence the name, who was an earth fairy. She knew all the homeopathic remedies. Peppermint for cramps, aloe vera to soothe redness like sunburns and ginger for your stomach. I was immediately hit with the smell of lavender, frankincense and orange. I felt my anxiety shift from the forefront of my brain to the back. I always wondered if Pricilla added a sprinkle of magic to make her shop relaxing or if it was just the blend of herbs and essential oils.

She was sitting at a table that was swamped with herbs in jars and liquid bottles that were labeled as different oils and waters. I found myself smiling. She was concentrating on the bowl in front of her. Her hands glided across the table and drizzled ingredients. I reached my back pocket to grab my phone. Candid videos were my favorite to capture.

Pricilla's dark brown hair was pulled back by a purple hair clip, matching the lavender streaks in her hair. Her tawny skin glowed as the sunlight poured in. Her whiskey colored eyes looked as if on fire as magic poured out of her and her stained lips made quick movements as she softly spoke. Something about the smell near her work table called me over. Citrus and sandalwood mixed with something else that I couldn't spot. I felt a tickle in the back of my head.

She placed her right hand over the bowl and closed her eyes with a smile, whispering, "Thanks."

I admired the way she was so in tuned to her magic. It wrapped around her like a cardigan. I always felt a seed of jealousy. While I loved my magic, I was also aware of the fact I couldn't keep it under control half of the time. My emotions had always been big. So big that they would overrun my brain, my body and my control.

"Lily," A soft voice broke through my thoughts. I opened my eyes to see Pricilla's arms, outstretched for a hug. I stepped in immediately. I felt like I was hugging Mother Nature herself. Pricilla squeezed me and I relaxed. "You totally caught me on video when I was in the zone didn't you?" she asked sweetly, pulling away.

I waved my phone. "Yep, and it was beautiful as usual," I said triumphantly. She rolled her eyes.

"You're going to be filming a few clips right?" Pricilla moved to pour the herbal mixture into a canister.

"Yeah. I have a few ideas. Should only take an hour," I confirmed. The fairy nodded.

"Well, I'm all yours. Do your thing, Lily."

OKAY SO, it didn't take an hour but three. Lip syncing sounds would forever be my biggest annoyance and customers were coming in and out of the shop. I bit my lip. Out of all the places I needed to grab promos for, the next stop would be the hardest. Drunken Fairy Tale Tavern. Caleb did an amazing job running the place despite not being the biggest fan of socializing.

Making my way down the street, I tried racking up the ways I could probably strong arm him into listening to me. A date with Eleanor? No. I couldn't use my bestie. Although those two have had years of sexual tension and they would probably be game. I laughed. No, I would let them handle *that* for themselves. I needed another way to convince him.

I stopped in front of Godmother's Patisserie. There was one other way through that tough elf's bubble other than Eleanor and it was sweets. I smiled as I pulled open the glass door and the smell of pumpkin spice coated my senses.

"Lily," a voice from behind the counter called. Greg was an elf with an affinity for baking. I swear, he could make the worst sounding combinations taste out of this world. As I walked towards the counter I noticed Flynn was picking up some sweets.

"Hey Flynn," I said. Flynn smiled, grabbing a pastry box from his older brother. Both of these men were Caleb's brothers. Greg, Caleb, Flynn and Bridget, in that order. The Kiernan siblings.

"Hey there, Lily. Heading to the tavern?" he asked. Flynn was around my height with shaggy dirty blonde hair and brown eyes. Flynn always had an easy smile but Caleb's temper. Greg on the other hand came up around my shoulder with light brown hair braided down his back. His blue eyes were bright like the ocean and his cheeks were rosy like cherries. An idea sparked in my brain.

I nodded. "Yep! If you're there, could I get some clips of you? If you have your family's whiskey I can add it to the clips and tag you guys," I offered. Flynn smiled. The Kiernan Family owned Kiernan's Whiskey Distillery. Caleb and Greg didn't care for helping run the company but Flynn always had an interest. He even became a horticulturist to have a deeper knowledge on vegetation to create different whiskey flavors.

"Perfect. I'll see you there then," Flynn said, waving off. I turned to Greg with a cheeky smile.

"Hey, so I need something special to get Caleb to cooperate," I pleaded. Greg let out a hearty laugh. It reminded me of Santa Clause. While I grew up with Greg, Flynn and Bridget, Caleb didn't grow up in Lavender Falls. I don't know the whole story except that their parents divorced and Caleb stayed in the city with his dad.

"Have you thought about telling him you could get Eleanor to go on a date with him?" he asked with a twinkle in his eye. I giggled.

"I thought about it but I'd rather see what naturally brings those two together," I said. Greg sighed.

"Hopefully," he said with a weird tone as he walked up and down the dessert case. I wonder what he meant. He stared into the cases to find the perfect treat to soothe his younger brother. Behind the glass were the normal desserts for tourists. He had things like different pies, puddings and cakes.

The more unusual stuff was in the back. Some of my favorites included basilisk cheesecake that used phoenix ashes or dragon turtle rolls which was like a Swiss roll but with a special dragon berry jam center. Dragon berries only grew in the hottest of climates and made the sweetest of jams.

"How about cinnamon bread with chocolate chips?" Greg's blue eyes glowed. I could tell he was mixing his magic into the bread. I pulled out my phone to record. "It's his favorite. This should help him be less grumpy since he's been a bit stressed lately." Greg eyed the bread. I wonder what was up with Caleb.

"Who knows, maybe my charm will win him over," I said. Greg snorted, packaging the bread.

"You know my brother Lily."

It was mid afternoon by the time I left the bakery. I decided to grab some clips of Greg working. There was something magical about watching experts create and extra footage was always great.

Thankfully, there wasn't too much happening at the tavern today. I sighed gratefully. If the tavern was busy, no amount of cinnamon bread with chocolate chips would deter Caleb's attention. He was even at the tavern on his off days.

Caleb was standing behind the bar cleaning glasses. His blue eyes were lighter than Greg's. It wasn't the paleness that sometimes made me feel unsettled but the way he watched you. Like a predator. I never understood why Caleb always seemed to be on guard. Especially with Greg the opposite. But then when were siblings ever the same? His hair was nearly silver and braided back. Caleb turned around as if he hadn't seen me walk in.

"Caleb," I called out. The man began walking to his office behind the bar. The asshole agreed to me filming and was now escaping. Fuck no. We had an agreement and I needed to do whatever it took to raise ticket sales. "Caleb I have cinnamon bread," I yelled. He paused at his office door. He slowly turned around.

"Is it from Greg's?" he asked with a raised eyebrow.

"Where else would I get something to bribe you with?" I raised an eyebrow back at him. He sighed heavily. I rolled my eyes. Could Eleanor be dramatic? Yes, but Caleb was the literal definition of drama. He stomped his way back to the bar, hand outstretched. I smiled, taking a seat on the bar stool.

"Fantastic. It will help make this whole ordeal as painless as possible." I pulled out my notebook with ideas.

"I doubt that," he said into his first bite. Caleb's shoulders relaxed as he ate. Was the magic working already? Mid chew he glanced at the bread. "Fucker," he grumbled.

"What?" I asked, pulling up my sound list.

"It's good," he huffed. I shook my head.

"Listen, you yourself won't be in the video, just your hands. I'll get clips of you making drinks, the bar and the tavern itself. It won't take long. I pinky promise," I said, holding up my pinky. The corners of Caleb's lips twitched.

"My hands?" he asked skeptically. I smiled at his innocence.

"Yes, hands. Hands are attractive. Especially when they're doing things like making drinks. Plus, you have strong forearms. People will be attracted to that and wonder who the mysterious bartender is." I wiggled my eyebrows for effect. He rolled his eyes.

"I want people to come here to drink and eat, not watch my hands." He took one last bite before throwing the brown paper bag away.

"Have you ever seen the 2005 version of Pride and Prejudice?" I asked. He shook his head.

"Period pieces aren't my thing," he said. A smirk pulled at my lips.

"Well if you want to understand the importance of hands you should check it out." He made a noise in the back of his throat. "It's also Eleanor's favorite movie," I added. I snuck a glance at him. There was a tick in his jaw.

"Fine. Do whatever," he grumbled. Eleanor had no idea just how much she had Caleb wrapped around her pixie pinky.

As I MADE my way to Siren's Saloon a headache was beginning to form. With the cinnamon bread in Caleb's tummy, he was more compliant. What I thought would be an hour turned to two hours of recording patrons enjoying their post work time routine as they came in.

The sun was beginning to set and all I wanted to do was crawl into a bubble bath and relax. Hopefully all the clips I got would work. I was already mentally scheduling them. I needed to be consistent more than ever this week.

The Siren's Saloon was a tad crowded for my taste. I made my way towards the bar, waving hi to the townspeople I grew up with. I ignored the pressure that was building in my chest and pasted on a smile. I could get through this. The saloon wasn't as packed as

Saturday night. But that night I was just having fun. My mindset was different that day.

Today, I was working and the slew of people around had me teetering at the edge of feeling confined. I caught Sailor behind the counter. A warm smile broke across his face.

"Hey Lily!" He gave me an easy smile as he waited behind the bar. His presence eased my nerves slightly.

"Hey Sailor!" I leaned across the bar to press a kiss into his cheek. "I'm going to need your face in these shots," I said, pulling out my phone and tripod. Sailor swallowed.

"Anyway we could avoid my face actually?" he asked. My brows furrowed. His blue eyes seemed tormented. I didn't want to pry.

"Whatever you're comfortable with," I said smiling. I didn't press Sailor but I knew there was more behind his sunshine smile.

TWO HOURS LATER, I got everything I needed. We had to take breaks in between filming so that Sailor could attend to customers. The place was nearly packed. Thankfully Sailor was making me laugh, taking my focus off of the tight feeling in my chest.

I felt a warm arm around my shoulder. I turned to see Carrie who was a tall woman with fiery red hair that hung down in waves. Her face was dusted in freckles and her green eyes were hypnotic. She was a fierce woman who could make anyone bend to her will.

But something in her face made my stomach tighten. Something was wrong. I could tell by the tension in her shoulders. I took a deep breath. I needed to relax. If something was wrong it most likely had nothing to do with me. Carrie's arm dropped away from me as she looked at Sailor.

"We need to talk," she said. Sailor cocked his head.

"I'll just go," I said softly, reaching for my bag. But then Carrie's next words made me freeze.

"This involves you too Lilianna." My stomach dropped. I turned to look at Carrie who was already headed towards her office. I glanced at Sailor who shrugged his shoulders, making his way out the bar. I trail behind them. Did she not want me filming? She never had a problem before. Was it because I almost swam in the aquarium?

With every step towards the office my mind was running through scenarios. There were endless possibilities that had me on edge. Carrie sat behind her desk. Her eyes were glued to the computer. So it was the ticket sales. She motioned us to sit in the two arms chairs. I sat down, unable to control the shake in my leg.

"Something is wrong with alcohol delivery," she said. Alcohol delivery? That caught me by surprise.

"What do you mean?" Sailor asked. I bit the inside of my cheek.

"We've had to order a bunch of extra alcohol to prepare for the festival, especially for the bar crawl. But something is wrong with the shipment. There's a major back order. They're not sure if the alcohol will arrive on time." Her eyes met mine. Something began rattling in my chest.

A memory of Caleb looking pensive as he shifted through the bar's bottles. A shakiness began to take over. We were at a stop sign and I shifted my brain into drive.

"You could contact the other bars. Split the alcohol with them? And have that as a backup plan until this issue can be resolved." I said, my voice as steady as it could be. And right before the rattling in my chest could disappear Carrie's next words sent my heart into overdrive.

"Lilianna I'm talking about the alcohol for all of the pubs. If the shipment doesn't get fixed no one will have enough for the bar crawl." Her voice sounded far away.

The bars all had to order extra alcohol because of me. It was my idea to have a bar crawl. No alcohol. No bar crawl. No promotion. I felt my breathing begin to pick up. We were in a small town. Sometimes shipments were slow to arrive. But we were a magical town. There had to be a spell? Maybe other towns we could go too.

I stared at Carrie's hands that were folded on the desk. It was all on me. I needed to fix this. My leg began shaking violently as my brain racked for solutions.

"Lily?" Sailor's voice was far away.

But could I fix this? First ticket sales, then the mystery surrounding The Drunken Fairy Tale and now this? Something in the back of my head began pulling for freedom. My heart was pounding so hard against my chest I swore it was going to burst.

A touch on my arm caused me to jump. A spark of my magic lashed out pushing Sailor away and caused the books on Carrie's desk to tumble to the ground. My eyes widened. Not again. Not now.

"Lily," Carrie said in shock. She stood up to make her way towards me. I threw up my hands. I needed to calm down. I needed to breathe. I felt it again. The pull from the pit of my stomach was leaching out and squeezing my lungs.

"Just give me a second," I choked out, trying to breathe through my nose. My throat was constricted. A tornado of thoughts kept swirling in my head. I *needed* the bar crawl to be successful. But I was failing. This was failing. I messed up. I smelled the torrent of my magic in the air. I was going to burst. Everything was bright and loud.

"Lilianna," Sailor's voice slipped through the cracks of my storm. The sound of my name twirled around me, binding my thoughts together. My breathing slowed as the smell of the ocean took over.

"Breathe," Carrie said. I felt the gentle graze of her warm fingers at my temples that made my body feel weak.

"It's okay," Sailor said. I opened my eyes to see Carrie and Sailor each holding a hand.

"Sorry," I said, tugging my hands away, the warmth disappearing.

"It's okay. It happens," Sailor said, offering a smile. I nodded weakly.

"I'll figure it out, don't worry. Let me see what Leo says. He might have a magical way around this," I said. They looked at each other before looking at me, worry written all over their faces. Sailor wrapped his arm around me.

"How about some water and fries," Sailor offered. I relaxed into his arms and nodded.

This was going to work.

THE NEXT DAY I still had the headache despite caving into medicinal remedies. I groaned into my pillow. I had to tell my boss about the crisis that was happening. But what would he say? Would he be upset? Was there a way to fix this? I pushed the negativity away. If I kept those thoughts running around it would lead into a slippery slope that would end with me having another anxiety attack and this time no one would be there to pull me out.

There was a solution. Of course there was. I pushed off my covers and went to get ready for the day.

Outside, the sky was overcast. I rolled my eyes. Rain or shine I wasn't going to let anything stop me. But I couldn't shake this feeling in the pit of my stomach. Recalling the previous day, I started to shiver.

My magic had sparked. My anxiety took over my body and who knows what would have happened if Carrie and Sailor hadn't used their magic to calm me down. I groaned. They both used their magic. It took two sirens to coax me down from having an attack and my magic running haywire.

I flinched when I remembered that I shoved Sailor. I could have hurt him. Only two people have ever seen me have an anxiety attack. My mom and Eleanor.

I still remember the shock on my mom's face. It was during finals week. I was home on a small break but still working. I had made the dumbass mistake of agreeing to two internships and attending classes full time. I had overslept because of one of my internships and accidentally spilled coffee on my marketing analytics project.

I remembered staring at the stained papers in shock. In an instant my brain had cracked. My throat tightened so much I couldn't get air in. I started choking. My body was screaming to breathe while my brain lashed out viciously saying how stupid I was. My magic began sizzling and my books began floating, pages being ripped out by themselves. The sink was spouting out water. I didn't know I was shaking until my mom was in front of me counting. She was hoping numbers would gain my focus and calm me down. It distracted me enough to relax.

Without realizing it I had arrived at the office. It was now or never.

CHAPTER 22
ANXIETY MONSTER IS FIGHTING

I sat nervously in front of Leo the following afternoon recounting what Carrie told me.

"What?" Leo kept his voice soft. He could see the look in my eyes. I bet he could sense the nerves rolling off my body. I was doing a good job of looking relatively calm but that was only surface level. Leo has known me long enough that he could tell I was trying to keep it together.

"Maybe we could go into local towns and grab the alcohol there," I suggested. I was pulling ideas out of thin air. He scratched his beard.

"Yeah. Mhmm. I'll look into other distributors that we can pull from. If anything we could always portal the alcohol even though that can sometimes be dangerous," he said. I sighed. Leo sent me a small smile. "It's okay, Lilianna. Thank you for telling me. I can also find some people to send to nearby towns," he said. I nodded, biting the inside of my cheek. "Just focus on the videos and the crawl. That's all I need you to do," he ordered.

20 year-old me would have pleaded, saying I could handle everything and offer to drive to every supply chain within 100 miles, but after yesterday and being somewhat wiser, I agreed with him. Maybe

giving my brain two things to focus on would ease the torrid waves inside me. I stood up and headed for the door.

"Work with Celestino," Leo said before I had a chance to escape. I opened my mouth to fight back. "Lilianna, he's there to help. Don't do everything on your own," he said firmly.

"I see what you're doing," I said back to my boss, opening the door.

"I don't know what you're talking about," he yelled out as the door closed.

Speaking of the warlock. Celestino stood before me. A smile twitched on his lips. He was dressed in black fitted slacks and his gray dress shirt was tucked in. A single golden chain laid around his neck. I wanted to grab it and yank him to me.

"Posey," he said, waving his binder. I shook the perverted thoughts from my head.

"You're coming with me," I demanded and made my way to the elevator.

"Yes ma'am," he said, his voice low.

We stopped at the haunted house so Celestino could grab some invoices and check on the progress. We needed to go back to the library to look up some old records. Hopefully that would clue us in on who owned the tavern because there was no way I was going to leave this mystery unsolved. Sailor walked in on his way to decorate one of the rooms and Celestino waved him over. Oh, no. Would he mention yesterday? Celestino handed him some papers with designs.

"Hey guys! Lily, I heard Leo is handling the distributors. Carrie is relieved," Sailor said. I nodded. News travels fast in a small town. Thank the stars he didn't mention my near anxiety attack. "Are you feeling better by the way?" He placed his hand on top of mine. Dammit Sailor.

"What do you mean is she feeling better?" Celestino's voice cut through the magic. We both glanced at him. Celestino watched as I slipped my hand out of Sailor's, his eyes were glowing a brighter shade of green.

My stomach twisted. I was keeping my anxiety from him and it was starting to eat me up inside. Sailor knew about it. He was a siren and could sense my emotions better than me.

"It's nothing Celestino and yes, Sailor, I am. Thanks again," I said. I was being cryptic. It was stupid. Celestino was my best friend. We grew up together. But I cared what he thought of me. I didn't want him to look at me as weak. I couldn't handle that.

"Well, I'm glad. If there's anything you need, let me know. Can't wait to see the video too!" Sailor glanced at Celestino and gave a tight nod, leaving us alone.

"Posey." Celestino's voice sounded demanding. I hatcd that I liked it.

"Celestino," I said, sending the attitude back at him.

"You're really not going to tell me?" He raised an eyebrow.

"Nope," I said. I could tell by the tick in his jaw he didn't like that.

"I'll find out sooner or later," he said, grabbing his bag. I rolled my eyes.

"And how do you know that?" I asked.

"Because I'm a very determined warlock," he said, stepping in front of me. I snorted. What was he, a character in my romance novels?

"And I'm a stubborn witch," I said, taking a step closer to him. Our eyes connected in a silent battle that I desperately wanted to win.

"I've always liked a challenge," he said, his arm slipping around my waist. I gasped as he pulled me close. He smirked. His green eyes stared back at me playfully.

"Not going to give up?" I softly asked.

"Never." His eyes bore into mine. I bit back a smile. I pushed him away before his eyes could make me spill my guts. We needed to head to the library before it closed.

CHAPTER 23

DISCOVERING KINKS

Walking into the library, we made our way towards the head librarian, Ms. Glade. She also happened to be the record keeper for the town. She was one of the oldest and sweetest witches in Lavender Falls.

"Everything is in the basement! Look through whatever you like Lilianna. You should be able to find what you need there," Ms. Glade said. She handed me the key before turning to Celestino. "Celestino, so glad you're back," she said.

"Glad to be back," Celestino said, smiling warmly. The records were kept in the basement of the library. I followed behind Celestino as we descended the stairs. The air around us cooled as we walked down. I couldn't stop my eyes from wandering from his wide shoulders to down his back.

"Posey?" I heard Celestino say, interrupting my fantasy. I needed to relax. *Focus.* I used the key Ms. Glade gave me to unlock the room. Stepping in, the room was filled with filing cabinets and off to the side was a table and a few chairs. I turned around to see that Celestino had a little smirk. I knew he caught me checking him out.

"So what year are we looking for?" he asked, not calling me out on my lustful longing. I set my bag on the table.

"Probably around the 1940-50s," I said. He nodded and went off towards one of the cabinets. Was he really not going to bring up rule six? I inwardly groaned as I remember the dream I had during our unexpected sleepover. We were making out. Our hands roaming each other's bodies.

I blushed at the memory. It felt so real. I glance over at him to see him flipping through files. I was being distracted by my own thoughts. We needed to finish this assignment. And maybe when everything was finally over I could answer his dare from the closet.

We were surrounded by papers. The dull pain in my head came back as I shifted through the files. I clutched my head. Why was this so hard? This was seeming to be hopeless. So far we haven't found anything. It had to have been a spell to have this much erasure.

"We'll find something," Celestino said, encouragingly. I felt my eyebrow twitch. My chest was tight again.

I looked around at all the papers. We needed to figure out who the owner was so I could finish the script for the Cursed Bar Crawl. With the script done I could focus more on promoting. I *needed* this to be successful. I *needed* to show Leo and Mayor Kiana what I was capable of. I had to trust my gut. Or was my anxiety talking?

"Posey?" Celestino's voice was quiet. I took a deep breath. I could feel irritation seeping in and that wasn't fair to him.

"I'm just tired," I said.

"We can go home. Come back tomorrow. It's been a long day," he suggested. Coming back fully rested with fresh eyes was a good idea. But I was stubborn. I shook my head.

"There has to be something," I said through gritted teeth.

"You know we could always make something up," he said tentatively.

" No. I can't explain it but I need to figure out who the person was."

There was also the problem of ticket sales and the alcohol. There was so much. So fucking much. I barely heard the scrape of a chair as my breathing quickened. He turned my chair to face him and tilted my chin up.

"You need a break," he whispered. I felt my heart rattling against my chest.

"There's so much I have to do," I practically pleaded. The papers were shaking between my fingers. Celestino leaned closer.

"You need a break," he said again, his eyes serious. My eyes flickered to his full lips. Glancing back up to his eyes they were glowing, pupils becoming dilated. "Posey," he said. His hand was light as it slipped down my throat, creating a trail of heat. My body was slowly burning up. Was it finally happening? Was this the moment?

"I caught you in the staircase. Rule six, truth or dare," he said. This was the moment. I had been waiting for him to say something. I knew my answer.

"Dare," I whispered.

"I dare you to take a break," he said, gently kissing my forehead. His hand fell away from my neck.

It felt like a cold bucket of water was thrown on me. That's what he chose for a dare? Sure, he kissed my forehead which made me want to melt but my lips were right there!

Something in me snapped. This is not how I wanted this to go. I was frustrated. I was tired and the stupid dream had been filling my head. I glared up at him.

"What," he asks, batting his eyelashes. The warlock knew what he did. Anger and frustration began taking over. The thinking side of my brain had officially decided to say fuck off. I didn't care anymore. "Posey," he said, curiously.

"Sit in the chair," I say, getting up from my seat. I didn't know what I was doing. I was scrambling to grip onto control. He obeyed silently. His hands gripped his thighs.

"*Querida*?" he questioned. I swallowed.

"Rule seven, truth or dare?" I asked. He tilted his chin up, fighting back a smile. I always enjoyed him having to look up at me.

"What did I start?" he asked with a smirk.

"You know what you did back there. Now, truth or dare," I said, breathing heavily. He sat watching me, his eyes traveling down my body. My hand reached to hold his chin and force his gaze. "Pick Celestino."

"Dare," he whispered.

"I dare you to kiss me." The words were barely a whisper and he reacted instantly. He reached for my waist, pulling me onto his lap. I gasped.

"Are you sure?" he asked in a rough voice that felt like sand against my skin.

Even though this was about to blow our friendship out of the water, I wanted him to kiss me.

"Celestino, I need to not think. Please," I said, my fingers playing with his shirt collar. His hand slipped to the back of my head, pulling me to kiss my cheek, gently.

"I'm not rushing this okay," he murmured. I nodded wordlessly as he swept kisses across my other cheek, down my jaw and across my temple. It was like he was easing us into the inevitability of our lips joining in blissful unison. Just like how I imagined in the library the other day. It made my heart swell.

He pulled back to look at me again, taking a deep breath.

"May I?" he asked. I nodded. I felt his hand drop to the back of my neck while my hands slid around his, pulling him closer. His mouth slanted over mine and my fingers tightened in his hair.

Finally.

Our bodies relaxed into each other as we kissed. I could almost hear the Fates rejoicing. It was a kiss that spoke to the deepest part of me. The thread that linked our souls finally intertwined into place after being trailed around for years.

He pulled back, slightly out of breath, pressing his forehead against mine. I could feel the slight tremble of his hands holding me against him. We stare at each other wide eyed.

"We kissed," I said in a shaky breath as he tucked a strand of hair behind my ear. He gave me a soft smile, his eyes crinkling on the corners. My favorite smile.

"Would you like to again?" he asked. I looked at his plumped lips.

"Yes," I said. His smile grew until I was being basked in his glow. I leaned forward, tilting my head to get closer. I was kissing my best friend. His lips were tender as they coaxed me closer and closer. My hands slid down to grip his shirt and pull him towards me.

Desperation was beginning to set in. His other hand pressed into my lower back until we were flushed against each other. I needed to be closer. I nipped his bottom lip and he shivered. I couldn't help but smile.

"I can't kiss you if you're smiling," he grunted. I pressed my forehead against his, smiling wide. He tugged my hair back and I gasped. Celestino took advantage and slipped his tongue. My heart was rapidly beating. My body was being consumed by fire. I threw my hands into his hair.

I needed more. He groaned, deep in his throat as I tugged. He licked and nipped a heated trail down my throat and a whimper poured out. My body trembled against him. It had been so long since I felt this way, since I felt devoured by these sensations.

"Fuck," he whispered against my skin. His shaky hands wandered, squeezing, pushing my body as if trying to mold me into his as they explored. I rocked my hips against him, needing friction to dull the ache between my thighs. His hands lowered to squeeze my ass. "Lilianna," he whispered, finding my mouth again. My name on his lips had me falling deeper into this moment.

"More," I begged. I needed more from him. He filled my heart and my mind for more than half of my life and now that I've tasted him I wanted to be consumed.

"Fucking greedy," he whispered as he bit the spot between my neck and shoulder. Celestino rarely cursed and it sent a wild thrill down my spine to see him come apart. He bucked his hips and I gasped, wrapping my arms around him.

"Like that?" he asked, tugging at my earlobe. His fingers brushed underneath my breast, making me arch.

"Yes," I hissed. I pulled his face back. I wanted more of his kisses. They were addicting.

This time there was no gentleness. It was fire clashing against fire and we were burning each other. I dug my nails into his back, clinging to him as if he was the only thing keeping me grounded to Earth. His hands dipped back down, digging into my ass, rocking me into a delicious rhythm. I felt myself floating higher and higher.

This is what I needed, a moment to forget the world. I could feel his magic caressing me, massaging me. It was intoxicating.

"Lilianna," Celestino hissed.

The sound of knocking broke us apart. I scrambled as I ran over to a filing cabinet to look busy. I took in a deep breath, trying to settle my nerves.

"Hi guys. We're closing up okay?" Ms. Glade poked her head from behind the door.

"Okay! We'll be out soon." Celestino answered as I tried my best to get my body to calm down. My body was hot and my lips felt swollen.

I just fucking made out with Celestino Nuno Santos. *My best friend.* My hands trembled as I mindlessly flipped through files.

"Lilianna," he said from behind me. Not Posey. Lilianna. At this moment I wasn't Posey, his best friend who would read books at his soccer games but Lilianna, the witch he let dry hump in the basement of the library.

"Y-yes," I stuttered. Fuck, I needed to get a grip. He braced a hand on either side of me, holding onto the cabinets and pressed against my back. A whimper escaped my mouth. He was still hard and it felt so fucking good.

"We're not done. Use rule nine," he whispered as he placed a soft kiss on my shoulder. I turned around. He still wanted this? Staring into his eyes I knew things were different. We crossed a line that was becoming blurry. But he was giving me control.

"Truth or dare?" I asked, regaining composure.

"Dare," he said with unwavering desire. His pupils were blown and he was breathing heavily. He pressed his forehead against mine. "Dare, *querida*," he whispered. Celestino traced a line with his fingers along my jaw and down my neck, stopping at my collarbone.

"I dare you to come back to my apartment." I don't know where this dominant side of me came from but I was letting her take the reins.

"Yes ma'am," he said.

I really was developing a kink.

CHAPTER 24
MORE. MORE. MORE

My hands were shaking as we walked back to her apartment. This wasn't how I planned my night but who the fuck was I to deny my witch what she wanted. I could still feel her ass in my hands. The way she rocked and panted against me.

Stars, she felt like a fucking celestial being against me. I needed to worship her. I needed her to scream my name.

The line was blurred. We both knew it. I had no idea how the rest of the night was going to go or how she would feel tomorrow but I knew one thing for sure. She was going to come by my hands. I knew the second we were walking down the basement steps that something shifted in her. She could barely focus in that room. Her face was flushed and she kept twitching. She felt frustrated.

Her hands were shaking like mine as we entered her apartment. We slipped out of our shoes when she finally spoke.

"Celestino?" she asked, pulling me from thoughts.

"Yes *minha alma*?" I asked. She turned to me, eyes filled with concern. Pain washed through me. Was she regretting this? "What's wrong?" I asked, cupping her face. She sighed.

"I liked kissing you," she grumbled.

"I liked kissing you too," I teased, tapping her nose. She bit her lip and I pulled it away with my thumb. "Lilianna?" I needed to know what was running through her mind.

"I'm just afraid," she confessed. I dropped one hand to her waist, pulling her in.

"Why?" I asked softly, kissing the side of her head. I didn't want her running away from me.

"What if it doesn't work out? What if we're not compatible? What if I break your heart? Will that ruin our friendship? Will that make our friends choose between us? Will-"

I kissed her quick and hard, interrupting her. I needed her to stop talking about us ending before we even began. She leaned into our kiss, giving in quickly and easily.

"Not compatible?" I asked with an eyebrow raised. She rolled her eyes, cheeks flushed.

"Okay…maybe we are but what if-"

"Lilianna," I said, cutting her off with words this time. She was looking off to the side now, afraid to meet my eyes. I gripped her chin. "There's a chance it might not work out," I said truthfully. She breathed in sharply. "But there's a chance that this could be the best thing that has ever happened to us," I continued. Her bottom lip quivered.

"I'm really scared," she choked out. My heart clenched. I pulled her into a hug.

"And you don't think I am?" My voice cracked at the end. I've been in love with her since we were kids. I always dreamt of the possibility of this happening. Now here it was. There was no way I was going to fuck this up. Lilianna and I have been intertwined since we were kids and there was nothing that could break us apart.

"Our friendship has always been one of the most important things in my life. You've always been my center," I said. She pulled back.

"Really?" she asked in disbelief.

"You keep me tethered to the world. You're my gravity," I said, smiling, tucking a strand of hair behind her ear. Her brows furrowed.

"Wait…have you liked me this whole time?" she asked. I chuckled.

"Was it not obvious?" I asked. She pushed away from me.

"No! I've had a crush on you since…forever," she confessed. My heart surged. She's been feeling the exact same way this whole time. And I bet a thousand comets that Eleanor and Lola knew.

"Well we don't want to waste any more time," I said. Her cheeks flushed. "Or should we take it slow?" I asked.

"I mean I was dry humping you earlier. That's at least second base," she said. I shook my head, unable to stop the grin on my face. I began walking towards her. She took a step back. I raised an eyebrow.

"Posey?" I asked. She bit her lip smirking and took another step back.

"What?" she asked innocently.

"Why are you stepping away when we just confessed a life long crush on each other? We should be making out right now amongst a few other things if you're down," I said, taking another step. We continued this dance until only the couch and coffee table separated us.

"Maybe I like making you work," she flirted, eyes excited.

"You're such a temptress," I said, crossing my arms.

"I like tempting you," she said. My dick twitched in my pants. I was fucking falling for this confident flirty side of her. I needed more. I placed my hands on the back of the couch.

"What else?" I asked. My eyes dipped to the rapid fall of her chest.

"I like being on top."

I sucked in a breath. She crossed her arms and once again my eyes were on her breasts that were peeking from the neck of her blouse. A memory of the elevator resurfaced, her braless and pressed into my chest. My hands itched to feel them. I walked around the couch and sat down, arms spread out. I raised an eyebrow. She walked towards me, slowly, her eyes never leaving mine.

"Hands stay on the couch," she said. I groaned, clutching the couch cushion with my hands. She was really going to torture me. She settled in my lap, straddling me. I hissed as she rocked her weight against my cock, a smirk on her perfect face. Fuck, I loved confident Lilianna. Before I could think further into that, she fully settled her weight on me.

"We're doing this," she said softly. I nodded. She dragged her hands up against my dress shirt, smiling. Her fingers trailed against the collar, gently brushing my skin.

"Lilianna," I growled. Looking at her I still couldn't believe this was the same Lilianna. "You can take it off if you want," I said, my voice hoarse.

"I used to dream about you saying that," she confessed. My heart rate kicked up.

"You dreamt about us?" I asked. She nodded, eyes darting away quickly. I tilted my head and she looked at me. "I want this to be good for you," I said.

"For *us*," she said quietly. I nodded. She leaned forward and brushed her lips against mine. She rocked against my dick and I groaned out loud.

"Did you dream about me while wearing my hoodie?" I asked the questions that were burning me. She pulled back smiling before nipping my bottom lip.

"Use rule six," she said softly against my mouth. I chuckled.

"Truth or dare," I whispered. She dragged her fingers into my hair.

"Truth," she said with a small smile.

"Did you touch yourself while wearing my hoodie?" I asked. My body tightened in anticipation.

"Yes," she said with a grin. I groaned and leaned forward to connect our lips.

Kissing Lilianna felt like getting caught in a thunderstorm; her touch was like lightning dancing across my skin, and I was ready to drown in her downpour.

I felt her thighs squeeze as my tongue slipped between her lips. She moaned as my tongue slid along hers. Her hands were sliding from my neck to down my chest. Our lips kept crashing into each other and I could feel our magic around us tingling.

Lilianna refused to let up. She was kissing me as if it was our last day on Earth. As if this was our one and only moment to surrender to each other. She kept grinding into me, seeking release. If only she would let me touch her. She moaned as I sucked on her bottom lip.

Stars, it had been so long since I had a woman's touch. Between her rocking against my dick and her moans and whimpers I was ready to come. I lean my head against the back of the couch, panting as she bit and licked her way down my neck.

Who fucking knew my little witch was so aggressive. I was probably going to have a hickey. I smiled at the thought of her marking me and everyone seeing it.

"Lilianna," I panted. She mumbled something against my throat. Her tongue flicked against my heated skin and I shivered. "Let me touch you," I said as I rolled my hips. She pulled back, her lips fucking swollen. There was a wicked gleam in her eyes again.

"Beg," she said. My eyebrows rose.

"Beg or play our little game?" I asked. She bit her lip before grinning.

"Rule nine, truth or dare," she said as she began rocking faster against me. Fuck, I was going to finish in my goddam slacks. I leaned forward, brushing my lips against her as she leaned back.

"Lilianna Maria Rosario" Her eyes widened as I said her full name. I slowly brought my hands closer, grazing her legs. "I pick dare because I want to fucking touch you." I kissed her cheek as my hands traced her thighs. "I pick dare because I need you to come by my fingers," I whispered into her ear.

"And I pick dare because I need you to scream my name." I bit into the tender flesh below her ear. A small whimper escaped her lips.

"I dare you to touch me," she whispered, voice pleading. I smiled. *Fucking finally.*

We reached for each other again. My hands gripped whatever they found. The back of her neck, her hips, her ass. It was like I couldn't get enough. I needed more. I was blissfully drowning in my best friend.

She pressed into me as my hand slipped under her blouse. I stroked her soft skin with lazy lines, tracing the hem of her pants. As our tongues tangled, I dragged my nails down her back under her bra line.

"Yes," she hissed.

"Can I touch you here?" I asked. My hands were aching to feel her breasts, to roll her nipples between my fingers. Lilianna's hands tightened around the collar of my shirt.

"Lilianna?" I asked, pulling back. Her face was flushed, eyes hazy with lust. "Can I touch you here?" I asked more clearly. She laid her head on my shoulder, arching her back as my hands kept digging into her muscles.

"Yes," she whispered. I lifted her up and her legs immediately wrapped around my waist. "W-where are we going?"

"To your bedroom where I can lay you out properly and fulfill both of our dreams." She let out a carefree laugh and I bottled the sound. I planned on spending the rest of my life making her smile, laugh and especially moan.

CHAPTER 25
YES. YES. YES

I held onto Celestino. My heart was pounding. He felt so good in my arms. My body was igniting. I needed more of him. But a tiny part of me was still nervous. It had been so long since I had been intimate with someone even though with Celestino it felt right. It felt natural and that was scaring me.

He pushed open my door, still holding onto me. He squeezed my ass hard and I pressed against his cock with a moan.

"Rough?" he asked, breathless as he dropped me on my bed. His eyes were dark and filled with desire.

"I think so," I said honestly. He cocked his head to the side.

"Why don't we take our time and find out?" he asked. My heart swelled. This man was going to be the death of me. I nodded.

"I'm going to take off my shirt," he said, slowly unbuttoning it. I swallowed. How many times did I fantasize kissing his body? Tracing his tattoos with my tongue? Celestino threw his shirt over to my dresser revealing his inky tan skin.

My fingers shook, reaching out towards him. He smiled and motioned me to scoot back. I pushed my way up my bed as he crawled towards me. A fucking sight, watching him on his hands and knees to worship me.

"When did you get the tattoos?" I asked. I needed to distract my brain from overthinking what we were about to do. He smiled.

"This first part here," he started as he pointed to his left pec. "It was freshman year. I didn't go back for the fall festival. I wanted something to remind me of home." I bit down my lip and blinked my eyes a few times. His tattoos were a mixture of lavender and waves intertwining.

Ocean waves.

His hand slipped to cup the back of my head. I was definitely going to die of bliss. Celestino was going to murder me with happiness but hopefully after I orgasmed.

This time when we kissed it was like the first time, sweet and gentle. We took our time relaxing into each other's touches. My hands wandered up and down his back gripping and pulling at his heated skin.

As he made his way to the sensitive spot on my neck I began tugging up my shirt. He pulled back with an arched eyebrow, asking if it was okay. I nodded and sat up. He helped me pull off my blouse and sat back on his heels. His chest was rising and falling fast. I suddenly wished I wore something other than a plain nude bra.

We looked at each other for a moment. His eyes wandered up and down my body, taking me in. The blurred line was about to be erased. His fingers came up to play with my bra strap.

"I feel nervous," I confessed.

"Same." He let out a chuckle.

I tucked a hair behind his ear and leaned in for another kiss. Taking a deep breath I reached back to undo the clasp. He pulled off my bra and tossed it to the side. Celestino groaned. His hand lightly grazed the side of my breast as he stared at me.

"You're beautiful," he whispered. A noise escaped my lips at the light feel of his touch. My breathing hitched when he pinched my nipple.

"*Minha*," he whispered. His eyes roamed down my body, taking in the sight of my naked chest. He pushed me back until I was laying against the bed. "Pants?" he asked. I reached for the button. Celestino moved my hands away and began kissing down my stomach as he pulled my pants off.

After pulling off his own, he made his back between my thighs, pushing them apart. I rocked my hips needing his mouth on me. His finger brushed down the center of my panties and my body twitched.

"Not yet *meu amor*," he whispered.

His lips found their way back to my mouth and then down my neck until he reached my nipple. He flicked with his tongue and I gasped loudly, thrusting my hips against his. I clamped a hand over my mouth and I watched as he licked his fingers to play with the other at the same time. I squeezed my eyes shut. Watching him felt erotic, over-whelming.

"I want to hear you, Lilianna," he whispered as he sucked and nipped at a torturous pace. I whimpered, grinding my hips. He yanked my hand from my mouth and my eyes shot open.

"Neighbors," I said, glaring at him. He placed a tender kiss on the center of my chest.

"Good thing I know magic." He smirked, his green eyes glowed violet slightly and a faint whisper of magic seeped into the room. He gripped my hips and rolled me over so I was back on top.

"Now, be as loud as you want my wicked witch," he said, voice rough. I rocked against him as he thrusted up. "Fuck Lilianna. *Linda.*" His hands ran up my body, squeezing my breasts together. I shivered. It still wasn't enough.

Then one of his hands made its way around my throat. I sucked in a breath as he squeezed lightly. I moaned, rocking harder.

"Use me Lilianna," he whispered. "Ride me until you come," he said, fingers digging into my hips. "Lilianna," he said as he bucked up. I grunted in frustration. My brain was refusing to switch off and was getting in my way.

"So close but-," I struggled to get out.

"Tell me what you want," he said as he reached up to take my nipple back in his mouth. I moaned as his tongue flicked and his teeth nipped gently. Fuck, the things he could do with his mouth. I took a shaky breath. I could feel my orgasm just out of reach. My brain was completely consumed with thoughts and letting go felt unattainable. My hands tightened on his shoulders in frustration.

"Hey, what's wrong?" Celestino asked, pulling away to look me in the eyes. I traced the wave that was tattooed across his left pec as he began massaging the top of my thighs.

"Sometimes…because my head is so filled with thoughts, I have trouble just feeling," I said as best as I could.

"I guess I need to do better at distracting that beautiful brain of yours," he said. It took a second for his words to sink in.

"I guess you should." I said, shrugging my shoulders, biting back a smile.

"I don't care how long it takes, I plan on learning every inch of your body." He pressed the promise across my collarbone with his lips. My head tilted back and my hips rocked against his cock slowly this time. I gasped when he lightly smacked my inner thigh

"But I *need* you to tell me what your body wants." He arched an eyebrow. I bit my lip. "Rule nine, truth or dare," he said as his fingers traced my panty line. I felt my head swimming as waves of pleasure rolled. "Truth or dare, *querida.*" His tone was impatient. But I was losing focus. I mumbled truth as his fingers brushed my panties.

"What do you want me to do?" he asked.

"I want you to eat me out," I said timidly. His eyes lit up with excitement and I swear his cock pulsed under me.

"Thank fucking stars," he whispered.

"I think you mean Lilianna," I said. He rolled me on my back and pressed into me. His body was a delicious weight. "Celestino," I moaned. He smiled sinfully, pressing his forehead against mine.

"I'm going to pull your panties off now and I want you to watch me," he demanded. I nodded weakly. His hands slipped under my waistband and tugged them down to my ankles. Sitting back his eyes roamed all over my naked body. He was breathing fast. A part of me wanted to cover up and hide. I fought that urge down. With him, I was safe. I knew I was.

His fingers slipped between my folds and he let out a deep groan.

"Are you really this wet for me, little witch?" he asked. I nodded weakly. Celestino's lips stretched into a wicked grin. He gripped the back of my thighs and hauled them over his shoulders with ease.

I yelped. My ass was pressing against his chest and I reached behind me to grip the pillows for some support.

"Eyes on me *querida*, while I eat this pretty pussy." His voice was hoarse against my inner thigh. He parted my lips and his tongue circled my entrance. My legs immediately tightened. I rocked my hips, needing to ride his face.

This is what I wanted. His tongue continued there path up until he found my clit. I bucked as he found the spot and he chuckled. My hands dug into the pillows. I felt myself getting closer and closer to the edge.

"There," I yelled when his tongue hit the perfect pressure. I kept my eyes on him like he asked. He flicked his tongue back and forth on my clit and then sucked. My thighs were trembling as he worked me. It was becoming too much but he was reading every movement I made as his mouth devoured me.

He continued the pattern until I could barely breathe. I could feel the blood rushing to my head because of the angle. His tongue slid back down teasing the aching hole that was begging to be filled.

My hand gripped his hair, pulling him closer. He gave a rough lick on my clit that had me arching off the bed as he slipped a thick finger inside.

"Fuck Lilianna," he mumbled. My hips bucked, trying to meet him with every thrust of his finger. "All of this is for your best friend, uh," he said, grinning. My core tightened. He sucked hard on my clit and my legs tightened around his head.

I glanced away from his adoring face to flick my hand towards the dresser. Without too much thought my magic opened the draw. Celestino pulled away in question.

"Toy too," I gasped out. "Please," I hissed.

"I've been dreaming about using it on you since I found it." He reached over to grab the blue vibrator. It curved slightly at the end and according to directions had different vibrating speeds.

"This is going to be fucking fun." He smiled wickedly, his beard glistening.

He laid my body back down and nudged my legs further apart. He slid the toy between my folds, getting it wet. I sucked in a deep breath.

"I got you," he whispered as he licked my thigh. I hissed as he slowly pushed it in.

"I can't wait for you to take my cock," he said. He pushed the toy further in and my body tightened. "Stars, you're fucking tight," he said. I nodded frantically. I could feel myself straining to open up. Celestino must have sensed it because his lips found my clit again and he turned the vibrator on to the first setting. It pulsed in a slow rhythm.

My body relaxed at the new sensations. He took his time thrusting the toy while tracing circles on my clit with his tongue until my body gave in to his torture.

He messed with the vibration setting until he found the pace that was making me tug his hair and my thighs tremble. I began moaning louder as the toy slipped in easier.

His name was mixed with a slew of curse words. My heart was threatening to jump out. My senses became overwhelmed. I felt like I was riding on a cloud higher and higher.

"Celestino. Y-yes," I hissed, as his pace picked up. His magic pressed into me, grounding me. The books on my shelf began shaking as I felt my magic crackle through the air. His hand lowered, shifting the angle of the vibrator.

"Come for me *meu amor*," he whispered.

I threw my head back, eyes clenched close as the wave of my orgasm shoved me over the edge. I cried out his name and my body shook uncontrollably. But it didn't stop. My orgasm crashed into me again and again as he kept thrusting the toy. His tongue refused to let up.

"I-I can't," I stuttered.

He shushed me, pulling out the toy as his mouth kept torturing every last drop out of me until I was no longer trembling. He pulled away to look at me with hooded eyes.

"Holy stars," I said, trying to get a handle on breathing normal. My legs felt like jelly. Celestino smiled, eyes raking up and down my body.

"Now imagine how it'll feel with my cock inside you," he said, pressing a kiss to my shoulder. I shook my head laughing and reluctantly moved to get up. Celestino caught my hand.

"Where are you going?" he asked.

"I have to pee now," I said. If I didn't go now I would not be getting out of the bed and my body would hate me. He let go of my hand. I slipped his hoodie that was on my corner chair before running to the bathroom.

Once I cleaned myself up, I stared into the mirror. My hair was frizzy and my face flushed. I was a mess but I looked happy. I was happy. He just made me have the best orgasm of my life. Celestino Nuno Santos made me come. He touched parts of my body I only dreamed about.

I made my way back to the bedroom ignoring the millions of questions running through my head. I needed to savor this moment.

"Hey," he said once I was back in the room. He held his arms out and I let him pull me into his chest.

"You curse more when you're horny," I stated. Celestino never really cursed much but behind closed doors? It was like he let go of something. He chuckled.

"I guess I do. But we need to do one thing right now." His eyes were filled with mischief. I glanced at his still hard cock, my hand already trailing down his tattoo. He let out a laugh.

"Don't worry about me. This is about you, *querida*." I blushed at the endearment. I moved to straddle him, already enjoying the feel of his cock under me again.

"Yes?" I couldn't even begin to guess what he had planned.

"How's my neck?" he asked. I inspected his neck in confusion.

"There's like two hickeys from when I was kissing you," I admitted embarrassingly. He smiled and grabbed the back of my neck, pulling me forward. We smiled at each other. My heart, my body, my brain felt like they were floating.

"Good because I want you to mark me." My eyes widened. I was not expecting that. "You've made me discover that I might have a kink." He slapped my ass playfully and a startled gasp poured out. "Now come on, my wicked witch. Do your worst."

And who was I to say no when given a task?

CHAPTER 26

FIRST DATE

I woke up in bed alone the next day. After giving Celestino a few hickeys he left. He didn't want anything else from me. I clutched my pillow. I couldn't wrap my head around what happened last night. The confession, the kisses, the touches. Memories from the night filled my brain.

"I CAN'T BELIEVE you still have this," Celestino said with a warm smile. He was playing with the hem of my hoodie. I nodded, my cheeks heating up. He gave me his hoodie when we were seniors and the soccer team won their championship. We were having a senior class bonfire.

"You were sitting by the fire, shivering in that flimsy cardigan," he said. I nodded again, my fingers tracing his cheek. "I handed it to you and you looked so cute wearing it." His fingers came up to trace my cheek. "I wanted to kiss you then," he confessed. My hand slipped into his hair. He met my eyes.

"I wanted to kiss you in that moment too," I said. He swallowed, eyes filled with regret.

"But it didn't quite feel right," he said. Which was true. It didn't feel right. Under the fire's glow, surrounded by our friends drinking, it didn't feel like the right moment for us.

"I tried to give it back to you," I pointed out. Celestino chuckled and brought me tighter to his chest.

"Yeah but I wanted you to keep it. I wanted you to have something of mine for when we separated for college," he whispered. And I wore it all the time, even now.

Because having a piece of him was having a piece of home.

I COULDN'T STOP the smile stretching across my face. But what now? It was early enough that my brain was spiraling without my permission. What did this mean? We haven't gone on a date. Are we together? We confessed. Do I ask him out? Does he ask me out? More questions kept floating around my head.

I shook away the thoughts and headed for a shower. I was over-thinking like normal. None of these questions would be answered until we had a conversation. But we also still needed to find the owner of The Drunken Fairy Tale Tavern.

After pulling on a shirt and some jeans I made my way to the kitchen for a cup of coffee. I could feel my phone burning in my back pocket. I hadn't messaged Celestino and he hadn't texted me either. But then again, it was just 7 am. I sighed, watching the water heat up.

A tingle ran down my spine. Without thinking, I headed towards my door and threw it open. Except the hallway was empty. I could have sworn I sensed Celestino. Ever since he came back it was like my magic was constantly seeking him out, aware of where he was. I heard a tapping from inside my apartment.

"What," I said under my breath. Closing the door I walked back into the living room. The sounds of birds singing by my kitchen window caught my ear. For once their melodies didn't make me want to set them on fire. A small white dove was pecking at the glass.

"What the stars," I muttered. Walking closer to the window, there were three birds randomly hovering outside. One was carrying a small paper while two were holding a flower crown. "What the fury fuck," I said while opening the window.

A breeze surged in and the birds flew in dropping a flower crown and an envelope. As fast as they came in, they flew out. I stared in disbelief. I pinched myself. Surely that did not just happen. Am I Snow White? Cinderella? I picked up the white piece of paper and unfolded it.

Good morning minha alma,

I'm still in awe about last night. Who knew (other than the town) that we've been crushing on each other our entire lives? I bet you're actually wondering what all of this means and you'll find out soon.

I wanted to know if you would accompany me on a lovely picnic. And yes, it is a date. Our first date of many if I'm being optimistic. If it's yes, please place the crown on your head. If no...well no hard feelings. Like I said, we'll take it as slow as you want.

Meu coração é seu,

Celestino

P.S. don't worry about work I have an idea

My heart was pounding. Tears pricked my eyes. This was like a fairy tale. This was something out of one of my romance novels. I stared at the paper until the words blurred with my tears. I closed my eyes tightly, taking a deep breath.

I grabbed the flower crown that was adorned with baby's breath, carnations and daisies. Simple and beautiful. Just how I liked things. I smiled. He knew me so well.

I was going to go on a date with Celestino.

I placed the crown on my head and a puff of pixie dust exploded. The clothes I was wearing began to transform into black jeans with a cropped burgundy sweater.

A knock on my door stole my attention before I could think about what just happened. It was him. I could feel it in my bones.

Throwing the door open, Celestino stood with a bouquet of white carnations.

"*Meu coração*," he said, handing me a bouquet of carnations. He wore black slacks with a cream sweater and sneakers. I blushed.

"Again with the names," I said, teasingly.

"You better get used to it." His fingers wandered to my hip, pinching the sweater as his eyes softened. "Shall we go?" he asked.

"This is too much," I said with a grin. He cupped my face and placed a soft kiss on the corner of my mouth.

"We'll work on that."

I HAD no idea where Celestino was taking us and for once I honestly didn't care. Okay, that was a lie. Throughout our walk my brain kept jumping between the fact that he was holding my hand and trying to pinpoint the possible area our path was taking us.

It wasn't until we were walking by Boogeyman's Bar that I figured out we were heading towards the Gasping Greenwood Forest.

"The forest?" I asked. Celestino didn't respond. Instead he kept smiling and tugging me along. I actually liked the Gasping Greenwood Forest despite its name. It was a normal forest although a few sprites and creatures dwelled within it. They named it that to entice the tourists. The forest laid around the edges of Boogeyman swamp by our community garden.

As we crossed the swamp I waved hi to the water sprites. It's good to always be polite so they wouldn't feel the need to play tricks. A chill seemed to breathe out of the woods as we stepped in.

"Ready?" Celestino's voice cut through. Leaves crunched beneath our feet. Tree branches twisted into each other as if to embrace one another in solace as their leaves broke and floated to the ground.

We followed the marked path, most likely heading towards the clearing. It was one of the few places in Lavender Falls that I felt completely at peace. Probably because it was the area where multiple ley lines crossed. It also happened to be a popular spot for picnics and ceremonies.

After a few minutes of walking, we made it to the edge of the clearing. Golden rays cut through the boney branches painting the scenery like a kaleidoscope of autumn colors. In the middle of the clearing was a blanket and a picnic basket. I turned to Celestino smiling.

"*Querida,*" he said, stretching out his arm for me to continue walking. Upon closer speculation it wasn't just a blanket and a basket. There were pillows, a bottle of sparkling wine and books.

"Are those books about the town?" I asked, my eyes widening. He came up from behind to wrap his arms around me. I melted into his warmth.

"I knew there was no way you would be able to focus on our date when we still haven't figured out the pub situation and there was no way in hellhound's lair I was going to wait until after the festival to take you out." He squeezed me. "So why not have both," he whispered in my ear. My chest tightened. I bit my lip. How could he know me so well?

"I'm sorry," I blurted. He spun me around.

"Why?" he asked in surprise.

"I'm a workaholic," I stated. My heart skipped with trepidation. This was a date and Celestino was willing to turn it into a work date. Guilt began settling.

"Hey, Posey. I'm okay with this. I thought of this. I wouldn't be doing it if I wasn't sure." He tilted my head slightly down. "Look at me," he said softly. I couldn't deny him when he used that tone.

"You're okay with it?" I asked again, needing confirmation.

"Yes and you know why," he said, his tone switching to playful. He pulled away to scoop up the bottle of wine. "Because we're going to have mimosas and mimosas make everything better." Laughter broke out of me. Only this man could soothe my soul in a matter of seconds.

"Why does that sound like something Lola would say?" I asked, crossing my arms. Celestino zipped his lips and I couldn't help but laugh. "Well I hope you brought food too because we're going to be here for a bit," I said, settling down by a pillow.

Celestino smiled and in that moment I knew that even though this was scary, with him I'd be okay.

CHAPTER 27

FIRST DATE GONE WRONG

Last night I got to kiss Lilianna. By the stars, I did more than that. And she responded. Every graze of my fingers made her shiver. Every time I whispered words against her skin she whimpered. She caved under my tongue. It was like her body was made for mine. It was incredible. Her glowing eyes, swollen mouth and flushed cheeks when she came nearly made me bust in my pants.

Lilianna was curled against a pillow with a book. I smiled. This date wouldn't have even happened without Eleanor and Lola. I cringed inside as I remember Eleanor yelling at me on the phone.

"You're so fucking lucky I'm awake and I like you," she said. I chuckled. I forgot how against mornings Eleanor was.

"I know. It's just that last night Lilianna and I kissed. Well we did more than that and I know she's probably waking up right now, probably asking a million and one questions about us and so I want to ask her out on a date. But make it magical you know? She deserves all the

fairy tales and stuff so does she still like carnations?" I sucked in a deep breath. Holy stars, Lilianna's rambling was rubbing off on me. Eleanor was quiet. "Ellie?" I asked.

"YOU FUCKING KISSED AND SHE HASN'T EVEN TEXTED ME ABOUT IT?"

"I'm telling you..." I mumbled.

"She should have told me last night," Eleanor said.

"Okay but I'm telling you," I grumbled.

"Holy fucking shit you guys are together," she squealed. I couldn't help but laugh.

"Well not officially. I have to ask her on a date first and then ask her to be my girlfriend. Like I've asked, does she still like carnations," I asked again.

"Let's call Lola."

I WAS FINALLY GETTING the witch of my dreams. Now all I needed to do was help her achieve her dream. I glanced up from my book to look at Lilianna. The sweater made her skin glow and brought out the vibrance of her cheeks. She shivered slightly and I leaned closer so she could feel my warmth. A small smile graced her face. Her wavy hair was down and her baby hairs were beginning to frizz.

I made her a mimosa and passed it to her. She looked up from her book. Her brown eyes lit up. They were a soft brown with golden streaks bleeding from her pupils. She was a work of art that I could spend the rest of my life admiring. I felt my cheeks flushed.

"I can't believe we're trying to solve a mystery," she said, breaking the silence.

"I mean it wouldn't be Lavender Falls if we weren't sent on some mystical adventure before the Full Moon Fall Festival," I said, taking a sip of my drink. Lilianna shook her head, laughing.

"So it's some quarter life crisis rite of passage?" she asked. I shrugged my shoulders. Strange things were always happening here. My thoughts fell back to the meeting and the look of panic she desperately tried to mask.

It broke me. I never realized how much of herself she hid from the rest of the world. Thinking back to our childhood, how many times did she pick at her nails? Tug her ears? Bit back the urge to say what was really on her mind? Was I to blame?

I knew Lilianna tended to be more shy in certain situations. I knew she enjoyed just being the observer. Or was that my own perception of her? I flipped a page absentmindedly. I wasn't reading although I should have been. This was only our first date and I was already doubting myself the same way I doubted where I belonged.

"Have you found anything yet?" The sound of her voice brought me back to reality. I shook my head. She bit her bottom lip as she tried to get a read on my face.

"Is this awkward?" she asked, eyebrows pinched. I immediately cupped her cheek and she leaned into my hand.

"Do you see what you're doing?" I asked. She looked at me confused. Not only has she been leaning into my hand while I stroked her cheek, her other hand was clutching my knee. "What we have feels natural. My magic naturally seeks yours. My hands crave yours. It's never been awkward to be with you, Lilianna. I just can't believe we're finally here," I said earnestly. She blushed and sighed in relief.

"Okay. Just checking," she said, letting out an awkward laugh.

"Stars, you're fucking cute," slipped out of my mouth. She rolled her eyes and handed me a sandwich.

"Here, eat and work," she said in an attempt to change the conversation. A witch of few words.

WITH THE BOTTLE HALF EMPTY, and sandwiches eaten we were laying down still flipping through pages when Lilianna sat upright.

"I'm such an idiot. Well I'm not. I just-" she cut herself off and started flipping through one of the books.

"What?" I asked, sitting up. She threw a glance my way.

"G.G," she said excitedly. G.G was the initials of the owner. But we couldn't find anyone with those initials.

"And?" I asked, clearly confused.

"Well we've been looking for someone with those initials when we could have just been looking for someone with a last name that starts with G." Her eyes were darting rapidly across the pages. Oh, shit. I grabbed one of the books.

"Because chances are the person that casted the spell erased *their* first name, not their family's name," I said, everything clicking.

"Exactly," Lilianna exclaimed. She was practically buzzing as she scanned the pages. This was it. This was the key. And it was in front of us the whole time! I needed to find someone with the last name that started with a G. Thankfully the list was very short.

Very quickly a fog rolled in. I looked over at Lilianna. This wasn't a normal fog. She seemed entranced by the fog that seemed to be getting thicker and closer. My magic buzzed.

The Gasping Greenwood Forest was home to some supernatural creatures. But if you left them alone, they left you alone…at least sometimes. The smell of honey filled the air. Something was off. I tapped her shoulder. Her eyes were fixed on a clump of fog swirling in front of her.

"What creature is this?" I asked reaching to pull her up.

The fog kept rolling in around us. What was this? I racked my mind of the possible creatures that could create this fog. If Lola was here she would know. Celestino pushed me behind him.

"Lilianna," Celestino hissed. I gasped. The fog had swirled its way around his body, slowly tightening its grip.

"Um, how about we don't do that," I said out loud. My magic was swimming around my body, itching to be released. But I couldn't. Something could go wrong.

"Lilianna," Celestino hissed again. I looked up to see the fog slither around his neck.

It was…stroking his cheek. What the stars?

"He's sort of taken," I said. My hands were trembling. My magic pulsed again. Then the fog bopped his nose and I heard a giggle. What was going on?

I closed my eyes. I needed to concentrate. I needed to save him…I think. The more I stared at the fog the more it seemed to caress Celestino which I didn't like. I shook my head. I needed to bond with my magic, not have it lash out.

The smell of honey was all around me but I needed to find its source. Wherever the smell was coming from is where the trickster creature was. I remember helping Lola study for exams and there was a section on tricksters. I reached out tentatively with my magic. I needed to coax the fog into giving its secrets.

"What are you doing?" the voice asked. I shifted my hand around the fog, watching it wrap around my hand. I called out to it.

"Hidden beneath the fog is where the truth was all along. Now reveal to me, the face that is unseen," I whispered into the air. The creature hesitated. I smiled. I kept moving my hand back and forth in the air. I focused on it. I watched it as it took shape. I was right about it being a trickster. Big pointy ears popped out.

"Hello there," I said to the fog that was becoming more tangible. It began to take the shape of a fennec fox. Unusual for these parts. The fox had cream colored fur, ears too big for its face and round dark eyes. There was a twinkle there. I felt a tug towards it.

"Caught me," It said while walking around my legs. "You're smart for a witch," It giggled. The fog began to dissipate and Celestino coughed, gasping for air. "And you're good looking," It said towards Celestino.

"You little fu-."

"The name is Fabian hottie with a body," Fabian growled. Celestino stood up, walking to stand next to me, protectively. I stepped to the side.

"I got the F part right," Celestino grumbled. I couldn't help but giggle. We were having a date, on the verge of discovering who the owner of the Fairy Tale Tavern was and this mischievous fox named Fabian showed up. I knelt in front of Fabian who came up to me, begging for head scratches.

"Um, hi there. I would appreciate it if you didn't flirt with him," I said gently. Fabian narrowed his eyes on me. "Any reason you came to us?" I asked. The fox cocked his head. He glanced at Celestino who glared back, placing a hand on my shoulder. Fabian rolled on his back and I scratched his belly.

"Please?" I asked again. The fox was wasting time. We needed to get back to work. The sun was dropping and I didn't want to be in the woods at night. We were lucky it was just a fox and not the other monsters that sometimes lurked in the shadows.

"Listen fox-"

"Fabian," he hissed, cutting off Celestino.

"Fabian. Are you going to answer or not?" Celestino asked, annoyed. Fabian scratched behind his ear. The fox looked at me and I felt like I couldn't look away.

"You're looking for the owner of the Fairy Tale drinking place," Fabian said. My heart raced as I gripped my sweater. Celestino squeezed my hip.

"Yes we are," I said. Was this the moment? Was the mystery finally coming to an end?

"He came through the forest. Sad. He seemed lost. He grumbled something and then turned to head back into town...," Fabian trailed off, glancing around.

"Great. Did you see where exactly he went? Maybe where he lived?" Celestino asked. The fox giggled.

"He doesn't," Fabian said.

"He doesn't?" I asked.

"Nope," he said, his big ears twitching.

"I'm confused," Celestino said, taking a step forward. Fabian glanced over at him.

"I guess you're just looks," Fabian huffed.

"What's that supposed to mean?" Celestino asked, taking another step. Fabian raised on his hackles, ready to pounce. I moved, getting in between them.

"Let's not lose track here. Can you clarify where we can find him then?" I asked, hoping to calm the tension. Fabian walked past Celestino, head and ears tall.

"Sure, follow me, pretty witch."

I met Celestino's gaze and he shook his head.

"Clearly it likes you," he said, packing up everything.

"It's Fabian, puny warlock," the fox called out.

We trailed behind Fabian on our way back to town. I had a sinking feeling. I could feel my anxiety bleeding out. Celestino reached for my hand. I smiled at him. This was crazy. We were following a random fox to who knows where.

But Celestino was by my side. He always has been. I needed to to trust myself and the people around me. Especially those who already had my heart.

CHAPTER 28

GRAVEYARD OF SECRETS

Of course we ended up at a damn graveyard. We had to take a stop at the vet clinic to pick up a treat for Fabian who was famished. By the time we arrived at Lavender Falls Cemetery the sun was officially setting.

"I have an annoyed feeling about this," Celestino muttered. I glanced at him. He had been quiet the whole walk to the cemetery. He glanced at me and kissed my temple. I really liked Celestino. Stars, I loved him. I always have. I just needed to trust myself to be with him.

We stopped at the entrance. The cemetery was about 15 acres surrounded by a stone wall. We stood in front of the iron gates.

"Go talk to Greg," Fabian said with a yawn. The fox was really cute. I bent down to scratch behind his ears.

"Thank you," I said smiling. I looked into his dark eyes. Something about them felt familiar. The fox smiled.

"I like you. I'll see you again very soon." Fabian booped my nose with his. I giggled as he disappeared into a cloud of fog. Celestino chuckled, shaking his head.

"You're gonna end up with a fox as a familiar," he said. I rolled my eyes.

"A fox would be unusual," I pointed out. He gave me a lazy smile and the nervous feeling in my stomach seemed to settle.

"You're anything but normal," he said gently. I bit the inside of my cheek and nodded. I walked past him to the gate but his hand wrapped around my arm. "There's nothing wrong with that." His voice felt like a caress.

Our eyes met and I nodded again. I wanted to hug him. To feel his body wrapped around me. Not now though. We needed to get through this first.

"Lilianna," he said gently. I've heard him say my name in different ways. It terrified me how my name from his lips owned me, consumed me.

"Let's get this over with…first." I squeezed his hand before pulling from his grip and stepped into the cemetery. He nodded.

"I know where Greg might be," Celestino said, grabbing my hand again. He was definitely touchy. I bit back a smile.

Celestino's family were necromancers. He was basically raised in a graveyard. It was peculiar how a man filled with such warmth could be a warlock that could raise the dead.

He seemed to glide between the graves. Up ahead we saw a tall skinny figure bent over a grave.

"Greg," Celestino called out. Greg slowly turned around. Greg was a zombie with a willowy frame. His dark eyes were sunken in and his cheekbones stuck out as if they were stretching across his bones. He had been around for what felt like forever.

"Mr. Santos, hello," his voice was scratchy. He probably wasn't used to having to talk a lot being a graveyard groundskeeper.

"Greg, you know you can call me Celestino," Celestino corrected him. Greg shrugged his shoulders. I placed a hand on Celestino's shoulder and took a step forward.

"We need your help. We were told you could help us find the original owner of The Drunken Fairy Tale Tavern," I said. Greg's frayed eyebrows shot up. I wasn't sure if it was possible but his pale cheeks became an ashy tone of gray. Could zombies blush?

"Um…the owner of The Drunken Fairy Tale?" he asked. Celestino nodded.

"According to a furball from the forest, they came through here." Celestino's eyes narrowed. Greg scratched the back of his scalp.

"Yeah I know who he is." Greg's eyes darted across from us to a grave. His right hand tightened around the rake he was holding.

"Greg, what are you hiding?" I tentatively asked. The zombie sighed.

"So the thing is…" Greg trailed off once again, eyeing the grave. Celestino slapped his forehead.

"It's YOU," he exclaimed. Greg gave a wry smile.

"Hi," he rumbled.

"Wait, you're the owner," I practically shouted.

"Yes. I wasn't always the best at talking to people." He stared at his bony hands. My throat closed. "I was always messing up. My father handed me the tavern, thinking the responsibility would keep me focus. But I made things worse," he said, staring at the ground. "I left thinking it was better that way. I managed to cast a spell to make people forget me despite my magic being a little unpredictable."

He glanced at me with sad eyes. My eyes pricked with tears. Greg was describing everything I've always felt growing up.

"I was walking through the forest to leave town. Then I realized what I did was dumb and decided to turn back. I stopped to eat some fruit before coming back, one of those magical berries. I ended up getting stung by a bee. Turns out I was allergic to bees and died," he said grimly. "That fox you entered with woke me up by trying to chew my ear off. Since I had ingested the berry right before croaking, it kind of turned me into a zombie," he said.

We stared at him in shock. "What are you doing here then?" Celestino asked. Greg smiled at him. The kind a father would give, at least that's what it looked like to me.

"You," he said with a small smile. Celestino stared incredulous.

"I stayed quiet for a few years. The Kiernan family was doing great with the pub. I went back and forth on what to do for years and years," Greg began. He shuffled his feet. "Your family was happy to have me in charge of cleaning the cemetery and I liked the quietness," he said, smiling softly. "There was also you." He glanced at Celestino who let out a chuckle.

"You helped me realize the good my family's magic provides, the peace we bring," Celestino said. I smiled warmly.

"I realized working here was where I belonged. " Greg stared at his shoes.

"Greg, it's okay. Honestly Caleb is happy running the tavern but the thing is we're doing a bar crawl. And well, we need some history facts about the tavern hence us trying to find you," Celestino said. An idea sparked in my head.

"Greg? Would you like to participate in the Cursed Bar Crawl?" I asked. Greg looked back and forth between us.

"A-are you sure," he stuttered. I stepped up and took his cold hand in mine.

"Absolutely, trust me. You know sometimes I feel like I'm out of place in town…in this world. But something I'm learning is that there are people out there who appreciate you for those differences. There are people who will be there for you." I stared into his sullen eyes. Greg sniffed.

"I know that. That's why I came back…for my sister. She was always there for me even when people made fun of me or got frustrated with me." I nodded in understanding.

"Greg, would you like to talk to your sister?" Celestino asked gently. I turned to him slightly in shock. Greg looked surprised.

"I could never ask that of you Celestino," he said. Celestino gave him my favorite smile. The one where his green eyes softened and crinkles appeared on the side. His dimples deepened.

"Greg. You're my friend and I'd do anything for my friends." My heart swelled. This was another reason why I loved Celestino. His self-lessness.

"I…I would appreciate it," he confessed.

"Look at all of us healing and bonding," Fabian said, appearing.

"Where the fuck did you come from," Celestino said. Fabian scratched the back of his ear.

"I had to check that my girl didn't get zombified but apparently you keep interesting company."

I bent down to pat his head. "That's so sweet of you," I said.

Celestino snorted. "Your girl?" He glared at Fabian.

"Yeah, mine," Fabian snickered. Celestino placed his hands on his hips.

"Since when," he fired back. I rolled my eyes at them.

"Did you not see our connection back in the forest? Are you just a pretty face?" Fabian asked, stretching his back, bored of the conversation.

"Maybe we should focus on the task at hand," I said, hoping to steer the conversation.

"I'll let you go to do your sparky magic. Lilianna, if you need me you just have to say my name three times."

"Like Beetlejuice. Got it," I said.

As fast as he appeared, Fabian disappeared.

"I'm going to murder that fox," Celestino said through gritted teeth.

"We don't send friends to an early grave," I tsk. Greg eyed us both with a small smile.

"What?" Celestino asked.

"Nothing…anyway this way." The zombie led us across the way while humming.

I FELT NERVOUS. We were standing in front of a gravestone that read,

Gertrude, Griffin. 1929-2008. Beloved Sister, Wife &
Dog Mom.

"Are you sure this will be okay?" I asked. Greg nodded.

"Yes. I need to apologize," he said. Celestino patted the gravestone gently. Greg sat down in front. Taking a deep breath, I faced Celestino. His whole body seemed relaxed. He sat cross legged on one side of Greg.

"Um…do you…like need anything?" I asked. He looked at me, his eyes softening.

"No, but if it makes you more comfortable you can sit off to the side. Things get a little…intense," he said gently. I kissed his cheek quickly and sat across from him. I watched him close his eyes, the muscles in his whole body going limp. Unlike back at my apartment where his magic was borderline electric and deadly, this time it flowed out of him.

If I concentrated hard enough I could see a faint glow of violet seep off of him and into the ground. I was in awe. I was rarely at peace with my magic but Celestino navigated his easily. I never witnessed him use this part of his magic. I felt hypnotized. His mouth moved but I couldn't make out his words. He took one final breath, placing a hand on the ground.

"Gertrude, I have someone here who would like to talk to you." His voice was low, graveling. I bit the inside of my cheek. When his eyes opened they glowed pure violet, no longer green. From the gravestone, smoke poured out taking the shape of a plump woman in pajamas.

"Ugh. A Santos. What do you want?" Her voice was shrilled.

"I have someone here who would like to say hi," he said shortly. She glanced at me, ignoring Greg.

"Fine. Hurry up. I have poker night with some ghosts from the 80s," she said, in a bored tone. Celestino took a deep breath.

"Do you recognize the person sitting in front of your stone?" he asked softly. His tone sent shivers down my spine. Gertrude the ghost seemed to turn a shade of unnatural green.

"Should I?" she asked, bothered. Greg's shoulder trembled a bit. A sniffle escaped.

"I'm sorry, Gertrude." His voice broke. Gertrude leaned closer.

"You…seem familiar." Her eyes bore into Greg's. She was struggling. My eyes widened.

"The spell," I whispered. Celestino briefly glanced at me. The spell Greg casted was still in effect, even in her death. Gertrude wouldn't be able to recognize him until it was broken. I noticed Celestino began to tremble. There was no way he could break the spell when trying to keep an open line of communication with Gertrude. Greg couldn't break it because he was a zombie. That meant it had to be me. I stared at my hands. I had to break the spell.

But what if I screwed up? What if it backfired? I looked back at the siblings.

"It's me, Greg," he croaked. I *needed* to break the spell, for Greg. Because his sister was the one person who allowed him to be himself the way my friends do for me. I closed my eyes. I could do this. I was a Rosario.

I took a deep breath, trying to settle my racing heart. The smell of sea salt began mixing with sandalwood. I took another deep breath. With Celestino's magic in the air, it called me deeper into my own. I felt invigorated.

For Greg.

"Hide and seek, lock and key. Memories hidden, let be seen," I whispered. The cool breeze around the cemetery picked up and leaves began flying through the air. I could feel my magic floating higher and higher as it tangled with Celestino's. A glow began emanating from Greg and blew away from him, spreading across the cemetery.

"Greggie?" Gertrude's voice sounded small, younger. I flicked my eyes to Celestino's. His eyes were wide, a faint blush across his cheeks. I felt my own flush. Our magic was still intertwining, making me feel higher.

"Gertrude," Greg cried out. Gertrude placed a ghostly hand on his cheek.

"You idiot! How could you leave us," she begged. Greg covered his face.

"I'm so sorry," he exclaimed. Tears fell down my face while watching the siblings reconnect. There was a rustle across from me. Celestino was getting up.

"Don't you have to…" I pointed at the siblings. Celestino shook his head.

"She has unfinished business now that she remembers Greg so she doesn't need me to keep her around." Celestino tilted his head to signal me to get up.

Greg turned around quickly and reached out to Celestino, embracing him. Celestino smiled, patting his back. Greg took my hand with a smile.

"I-I'll help you guys out," Greg stammered.

CHAPTER 29

THE ANXIETY MONSTER IS HERE

"Thank you Greg," I said sincerely. Greg turned to go talk to his sister while Celestino and I left them in peace. "Are you okay?" I asked. I could still see hints of violet in his eyes.

"I'm okay," he said. His eyes traveled around my face. "Are you okay?" he asked, fingers grazing my cheek.

"I think so," I said, softly.

"I think this is now the second time I've really seen you use your magic," Celestino said. I turned away from him.

"Yeah…" I felt my throat closing. My hands began trembling. One seemingly harmless sentence had the power to send my body into fight or flight. A wave of uneasiness washed over me. Could I tell him why? Could I share that part of me that kept me away from truly living? I looked across the moonlit cemetery.

"Do you want to tell me why?" Celestino asked gingerly. "You can tell me," Celestino said. I *knew* I could talk to him. But taking that first step was terrifying.

"I know that," I said. I regretted my tone instantly. "It's hard, okay?" I said a bit more gently. I felt the pull of his hand.

"I know it is," he said. I shook my head.

"No you don't. You have no idea what it is to worry about everything, all the time." *Fuck*. My stomach twisted. I needed to calm down. I felt it in the pit of my stomach. This was it. The thing I had been keeping at bay for the past couple weeks was beginning to finally boil over. With my magic already in the air I felt my control slipping.

"I do," he said again, taking a step towards me. I stepped back. I felt my magic rattling within. He needed to stop.

"I worry about everything and anything all the time. It's nonstop. I need to get this done, that done. I can't forget that. Why did they have that tone of voice? Was it something I said? Something I did? I need to fix it." Everything began pouring out as my heart pounded in my chest. "I need to be better. I need to calm down. Everything in my head is too much."

The air became electric. If I didn't stop, my magic would be unleashed and stars knew if I could control it.

"You are *not* too much Lilianna," Celestino said, taking a step towards me. I shook my head.

"You weren't there in college when I would get anxiety attacks. When I would screw up." I tried to take in a breath. "Sometimes I feel like I'm battling myself. Who I really am and who the world needs me to be. It's exhausting."

Hurt flashed across his face. "I'm here now," he said softly. Tears welled up in my eyes.

"I don't want to screw this up. I don't want to be too much for you, for anyone." My voice broke. I took a step back. I didn't need him any closer. My throat started closing. My breathing was becoming short. I felt a warm hand grasping my arm.

"We're in this together," he said. My magic was whipping around.

"I can't keep it in," I said through gritted teeth. He wrapped both arms around me. I closed my eyes. Everything was becoming over-whelming. Voices began entering my head.

The bar crawl, don't panic, you keep making mistakes, you're dumb, breathe, just be normal, the event will be a disaster, it's all your fault, breathe, dumb.

The air became hot with my magic. "L-let go," I said, voice cracking. This was too much. Everything was too much. I hated this feeling of being out of control. The breeze was grating against my skin. My skin was covered in cold sweat. The claws of my anxiety began cutting off my air. I needed to breathe. But how? I couldn't remember how. I felt myself gasping for air. The world was collapsing in on me.

One side of my brain kept telling me to breathe and relax but the anxiety monster was taking control, spewing wretched thoughts, one after the other. I was battling myself and it was becoming unmanageable. I could feel my magic rushing through my veins, begging to be released.

Celestino's arms tightened around me, securing me. I didn't realize I was shaking so much until I felt his warmth and his steady heart beat against the palm of my hands.

"Let it out," he whispered in my ear. I shook my head. The voices were still ringing in my head. "It's okay. You don't have to be in control around me," he said. Tears poured down my face. Everything was hurting. Celestino squeezed me. "You are the kindest witch I've ever met," he whispered against my cheek. I sucked in a deep breath.

"You are strong and funny. Your magic feels like a summer day at the beach. You are beautiful inside and out." And with his words laced with love and acceptance I broke, crying out.

A burst of magic flung from my body and my knees gave out. The wind roared as it whipped around.

Celestino caught me. I couldn't stop the tears and frustrations from pouring out. His magic filled the air, wrapping around me like a warm blanket. I cracked open my eyes to see the remnants of my magic float in the air like tiny stars. He kept wiping the tears from my face as I tried to get my breathing under control.

"It's okay, Lilianna. I'm here," he said, rubbing my shoulders. I buried my face in his shoulder, letting him soothe me.

"You-" I began to say but he squeezed me instead. He used his own to cocoon us and keep the burst from causing any damage. He let me expel my energy despite the fact he was recovering from summoning a ghost. I squeezed my eyes shut. I couldn't believe he had done that for me.

"Celestino," I cried out, feeling selfish. I felt his fingers slip between my hair to massage my scalp.

"It's okay," he whispered in my ear. I shook my head and pulled back to see his face. His green eyes were playful, his smile carefree but there were bags under his eyes. My eyes watered again. "Breathe with me," he said. I kept my hands on his chest and followed him. My shaky breathing became steadier slowly. He pressed his forehead against mine.

"Sometimes things can be overwhelming and they pile up. I'm so busy running around and trying to be in control it eventually explodes." I took a deep breath. "It's like my brain runs on two different train tracks simultaneously." I fumbled with my words. "Sometimes I think if I could just think and feel like everyone else, things could be easier," I said, sniffling.

"You mean it could be easier for everyone else," he said, rubbing my cheek. My bottom lip wobbled and I weakly nodded.

"When Sailor asked if I was okay, it was because I was with him and Carrie when I found out about the mishap with the alcohol shipment. I felt responsible and started to have an anxiety attack. My magic flared and I shoved Sailor. They both had to use their magic to calm me down," I explained. Celestino continued to stroke my cheek with his fingers.

"I felt horrible. I could have hurt them," I said. Celestino tapped my nose. I met his gaze.

"There's nothing wrong with seeing the world through a different lens. You see a kaleidoscope of possibilities and beauty unlike the rest of us. It's beautiful." he said. I looked away from the intensity of his gaze.

"I'm exhausted by my own brain half of the time. How do you know you won't be?" I asked, my voice feeling small.

"Faith…trust…," he started to say. I let out a shallow laugh.

"Don't say pixie dust." I finally met his eyes.

"Got you to smile," he teased me. I rolled my eyes.

"You always do…it's frustrating," I muttered. His smile made me feel like I was getting kissed by the first rays of a sunrise.

"Frustratingly charming?" he asked. I pinched his cheek.

"Stop that," I said, giggling but he kept smiling.

"I'll be here for the overwhelming days, the quiet ones and the loud ones. I'll be there by your side to take your hand when and if you need me to." His fingers tucked a strand of hair behind my ear. He did see me. He always did.

His thumb swept my bottom lip and I felt my body tighten with anticipation. He let his finger follow my jawline, down my neck and across my collarbone. My heart fluttered and my stomach dipped. Our magic was still intertwined, bringing us closer.

I wanted him to caress me in a way that made me forget everything just like that night. I wanted to forget the bar crawl, the videos I needed to edit for work and how I needed to help Eleanor plan her festival outfit to get Caleb's attention. I didn't want to have my brain piled with thoughts anymore. I just wanted to be with him.

Celestino's eyes met mine. I bit my lip. There was an emotion in his look, one that suggested deep unwavering adoration. It ignited the possibilities of happy ever afters. For once I didn't want to run from it.

"Let's get you back home," he said, placing the softest of kisses on my lips.

CHAPTER 30

FEELINGS ARE A LOT

Lilianna was leaning heavily on me as we walked back to her apartment. My mind was swirling with thoughts. Her eyes brimming with tears and shaking uncontrollably was imprinted in my brain. It broke me to see her like that. It destroyed me to hear the things she said about herself. I wanted to hunt down every person for making her believe she was something that needed to be changed.

And now I know why she's been so nervous about us. She had trouble trusting herself and her emotions. I took a deep breath. I would wait. However long she needed. After tonight's success with Greg that would be one less thing on her plate.

Greg.

I couldn't believe it had been Greg all along. I felt myself smile. I've always loved Greg. He was always a little quirky. He constantly worried about weeds and making sure each gravestone was polished. And he was sweet and listened. He reminded me of Lilianna actually.

"Come on, Posey," I whispered, placing a kiss on her temple as we made it into her apartment.

"I'm sorry," she said, sitting on the couch. I shook my head. I moved to the kitchen to make a cup of tea.

"You don't have to apologize, Posey." She picked at her jeans that were covered in grass and dirt. She nodded silently.

"A great first date, huh," she choked out. I chuckled. I placed the mug on the coffee table and wrapped an arm around her shoulder. She relaxed into me.

"The date technically still isn't over," I said. She turned her head to face me.

"Most dates end with a kiss," she said softly. I bit the inside of my cheek. She looked a little pale, shadows under her eyes.

"Maybe you should just rest," I said cupping her cheek.

"Just one…please? If that's okay," she said. I smiled. How could I say no to her?

"Rule nine," I said softly. Her eyes melted. "If you feel like doing something do-"

She cut me off mid sentence with a brushing of her lips against mine. I practically sighed at the feeling. I leaned forward gently, afraid that this was all a dream. I pressed her closer to me. I needed her to feel that I was here for her. I would always be here for her.

My hands slipped back into her hair, anchoring her to me. I bit her bottom lip softly causing her to jump. I chuckled and started to pull back to apologize.

But she shifted closer and wrapped her arms around my neck. Her tongue slipped inside, gently coaxing mine. I was taking my time with her, letting her open up to me. My hands fell away from her hair and I gripped her hips to lift her up onto my lap. My hands brushed under her sweater to massage her back. I wanted to relieve every intrusive thought that she was hyper fixating on.

"Relax," I whispered as I placed kisses down her neck. She shivered. I bit down on the pulsing vein and Lilianna let out a moan, her legs shaking.

"Fuck," I whispered against her neck. She was so fucking sensitive to my touch. I sucked on the tender skin and she shivered again. "I've been wondering since last time how rough you like it," my breath was hot on her skin and she tightened her hands in my shirt, pulling me closer, needing more.

Instead of responding with words she gripped my face and kissed me with urgency. My heart pounded.

"Just a bit longer," she pleaded against my lips. She kissed with a hunger I wasn't expecting, but stars, did I fucking love it. A tiny part of me knew she was using this moment as a way to forget everything. I groaned as she pressed her hips against mine.

"Lilianna," I murmured against her ear. Her hands fisted my sweater. She began rocking more, faster. She was begging for friction. I gripped her hips, rocking her against me as we kissed.

"*Meu coração*," I said as I laid playful nips down her neck once more. My hand slid to cup her breast. I gave a hard squeeze. Lilianna let out a whimper. She pulled back to meet my gaze, her eyes filled with lust. I loved this confident side of her. I was about to ponder how the word love felt right when I felt her hand brush down my chest.

With a steady sure hand, she continued down. Air escaped my lungs and she smirked. If she kept this up, I was very much willing to take off my clothes and take her on the couch.

"You wicked witch," I said, pulling at her hair, causing another sweet melodious moan to escape between her plumped lips. But I couldn't. Today was an emotional rollercoaster for her and I used an intense amount of magic. We were not going to take that step yet.

"As much as I would love to continue this, today was an intense day. I think we should probably stop and sleep," I said softly.

With her face flushed, she glanced away. I could tell she didn't want to but I didn't want our first time to come from a day of confusing emotions. I could tell there were things she needed to work out. I pulled her in for a slow kiss.

"I want us. I want this. But when you are 100%. It was a heavy day but still a great first date," I said. She tugged on her ear lobe. The confident sexy witch I was making out with was retreating back to her shell.

"I hate it when you're right," she grumbled. I laughed, squeezing her into a tight hug. "Want to watch a movie?" she asked. I nodded.

I couldn't wait until she was officially mine.

Minha bruxinha.

I woke up with a smile on my face. For a few blissful moments, I enjoyed the feeling of my flushed cheeks and uncontrollable smile. Kissing Celestino was like bathing in sunlight; slowly igniting my entire body, and I reveled in his flames. I missed the feel of his hands kneading away every worry from my body. He was with me through my anxiety attack. He was there to listen to me shift through my thoughts and emotions. He's *always* been there for me.

My phone vibrated and I lazily reached over to my night stand. It was Eleanor and Lola. I groaned again into my pillow. They were going to scream.

ELLIE

So how was the date

LOLA

Yes spill!!

A lot happened

I texted cryptically. I snorted. Cryptic. Graveyard.

LOLA

I'll grab the wine and juice

ELLIE

I'll grab the food and coffee

See you soon!

Eventually there was a knock on my door. Eleanor and Lola came in with breakfast. Once we were settled on the couch Eleanor handed me a cup.

"My sweet clueless anxious witchy sister from another mister, good glorious morning. Here is your coffee. Sip and spill," Eleanor said.

"Yes please. Remember I'm living through you," Lola said, tucking her feet underneath her. I rolled my eyes. She smacked my arm. "As a bonus," she pointed out.

I cuddled up into a couch pillow as the taste of sweetened caffeine warmed my body. Memories flooded back as I stared at the spot Eleanor was in.

"Oh fuck no, switch seats with me," she squealed, reaching for Lola.

"What? No!" Lola shoved Eleanor. I threw my head back laughing.

"Don't worry it was my seat and nothing dirty happened…really," I said with a wink. They giggled and looked at me with eager eyes. The events of yesterday tumbled out with a series of bewildered expressions, giggles, nerves and a flushed face. I had stopped before mentioning the part of my anxiety attack.

Eleanor and Lola didn't make a single comment until a puff of fog appeared in the middle of the couch.

"Fabian," I yelped as Eleanor and Lola jumped in surprise. Fabian sat on the couch, scratching the back of his ear.

"Aren't you gonna tell them about the kiss?" he asked innocently. My eyes widened.

"Kiss," Lola screeched.

"I thought you were a fox, not a rat," I hissed.

"You didn't tell us about the first kiss," Eleanor trailed off threateningly.

"Exactly. We're still offended by that," Lola said, crossing her arms.

"Honestly I'm surprised the apartment is in one piece. The magic between you two was sizzling," Fabian said indifferently. They gasped loudly.

"Sizzling," Eleanor practically yelled. I shushed her.

"I have neighbors," I hissed.

"All I'm saying is you could fry a steak from all the sizzle of that kiss," Fabian continued. I slammed the pillow against my face and groaned in embarrassment. Lola reached to pet Fabian who immediately laid in her lap. I smiled. Creatures have always been drawn to Lola. She was going to be a great vet.

"Lilianna Maria Rosario," Eleanor ordered.

"Okay, okay," I said, giving up. I spilled everything to them including the anxiety attack and kisses.

"Are you okay?" Lola asked in a quiet voice. I picked at the fur that was coming off of Fabian. There was going to be a lot of fur hanging around my apartment from now on. Maybe I could cast some sort of spell to keep him from shedding.

"I'm fine. I have everything under control," I said, not meeting their eyes. I was afraid they would reveal too much.

"You're not. You're under way too much pressure. Pressure you put on yourself," Eleanor pointed out. I looked around the room. I knew she was right but I wasn't ready to admit it out loud.

"You also don't need to control everything," Lola stated. The remote on my coffee table trembled as my magic flared in the air. They didn't look away from me despite hearing it. I pointed at what my magic was causing the remote to do. Lola shook her head.

"You need to accept your emotions," Lola said. "It's okay that you feel big emotions. It's who you are. You need to accept yourself and see that others can accept you just the way you are. *Not* the different versions you act as," she said softly. I bit my lip, tears swelling in my eyes. It was easier to hide behind a mask.

"When are you gonna come down out of your ivory tower and see that the evil dragon keeping you locked up is not him or work," Eleanor said, placing her hand on top of mine. Warmth began spreading throughout my body. The smell of cinnamon filled the air. I could tell Eleanor was using her magic to help calm the growing waves within. Lola reached over and placed hers. The smell of sage eased me. Tears began spilling out.

"He's trying to be your Prince Charming, not a wicked warlock," Lola said, squeezing my hand. I nodded, knowing everything my best friends were saying was right.

"Well in the bedroom he might be," Eleanor snickered. I tossed my couch pillow at Eleanor who smiled.

"Why is he different?" Eleanor asked, recovering from my attack. I took a deep breath.

"I'm worried that one day he might see how broken I really am. The greater the love, the greater the fall and no magic can fix a broken heart," I admitted. Fabian rubbed my thigh with his head. "But I don't want to let him go. With him I feel safe and happy," I said, feeling my heart swell.

"And you like kissing him," Fabian pointed out.

"He's a really good kisser," I said, blushing.

"Gross. He's my best friend, don't say that," Eleanor teased. We erupted into a fit of giggles. Fabian sat back, a smile tugging.

"Alrighty, so brunch now?" I asked. Eleanor nodded.

"Bad bitch brunch begins now," Lola said.

Eleanor stood up. "Alrighty besties the spilling is done and we may go back to sipping!" Eleanor stood up excitedly. The walls around my heart were crumbling down.

The girls and I finished a bottle of Prosecco with very little juice and watched romcoms the rest of the day. Later on Lola asked if cemeteries were sexy and I couldn't help but laugh. But I did tell her yes.

A few days passed with us not talking. I knew she needed space. She needed to work on things for herself.

Everything was slowly coming together with the Cursed Bar Crawl. We had someone lined up to be the tour guide. The script was complete and Greg's sister was finally at rest after her poker night with some ghosts from the 80s. Lilianna's spell broke the memory wipe that Greg casted on the whole town.

The Griffin Family welcomed Greg with open arms. Turned out he was a great uncle! Caleb offered the Griffin Family a portion of the tavern. He said he didn't feel right owning something that belonged to them. Now the pub was owned by Caleb and Tatiana Griffin. Everything was falling into place and I felt myself falling into step with my town.

I sat at the tavern, picking at the beer label. I would be meeting with Ben, Leo and Lilianna to make sure the bar crawl was officially set.

"Hey there boss man!" Sailor said, sliding into the stool next to me. I couldn't stop a chuckle from escaping. "Interesting mood," he commented.

"What does that mean?" I asked, eyebrows raised.

"You seem...more at peace." His blue eyes shone brightly. I glanced around at the smiling patrons that I grew up with. Caleb was taking an order. Flynn was staring at his whiskey bottles. The door chimed and a zing ran down my spine. I turned to see Lilianna walking in. She flushed with a smile when she met my eyes. I looked back at Sailor.

"I think I finally am...friend," I said, nudging his shoulder. Sailor's eyes widened and he threw his arms around me. I nearly fell off the seat.

"I knew we would be besties," he exclaimed. I barked out a laugh.

"I said friend not best friend. You have to work for that," I said. He rolled his eyes. Sailor was right though. In the city, I felt lost. But here, in Lavender Falls surrounded by people who just let me be me, I was at peace. I didn't need to try to be the star soccer player, top student or the best event planner in the state. I just had to exist. I felt tethered to this place and its people. I could *finally* breathe. I glanced back at Lilianna. She waved.

"I have a meeting. Guys night later?" I asked Sailor.

"I already named the group chat," he said. My phone pinged. I glanced down at my phone. I was added to the group chat: *Magic Men* with Sailor and Caleb. I snorted. Of course. I left the guys and headed towards my love. I smiled. *Love.*

I was nervous sitting at The Drunken Fairy Tale Tavern. I sat at a booth, legs bouncing. Celestino was talking to Sailor at the bar. He looked happy. I kept chewing the inside of my cheek. I wasn't nervous to see my boss or talk about the crazy adventure I went on for the bar crawl. I was nervous seeing Celestino again.

It had been a few days since our date, the kiss in my apartment and my anxiety attack. I had never been that vulnerable with him. He tempered my magic when I lost control. I crafted myself to control my magic and emotions. But the more control I tried to manipulate the more it escaped me. Celestino allowed me to let go because I didn't need to lose myself to let go. I just needed to simply *be.*

I glanced around the bar. People were laughing and smiling. I felt myself smile. My town was filled with people from all walks of life and all types of supernaturals. Sometimes I wondered what it was like to not worry about things. To live carefree. That was always the problem. My mind was at constant battle with itself. My logical side and my anxious side. I stared at the cup of water in front of me. But I didn't need to fight myself. Just learn to love how these different sides of me could coexist.

Greg didn't feel like he belonged but he had his sister. He needed to accept himself and that there would be people like Gertrude who would be there for him. So did I.

The smell of sandalwood slipped under my nose and I felt my shoulders drop.

"Hey." I turned to meet a pair of warm green eyes. There were a few shadows under his eyes and his hair was pulled back in a messy ponytail. He wore a wrinkled shirt and joggers. On instinct I reached up to brush his cheek.

"Are you okay?" I asked as I met his gaze. His eyes softened and a small smile poked out.

"I'm fine *amorzinha*." My cheeks flushed at the endearment.

"Is it the haunted house? Do you need help?" I asked quickly to deflect from what he just called me. I could tell he knew by the way he smiled. Celestino knew now how easily he could affect me with language.

"It's coming along. Almost ready. I just stayed up late." He grabbed my cup of water to take a sip. I followed the movement and watched the way his throat bobbed. His eyes narrowed at me.

"You okay *fofa*?" he asked. Before I could respond our bosses showed up. The twin werewolves strolled by. With the festival at the end of the week everyone was working more hours. Their eyes darted back and forth between us.

"Is the bar crawl set?" Leo asked. Celestino snorted.

"We dealt with a fox and had to summon a ghost, but yeah," Celestino said, stretching in his seat, his arm coming around my back. I leaned back into him. The brothers nodded, smiling as if us going on a wild adventure was normal. But then again we were a magical town.

"Any compensation you need just send it as an invoice," Ben said. I laughed.

"So you're going to pay me for the distress?" I asked jokingly. My boss looked at me.

"Of course, you're also taking a mandatory vacation after the festival," Leo said. I was about to argue when he held his hand up. "I know for a fact this has been causing you stress and you've been doing a great job Lilianna. It's okay to have a break." Our bosses glanced at each other.

"What?" Celestino asked. Ben was beginning to look uneasy.

"We know how much work you've also put in Celestino so you're going on vacation too," Ben said.

"Both of us are going on vacation?" I asked. I could tell Ben was forcing himself to not look away from my eyes. I loved Ben. He was great but he was a horrible liar.

"We just think you guys deserve a vacation. And you know…you could save money if you do it together," Leo said, scratching his arm. I blushed.

"Right," Celestino chuckled. These wolf men were too much.

"Fine, fine. Anyway, how's the alcohol?" I asked, laughing.

"Right, well with some magical spells and help from Kiernan's Distillery we'll be fine," Ben said happily. Celestino and I sighed into our seats. The twin werewolves smiled. An idea trickled in my head.

"Hey, could you go to each pub to double check their special cocktails? When we did a test run the drinks had interesting effects," I said. Leo smiled.

"Ben and I would gladly do that." Leo looked at his brother.

"Why are you volunteering for me?" Ben asked. Leo rolled his eyes.

"You do know this means we can try the drinks right," Leo gave his brother a look.

"Let's go," Ben said, getting up. Our bosses waved us off. I shook my head.

"Well that's all done," I said. Celestino pulled me into his arms and squeezed. He grazed my cheek with a soft kiss.

"I have to finish up some work, okay," he said. I nodded and watched him walk out the door with my heart. I definitely needed to officially answer that closet dare.

CHAPTER 31

A CINDERELLA MOMENT

I had finally posted the video that Caleb was fighting tooth and nail against me for. The sunlight was glittering in through the windows of The Drunken Fairy Tale Tavern. I had the camera focused closely on the beer he was pouring before panning out with him coming into full frame. Right before stopping the recording, Caleb's pale blue eyes flickered towards the camera. I remembered thinking how perfect the video was.

After I edited the video I sent it to him to be approved. I had told him it would just be his hands but decided to test him. I told him I could cut the video but he ended up saying it would be okay if it helped with tickets. I knew the video would do well. I just wasn't expecting the view counts to sky rocket the way it did.

Over a hundred thousand people had seen the video with the likes nearly matching the view count. I woke up from all caps text from Eleanor who was feeling hot and heavy.

I don't want to hear about your libido this early in the morning

ELLIE

You know what this means right?

> You need a sexy costume for the festival to
> have Caleb on his knees?

LOLA

I have leftover fishnet and seashells from
making costumes for one of the baby
dragons.

> Oooo Ellie as a sexy siren

ELEANOR

This is going to be great

I shook my head laughing. I grabbed my laptop off my nightstand and opened to check on ticket sales. My eyes widened. Sales had doubled overnight. I broke out in a giant grin.

"Yes," I yelled. This was going to work out and just in time.

Tomorrow was the festival and while social media was scheduled and ready, I wanted to double check on the alcohol. I pulled on an oversize cream knitted sweater with skinny jeans and sneakers. My bookcase caught my eye.

It was taller, the shelves were longer and the edges had carvings of waves. I noticed it a few days ago. I had asked Eleanor and Lola if they had anything to do with it and they refused to disclose any information. It was beautiful just like the person who made it. My phone vibrated again. This time from Celestino.

CELESTINO

Alcohol has arrived at the pubs. I didn't want
you to worry. See you soon

THE SMELL of pumpkin spice was in the air. Fall was in full effect and I was happy. I ordered two coffees. A small blush formed on my face as I grabbed the second cup. I walked down the street feeling myself slowly relax. Everything had worked out. Well, almost everything. There was still the matter of officially expressing my feelings for Celestino.

I glanced to the side of my office building where mother Hulk duck sat with her ducklings. The babies looked bigger. They all gave me an evil glare. Ducks glaring was now a new fear.

I hurried through the door, praying to not get attacked. Everyone was sitting in the meeting room, all except Celestino. I placed the coffee in front of his empty seat. Everyone exchanged pleasantries.

The meeting opened with everyone talking about their different duties for the festival. All the vendors were accounted for. The maps were being printed. Decorations were in place and tickets sales were jumping through the roof. Everyone clapped for me. I awkwardly said thanks, wanting the attention to shift. Celestino walked in just then, hair filled with sawdust.

"Sorry guys for being late. Just making sure the haunted house was good," he said.

"Just needs a few more decorations at this point though right?" Ben asked. Celestino nodded, taking a seat across from me.

"Just a few cosmetic things and she is ready!" He smiled. His eyes flickered to the coffee and then me. I gave a small smile. He mouthed thank you before taking a sip. I saw his shoulders relax into the chair as he drank. He must have woken up early if he checked the pubs and then the haunted house. My heart squeezed. He gave kindness effortlessly and I planned on working to receive it the same way.

"You all have done such a great job! So much has been able to get done despite some setbacks," Mayor Kiana said, smiling at us. "What's most important now is that everyone has fun this weekend. Yes, some of the tourists will more than likely cause a few hiccups but know that you all have done a stellar job," she said, concluding the meeting.

Everyone began shuffling out. Celestino hadn't looked my way the whole time besides the coffee moment and I hadn't realized how much I missed his eyes. I missed the way we would find each other occasionally throughout meetings. Without realizing it, I got up and before he could walk out, I reached for his hand. He turned around, surprised.

"Morning," I squeaked. His eyes softened.

"Morning," his voice was rough. The shadows around his eyes are only slightly lighter.

"Hi," I said awkwardly.

"Hi," he responded. Silence passed between us. I didn't like this. I missed our banter. The way he seemed to always read my mind. I opened my mouth but my body tightened.

"We're okay," he said softly. "Thank you for the coffee Lilianna." He said my name softly, like a feather floating down, slowly, gently.

SITTING at my desk I began picking at my nails. I could have answered his dare at that moment but I froze. Fucking froze. Eleanor came into my cubicle.

"Lily," she began. I glanced at my best friend who was dressed in a hot pink blouse tucked into grass green slacks and yellow pumps.

"Yes," I responded.

"You know I can see your problem," she said.

"Which problem are you referring to?" I asked as she sat on top of my desk.

"Please, sit on my desk." I scooted my chair back. Eleanor smiled.

"You're not the best with words. You're more of an action person," she said. I cocked my head to the side.

"You don't express your love with verbal words," Lola said appearing. "You get awkward but you love helping others and surprising them with gifts."

"Lola? How come you're here?" I asked in surprise. She bumped her hip against Eleanor's legs.

"I have something to discuss with Mayor Kiana," she said secretively. Eleanor cleared her throat.

"You buy me my favorite tea occasionally. You love bringing in sweets for the office," Eleanor said.

"And you surprise me with new plant seeds you find in stores," Lol interjected.

"You bought Celestino coffee," Eleanor pointed out. I thought about it for a second.

"And it's obvious you have feelings for him," Eleanor said. I blushed and nodded. "Celestino likes to hear words. But you like actions. So he's been showing you his feelings this whole time. Like the man makes eyes at you all the time," she said.

"He helped you at the library, on your period, made your first date be a work date. Did you notice how he always smells like sandalwood and citrus," Lola added. I looked up at her quickly.

"I knew it! He does, doesn't he," I blurted. They giggled.

"Yes and do you know why?" Lola asked. I shrugged my shoulders. "It helps to reduce anxiety. I saw him buy some from Pricilla," Lola said, leaning against my desk. My eyes widened. "I was there to talk to Priscilla about something and I overheard him asking her what were some good scents to help with anxiety. She made him a *special* cologne," she said, smirking. Eleanor wiggled her eyebrows.

"That explains it and I bet he made the bookcase," I said. Eleanor leaned forward.

"I wonder who let him in," Eleanor said innocently. I pulled at my blouse.

"Well it's really pretty and he always smells nice," I muttered.

"Like you want to cuddle in that nice wide chest of his, possibly with clothes off." Eleanor had zero shame. My face flamed.

"Eleanor," I hissed.

"Is she wrong?" Lola asked. I glared at them.

"Do you have to double team me?" I asked. They looked at each other first and crossed their arms.

"Yes," they both said. I groaned.

"I don't know why I can't just say how I feel to his face," I said.

"You can't let the fear of striking out keep you from playing the game," Lola said, twirling her pink hair.

"Really? A Cinderella Story," I said.

Eleanor snapped her fingers. "But you're not Cinderella in this scenario," she said. I stared at her for a moment.

"So I should give Celestino a Cinderella moment?" I asked. I felt myself begin to smile. Actions would help me say the words and get my feelings across. I could do that.

"Can you guys help?" I asked. Both of them smirked.

"Time for big brain bitch energy," Eleanor said, wrapping an arm around Lola. I snorted.

"Leave everything to us," Lola said.

I HAD monster zombie butterflies flying throughout my stomach as I finished off my dark lipstick. I was wearing a tight black dress with a plunging neckline that skimmed over my curves and fell down in pools of black. Lola had made the dress a few years ago and made a few adjustments to have it fit me. Thankfully we were both around the same height. I straightened my back and flicked my hair back over my shoulders.

Today was the day I would confess to Celestino. My heart pounded. I couldn't keep living a reclusive life. Life was meant to be lived even if it meant there was a chance of getting hurt. Because at least with pain there was always hope for happiness.

Walking out into the cool night air I broke out in a smile. The streets were littered with people. Some dressed in costumes and some in full fall aesthetic. Pumpkins and hay bales lined the sidewalks. Some shops had their doors propped open. The smell of apple cider and cinnamon filtered out into the street with music everywhere. I sighed happily. We all did it.

I looked across the street to see the town center. A group had gathered. This was the group for the bar crawl. They were all buzzing with excitement. I waved to Hallie who was the ringleader for the tour. Greg stood next to her, smiling. I could hear the clicks of cameras in the distance. The photography club at the high school was helping out with catching film and photos.

After my confession to Celestino, I promised myself I would get a few things for social media before hanging out with the group at the tavern.

At the end of the street was Atticus's Antiques which had completely transformed into a haunted house. Fog leaked throughout the windows and doors. A line had gathered outside.

"You're here," Eleanor yelled from the the line. Sure she could have probably cut the line but I knew Eleanor wouldn't have felt right doing so. She was dressed as a zombie siren with pearl scaled bra and a skirt that was made of netting; shorter on her left leg and angled down to her right knee. Her pink hair was down in smooth waves with a few braided pieces and shells. Her face shimmered with glitter.

"You look fucking hot," she said excitedly. I rolled my eyes.

"You know I dress up occasionally," I said pointedly.

"Yeah but your boobs look great," she said, shimming her shoulders. I giggled.

"Okay okay. Well I can't wait to see how Caleb looks at you." I said. Eleanor shushed me.

"Hurry and get inside," she said. I furrowed my brows.

"Where's Lola?" I asked, scanning the crowd.

"She's at the petting zoo making sure the baby dragons are behaving but she'll meet us later for drinks," Eleanor confirmed. I nodded.

With a deep breath I made my way into the haunted house. The workers stayed in character, attempting to scare me. They were hiding behind furniture and blending into the walls. There was even a grandfather clock that one of them hid inside. Everyone seemed to be enjoying themselves.

Fabian appeared onto the staircase.

"Are you ready?" he asked.

"I feel like I'm going to throw up," I said. Fabian's nose twitched.

"I think that means you're ready," he said. I nodded and with a snap of my fingers the candles that stood on either side of each step lit up. I smiled, feeling my magic dance around me. We were in sync, finally. With a deep breath I began to walk up the steps.

CHAPTER 32

ADAMS FAMILY LOVE STORY

I didn't know why Eleanor requested my presence at the haunted house. I also didn't know why she made me dress like Gomez Addams. Sure it fit the theme of the haunted house but I wasn't really going to be participating in it or anything. I tugged at the black tie of my pinstripe suit.

"You look good," Eleanor called out from the front of the line. I ran my hand through my hair, pulling it back. "Still upset you didn't put on the mustache," she said, glaring at me.

"I would like to not have a dead caterpillar on my lip when I can grow one," I said.

She rolled her eyes and leaned in to say quietly, "You could have just used the magical hair grower from Pricilla's shop." I let out a chuckle.

"Yes, but there are some things I would rather let happen without magic." Eleanor shook her head, glitter falling.

"Anyway, go inside," she said, pushing me towards the door.

"Why?" I asked. She hadn't really explained why my presence was needed. Ben and Felix didn't call me about anything so clearly nothing was wrong. "What's wrong?" I asked.

Eleanor huffed. "Nothing," she said.

"Then why am I here?" I asked again. I just wanted to be at the tavern drinking and hoping to at least catch a glimpse of Lilianna. I knew giving her space was the right thing but I missed her. I missed the calming effect she had around me. I missed the way her eyes noticed every detail or the way her hair frizzed in the heat and her cheeks turned pink at just about anything.

"I swear to the stars if you don't get into the haunted house I'm going to throw you into the swamp," she said. I laughed.

"Okay, okay. I'm going. I don't want you to ruin my suit anyway."

I made my way into the haunted house marveling at the work everyone had done. Floating candles glittered the ceilings. The mundanes probably thought they were being hung by strings and not actual magic. Fog covered the floor. The sounds of screams and laughter made me smile.

The staircase caught my attention though. Long black candles were lit on each step. I wondered who did it. Then my eyes found Fabian. He had a black bow tie around his neck. I stifled a laugh. If the fox could roll his eyes, I was sure as the stars above he just did.

"This is so humiliating and I will make you pay for it if you say anything. Now, follow me." Before I could respond he began walking up the stairs.

"Okay," I muttered. Walking up the steps towards the attic, I could smell sea salt and lavender. For some reason my hands began to sweat. The door was slightly ajar and fog leaked out. When I opened the door I nearly choked.

The floor was scattered with black rose petals. Candles were lit around the room. Moonlight filtered through the window bathing the woman in front of me like a goddess. She was in a tight black dress that accentuated every curve she had and I wanted to sink my fingers into the soft fabric. My eyes followed the dangerously low neckline and my mouth watered. She looked ravishing. I saw her eyes travel up and down my body, her cheeks turning pink.

"Posey?" I questioned. My heart rattled against my chest. Despite dressing like a sexy vixen, I could see the nerves in how her shoulders were tight and the unease in her eyes. "Is everything okay?" I asked, walking towards her. She held her hands up when I was only a few feet away.

"You're dressed like Gomez Addams," she blurted. I chuckled.

"Per Eleanor's request," I said, cocking my head to the side.

"Gomez Addams is sweet. He isn't afraid to love or show his love. He constantly expresses himself unapologetically. He's passionate and romantic." Lilianna's voice was shaky.

Was this what I thought?

"You're like Gomez Addams," she continued. "Romantic, kind, funny, confident. You're not afraid to use your words." I took a step towards her. I needed to be close to her. She backed away, closer to the window, a small smile on her dark lips. "And…and I'm dressed like Morticia." I looked her up and down and nodded.

"You look bewitching," I said softly, smirking.

"Shush, yes I know. Let me get this out."

I zipped my lips which made her giggle. She took a deep breath. I knew this was hard for her.

"She is tough. She may seem a bit quiet but she loves fiercely. She cares fiercely. And she is with someone who lets her be her. Someone sincere, trustworthy. He understands her and supports her through everything." She took a breath, eyebrows scrunching. "But she also seems cold and I don't think I am. Okay wait. Focus." I felt my heart pounding my ears.

"You push me to come out of my shell. You push me to experience the world. Loving others has always been easy for me. But letting someone love me when I've only felt broken is terrifying. You've shown me that I'm not broken. My puzzle piece is just different and yet you fit me. I want you to be my person, my Gomez. I…accept your dare."

I broke out in a smile and without thinking moved to gather her in my arms. My hands gripped the soft fabric. Lilianna giggled, her hands wrapping around my neck. She pressed her forehead against mine.

"I will climb every tower and slay every dragon. I will count the stars until you fall asleep. I'll pick up the glass pieces and build you a library to hold your sexy romance books. I'll work to make you feel like you're in the books you love reading because you deserve that and more," I said.

My eyes welled with tears. This was feeling like too much and I loved it. I loved the overwhelming emotion. It felt like a rollercoaster and I was riding along, hands up, wind whipping around. I deserved this. Everyone deserves a love that feeds fire to their soul and pulls them out when they feel like they're drowning.

Celestino grabbed my chin and looked into my eyes. "You deserve someone to give you the love you give to everyone," he whispered. My cheeks felt wet with tears.

"Are you trying to outdo me," I choked out.

"You and I both know I have a way of words," he said, smiling. I rolled my eyes.

"And I'm better at showing rather than telling," I said. He raised an eyebrow.

"Is this the part where we have a hot steamy make out session in the attic of a haunted house?" he asked teasingly. His green eyes glowed against the moonlight. I slipped my hand into his hair, pulling him closer. I pressed my lips against his.

"I can't kiss you if you're smiling," I said, against his lips. His chest rumbled. Our arms tightened around each other in an embrace. He nipped my lower lip and I opened up without hesitation. Our tongues met in a familiar dance. I felt his hand slip down my bare back.

Kissing Celestino like walking on moonlight. My power surged throughout my body but this time I wasn't afraid. This time my magic was flowing with love and acceptance. Celestino pulled back, his eyes melting into mine.

"Too much?" he asked, his voice sounding hoarse. I shook my head.

"Not anymore," I whispered. Celestino's eyes wandered around the room. He pressed his lips to my cheek.

"Not to freak you out but your magic has us floating." My eyes looked around. We were a few inches off the ground. I met his gaze and smiled.

"What can I say? Love is magic," I said. Celestino raised an eyebrow. My eyes widened. The L-word slipped out.

"Um…what I mean is…."

Celestino tilted up to kiss my forehead.

"It's okay. We can wait. I'm a very patient warlock," he said, cupping my face.

"I know," I said, smiling. A puff of smoke appeared behind Celestino on the ground. Fabian scratched at his bowtie.

"Less talking, more kissing," Fabian said.

Celestino groaned. "You're very lucky to be Posey's familiar." He turned to glare at Fabian.

A witch and a fox. Who would have guessed. Fabian shot him a foxy grin and disappeared. I kissed him again, this time sighing.

"I'm happy," I said. Celestino mirrored my smile. He made me feel like I was living in the fairy tales I've always read about and I've always enjoyed falling for fairy tales.

"You know I lost by the way," he said as we floated back down to the ground. I looked at him confused.

"Lost what?" I asked.

"I ended up making up more rules than you did," he whispered into my ear. My eyes widened.

"You were serious about keeping score?" I asked. His hands slipped back to the curve of my back. Something I was quickly learning was how much Celestino needed to be touching me. He nodded, enthusiastically.

"What do you want?" His voice dipped, sending shivers down my spine.

"What do I want?" I questioned. I glanced around the room, taking my time to make him squirm. I met his steady green gaze. "I would like for you to be my boyfriend," I said. He kissed me hard.

"Yes," he said grinning.

"Thank you," I whispered.

"For what?" he asked as his hands squeezed my hips.

"For letting me be me and also the bookcase," I said. He chuckled awkwardly.

"Well, eventually it'll be our bookcase. I was just thinking of the future," he said. I threw my head back in a laugh.

"Silly warlock. Do you know how many books I have? It's mine."

His hand reached to cup my face.

"And you're mine," he whispered. Our lips met once more. His body relaxed as he let me lead. My teeth nipped his bottom lip, needing us to feel more connected. His hand slipped to massage the base of my skull. I groaned as a thought pulled me away.

"As much as I would love to stay making out with you in a haunted attic, the only way I got Eleanor to help me with this whole Cinderella moment was if we help her with Caleb tonight."

"And Lola?" Celestino asked, slipping his hand into mine. I smiled.

"She has a special project she wants my help in," I said. That project was going to be interesting.

"Well, we can't be the only ones in Lavender Falls with a fairy tale ending," he said, pulling me towards the stairs. With a flick of my fingers I let my magic blow out all the candles in the room, the rose petals dancing in the moonlight across the floor. I turned back to face Celestino.

"Ending? This is just the beginning," I said, smiling.

The End

EPILOGUE: SEXY TIME

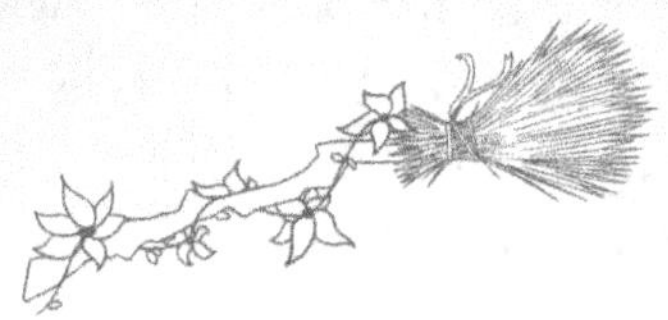

"Fuck," he hissed. His fingers digging into my hips. I nodded, soundlessly. "*Querida*, you got to relax," Celestino sounded strained. My eyes snapped to him. My thighs were braced on either side of his body.

"I swear to the stars Celestino if you tell me to relax one more time I'm hopping off this bed, grabbing my vibrator and kicking you to the couch," I snapped. He let out a chuckle while swirling his hips. I took a deep breath, relaxing my body. Finally his cock slipped all the way to the hilt and we groaned in unison.

"See *meu amor*? Once I got you out of your pretty head it was much easier-" I cut him off with a rock of my hips. He arched his back.

"Less talking, more fucking," I hissed.

"But you like when I-" This time I lifted my hips up until he was close to slipping out and slammed down. His eyes were vibrant green but if I looked closely I could see flares of violet. Our magic was mingling together in the air. The drawers on the dresser began rattling.

"Got it. More fucking," he groaned with a wicked grin.

After the success of the Full Moon Fall Festival, Celestino and I took a little vacation. Sailor let us borrow his place in Coralia Coast. A coastal town tucked into the corner of the northeast. He warned us that sometimes the people here could be a bit standoffish.

It was our first night away and I couldn't wait to rip his clothes off. Eleanor and Lola slipped a bunch of lingerie and condoms into my bag and I was forever grateful.

The moment for taking our time and savoring each other was out the window though. I hadn't even had time to put on one of the things they gave me because Celestino was already tugging at my clothes the second we were inside the cottage. I needed him hard, fast and now.

I rocked harder against him, giving my clit the friction it needed.

"Fuck your breasts are beautiful."

I cracked open my eyes to see him staring at my chest in admiration. His hands came up to squeeze them, earning a delicious moan from my lips. His hips bucked to keep up with my rhythm.

"Yes Celestino. Please," I muttered. His hands slid back down to grip my hips, taking over the pace. He was relentless. A warm ball of electricity was building up. Our magic was mixing in the air, making the room hot, pushing us.

"You're so fucking perfect for my cock. *Perfeita*," Celestino punched out. I nodded wordlessly. I felt myself climbing higher and higher. My nails were digging into his chest. My thighs squeezed as he thrusted again and again.

"Celestino." I chanted his name over and over again to help me get closer to the edge.

"Lilianna I need you to fucking come," he hissed as he slapped my ass. I yelped. He flipped me over before tossing my legs over his shoulders, driving back into me again. This angle was hitting just the right spot to make me see stars. He pressed himself tightly, hitting my clit with the pressure I needed. Our lips found each other again and our tongues stroked each other into the tempo of our hips. It was building back up again. The pressure in my lower belly. I slapped his shoulder, my eyes closing as I let the sensation take over.

"Fuck...*minha...alma*...Lilian...ah...*perfeita*." He panted into my neck. I clung onto him, helplessly, letting him take control. I felt my walls clamp and my thighs shook as waves of pleasure crashed into me over and over again. But he refused to stop. Celestino continued cursing as his thrusts became more and more erratic. Our magic slid along our bodies, making everything brighter and louder in the best way.

"Vamos meu amor," he whispered and I came again because when he spoke in our language I couldn't resist him

"Cel-Celestino…ah…Celes-" I bit into his neck as he drove into his own orgasm, groaning out my name. I loved hearing him say my name. But like this? Full of need and desperation? It made me lose control in the best way.

Panting, we both looked at each other wide eyed. I was still trembling as his fingers found my clit. I shook my head.

"I can't," my voice sounded hoarse. He kissed me softly, his fingers kept tracing lazy circles around my clit until the trembles subsided. He knew exactly how to handle my body. He slowly slid out of me to dispose of the condom.

"You've ruined me, my heart and my cock," he said, pulling me into his chest.

"In that order I hope." I giggled. He playfully smacked my thigh.

"You know we're not leaving this bed," he said, kissing my shoulder.

"We definitely are. I have a whole list of things we can see here," I said, smacking his sweaty chest. Celestino groaned, his hand stroking up and down my hip. "But don't worry, I still want at least two more rounds before we go have lunch. There's a diner by the water with an amazing view," I said, lifting to face him. He smiled at me.

The smile that was only mine and radiated sunshine. The one where his eyes softened tenderly and crinkled on the sides. His cheeks flushed softly and his dimples popped out.

He was my sun and I was his moon. Our love was written in the cosmos and I finally had someone who was willing to watch the stars with me. He kissed my lips sweetly and I melted happily.

"Yes. Ma'am."

SNEAK PEEK OF BOOK 2

THERE WERE three women dressed like Tinker Bell flirting with Caleb and I wanted to turn them into pixie dust. The Fates, the universe, whoever and whatever must really fucking hate me.

I had been sipping on the same caipirinha for the past hour. And by sipping I mean my glass was empty and I was waiting for a refill. But the tavern was bustling with tourists and therefore I needed to wait.

Which was a good thing. It was the Full Moon Fall Festival. People were drinking, smiling and having a great time. Ticket sales had gone up and it was slowly turning into a success, all thanks to the amazing volunteers and city staff.

My best friend Lilianna had managed to become a marketing queen that helped create this success despite all her anxiety. On top of that she pioneered the Cursed Bar Crawl with our mutual best friend, Celestino, who recently moved back. And I bet right now they were confessing their love for each other in the attic of the haunted house.

How romantic.

I glanced at my phone. My other best friend Lola was still at the petting zoo, taming baby dragons in disguise. I eyed the stoic elf who was manning the bar.

His blue eyes that matched the same shade as my favorite flower, were focused on the beer he was pouring. His silver hair that reminded me of starlight, was braided back. His pale skin shimmered beneath his black henley. I chewed the useless straw attached to my empty drink.

One of the Tinker Bells leaned over the bar, pushing her breasts up to her neck and attempted to flirt with him. I snorted. She was bold but there was no way he would give her the time of day. However, I did applaud her attempt and her outfit was super cute. At least she was going for what she wanted.

Our eyes connected and mentally I cursed at the way my stomach dipped. My body always betrayed me when it came to Caleb Kiernan.

I hated his eyes. So pale and perceptive they unnerved me. He handed the Tinker Bell her beer without letting go of my gaze. His eyes followed the slope of my neck, over my scale cladded bra and down to my mishap fishnet skirt. With our fall festival being close to Halloween, many people came in costume. I decided to dress as a sexy zombie siren.

He took a deep breath, his hand reaching for the bottle of cachaça and the air fizzled.

I could imagine his hands on me, his fingers scraping the netting against my thigh until my flesh turned pink. I could almost feel his other hand slip up to wrap around my throat as his lips nipped at my weak spot right below my ear.

His hand tightened around the bottle as his eyes darkened in the haze of the tavern. My cheeks felt flushed. I could feel the body glitter slipping down my back.

This is what always happened. A stare down filled with desire, sly glances, flushed cheeks and the occasional breathless banter. But nothing ever happened. *Ever.* There was never a climax of any kind. We've known each other for four years and something or someone always got in the way.

Another Tinker Bell waved her hand for his attention, breaking our tug of war. I was five seconds away from blasting her but that wouldn't be pixie-like for someone who was deputy mayor of Lavender Falls.

Instead, I did what I always did where Caleb was concerned. I looked around for someone else to occupy my time. After the year I had I was tired of waiting for him. I was drained from our constant tango of sexual tension and I was exhausted from giving effort towards people who wouldn't or couldn't reciprocate. What I needed was to let go, a break. What I *needed* was a good fuck.

A nice, no strings attached, getting twisted in the sheets, sweaty and steamy lay. Sex was a great way to destress and with the end of the year being the craziest time in Lavender Falls, I needed to relax. A flash of blonde caught my eye. I smirked. The vampire at the end of the bar might do.

I did like when someone could sink their teeth into me.

There were about 85 people inside my bar which meant there were roughly 60 pairs of eyes I needed to stab. Why the fuck did she think she could come to my bar dressed like that?

My hand gripped the bottle of cachaça as our eyes undressed each other. It was the same tango we've been dancing for four years. I noticed Eleanor's drink was empty and was in the middle of making her a new one when some Tinker Bells showed up.

It must have been a cruel twist of fate to have three drunken women dressed as pixies badger me for drinks when the only pixie I wanted was across the room.

In my tavern's lighting, her honey eyes looked the same color but I knew better. One of them was the same shade as an olive. Her cheeks were flushed and by the rise and fall of her chest that was barely being covered by her bra she was feeling the same way.

My eyes traveled down to her skirt. Fishnet was wrapped around her hips and I wanted to dig my fingers into her flesh and feel her muscles tightened against me. Before my thoughts could spiral, another Tinker Bell waved her hand in my face. I glared at her.

"Yes?" My voice sounded bored.

"I was wondering," she pushed her breasts further up, "if you were busy later."

I looked back towards Eleanor but she had already disappeared. My eyes wandered around the bar, trying to find my pixie.

"I'll be busy," I said, keeping my voice short. She pouted. If she thought that was going to work she had another thing coming. My younger brother Flynn patted my shoulder. He was around my height with dirty blonde hair and brown eyes. A replica of our father.

"Excuse my brother. He's a stick in the mud but I'd be more than gracious to provide whatever your heart desires." I snorted. Flynn was always flirty with the customers. I didn't understand why. They ordered, we served. There was no need for small talk.

The Tinker Bells smiled. My brother waved his hand towards the end of the bar. My eyes narrowed at the sight. The bottle of cachaça in my hand was shaking. Eleanor grazed her fingers delicately on the vampire's hand, her eyes hooded. She was on the prowl tonight.

I recognized that look. It was the same look she gave me. She threw her pink hair back in laughter and I watched the asshole's eyes wander down her bronzed neck. There was no fucking way she was going home with him.

She's not going home with you either, a tiny voice whispered into my head. It's not that I didn't want to take her home, to my bed and then stay under the sheets until her body was sweaty and flushed. I did. But I couldn't. Not yet anyhow.

Not until I got rid of the stupid curse.

BAR CRAWL RECIPES

291

<u>Boogeyman's Booze</u>
1 ½ oz Apple Ciroc
1/2 oz Lime Juice
½ oz Simple Syrup
Sprite to your liking

<u>Siren's Song</u>
1 Can Peach twisted tea
1 1/2 oz Tequila
Sprite to your liking

<u>Love Potion #1</u>
Lemon juice
1 oz Raspberry ice tea
1 oz Tequila
Crushed Strawberries
1/4 tsp Pearl Dust

<u>Highway To Hell</u>
1 1/2oz. blanco tequila
3/4 oz. mango puree
3/4 oz. fresh lime juice
1/2 oz. Habanero Honey Syrup

<u>The Crone's Curse</u>
1 oz of Apple Vodka
Lemonade to your liking
Serve over ice and garnish with a maraschino cherry

ACKNOWLEDGMENTS

I want you to know that I, a reader never read acknowledgments. I also struggle to spell the word. Yet here I am attempting to fill this page with words and feelings. *Takes a deep breath*

Thank you to Kizzie and Dom who in the very beginning of writing kept me accountable. Without you guys who knows if this story would have gotten finished. I do have notebooks and files of unfinished stories to prove it.

Thank you to my mom. I wouldn't have been able to put out this book or afford to without you. We've gone through so much pain in this life and my promise since I was eight years old was that one day I would pay you back for all the sacrifices you made. Thank you for teaching me to read and falling in love with books when you couldn't speak English well. My favorite memories will always be going to work with you on Saturdays and spending time in the library.

Thank you to my best friend Jennette who not only designed the cover but helped me edit this book. I have the worse grammar skills and I'm so sorry. I'm very grateful we met. I'm so happy to take you on this journey with me. Like I said we're in this TOGETHER and we'll make it together.

Thank you to Anaija, Ime and Michelle. I'm not sure if you guys know this but your friendship and support for me helped inspire these characters. I wanted to write about a group of friends who are there for each other and care for each other. You each have been with me through happy moments and sad moments. I'm so glad to have you in my life.

Thank you to Bear. Thank you for letting me be me. Thank you for being there through my anxiety attacks and for the days I'm feeling overwhelmed. Thank you for thinking that my random facts and rambling are normal. Thank you for showing me that I'm worthy of love.

Thank you to everyone who has reposted a video, a graphic and even messaged me about their excitement for this book. If I'm being honest, having people be excited for something I've created is really scary. It's hard for me to trust people who genuinely support me. The people pleaser in me doesn't want to disappoint you guys. So if you ended up not liking this book I hope you decide to pick up the next one. I think it'll be better.

Thank you to me finally. We've been through a lot haven't we Isabel? You never thought you would get here and now look at you. I know you're still struggling but we've been taking baby steps towards our future for awhile and we'll get there. YOU deserve this. Fifth grade Isabel is looking at you so proudly. I'm so proud of me.

Takes bow

About the Author

Isabel Barreiro is an anxious bookworm who loves being a dork and knowing random facts. Did you know a bumblebee bat is the world's smallest mammal?

During the day she's a freelance social media manager and at night she's binging anime shows or sewing clothes. Her brain has five hamsters running around on fire which makes the day to day interesting.

Despite being born and raised in Miami she prefers mountains and the fall/winter season. Maybe one day she'll have her small town life that she loves writing about. She loves cooking and crafting and being an extroverted introvert.

You can follow her on Instagram/TikTok:
@bell.books.and.coffee
You can receive my newsletter on substack:
A Bookworm's Diary by Isabel Barreiro